INFECTEDS

Enjoy some
light-hearted
reading!
Paul Bond

INFECTEDS

BOOK ONE:
EVE OF THE PANDEMIC

PAUL BREIDING, M.D.
JACKSON BREIDING

gatekeeper press™
Columbus, Ohio

Infecteds: Book One: Eve of the Pandemic

Published by Gatekeeper Press
2167 Stringtown Rd, Suite 109
Columbus, OH 43123-2989
www.GatekeeperPress.com

The editorial work for this book is entirely the product of the author. Gatekeeper Press did not participate in and is not responsible for any aspect of this element.

Library of Congress Control Number: 2021934088

ISBN (paperback): 9781662910319
eISBN: 9781662910326

CONTENTS

Chapter 1

FAIR WARNING

I WAS DEEP IN paperwork one evening after a long day at the office when the back line rang at my practice. It was after 6 pm and no patients had that number. It was probably the hospital but I wasn't on call. Fortunately, my secretary hadn't left just yet and picked up the call. A moment later she called down the hall, "Dr. Braden, it's Dr. Ashworth from the hospital. He really wants to talk to you."

"I'll take it in here." I called out to her. "It's late. You should get home to your kids."

Jenny was a fantastic secretary and often stayed late just to help me out when it was busy. She knew I did not like to be disturbed unless it was my family or something truly important.

"Okay." She called back from the front desk. "I'm gonna take off Dr. B! See you bright and early!"

"Goodnight." I answered as she walked out the door. I peeked at my watch as I picked up the phone.

"Hey, Tom. It's kind of late for you to be working." Which really wasn't true. Dr. Tom Ashworth was an old school type of doctor and a good friend. He was a practicing neurologist and did a lot of teaching at the local medical school. If that wasn't enough he recently was making quite a bit of progress in a vaccine trial that he was piloting.

"I called you at home but Kristin said you were still working. I wasn't surprised . . . I was actually relieved you weren't at home. There's a situation." he paused for a moment. "It has to do with phase II and I want you to know what's going on."

Tom is usually a pretty upbeat guy but I could tell from his voice he was serious.

"What's the latest update?" I asked. "Your vampires want more of my blood? Sorry Pal, I told you I was all done after that phase I debacle. I know I don't need to remind you what happened to me that night!"

I expected a chuckle or a wise-ass comment but he didn't pause at all.

"No, it's not about that. Well, that's not entirely true. Just *listen* to what I have to say, it's complicated but I only have a couple of minutes."

He proceeded to give me a summary of what was going on today not just at his vaccine lab but at multiple study sites all over the world. It was clear why he was so serious and why he needed to talk to me.

"Paul, I saw the video with my own eyes. Not just at my lab but everywhere! Every single participant in the sleep labs seems to be affected. At first we thought it was some type of an adverse reaction, something far worse than what you experienced. But over the last 48 hours what looked like a bad reaction became more of a transformation into something . . . unreal. This is really bad. Oh God!" I could hear his voice change. I never heard him like this before and it was quite unnerving.

"Tom, you better pull the plug on this study, take it from me." He knew how sick I got after I received my injection. It was the main reason I bailed out of the trial.

He cut me off abruptly. "That's the reason I'm calling you.

I don't think we have that option! It's too late. The patients are running around the study sites and it's a bloodbath. The staff were all attacked and they're all gone, dead. And it's not just at the labs. There's word that this is starting to happen in the communities but it's not being reported yet. He gave me all the details and I couldn't believe what I was hearing except his voice was as agitated and serious as I ever heard him sound. He described the horror show at his sleep lab and at multiple locations on all continents. He even forwarded a video clip from one of the testing sites. He thought I may need some sort of proof but I really didn't. The last thing he told me was the *reason* he needed me to be one of the only people who knew about this. All I could do was listen to this chilling information and try to absorb it all. Then he seemed like he was needed urgently and he hung up. I sat there for a minute, my mind racing. I knew the clock was ticking and I had a lot of work to do if I was going to save my family from what sounded like a man-made epidemic of biblical proportions. Tom gave me a lot of top-secret information and some evidence of the atrocities that were happening in sleep labs all over the world. But most of all he was giving me something even more critical, a head start.

Chapter 2

SLEEP DEPRIVED?

I WAS NEVER A good sleeper. As far back as I can remember I was never tired at night and I couldn't stay asleep for more than four hours. I never knew what it was like to *want* to go to bed or to sleep in. I was jealous of whatever everyone else seemed to appreciate when they slept. It appeared to be something that ran in the family, a family curse. My father told me it was the same for him growing up and into his seventies still. He seemed to know what I was going through and why I was so frustrated. Whenever I seemed to be bored late at night when other kids were sleeping he always made sure that there was something I could be doing to keep me entertained or occupied. In the early morning hours when I wished I could be sleeping like all my friends he always tried to make sure I had something else to do. In my childhood it was mostly reading or watching videos. Not typical kid stuff but it was usually satisfying enough. Often it was science-related material, some history and cultural topics. He was trying to make it seem fun but when I look back just about everything had a lesson or a purpose. It wasn't just at night or in the morning. When our homework was done in the afternoon my older brother

Mark and I could always count on some type of activity Dad had prepared for us. Early on it seemed like fun and games but there was always a lesson or a goal. As we got older there was plenty of physical training too. From martial arts to marksmanship to survival training my father always wanted us to be learning new skills and realizing how much there was to absorb. I'm pretty sure he felt guilty that we inherited some type of sleep disorder from him. He seemed to think that if you can't change it you might as well take advantage of it. It didn't matter ultimately. I still wanted to sleep more and I guess I still do.

I really thought I had some kind of defect or flaw. In high school I spent a lot of time reading about sleep and researching what the hell my problem was. There's a lot of science and research out there but still a lot of unknowns about what sleep does and why people need it. There is the energy conservation model that the brain needs to shut down or hibernate but few people accept this as an adequate explanation. The restoration theory maintains that the brain needs to clear out toxins and rebuild energy stores. It makes some sense and there is an accumulation of byproducts in all organs, but still not a good enough answer. More recently there is the idea that the brain needs downtime for the processing of information and memory consolidation. We have learned about the connectivity and plasticity within the brain that is required for problem solving and complex learning. This process involves many neurochemical connections that occur almost exclusively at night when we sleep. All still theory.

I did have some long discussions with our family doctor but within several minutes it was clear he knew very little beyond the basics. He was quite interested in hearing what I had learned and was impressed at how well-versed I seemed to be. He was not embarrassed at all to ask me very rudimentary questions about what type of sleep therapy was out there beyond the popular pharmaceuticals he commonly prescribed. I even tried to contact experts in the field. Most of them tried to teach me about sleep hygiene (common sense behavioral recommendations) or were quick to recommend prescriptions rather than try to fix the problem. I felt like there really weren't any answers to my questions. I kept looking for my own solution and did tons of reading. Most likely that's why I ended up going to medical school after college. I had a natural interest in medicine and quite a bit of time to do all the studying required. It was a good fit. Late nights and long study sessions with other students made the insomnia more tolerable and I did enjoy the challenge.

My father always liked to remind me that he trained me for this type of life. I can see the same affliction in my son Jackson but not quite as severe. Jackson never slept much as a baby and we thought it could just be colic or gas but deep down I knew the truth. He inherited the curse of sleepless nights. My father and I were affected and to a lesser degree my brother. I had hoped Jackson would be spared this fate. Ultimately, I turned into my father providing the poor kid with extra books, videos and projects that I hoped he would enjoy. He usually would accept them and I would try not to make it seem like the eternal boot camp that my father ran. I tried my hardest to make it all seem voluntary and not force-fed. My daughter Casey on the other hand, forget it. She could sleep til noon on a Saturday and still give someone hell for knocking on her door and waking her up. I loved that. I didn't mind being yelled at just to know that she loved to sleep in! Thank God.

*   *   *

I often look back and think of all those years of sleepless nights and long days. All the mornings I got out of bed at 3 am because I just couldn't stare at the ceiling another minute. Whatever my sleep flaw is just may be what saved my life and cast me in a role I never would have expected. All because of some type of faulty wiring or glitch in my sleep system.

Chapter 3

MED SCHOOL

IT WAS IN medical school that I first met Dr. Ashworth. He was my advisor during the first two years and we hit it off pretty well. All the entering students were paired with a practicing physician within the academic community. He was a neurologist and did a lot of research at the medical school and local teaching hospital. He had a sub-specialty in sleep medicine and conducted research in that area. I can remember our first meeting at his office. He revealed that he had requested to be my advisor largely based on a shared interest—sleep. The medical school application included some essays about why we wanted to go into medicine. My three paragraphs about sleep and the black hole of understanding sleep medicine perhaps helped get me a spot in the class. Someone forwarded that essay to Dr. Ashworth and he revealed to me at our first meeting that we shared some strong opinions.

"Paul, I really think you underestimate what we know about sleep and the processes that happen when our brains go offline every night. To me it's a beautiful physiologic mechanism that developed over hundreds of millions of years. The biochemistry and physiology behind REM sleep and our understanding of sleep science has come a long way over the past ten years and I personally think we'll see some exciting things over the next decade."

He shared with me early his passion to help people who suffered from insomnia. He helped me understand that while many people suffered from self-induced sleep dysfunction there certainly were people with genuine "disorders." It's well known that between alcohol, caffeine, nicotine, and assorted drugs of abuse that many people sabotage any chance they have of real sleep. Most recently—and it was well represented in my classmates on a nightly basis—neurostimulants represented a highly abused (and profitable) player in the sleep disorder world. For every ritalin prescription there seems to be an ambien prescription. The ever-increasing number of prescriptions filled each year was staggering. It was frustratingly clear that medications couldn't fix the problem most people had with their sleep. Trying to help insomnia sufferers 'change their ways' also seemed futile to Dr. Ashworth. He put in many hours at the bedside or in the exam room discussing sleep hygiene and behavioral therapies. He, like many physicians, found himself playing the role of motivational speaker. Unfortunately, that approach rarely made a difference and didn't pay the bills.

As a department chair and respected name in the field of neuroscience research Dr. Ashworth was constantly approached by pharmaceutical reps. Sadly, many doc's caved in to the easy money of drug dinners, speaking honorariums, and bogus positions on company boards. Dr. Ashworth was unwilling to give in to any of that. He would rarely listen to any of the reps in the business until the 'stars aligned' one day several years ago. He shared with me some of these new developments while we grabbed a late night dinner after work.

"It is finally happening!" He said with an excited grin. "The shift in the field of sleep medicine has reached a point that I wasn't expecting for another five to ten years Paul!

He had talked about his theories of a "sleep vaccine" since some of our earliest meetings. He was an expert in the physiology of sleep and was convinced that there was a way to help patients find restorative sleep without the endless string of pharmaceuticals and the exhausting lectures he was tired of giving to stubborn patients.

"I know we can help people like you, Paul." He seemed really excited as he went on. "People who can't enter the deeper stages of sleep or who wake up after only a partial cycle. Most people suffer greatly with these disorders. Not everyone figures out how to turn it into a strength!"

He gave me almost an annoyed look but I knew from previous talks he marvelled at how I adapted to such sleep depravity. He had actually studied my upbringing and had quite a few conversations with my father. He was truly intrigued by how we all seemed to be hard-wired with our sleep limitations. He cared about me and cared about making a difference in the world of sleep science.

He described getting a pretty typical visit request from a pharmaceutical company but it was from a different company than he was used to. Most of the reps in the business tried to minimize their interaction with him—he wasn't the easiest guy to deal with. Many of the private practitioners would get friendly, othen *too friendly.* with these sales reps. Free lunches for the office, nice dinners or shows, why not? Some friendly banter that seemed harmless enough on the surface. A brief discussion about new products or new equipment was just part of the deal. The smooth-as-silk salespeople knew that the friendly chats and subtle perks would eventually make a difference in the prescriber's decision-making. The bigger business was in hospitals and institutions. Big contracts were in the balance. Dealing with the sales reps was another job for the chief. Dr. Ashworth was a great physician and researcher. He was also a shrewd businessman and didn't put up with bullshit. Unfortunately, the sales reps had to go through him to get access to the hospital pharmacy and formulary. He would almost relish the debates he had with these poor people. He realized they were just men and women trying to do their job but they did represent "big pharma" which he detested.

Tom was somewhat surprised that someone from an unusual company, Sonosphere Pharmaceuticals, came to see him and it wasn't a polished salesperson in a nice suit. This was a regular looking guy in a lab coat who looked the part of a scientist and it turned out, he was. He represented the development arm of the drug business that usually didn't make these types of visits. His name was Steven Glassman and he was a Ph.D. who had been working on a new treatment for treating insomnia. The treatment incorporated a biologic approach and a gene therapy approach as a hybrid. Now biologics have been around a long time, decades. From human insulin to cutting-edge cancer therapies most people have heard of these drugs and are annoyed at the constant commercials we're bombarded with. Every day it seems there's a new product that no one can pronounce with the memorable catchphrases and the annoying music you can't erase from your memory (all part of the master plan, of course!) Like it or not, these biologics were at the forefront of modern medicine. The new paradigm.

Gene therapy was also well known and has been vital in many areas of medicine including oncology, immunology and now—neuroscience. Amazing results have been seen over the past decade that no one could have predicted. From the practitioner's perspective it has been exciting to see the remarkable progress being made in nearly every branch of medicine. It was undeniable that we owe much of that progress to the bench researchers and lab workers employed by companies like Sonosphere.

"Thanks for agreeing to meet with me, Dr. Ashworth. I know you're a busy man and have many other things you could be doing. I appreciate you giving me a few minutes of your time." Dr. Glassman offered as he extended his hand.

"Come on into my office. I'll admit I'm more accustomed to three-piece suits than well-worn lab coats. I guess they still have a few new tricks up their sleeves to get our attention." and Tom led this rep to a chair in front of his enormous and imposing desk.

They sat down and Tom made it clear the clock was ticking. Steve Glassman didn't have the smooth conversational skills of a sales rep. He wasn't particularly good looking and didn't bring any gifts or swag. What he did do was completely blind-side Dr. Ashworth with an amazing description of how his company had developed a completely new treatment approach for insomnia and had basically kept it all completely below the radar, until today. He didn't waste time explaining to Tom the intricacies of sleep and the conventional understanding of the very complex biochemical pathways that he lectures on. He described how at Sonosphere they were essentially ready for a trial and needed someone from the outside to help negotiate some of the FDA hurdles that Tom was familiar with. Tom was no pushover but he was captivated by the science and amazed by the technological breakthroughs that were being revealed to him. This unassuming research scientist in front of him seemed just as excited in describing how they had made such staggering leaps and managed to keep it all quiet.

"It has been quite thrilling compared to what happens in most research labs that often work years if not decades to make any advances. Making progress in each step along the way has been rewarding and dizzying. The initial idea of using such a common virus as a vector seemed plausible but we weren't expecting such immediate confirmation."

Dr. Ashworth was somewhat surprised they had used a modified parainfluenza virus as a vector. Viruses have long been recognized as a way to deliver a new message (often a gene or DNA code) into a host cell. The virus is able to bind to the host DNA and introduce genetic material as part of the replication cycle. The genetic material contains basic 'instructions' of how to produce more copies of the virus or to produce other types of messenger proteins.

This virus was able to cross the blood brain barrier and enter the brain. The target of the research was the reticular activating pathway in the mesopons, an integral part of the complicated sleep pathway. Activating the cells that produce dopamine and noradrenaline in a pattern that would permit longer stages of REM sleep and increased total sleep was the goal. The animal models were showing great promise and the potential impact on the sleep medication market ($30 billion/year) was staggering. Dr. Ashworth was enthralled with the beauty and elegance that he was hearing but he tried to remain skeptical. He had many questions but Steven had smart, immediate answers with an honest exuberance that would make any sales rep jealous. Tom had promised this unassuming fellow five minutes then sat transfixed for ninety minutes. He would have listened for ninety more. For Dr. Ashworth he had never had such a meeting end so differently than how it started. By the time they shook hands Dr. Tom Ashworth was the new medical director and principal investigator for Sonosphere's division of research. He would also be the lead investigator of the potentially blockbuster insomnia cure, REMfab.

Chapter 4

TIME FOR ACTION

A FTER I HUNG up with Tom I knew I had a huge number of decisions to make and things to do. My mind was racing like never before but I knew I needed to check my emotions. Part of my brain wanted to panic but I knew I didn't have the time. I sat there for about five minutes and penciled out a few lists and tried to figure out where to start. When I look back I was surprised that I could be so composed when I called my assistant Jenny at home.

"Sorry to bother you at 6:30 on a Wednesday night, Jenny."

"Do you need help working the fax machine again?" she laughed. I had made that call of shame several times over the past few years.

"No, somethings come up and I'm not going to be here tomorrow or Friday. Would you mind letting patients know?" I asked knowing she didn't mind. All she heard was "four day weekend!"

"That's fine with me. I'll send out a robo-call from home." She answered.

"I'll sign out to Warren and let's just shut the office down entirely. Spend some time with your family.

"You know I have tons of crap on my desk and I think I can . . ."

"Not tomorrow or Friday, Jenny. It can all wait. The office is closed." I said sternly enough so she would go along with the directive. She knows I appreciate how hard she works and her dedication to the patients. I thought about telling her what was really going on but I didn't. That was one of the first real ethical decisions of many that I would have to make over the next few days. Such a weighty decision made in a split second. Unreal. "Do something fun, doctor's orders!" I said before I hung up.

The next call was to my wife. That was maybe the hardest call I had to make because she needed to know everything and had to believe everything I said. How can you convince someone that the world is about to plunge into a chaotic freefall unlike anything that's ever been witnessed, even on cable TV. I realized that I would be doing this quite a bit over the next few days. I would have to be very good at delivering terrifying news in a believable way so that people, especially family, would hear my words and accept them as reality. Moreover they would really have to be ready to engage and rise to the huge challenge of this new reality very quickly. I almost laughed . . . It's just like the emotional grind of being a doctor. Patients need to hear that there is bad news, process it, hear the treatment options and decide on a treatment plan all in very short spans of time. It was never fun being the bearer of bad news but being able to do it in a gentle, sympathetic, and empathetic way is a real art. Those early dialogues truly set a patient's mindset and they don't ever forget how they felt when you sat them down and had that talk with them face to face.

*   *   *

The phone was ringing and I hoped she would pick up. Not exactly an easy message to leave but I knew she was home and waiting for me. We had made plans to have a nice family dinner, something we didn't do enough and now felt like something I shouldn't just eliminate in an effort to create more time. Fortunately she did pick up.

"You're late again." she said like someone who was used to it. "But it's actually good. The kids are getting along well and I'm a little behind schedule too. It smells good though. You are gonna smell the garlic when you pull in the driveway!"

Another split decision. I'll give her the real details a little later I decided. Another chance to have a family dinner like this may not happen again in a long time. "I think I can smell it from the office! I'll be home in 20 minutes. I do need to change our plans a little bit. I need to have a little meeting tonight with some neighbors."

"Really? Another neighborhood meeting? Let me guess, an impromptu discussion about modifying the bylaws?" she teased me knowing how annoyed I was by some recent neighborhood association assessments. "Paul, I think everyone knows how you feel."

"No, I promise nothing like that." I caught myself smiling. "I'll fill you in when I get home."

I hung up the phone and looked at all the notes I had been making on my desk over the past twenty minutes. Tom had basically said I have three days to plan and prepare for a global pandemic that would be like nothing ever imagined. He informed me that the vaccine he had been working on for several years had mutated somehow and had turned all the participants into psychotic blood-thirsty killing machines. Even scarier was that the virus used to deliver the genetic code has developed self-replicating capacity and all the study participants had been releasing the virus like super-spreaders since they received the injection two weeks ago. This modified parainfluenza virus was now spreading through communities like wildfire and acting just like viruses act in nature. This version just happens to have a built-in timebomb that instead of fixing the sleep mechanism it turned the victim into a supercharged frenzied animal that seems to be wired only to attack and eat. The infected were essentially reduced to their most primitive core, a carnivore without much else in terms of cognitive function from what Tom could assess.

I couldn't help but chuckle a little. I had really felt guilty for pulling out of the vaccine trial after phase 1 but in hindsight it looks like I made the right call. Tom talked me into being a participant initially and I did receive the first injection of the modified parainfluenza vector less than one year ago. That version did not carry the gene-mutation and did not impact the sleep mechanism at all. It was kind of a trial run with no payload. What it did provide, according to what Tom's team believes, is immunity from the phase 2 recombinant virus. If he was correct (and he's pretty much the smartest guy I've ever met) then I am immune and anyone I was in close proximity to the day I received my injection may be immune. Those are all the people I need to talk to. Tonight.

Chapter 5

THE FAMILY MEETING

DINNER WAS ACTUALLY quite nice. I'm not sure how I was able to just kick back and have a good time but we had one of those fun nights when everyone got along and we enjoyed some great food. When Jackson and Casey get along I always tried to savor every minute of it. Casey at 14 is into theater and singing. She's really smart and a good athlete but right now in her life all she really wants to do is sing for us. She knows just about every lyric sung on Broadway and at this point I think the whole family does. I'm not sure when she's going to go boy-crazy but for now we are just happy she has other hobbies. Parenting her is tough because she is so strong-willed and stubborn. She really isn't like me or her mom, we were both pretty easy kids. She is sassy, challenging and mostly stubborn. So when she's in a good mood the whole family relaxes.

Jackson is 16 and a lot like me. He has many interests and reads just about everything he can get his hands on (It helps when you don't sleep beyond four to five hours a night.) He's a good student and a good athlete, pretty well-balanced. He does goof off and logs plenty of late night gaming hours with his friends. He's into girls but is pretty reserved and quiet about it.

He's our IT guy and is definitely going into the tech field. He has already told me he doesn't want to be a doctor. That didn't bother me. I'm not sure even *I* would do it all again but I am happy with what I have around me. Wouldn't give anything up.

We even lucked out and the kids offered to clean up after dinner. That's when I grabbed Kristin's hand and brought her out onto the deck.

"A fun family dinner and bonus dishwashing?" she was really happy.

I briefly thought about delaying the inevitable conversation but it had to come out now. She had to know everything. I had her sit and listen. She seemed to take it all in. She was smart enough to understand all the science. From medical school to residency and throughout my career she has always been my sounding board. She understands a lot of what I do and has always been interested in what I was interested in. She supported me when I decided to get the phase 1 injection of REMfab but she wasn't sure if I was doing it for me or for Tom. She knew I had great respect for him.

I told her everything and she nodded and had tears in her eyes.

"So I guess you made the right decision in not getting that second shot after all!" She said with a half laugh—half sob.

I guess our senses of humor are a lot alike too.

Tom had dropped off a small package before I got home. He told me he would bring it by and he had explained how to use its contents. Kristin had given him a hug and they spoke briefly but she could tell he was in a hurry and not in a chatty mood. I opened the package and pulled out a small test kit. It could give a rapid result whether someone was immune to this modified virus. I poked her finger and took a drop of blood and placed it onto a small medical device. It was kind of like a pregnancy test. We both had the same kind of nervous feeling as we reflected back to the last time we used one of those. We smiled and it felt okay to smile. This was definitely a different kind of apprehension. Two minutes later we read the test result and there was a "+" sign. She was immune.

We went into the kitchen and helped the kids clean up. We brought them into the living room and I pretty much said everything to them that I said to their mom outside. I was glad that they were able to hear it without being around anyone else but the family. They knew it was okay to cry or be afraid or ask questions. They both seemed to take it all in and even seemed to believe it. They were old enough to know when we were joking and when it was time to be serious. They could be very adult at times. Thank God they both tested positive. We were all immune.

"What if someone isn't immune?" Casey asked straightforwardly.

I'll have to admit I really hadn't thought about what I would do or say to someone if that happens. I better figure that out quickly.

"In a few days we are going to be seeing some really scary reports on TV and you are going to hear about all kinds of awful things." I was envisioning some gruesome images from the movies in my mind as I spoke. I also was thinking about the video Tom sent me. It was terrifying and made me realize how the truth really can be scarier than fiction. "Bad things are going to happen to people who aren't immune. Dr. Ashworth is working hard to find some kind of cure or antidote but he's not going to have anything soon enough to prevent what's happening out there. He was pretty sure I was immune and that you would be too. Now we have to find out who else is protected with these antibodies."

"Why can't you just call the government or police or the CDC?" Jackson asked next.

I told him what Tom told me. He had contacted them all and they have their best people working on containment. They had made no real progress and they had decided it was too early to let the media know. Some news likely will come out in the next day or two but it won't do much good. Based on Tom's projections the vast majority of people out there have already been exposed and only a few pockets out there were immune. We had to be careful about who we told because people who weren't immune were essentially "doomed" and those of us who were immune needed to work together to survive. That's what Tom believed and what I believe. That's what has to motivate us to do what we need to do over the next few days. It won't be easy but we had to find out who else was immune quickly.

We all hugged each other. We told the kids they can skip school the next two days if they want but they both wanted to go. They had quickly accepted that a lot of bad things were going to happen and most of the people around us would not make it through this.

Chapter 6

NOT YOUR AVERAGE NEIGHBORHOOD MEETING

During my call with Tom he informed me that my blood work revealed I was immune to this newly released modified virus. The REMfab phase 1 "prototype" had triggered an immune response to the novel parainfluenza virus in my system and I was protected. Additional testing within the trial had revealed that for eighteen to twenty four hours after the injection I was shedding this modified virus and anyone around me for at least a few minutes could also be immune. He had urged me to think about who could be "immunized" by that exposure and I had compiled a list of people that were close to me that day. It was pretty easy to remember that evening and that list of characters. After the call with Tom I had thought to myself 'Really? This is the group I'm going to have to rely on?' Convincing them that they are immune to a mankind-threatening virus, that we may never return to life as we know it, and that we all need to identify and fortify some type of safety compound in the next 48 hours? It was going to be a challenge.

Before I left the office I had called all the people I felt were possibly "immune" and fortunately they all had agreed to come over at 8:30 pm to discuss some important matters. I really didn't give any details to anyone except for Scott Lang. He was one of my oldest friends from college and we have been close since those days. I trusted him as much as anyone I knew and he was a really smart guy. He also served as my financial planner, not just because he was my friend but because he was absolutely the best. Most importantly he was honest and trustworthy. During our phone call I asked him to do something for me that he never expected.

"Scott, I'm glad you can come over later but I need something else that's really important. I'm not sure how to ask but . . . I need as much cash as you can get me as soon as possible."

"Really, Doc? Let's see. . . . You're in jail? No, not likely. Getting divorced? No way . . . what the hell's going on?"

"I'll tell you tonight but how much can you get me by tomorrow morning?"

"It will be two business days for everything to clear but I can bring over some paperwork in the morning"

"Scott, that's not gonna work. This is critical. I don't care what it takes or what penalties there are. It's urgent!" I realized I was raising my voice.

"Okay, okay." he conceded. "I can get you probably 250K if you don't mind some penalties. I can get you the rest Monday. What the hell is so important?

We went back and forth but eventually he gave in and agreed to bring me what he could tonight and the rest of the cash in the morning. He also promised to make a few calls and boost my credit card limits to the max. He had some concerns as an expert but mostly he was worried about me as a friend. I did ask him to take care of a few other things for me. He agreed and I promised he would know everything he needed to know in a few hours. It would be good to see him tonight. I could trust him and at least I had secured some capital to get some things that I needed. Some things I would need to buy.

Some things we will need to take.

* * *

The first knock came just before 8:30 pm. It was Dave and Lori Zanelo who lived two doors down from us. They had two teenage sons a little older than Jackson. Dave owned an insurance company and enjoyed camping and playing cards. Lori worked for the department of health and loved cooking and entertaining. They were good reliable people and I had Kristin bring them into the dining room where we had a little lab testing area set up. We had agreed that she would get everyone to provide the blood sample right away then bring them into the living room only if they were immune. I thought that would be the best way to be sure everyone hearing my talk was immune. I still wasn't sure what we'd do if anyone tested negative.

Next was Paul and Jaymi Stanford. Good friends with two boys the same age as our kids. Paul worked in the temp market, helping people get short-term jobs. Maybe someday that will come in handy again. I wasn't too sure. We did a lot of skiing and a lot of travelling with the Stanfords. I was hoping they were immune too.

Jason Izzo and his wife Kim arrived next. An orthodontist was good to have around but he did have another upside, he was into guns. That was going to be important. They had two kids, a boy and a girl who I knew were good with guns too. We had been to the local range with them a few times and they all knew what they were doing, even Kim.

Right after them Jesse and Jamie Browne showed up. He

sold cars and Jamie was super athletic. They had two kids as well and we all spent a lot of time together. I was glad they were here and hoped they tested positive.

Next, it was Peter Carlson and his wife Candace. Their daughter was Casey's age and they've been good friends since they were born. They had another daughter Samantha who had just started college.

Scott arrived next and gave Kristin a big hug. He gave me a hug too and I knew from the look on his face that he was worried about me. I noticed he was also carrying a full backpack.

Last to arrive were Kristin's sister Amy and her husband Allan Grey A nurse and a firefighter. Thank God they were part of this group. Both of them provided some useful qualities and skills we were going to need. They had two younger boys and lived in Newport, a twenty minute drive away. They left the kids with his mom and weren't really thrilled to be here so late on a Wednesday night.

We made sure everyone had a cocktail and managed to get everyone tested without too much pushback. They had no idea why we needed their blood sample and Kristin had done a great job getting all the guests tested without raising too much suspicion before they all came to our living room. I managed to make smalltalk with the group for a few minutes until Kristin came into the room and nodded at me. I didn't need anymore info . . . they were all immune.

I stood up in front of everybody. "Okay, let's get things going. I know you are all busy but I really do have some important stuff to talk about. This is not a joke. This is real." I was not used to addressing these people like this and it was strange. It didn't matter. "I'm going to explain it as simply as I can and I can only hope you listen carefully."

Everyone was looking right at me as I stood before them and started speaking. I was hoping they could tell how serious this was by my tone. "I learned today from a very reliable source that we, this country, really the world, are in grave danger. Something has occurred that has put all of us, all *people*, at risk." I noticed some shifting and some nervous looks but I still had their attention.

"Approximately fourteen days ago a pharmaceutical study entered phase 2 of a trial utilizing gene therapy targeting certain parts of the brain. This genetic therapy was delivered by a virus and was part of a major international study in twelve countries on every continent. I have been informed by a very reliable source that the virus, and the genetic component within that virus, has mutated. This mutation has rendered all of the subjects in all trial locations genetically altered. This genetic alteration results in a terrifying, horrific transformation."

No snickers. No laughing. I had their attention and I wasn't going to slow down. I looked at Kristin and she was doing the best she could to not cry. She kept wiping her eyes but it really didn't matter.

"I have been told directly that *all* of the study participants in *all* of the study locations have essentially turned into grotesque, horrible monsters. Real Monsters. Emotionless. Violent. Blood-thirsty animals without any mercy or off switch. It was a bloodbath in every test-center but that's just the tip of the iceberg. The virus was supposed to be a delivery agent only. Nothing more than a one-way vector bringing the DNA mutation into the brain without the ability to be virulent or infectious. Despite the most sophisticated controls in the realm of laboratory science, the virus somehow became virulent again. It replicated and reproduced inside each host and regained the ability to spread just like the flu, even faster. Every participant received this injection two weeks ago and the projections suggest it has already infected 95% of the world or more."

"The clock is ticking for the entire planet. This virus is

currently embedded in the DNA fabric of most people on earth and those people are going to start going through this transformation very soon."

"Wait. How come there's nothing on the news or on my phone? I don't see anything remotely going on in any of my feeds." Jesse said.

Dave followed, "How do you know any of this? Is this real or bullshit?" He had a little attitude in his voice but also some fear.

"And why are we all here finding this out from you, not the health department or CNN?" Kim asked. She was one of our good friends and I could tell she was a little scared. She knew I wouldn't be putting people through this without good reason.

"Listen, you all should be skeptical and I know I'm throwing a lot of scary shit at you but it's the truth and it's scary and it's happening. I learned about this earlier from Tom Ashworth. You all know Tom and what he does."

It's true. They all had met Tom at some of our parties and everyone who met Tom knew he was a brilliant man. He was well known as a prominent neurologist and as a researcher. Everyone knew I thought the world of him and that carried a lot of weight.

"Tom is a major player in all of this and believe me, when he called me it was crystal clear that he was scared. He was aware that this rogue virus has the potential to wipe out the population and he was reaching out to me! He was reaching out because I had received phase one of the REMfab injection and had already been exposed to this virus. I was not part of phase 2 so I don't have the altered gene mutation. Regardless, I had already been "immunized" during phase 1 of the trial and for twelve to twenty four hours after my injection anyone around me was theoretically immunized as well. Those people are in this room."

I looked around at everyone for a minute. It was clear they

were all pretty shocked and upset. I had to make sure they were absolutely convinced before the next part of the meeting. I grabbed my phone and linked it to my TV. I opened up my texts and played the video that Tom sent me. It was chilling. Everyone in the room was watching as a time-lapse video revealed a group of several dozen people in a sleep lab setting. One after another these study subjects all seemed to rise up from sleeping and start running around and attacking. Initially they attacked each other and the staff. They seemed to be in a frenzy of attacking, eating flesh, slamming into walls, doors and through windows. Eventually more staff came into the lab area and they were all slaughtered. The video was horrific and the audio was chilling. These "creatures" seemed to let out grunts, snarls, hisses and all types of inhuman sounds. Eventually the mob of infected poured out of the lab into the rest of the building and it just got worse.

I turned off the TV and looked again at everyone. They were all silent and some of them looked like they were going to be sick.

"Are you sure we're all immune and how do we know *you're* not going to turn into one of those things too?" asked Paul Stanford, somewhat suspiciously.

"The blood tests are the only way to know. We're all immune. I never got the second injection that causes this horrific . . . transformation. I had received the first shot at Tom's lab last year on my birthday. Some of you may remember the party we had right here. Everything seemed fine until after dinner."

"That's when you got really sick, I remember. I knew it was that shot!" my wife called out. "You were shaking and had such cold sweats. We sent everyone home early because of that. At least it *wasn't* the food after all." She looked around apologetically.

"I remember everything was so good!" Jaymi added, remembering that evening. "Kristin, I loved your meatballs. And your new crockpot had that adorable carrying case. It matched your apron! I saw a similar one and I was planning on ordering it . . ."

"Jaymi!" Paul interrupted her. She looked at him blankly for a moment until she figured it out. Everyone was staring at her but no one really reacted at all. That was just Jaymi.

"We didn't feel great the next day either." said Kristin's sister Amy. "Allan thought we might have picked up some kind of a bug at that party. . . . I guess we did." With a half smile she looked around and a lot of others seemed to nod in agreement. It all kind of made sense.

"What about all the kids?" asked Jesse. "They were all here too. Should we test them?"

It was something I had debated with Kristin. We thought it would be too distracting and divisive. "I would anticipate everyone that was here at the party is immune. You can test them in the privacy of your own homes later. The safety and survival of us here in this room *and* our children is critical. Which is why we really need to be prepared for what happens in the next few days. We need to start thinking about what we're going to do next so that we, and our kids, can survive." Everyone was watching me intensely. "It's time to make a plan."

Chapter 7

THE PLAN

So by now everyone had heard and understood the important facts that I had laid out. First, there was a life-threatening and globally-sweeping pandemic coming unlike anything humans had ever seen. Second, we were a tiny pocket of people who knew about this plague and were immune. Third, we had two maybe three days until the whole world around us looked like that video we watched. And fourth, we better come up with a good plan.

I was standing up in my living room and everyone was looking at me intently. I really didn't want to be in charge or leading this meeting but so far there wasn't much in terms of resistance or argument. I knew things were bound to get more complicated in the near future. Right now people seemed comfortable to let me direct this meeting. They trusted me and knew I was not trying to do anything but protect this group. We were all good friends and none of us really dominated each other in any way. We mostly enjoyed each other's company and rarely argued. I think another reason we all got along was that we were different. Different backgrounds and different interests. These men and women were all pretty bright and physically capable. I was actually quite happy to have them all here with me ready to help. Up until now I had felt alone and that I was keeping this giant burden to myself. Now I had a willing group around me and we all seemed to understand what was at stake. Everything.

The room was quiet but there was a palpable sense of urgency. Everyone seemed to be looking at me to start talking again. I decided I would take the opportunity to speak out loud some of the ideas I had only been thinking about since Tom hung up the phone. The truth is I had a lot of ideas and there seemed to be too many things to do and not nearly enough time. I knew we really had to come together and quickly develop a plan. We would need to all agree and buy into what we had to do. Many of the things I was thinking about were either financially difficult, against the law, or outright dangerous.

"I have been thinking a lot about this. Mind you I've known about all of this for less than three hours and you're all just processing what you've just heard." I said as I scanned around the room looking in everyone's eyes. It was late in the evening but they all still seemed wide awake. "We all have to appreciate the scope of what we need to do. This is not just us preparing for a bad hurricane or hiding out in our basements. We need to get everyone we know is immune to a safe place that offers protection from these things. Imagine the entire population of those bloodthirsty creatures running rampant in the streets, hunting down whatever they can sink their teeth into. Walls, doors, windows. . . . You saw the video. Nothing seemed to stop them. We need a safe place to be and we need to be together."

I paused for a minute and walked around a little bit while I thought. "We need to be prepared for a long, hard road ahead. We can hope for a cure or help from the army, but we have to be prepared for the scariest of probabilities. There may be no rescue for us any time soon. Food, water, medicine, weapons, we need to figure out how to secure enough to survive and a place where we can hold out for weeks, months, perhaps longer."

I could sense that everyone was getting more anxious by the minute. Husbands and wives whispering to each other. I gave everyone a moment as Kristin came over to me. I could tell she was a little freaked out. I thought she was going to say 'relax a little' or 'let's not get carried away' but she didn't. She hugged me for a few seconds then sat down next to Lori and looked at me as if to say 'I'm with you.'

It was time to get back to our planning, "As Kristin would say in her line of work, location, location, location." I winked at her as I spoke and she looked back with her eyes expressing 'really?'

"We can't stay in our houses or in this neighborhood. We're just too exposed and don't have enough protection here." I was about to keep going when Lori stood up and countered.

"We've all got generators and propane. We've got stocked pantries. Let's get as many supplies as we can get and ride it out." She sounded like she was confident but also like she was hoping that it would be so easy. Jamie Browne nodded in agreement like a good friend would but there was mostly silence as people really thought about what Lori said and what I had been describing. She was saying what some people were thinking. *Let's ride this out.*

"It won't be enough, Lori." Jason said but very politely. "We could last a few days or a week if we're lucky but we could also be putting ourselves in danger by trying to ride it out." He knew Lori was just pointing out that we all were prepared for hurricanes and blizzards around here but nothing like this. Nobody could be prepared for this. "How about getting everyone out to the farm? There's food, fuel, a generator, plenty of room for everyone and not a lot of people for miles." A lot of nodding and I'll admit I had thought of this as an option. His parents had a farm out in the country and we had all spent a few weekends there. Great memories and a pretty good location."

I could tell Kristin wasn't a fan of that idea. During our last visit to the farm her asthma acted up so bad it took her weeks to recover. There was no air conditioning either. There was no cable or wifi which turned out great as the kids were forced to all play together like in the good ol' days. The farm itself was old and probably not that sturdy. It would be a big gamble.

I nodded "I thought about the farm and it could be a good choice. Could be hard to protect but at least the farm provides food."

Jason reminded us all, "It's really just corn. My parents like how it looks and they have other people handle the crops. It may not be enough for what we really need."

"How about the club?" Kristin asked out loud. There was a little eye-rolling around the room. Kristin had been a member of the Warwick Country Club her whole life and we spent a lot of time there, maybe *too* much. "It's kind of in the middle of nowhere. It's got a big kitchen and tons of food in storage. I think it has a generator."

I think we were all imagining the scene there when all the members started to turn. What a transformation from a manicured golf and tennis club, everyone in their finest weekend attire, to a bloody carnage. We all knew that over the next few days we were going to see a lot of horrifying things. In the cities. In the country. Rich, poor, black and white. It didn't matter. The clock was ticking on the entire population.

"Imagine all those elitist yuppies tearing each other up on the tennis court!" Lori burst out. "I'd kind of like to see that!" Everyone let out a laugh. So did I and it felt good but just for a moment. Lori was sitting next to Kristin and grabbed her hand tightly. They looked at each other and Kristin laughed a little too.

"Sounds like ladies tennis on Wednesday mornings!" Kristin added squeezing Lori's hand back. They were like sisters. We all laughed and Kristin did not look mad. I looked at her closely and she gave me a subtle nod as if to say 'keep going!'

It was pretty clear everyone was going to need a thick skin from here on out. The club was a good idea but how long could we last there? It was old and exposed.

Allan put his hand up and people quieted down and listened respectfully. I motioned to him as if to say 'you have the floor.'

He spoke to the group "Last month Evan's cub-scout pack spent the night at Fort Adams."

Jaymi Stanford immediately commented "Oh, Evan must look so cute in his uniform but do they still have to wear those scarves? I never liked those on boys. Especially nowadays with what you hear about what goes on! Really scarves on boys?"

"Jaymi!" Paul said again, a little louder.

Allan didn't skip a beat. "This place is unbelievable. The location is great. It's surrounded on three sides by water out at the end of a peninsula, that's why they built it there." Everyone nodded and smiled. He continued, "It's got thirty foot walls that are impenetrable. They have an ingenious plumbing system and it has well water. The heat and cooling is all geo-thermal so you don't have to worry about that. I know they have a big generator and a huge propane tank. It's got some officer's quarters, and a kitchen with storage. "

I sat there and thought for a minute as he talked a little more about the fort. It seemed to satisfy everything we needed in a home base. He knew what he was talking about. Allan is a firefighter in Newport and sometimes he would have to work a detail at the fort if there was an event or function. He had made some connections over the years and he had arranged for the scouts to have their sleepover. There was access for other groups to spend the night but it was unusual. He made sure they had "all-access" during their stay. He had really scoped this place out and seemed to think it was a secure location. Everything he described sounded good and he made a pretty good argument. I had been to the fort years ago for a tour but never really saw the inner-workings of the fort like he had.

I thought a little bit but we didn't have a lot of time. I looked at him and gave him a real look of confidence. "Allan, I think that just may be perfect!"

We had our first vote as a group. Everyone agreed that Fort Adams would be our home base. How interesting that we would be resorting to a two hundred year old fort that didn't have many modern conveniences. A fort that was originally placed in a geographically strategic location to protect us from an invasion. Another thing just happened too. Everyone realized that Allan knew what he was talking about and that he had this great idea no one else thought of. Not everyone in the room knew Allan well. They knew he was a fireman and he was an "Islander." He grew up in Newport and loved his community. He knew everyone there and as a fireman he had access to just about everything. He was big and tall but unassuming and as nice as they come. He's the guy you want on your team when shit's going down. I was feeling better as I looked over at Allan. I felt bad that he got sick after my party but not *too* bad. Mostly because right now, shit is going down.

After the vote we took a minute to stand up and stretch. A couple of people grabbed a glass of wine or a beer. I couldn't blame them, it was a lot to take in. I still had a few things I wanted to discuss before everyone left. Scott came up to me with a little bit of a smile but I could tell he was a little rattled too.

"I'm glad you didn't tell me any of this earlier. You sounded a little crazy on the phone but if you started in with zombie talk and genetic mutations I would have never done what you asked." he said with a straight face. "Since that call I've been trying to figure out what the hell is going on with you. An affair? Divorce? Malpractice? I was never even close to this."

"Sorry. I would have preferred just about any other reason." I responded. "The more money we have will make the first day or two a lot easier. After that I'm not sure how much it's going to matter. I'm not sure we have enough for what we need to do. If we can get everyone's cooperation can you pull some more strings?" He knew what I meant. He was just about everyone's financial advisor and knew the whole group pretty well. His reputation was excellent and he was well known to be an honest guy. He was all about investing by the rules and doing things the right way. Scott had moved into the neighborhood after his divorce. He had three daughters who spent most of the time in Los Angeles where they live with their mom. He loved his girls dearly and they did come to visit once in a while. He travelled out to the west coast regularly to be with them. When in Rhode Island he spent a lot of time with our family. He was another guy you could trust with your life, not just your life savings.

"Now that I know some of the gory details you shared tonight perhaps there may be some more wiggle room in terms of cash flow." He was looking around the room as he spoke. "There's a lot of ways to get large sums of cash fast and unlimited credit."

"But earlier you said. . . ."

"Yeah, I know what I said and that's still my answer in normal times." Scott responded and really looked me in the eyes. "Things are all different now. I believe what you told us 100%. I think everyone does. Normally, I make sure everyone does the right thing with their money and investments. Now it's survival mode. By morning I can get everyone in here basically unlimited credit and a *lot* of cash."

"I thought you told me. . . ."

He held his hand up and smiled. "I know, I know. Listen, a

big part of my job is talking people out of bad decisions. None of this makes much sense in any other context. Paul, the clock is ticking for us. Let me take care of the financials." He winked and then gestured to the rest of the group in the living room all talking in small groups. "You get back out there and give this captive audience what they need. What *we* need. The plan."

I nodded and we returned to the living room. I went back to where I was standing earlier. I was in front of a large bookshelf and I briefly took in the imagery. All these books I collected over the years. A few pictures and mementos scattered on the shelves. These all reflected my years of preparation and studying. My training. Not just medical but everything I poured myself into since I could remember. I glanced at a picture of me in a taekwondo competition in high school. I could remember the stark emotions of excitement and clear-mindedness before any competition. Book after book that reflected my interests over the years. Apollo 13, I had thought about going into aeronautics briefly. I even got my pilot's license while in college. The Art of War. Interesting reading but really not relevant in today's day and age. That may just change pretty quick, I mused. Seeing all of these memories gave me a surge of confidence and clarity, mixed with fear and apprehension. I turned and faced these people who I cared for and loved.

Will what we end up doing be enough? Will I be able to keep my family and all of these people alive? Everyone was watching me as they were talking amongst themselves. Quiet came over the room as I stood and faced them all.

"We have a lot to do." I started off. "First of all I am really happy about agreeing on our home base decision. Fort Adams is ideal in a lot of ways and I think Allan's idea is great. But we're gonna need to get supplies that can get us through this and I don't know how long it will be until there's help. Or if there *will* be help. We need to go into this with the idea that it's not just camping for a week or two. We need food. We need weapons and ammunition. We need some tactical gear. From safe transportation to how we're going to communicate with each other. We won't get very far relying on what we have right now. Cell phones, wifi, cable, it's gonna be gone. What we do have, thanks to Dr. Ashworth, is forty eight hours to get what we need and to get somewhere safe."

Everyone nodded and seemed to be with me so far.

"Should we all just go buy guns tomorrow?" Dave Zanelo stood up as he asked. "I have an old rifle my dad gave me but I don't even know what kind of bullets it takes."

'Where can we get all this stuff?' seemed to be the consensus question. I had been thinking the same question but over the past four hours I had come up with a few ideas and I was hoping people would be on board.

"First of all, I cleared my work schedule the next 2 days and I recommend everyone do the same. Every hour counts." I stated and scanned the room. Just about everyone in the room had jobs but I was pretty sure taking a few days off was not a big issue. They all knew how rarely I took time off. For me to clear two days would be shocking . . . in *normal* times.

"I have taken the liberty of setting up some time at the local gun range tomorrow morning." I held my hands up, gesturing for everyone to relax. "We all need to have some comfort with a gun. I know everyone is thinking about the movies and about every zombie show on TV. I don't know what things are going to be like but we have to be prepared. If everyone here, and the kids, can meet at the rifle club at 9 am we will have the whole place to ourselves and hands on training for 3 hours."

"Can kids even go there?" Jesse asked. "I'm not sure my kids are capable of any of this. I get nervous when Ethan uses the weed wacker!"

"I know Jess. I wish this wasn't necessary but I really think it's a good way to get everyone feeling confident around guns and ammo. I hope we don't need to resort to weapons but every time I think about how things are gonna play out it gets pretty ugly and fast. We already told our kids about this and I recommend you all do the same. They aren't kids, they are young adults. I think they deserve to know what's happening but you all need to make those decisions. Tomorrow 9 am at the Pioneer Gun Range. The guys there are ready for us all and they're going to have a lot of gear and technical stuff for us to check out. Scott and I already paid these fellas a ton of money for the private range access, hands-on training, demos with survival gear and a few other things. I've already purchased guns for our group and as much ammunition as they could provide. It's a start. There will also be provided a five star all-you-can-eat breakfast buffet served at 9 am sharp." I smiled with that last bit. We had a very socially interactive neighborhood. People were always getting together. Parties, events, fundraisers. We all supported one another and also knew how to get people to be somewhere. We all knew everyone would show up on time if good food was promised.

Everyone seemed to be in agreement with this. There was no argument that we would all need to feel comfortable protecting ourselves from whatever evils we would be facing. The buffet just seemed to make all of this just a little more palatable.

"Speaking of food." Kristin asked. "Should we load up at the grocery stores? Even if we buy everything we can it's not going to last more than a few weeks. We can only bring so much. How are we going to know if we have enough food, Honey?"

I had been thinking about this a lot and had thought about ransacking a food pantry or large big-box warehouse. Stealing delivery trucks and filling up U-hauls with whatever we could get were all on the table. "I have several ideas for getting our hands on food but no matter how much we get it's a short term solution. First of all, thanks to some shrewd financial moves Scott has assured me that we're going to have plenty of cash and credit to purchase just about anything we want. We have two, maybe three days to execute this plan and the clock is ticking. We can buy, borrow or steal what we need but the next 48 hours is going to go by fast. Tonight may be a critical time to hit the web to amass as many supplies as we can get delivered. Try to think about non-perishable foods, clothing, medications, anything you may need. Whatever can be delivered overnight just buy it. Extra charges for overnight delivery don't think twice. Max out what you can get in terms of volume and size. We're not talking days, we're talking long term, folks. Remember, there is no financial obstacle." With that I gave Scott a quick look and a subtle nod.

Scott stood up and in as calm and reassuring fashion as possible explained what he told me earlier. "Give me one hour and I guarantee all of your savings accounts will be flush with plenty of cash and your credit cards will be limitless." He could tell people were uneasy with this notion. "This is no time to hold back. Whatever you need, get it tonight."

It was as good a time as any for us all to accept that breaking the law, lying, deceiving and possibly hurting other people were all going to be part of the deal. It's survival mode. Hands were going to get dirty.

Scott continued, "I grappled with this myself but I'm accepting it all as truth and I am buying into this plan. You all know I would never do anything foolish with financial decisions or break the law." Everyone nodded and remained quiet. "Paul had me really worried earlier today with some things he asked me to do. Now I know why. I know that in the next two days we can get so much more done with limitless cash and credit than with trying to steal what we need. I understand some things can't be bought but there is so much we can obtain with the unlimited finances we'll have for the next couple days. I don't want lack of money or credit to be the reason any of us suffer or die." He paused again looking at everyone. "I have already accepted that I can't approach decisions the same way anymore. Trust me. I will make sure nobody here is liable for any of the steps I'm taking to finance this. I have always followed the rules and always convinced people to invest the safe way. That doesn't mean I don't know a lot of tricks. Rest assured that whatever plan we come up with and whatever Paul asks us to do it's covered. We can afford it." He sat down again and our eyes met again. I could detect a shift in the energy in the room. What couldn't be accomplished if you had unlimited funding? Still, how much food can we buy and store for the future?

Allan's hand went up again and everyone was quiet as they listened. "I agree with Paul and Scott that we need to all buy into this plan and that it's going to get messy. No matter how much we can buy we'll only have enough for a couple weeks at most. If we are really going to survive and our kids are going to survive we need to be self-sufficient. I believe for the first week or two we will be in that fort and fighting for our lives. We can defend that place but at some point we need to look outside the walls for subsistence."

He was right but I hadn't figured out what the long term source of food would be short of holding out in a restaurant supply warehouse. Even that wouldn't do. "Any ideas Allan?" I asked.

Allan proceeded to give us all a little lesson on the history of the fort and of Newport itself. The fort was a former army post and vital defensive stronghold during five separate wars including the war of 1812. "I'm not really this smart." He assured us as he filled us in with more fort info "The cub scouts and all of the parents sat through a very long and thorough lecture on all of this. I'm surprised I remember any of this but it is pretty interesting." He explained that the location of the fort was based on the proximity to shipping lanes and access to Narragansett Bay. The fort was also situated at the end of a peninsula jutting out into Newport harbor which made it more defendable and harder to attack.

Because of the safety the fort provided over the past two centuries Newport became a burgeoning port with a very strong dependence on whaling and fishing. Surrounding the fort were multiple farms that prospered much like in a feudal system and a castle. The castle provided protection while the farms provided subsistence. Some of these farms around the fort were still active today and were located only a stone's throw from the walls of the fort. He also described how the fort kept the harbor safe and there was still a large, active fishing industry with working boats docked very close to the fort.

Allan looked at me and Scott. "Once we get through that first two weeks or so I don't see why we can't utilize these already existing resources like the crops and animals at the local farm and the local fishing boat industry."

He was right. I quickly brought up on some images of the fort and the surrounding landscape on my big screen (with some help from Jackson my IT guy.) Literally feet from the fort were docks and boats. Some of the boats appeared to be fishing boats. So close to the fort! On the inland side of the fort were a few athletic fields and what looked like pastures. Most people associate that part of Newport with mansions, beaches and an expansive golf course. We all could see the fort and how big it was but some small farms were situated very close to the fort and we never would have known that they were there and still operational. Interesting options for sure. The fort did look like a massive building with a large expansive field in the middle of it. Definitely big enough for us and whatever supplies we could get. We glanced through some other images of the fort on the inside. Not exactly a hotel but we all agreed we could make this happen.

Allan continued, "I know a couple of fishermen and for the right price . . ." he paused momentarily looking at Scott but proceeded, "I could get one or two of us on their boat and we could learn how to do it all. Right near that fort are boats outfitted to go out for fish and lobsters and they only need 3 or 4 guys at a time to haul in huge loads of fish all caught within a few miles of Newport Harbor. As far as the farm closest to the fort I'm sure they would be open-minded to providing some lessons to anyone who has cash and isn't afraid to get their hands dirty. I can call some people I know and visit the boat yard and farm tomorrow morning, if you think these are good ideas."

He paused but I had no reason to object to what he was saying. I had to trust that he really felt there was merit in these ideas. He also had a family he wanted to provide for and protect. "Keep going Allan. This is good." I reassured him.

He proceeded, "I would plan on needing two volunteers to go on the boat Friday morning. I'll make sure it is just a day trip. For the right price they will do whatever we want. From where they keep the keys to how they bait the traps we need to know everything. The farm may require more people. Planting, fertilizing, harvesting, livestock management. It's a big task to learn even a fraction of that in a day. Maybe three of us? For the *right price* I think we can get our people on a boat and on a farm Friday. He looked at me and Scott but I wasn't about to object to anything he said. I smiled and looked at Scott. We all did.

"I'm thinking they would prefer cash?" Scott asked without any hesitation.

"I think cash is the *only* thing that will get us all-access to the boat and farm experience." Allan responded. "But they'll want it up front. I'll need it by tomorrow morning. They leave the dock by 5 am.

Again Scott didn't hesitate. "No problem. Just let me know how much you think it will be Allan." We were all watching as such amazing things were happening quickly in my living room.

Allan seemed to do some math in his head as he spoke. "Two men, or women, or kids whatever we decide on getting onboard a boat which is probably illegal . . . learning everything they can from the fishermen, including the best places to go . . . losing some of the day's catch . . . twenty grand. The farm won't be as much, probably half of that.

Some people gasped a little bit but no one questioned it. How the hell would we know what it would take?

"You'll leave here with fifty grand." Scott replied again with no hesitation. "This is a critical step. Don't let some money get in the way of anything over the next few days." He seemed to be addressing the whole crowd but was looking at Allan. "I know some guys in that business too. Some of my clients are fishermen. Don't underestimate those guys. They are as smart and savvy as they come and aren't the most trusting. Hopefully you will be able to make this work, Allan. Something tells me there's no one better for the job."

"Great." I said after a few seconds of letting that sink in, "Allan, I hope you can make it to the range tomorrow after you conduct some local business."

"If you're supplying breakfast we'll be there!" he shot back without hesitation. Again we all laughed a little bit about the promise of a good meal. Allan and Amy have two boys Evan and Miles. They were only 10 and 7 but were big and strong. They looked and acted just like Allan.

"Have the boys ever shot guns before?" I asked not knowing, "It's been a while since I was in the cub scouts. They are welcome to come if you're okay with it." I directed this mostly at Amy who is Kristin's only sister.

As an ICU nurse and wife of a first responder Amy has made it clear she did not like guns at all. She resisted every nerf gun they bought the boys (they had them all I think.) "I don't love the idea of it but these boys are ready. All of our sons and daughters are going to grow up real fast. They need to be ready. We all need to be ready." She looked at me and smiled. "My kids eat a lot of food, Paul. I hope this breakfast lives up to the hype."

We discussed a few more items but I sent everyone home before it got too late. We were all planning on logging on to our computers and purchasing as much as we could as far as next day deliveries and bulk food items on-line. I'm not sure how much sleep people were going to get. Maybe I would get more sleep than some of them. That would be a first. I had a lot to do tonight too. I was used to these long nights. We were all going to have some long nights from now on.

We would see each other again tomorrow at the gun range.

Chapter 8

JACKSON

"Jackson what's going on down there?" Casey asked me as I came upstairs. Dad had needed some technical help so I was down there listening to what's going on. I could tell Casey was nervous. She had clearly been crying, her eyes were red and puffy. She was confused and didn't know how to act with her friends on-line or what to say about all of this. "This is too weird, one minute Dad's telling us everyone's gonna die and now my friends are wondering why I'm acting so weird. I don't know what to say or what to do!" She sobbed a little bit and she stepped towards me.

Now Casey and I aren't usually huggy-kissy but that didn't matter right now. I stepped into that hug and it felt right. It felt like we both needed to know that even though we fought most of the time that ultimately what mattered most was our family. She squeezed me hard and I squeezed back. A hug between us that happened organically without being directed or choreographed by helicopter parents—that was a first. "It's better to just act as chill as possible and not let anyone know what's going on. Dad's giving the neighbors the rundown and it's pretty bad Case. Things are going to get real bad, real fast."

"So like, are all our friend's gonna die or something?" Her

voice quivered as she tried her best to be cool. "What should I tell them? What can they do?"

"Honestly, I don't think there's anything you or anyone can do to change the fact that everyone we know, except for those people downstairs and their kids, everyone is screwed. Dad played the video to the group down there and he didn't need to convince anyone about anything. I saw it too and it was worse than anything in a movie. Probably because I knew it was real. Casey Dad's right. If there's some type of plague that turns people into those . . . monsters we gotta act fast and get somewhere safe."

"What do these monsters do?" She asked half crying as she continued to hold my hand. "Are they vampires or zombies? Do they have superpowers? Can we fight them?"

I brought her into my room and we sat down. I really summoned up my best reassuring voice as I went on, "I don't know but I listened to Dad and Uncle Allan and all I know is we have to be ready. We have a couple of days until this all happens and we have to be super-prepared. It's not just a weekend thing Casey this is like, a long-term plan. If you didn't know Dad you'd think he's going a little crazy with all kinds of credit card shit and fishing trips but he is serious! Even Scott is down there and on board. Everyone is kind of agreeing with what they're saying which freaks me out even more!"

She leaned in resting her head on my shoulder. I put my arm around her shoulder like my dad would do. She didn't pull away. I squeezed her a little harder. Usually this would be awkward but it really felt . . . nice. We both needed some comfort. Mom and Dad were downstairs and we were here together. I felt a strong feeling of attachment and felt like I needed to do whatever I could to shield this girl from badness. Whatever evil that was out there, whatever monsters we would have to face, it didn't matter. Keeping Casey safe and as happy as possible suddenly seemed more important to me than anything else.

Don't get me wrong. Casey could handle herself. She was probably as strong as I was and had no 'off switch' when she got mad. You didn't want her to be angry and my parents often went overboard to keep her from losing her shit. That meant I didn't get much leeway. If Casey and I were in a fight Dad always gave me a tough time. They seemed to rely on me to keep her from having a melt-down. It pissed me off but I knew there was some rationale there. I knew it didn't take much to get her pissed off and over-the-top angry. I also knew it didn't take more than a few kind words and an honest smile to get her into 'friend mode.'

Right now she was in friend mode and I think I needed this just as much as she did. "I'm not going to school tomorrow, Casey." I told her. "We are all going to the gun range to shoot and get everyone comfortable with guns."

She started to cry a little and I could tell she didn't know what to do. I squeezed her and she buried her head in my shoulder. I said truthfully, "Do what you want. You may never get a chance to be with your friends again . . . at least not like this. You should go and have fun. Don't even worry about the classes or the lectures, just enjoy normal stuff. It could be a while till we have that again."

She nodded and wiped her nose on my shirt a little just like she might with Mom. She realized what she just did and looked at me suddenly like she had crossed a line. I smiled and didn't let go. She seemed to calm down and everything seemed good for a minute.

I convinced her it was a good idea to go to bed so she could go to school and have a great day or two of just hanging out and "not learning." She ended up in Mom and Dad's bed cuddled up with Mom later on and that was okay because Mom looked like she needed some hugs. I went in for a little hug too. It felt great but after a minute I left them and went back to my room. They needed a little girl time and I was ready to focus on the new reality. The idea of what was going to happen the next few days seemed like a heavy weight around my neck. I wanted to feel comfort just like Casey did but I wasn't sure where to find it. I pulled out an old pellet gun I kept under my bed. I'm not sure why but it always seemed to make me feel safe. It was my dad's old gun and he used to practice with it for hours on end in the basement. I liked thinking that we both grew up with the same gun. I knew tomorrow I was going to go to that gun range and do a lot of shooting but for right now It felt good to hold that barrel close. I was less afraid as I gripped it tight in bed. I was pretty sleepy considering everything going down, I thought I would be able to sleep actually. I usually stayed up really late and Dad never seemed to mind. I always woke up really early, too. Just how it's always been. Neither me or Dad slept too much. Tonight I decided to set my alarm clock. I figured I should get up early and have a big breakfast. Then I thought for a minute about what Auntie said to my dad downstairs in the living room. I was going to wait to eat at the range. This breakfast better be good!

Chapter 9

THURSDAY MORNING AT THE GUN RANGE

I MET UP WITH Scott early at the range. I walked over to his pick-up truck and noticed he had all kinds of boxes and gear in the bed. I got in the passenger side. "Not enough room in the Porsche?" I teased him. He had several nice cars and could drive whatever he wanted. He usually ended up driving around town in this more unassuming option. The truck actually was quite a machine. It could fit five adults comfortably and haul a 25 foot boat without any hesitation. It had all the navigation and touch screen controls on the dashboard and a built-in generator behind the cab. Impressive bed capacity, big tires with big clearance, an all around good choice for the days ahead. We had decided to meet here early to discuss a few more things.

"Hopefully, Allan will have good news for us." he started. "Haven't heard from him yet. That's maybe a good sign, I guess." Scott seemed a little distracted and nervous, not his usual calm self.

I reassured him, "Allan will get it done. Knowing him the fishermen will want to take him out for free and the farmers will beg for him to stay for breakfast. Islanders." I paused for a moment. "What is it?"

"Tracy and the kids are flying out tomorrow." He responded without hesitating. "I called her last night and wasn't really sure what to say or how to say it."

"That had to be a tough conversation." I added, knowing what was coming next.

"As it turns out, she got a funny call from Tom Ashworth."

I really couldn't tell what his emotions were, so I just listened.

"She said he was going on and on about a *virus* and a *fiasco* and how she and the kids had to get some shot or they were gonna *die!*" as he summoned his best Tracy. While divorced they were still amicable and even travelled together sometimes. We all went on a family ski trip together last winter and it was surprisingly fun. Kristin and Tracy got along so well and even more surprisingly Jackson and his oldest daughter Cameron became *very* close. I think they still keep in touch on some kind of app or something. We still joke about that from time to time.

"Tom called Tracy? That's really strange. Did they get the shot?" I asked.

He looked at me and sighed, knowing I knew all of this. "While Dr. Ashworth was talking to her on the phone someone knocked on the door. Guess who it was? Tom was there with a team of doctors. They had vaccines and immunoglobulin injections for each of them. Fortunately, he is one smooth talker or she would have sent him packing. With a nosebleed."

He didn't have to remind me of the arguments they had over getting their kids immunized when they were little. I had a lot of conversations with Tracy and she eventually gave in. She felt better knowing that Kristin relented too only after the same prolonged debates. I knew Tracy had met Tom several times including at my wedding. She thought he was a great guy then and I imagine she still remembered him. Few people forgot Dr.

Tom Ashworth. While I had some mixed feelings about his most recent scientific efforts I couldn't deny that he was still one of my best friends and still a great mind. During my last discussion with Tom he mentioned he would be going out to a research facility in LA to work on finding some type of reversal agent or cure. I made him promise to do this favor for me and for Scott. I was a little surprised how easy it was to get him to do it.

"Scott, they got the shot but you know that doesn't mean they're immune. They likely were already exposed and it might not make a difference. We won't know for at least a few more days. They'll have to be quarantined." I told him in a friendly but guarded tone.

He nodded knowingly, looked at me and smiled. "They'll be here and that's all that matters. Thanks." Scott wasn't a guy who typically relied on other people for much and usually was the person people turned to when they needed things. We shared a little moment of pretty intense emotion. Unfortunately we had no time for any of that. A quick nod and a smile and that was it.

"There's plenty of room at the Inn." I responded after a few seconds. "I think we're gonna need even more vacancy however. I got a number of texts after the meeting last night. Apparently most of our neighbors are loving sons and daughters. We have a bunch of parents and several other families that simply need to be protected."

"Will it be safe to take them in? What about the virus?" he asked.

I held up a package that looked like it just came in the mail. "This is also from Tom. Just in case we had any other party-crashers." I smiled again. The package contained a dozen doses of the same vaccine and immunoglobulin that Tracy and the girls received. Tom had made it quite clear that they simply didn't have a reliable antidote or cure for the oncoming viral plague. The hope was that the immunoglobulin would provide immediate protection and the vaccine would allow the body to create its own antibodies within a week or two but there was no guarantee it would work. They only had a very small amount and couldn't possibly make enough to allow any type of mass vaccination. Only a tiny fraction of the populace would receive a shot. Mostly government, military, scientists and scattered select individuals.

The clock was ticking. The tidal wave was on the horizon and approaching fast. We were the only ones who could see it. Was there enough time to save some more people with these injections? It could be dangerous to allow some "non-immune" into our small band but we would have to take some risk, and some precautions.

"Good thing this fort has plenty of secure prison cells." I muttered. Scott seemed puzzled for a moment then seemed to get my message. It could be very messy. "I'm not sure how updated that wing of the fort is unfortunately."

I informed him that I had already used some of the vaccine/immunoglobulin injections with a few close family members and neighbors. He agreed that we should at least try to save some family and friends if possible. I had already gone to my parent's house, my brother's house and Kristin's parents house earlier this morning. I was getting better at summarizing how we were facing this catastrophic pandemic in just a few minutes. After some resistance and brief arguments I was able to immunize everyone and get them mentally prepared for the days to come.

"Just another Thursday morning for you, Doc." Scott joked knowing my tendencies of rising early and getting a lot done. Scott looked at his watch. "I've been thinking about some of the conditions at the fort. I think with a little effort and *a lot* of financial flexibility I can get some things done over there. Let me make a few calls." He punched in some numbers and we waited. He put the phone on speaker.

"Frontier RV." a young sounding lady answered on the other line. Scott looked at me as I rolled my eyes. "What can I do for you?" she asked.

"Hi, this is Scott Lang. I was looking for the Big Guy." Everyone knew Big John Mills, the owner of the biggest RV dealership in southern New England. And of course wouldn't you know it . . . another client of Lang's. "Is he in his office? This is important."

"Just a minute, Mr. Lang." came the response as she put us on hold.

Ten seconds later the ever-jovial Big John picked up the line. "Hey Langaroo you son of a bitch! I'm hoping you're callin' to tell me I can retire early. If not, I'm hoping I can put you into one of the finest luxury RV experiences you could ever dream of! Just imagine . . ."

"Big John" Scott interrupted his sales pitch politely but firmly, " I have some business for you that you're gonna like."

"If it involves me selling an RV today then I'm all ears, Buddy!"

Scott continued, "I've got an affluent client who needs to balance his books with some big-time philanthropy. He came to me and after brain-storming for a while we came up with a plan I thought could help a lot of people, including Big John Mills." There was even a little southern twang in Scott's delivery. "My client has deep pockets and he wants to provide an RV dream-home to ten local families and he's going to finance everything"

"I like this son of a bitch, Langaroo. Sounds mighty generous." We could practically hear Big John drooling. "I think I have the perfect solution for these lucky families. Ten of the finest, high quality, castles-on-wheels that money can buy."

"One catch." Scott interrupted, "We need them by tomorrow night."

After a momentary pause and some paper shuffling Big John cleared his throat a little and raised his voice. "You know who you're talking to and you know I can get that done. Getting it done by tomorrow just may require some added fees and transfer costs, if you know what I mean, Mr. Lang."

"Big John, I'm sure whatever fees, taxes, charges and sir-charges you think are necessary will be no problem to my client. I am prepared to make everything happen with no expense spared." Scott continued to talk to him while I got out of the car and made another call or two.

Scott was really smart. He was getting Big John to do a lot of the legwork that was otherwise going to take us time and energy. I quickly thought of a few calls I could make with the same purpose. If I get more people working for me to secure and deliver goods and equipment it would give me more time for other things. In these desperate times I found myself lowering my usual standards in a lot of ways. There would be lying, stealing, deceiving and using people. This could result in other people being harmed or worse over the coming days. These were all prices I had to be willing to pay to keep my family safe. My immediate family and my new *expanded* family. We were in survival mode now.

Scott got out of the car and grinned at me. "I even got Big John to close down all of his RV lots and enlist all of his staff on this project. Each RV is going to be tricked out with solar panels, satellite TV, a generator and crammed with five thousand dollars worth of non-perishable food items. And in appreciation of my referral he's letting me use his own personal state-of-the-art, (in his best Big John impersonation) one-of-a-kind custom-built giant RV that he just had constructed. He's going to deliver it himself with the fleet of RVs tomorrow!"

As Scott was saying all these great things it definitely got my brain working. We needed to have access to get all this stuff into the fort before things went south. I asked the leading question but I expected Scott was already way ahead of me. "So do we have any plans for actually getting into the fort? I know Allan knows a guy there. We could just use brute force."

"When I was dealing with Big John he seemed to want to do whatever he could when he found out it was all for a good cause. I know that the fort is really struggling with fundraising. I'm pretty sure if I contact the Preservation Society and dangle a big-time check from a deep pocket donor they will grant us whatever we need. They will bend over backwards if the amount is big enough. Some type of last minute event in appreciation of obscene philanthropy could be our entry ticket. And do you know what the preservation society excels at putting together?" he asked with some snootiness.

I smiled as the word came out of both of our mouths at the same time "Galas." Scott and I had attended our share of them in Newport over the years. It's the only place I could wear my seersucker three piece suit and feel right at home.

"That would be a great way for us to get our foot in the door." I thought out loud. We'd still need to iron out that plan but I had great faith in Scott's ability to get things done.

He seemed back to his confident, optimistic self. Fundraising, finance, raising capital. These were all the things that he was great at. Maybe the best. "I'll get to work on that this morning. I'm just hoping by Friday night Newport isn't turning into a sea of zombies." he spoke what both of us were thinking.

"Agreed." I said as he got back on the phone. "Looks like Mr. Stanton is here. Right on time." I left him to continue his planning and plotting. I walked toward the office.

Mr. Stanton was the owner of the gun range and had been here ever since I could remember. Scott and I were both

members of this rifle club and knew him pretty well. He knew
we were "good folk" and loyal to his range. My father started
bringing me to the range when I was ten years old. Now I
bring my kids here and have introduced quite a few friends
and neighbors to the range. I had thrown a few fund-raisers
in his on-site banquet facility and he appreciated the business.
When you met Mr. Stanton he was usually quite curmudgeonly
but after a while you realized he was just a businessman. A
curmudgeonly businessman but we got along quite well. We
didn't socialize with him much but he was always at the range.
He had no family. He and my father were old friends and they
used to hang out while I would practice shooting. He and my
dad still get together once in a while but usually it was here at
the range.

"Good morning, Mr. Stanton." I called out. He was unlocking
the office and motioned for me to come on in. There were
several larger trucks in the lot and few guys unloading some
gear. There was also a catering truck unloading food. They kept
bringing out more and more buffet trays of great-smelling food
and bringing it into the banquet hall that was adjacent to the
range. None of our crowd were here yet.

"I'll admit I'm a little tired, Doc. I was up pretty late getting
all your friends their gun licenses. I thought it was a nice gesture
for you to buy them all memberships here too. Much obliged.
Got the permits too. Had to pay a few hefty fees to get it all done
but you did tell me that was not a problem, correct?"

I nodded and smiled as he went on. "Got my best guys to
train you folks and take real good care of the younger ones.
Safety first of course. I know some of you feller's don't need any
help but I appreciate that your neighbors will be new members
here. I want them to feel very welcome. Breakfast will be ready
shortly but I think you miscalculated when ordering the buffet.
You have enough food going in there for one hundred people

at least!" He chuckled a little and shrugged his shoulders but it didn't really bother him too much. I had paid for everything up front. Just the way he likes it. Just then Scott came into the office and the two of them shook hands.

Mr. Stanton continued, "When you told me you were also looking to outfit the entire group with arms and munitions I wasn't sure what to expect. I did what you asked and acquired as much gear and supplies as I could get. That's what you see these boys unloading. I think you'll be happy."

"I think you'll be happy too, Mr. Stanton." Scott added with a wink. Yes of course, Mr. Stanton was also a client of Scott's. "You might even be able to take a day off!" Scott joked.

This was an enormous pay-day for this range and he appreciated our business although there was no gushing. He was all business but as a gun range and gun store owner he needed to be aware of just who he was dealing with and who he was selling to. He trusted us both. He didn't ask many questions about why we were doing all this or give us any resistance. That was priceless. The range was basically ours.

Chapter 10

BREAKFAST

EVERYONE STARTED TO roll into the parking lot just after 9 am. It was a beautiful morning with plenty of sunshine. It seemed strange that everyone wasn't smiling and laughing with each other. There was a different vibe (as the kids would call it) and it was palpable. Somber but motivated. It looked like people had been crying and up much of the night but they still showed up and were ready for action. I'll admit our house had felt pretty stressed out, too. Jackson and Casey were amazing though. Usually tension had a significant negative impact on sibling relationships. Our kids were often at each other's throats when the stress level was increased. They would feed off of our emotions and could sense when there was a heightened level of "nerves" around the household. This morning when I expected anger and yelling it was a pleasant, albeit unexpected, surprise when the kids got up early and were ready for action. They were getting along and helping each other. They knew they were supposed to be packing up their necessities for the "foreseeable future." They kept going into each other's rooms and seeing what they should bring. It was actually quite heart-warming to me and Kristin that they seemed to be bonding in this awful time. I had left for the range early and Kristin was going to bring the kids over at nine o'clock. Jackson and Casey had both decided that coming to the range was more important than classes this morning. It was their choice but I was happy they decided to be with us.

Jesse and Jamie arrived with their kids first. They entered the range and Ethan and Logan immediately headed to the banquet room where the buffet was. It did smell great and there was a huge amount of food and delicious coffee waiting for everybody. We needed to keep people energized and I really wanted them to be focused during the session this morning. While it would be great to get through the next few weeks or months without needing weapons I wasn't willing to take that chance. In fact, I firmly believed that being prepared with enough guns and ammo was critical to our survival. We needed to know that we could protect ourselves from whoever or whatever threatened our safety.

Jesse came over to me and we exchanged bro-hugs. He seemed a little anxious and looked around a little bit before he started probing me for some info. "Did you see some of the news this morning? Some hospitals and research centers reported breaches in their security systems. Not people getting in but some type of rogue virus being accidentally released and threatening the local neighborhoods. There was some video that looked quite edited but similar to what we saw last night. It looked like some military involvement was getting underway in a few countries and on the west coast. Do you know anything more?"

"Yeah, Jesse. I saw those reports and I have to assume things are starting to unravel in certain areas. I don't know when the government around here is going to mobilize or when the media is going to be all over this. We could start seeing widespread panic or there could be a quarantine. Tom just doesn't think there is any chance of a cure or quick recovery. You've seen those things. I'm not sure if there's anything the government can really do at this point. Soon enough there will be too many to fight and the people hiding in their homes are still infected with the virus. I just know it's not good. Just keep in mind. We have some time."

Jamie brought Jesse a coffee and gave me a kiss on the cheek. Mankind on the brink but she just can't be anything but cheery. "The boys tested positive for immunity. We told them all the gory details but what can I say, they're in the club and ready for action."

"That's good news. I'm hopeful everyone has the same results and the same attitude. We need to all be together from day one." These two were like family and I was happy they were here and engaged with this plan. "Tom's going to call me later this morning and we'll get an update."

I caught sight of Kristin and the kids driving into the lot. "We better get some food quick, Jackson just arrived and he hasn't eaten since an hour ago." I put my arms around them both and we went into the banquet room.

A few other families had filtered in. The Stanfords and Carlsons were all sitting at a table eating breakfast. It made me think of the last time we were all skiing together in New Hampshire. The Carlsons had a big house that was perfect for New England ski weekends. The best part of the trip was always eating together in the morning before the full day of skiing. Seeing them now made me wonder about that. Would we ever ski again? Vacations? What can we really look forward to? Too early for those thoughts. Hopefully, Peter was going to convince his extended family members to get to that house and spend some time together. What a great house to spend your last few days with the ones you love. Some good times just not a pleasant ending.

I said my good mornings and everyone seemed to appreciate the food. There were a few smiles and a little laughing. Jaymi had some type of camouflage yoga outfit on she said she bought just for this occasion. I couldn't figure out how she had time to go buy that. It actually looked great. I smiled at everyone and after some small talk I went to get some food.

I noticed Jason had come in and was talking to Mr. Stanton. Jason spent a lot of time, and a lot of money, at the range and was a favorite of Mr. Stanton's. They were opening a huge box and waved me over to see what was inside. I couldn't believe my eyes! It was clearly a lady's handgun set that was trimmed out with material that looked just like what they used to make my wife's favorite hand-bag. On closer look it had the exact same labelling and design. The pistol itself was a beautiful light brown color and I had to ask, "Is that tortoise shell on the barrel?"

They both looked at me and grinned. Jason looked incredibly excited and Mr. Stanton seemed happy for Jason but I could tell he was not quite as enthusiastic about what sat inside that box. There was a holster with exotic leather and several extended clips with labels I recognized only because my wife dragged me into those very stores on Newbury Street in Boston.

"I had this designed for Kim's birthday next month. She is going to love this. I think these are going to be the next big thing here." Jason smiled and nudged Mr. Stanton who seemed to want to look away from the atrocity in front of him.

"Dr. Izzo talked me into buying thirty sets of these for the shop. He thinks they're going to be big sellers. My goodness I don't know how he got me to do that. Those ain't cheap. I'm still not sure why he needed to call me up at 10 pm last night to get these rush-delivered today." He raised his voice a little but I could tell he wasn't really mad.

"Is that so?" I asked looking at Jason. He hadn't told me about this either. "Kim's birthday isn't for some time?"

"Well, it turns out Dr. Gunslinger is quite committed to the safety of all your wive's and children. He has already bought all of these guns and their *commemorative couture shoulder holsters* and intends to just hand them out to your group today. He made me drive up to Providence this morning to get these from the distributor." Mr. Stanton exclaimed with some degree of sarcasm. He seemed to be enjoying himself.

"That is perfect, Jason. Brilliant." I said honestly. The wives were not very into guns but put up with it for us. These were going to be game changers. They were going to love these and so would the younger folk, especially the girls. I can't even imagine what Jaymi Stanford was going to say.

"We'll bring these out at the end of the program when you folks are finishing up?" Mr. Stanton asked and Jason and I both nodded.

It was going to be a pretty standard entry level program designed to give everybody the basic understanding of gun safety and a working knowledge of guns, ammunition, and loading a weapon with careful attention to safety. I made sure we would have all the best teachers and full access to the range all morning. Everyone would be able to hold, load, shoot and compare four different guns and have plenty of time on the range with each. We were all going to need to trust ourselves and trust each other with these weapons in the coming weeks and months.

Jason and I made our way back to the banquet room and joined the other families. I sat down with Kristin and the kids. We were sitting with Dave and Lori and their boys Lucas and Colby. They were a little older than our kids but they were all comfortable hanging out together. The kids all grew up together and had a lot of memories, good memories, going back to their early days. What I couldn't figure out was who was putting the biggest dent in the buffet. Jackson and Lucas seemed to have the most food on their plates but Casey was definitely keeping up with them and maybe had the edge. There was a reason I ordered extra bacon, Casey always had room for more bacon. She wasn't shy at all around the Zanelo boys or any of the neighborhood boys at all. She seemed to be enjoying herself *and* the bacon. I could tell she was nervous but I was glad she wanted to be here with us all. I was especially glad we had this time to just kick back and relax.

Just then I heard another car pull into the parking lot. I could see Allan and Amy unload and start bringing the boys in. This was a good sign indeed. I looked over at Scott and we both seemed to be relieved that he was here. We asked a lot of him last night and he seemed motivated to do whatever we needed. There was no hesitation from him at all to do all of this this for the group. As I saw him walk through the parking lot holding his boy's hands I didn't really need to question his motives or intentions. As a firefighter he was used to putting his life at risk for strangers every day. Things were different now. For Allan. For me. For everyone. Everything we were doing now was to save our families. His boys ran to the buffet and quickly filled up plates of bacon and eggs. Everyone seemed to be settled in and enjoying a little bit of comfort and togetherness.

Allan grabbed a cup of coffee and sat his boys down at the next table. He got them situated then came over to us. He smiled at everyone but he looked tired. If he got any sleep it wasn't much but I know he's used to that. Some of my longest nights being on-call as a resident didn't come close to a busy "tour" or four day shift he typically worked as a firefighter. Being up days on end with non-stop physically demanding work was brutal. Add to that the dangers first-responders face with every call. Oh, and by the way the harsh effects of heat and smoke and poison gases. Working in a tempermental oven surrounded by intense flames and surprise explosions. Sometimes it's below zero and the job requires you to be in the freezing cold for hours on end. Ultimately, if the firefighter *isn't* there doing everything right and putting his life at risk other people die. It's that type of person who chooses that job and that's why he does it.

"Did you sleep in, Allan?" I teased him a little. We all knew he was up well before dawn and probably at the wharf by 4:30.

"Sure, how about you?" he joked back knowing that I probably never slept past 5 am in my life. "I actually had a pretty productive morning. Turns out you can get just about anything done with a bag full of cash. I'll give you all the details later but there's room for two on *The Flying Serpent* pushing off tomorrow morning at 5 am and they will be expecting 3 people at Hammer Mill Farm for the Introduction to Farming class at 6am."

"That's good news, Allan. Not everyone knows what it's like to be able to buy whatever and whoever you want with piles of cash!" I said as we both innocently looked directly at Scott who was listening attentively and enjoying his corned beef hash.

Scott nodded and smiled good heartedly. "Careful, Allan. Once you get the feel for that it's hard to go back to the real world!" He joked but his words lingered and we all realized the *real world* was soon going to be just a memory. He scanned around the room and people were still eating but listening to everything being said too. Scott offered in a more positive, upbeat tone something we were all curious about. "I'm interested to see who is going to sign up for those all-expenses paid scenic excursions tomorrow. They sound like fun!" It sounded like he might just as well be at an all-inclusive resort on a Carribean island.

Everyone sensed his effort at some comic relief. I could see a lot of families speaking quietly and probably talking it over.

Dave Zanelo stood up and all eyes were on him. He owned an insurance company but didn't look like he did. We all knew him to be a pretty rugged, outdoorsy guy and his two boys were also strapping young men who were comfortable camping and roughing it. Dave also has a reputation as a late night partier and was the usual suspect when someone got pranked. His boys followed in his footsteps. They were great students but both had early reputations for their share of fighting and trouble-making. "Colby and I are volunteering to go on the boat. We both love fishing and are interested in boating. I would enjoy seeing *The Flying Serpent* in action!"

Nobody seemed to object and I wasn't surprised that it would be Dave and Colby taking on that responsibility. They were really close friends of ours and we have spent a lot of time with their family over the years. I was glad they were stepping up and it felt good that they would be with us in the days and weeks and months to come. I was really appreciating more and more the people in this room. There was a lot of trust and a lot of love here. We were all really lucky.

"Okay! Zanelos, you got two tickets for the fishing boat excursion. I can't think of anyone better for that task. Thank you both." I said and I really meant it. They would fit in just fine on the *Serpent*. I smiled as I added, "Dave just try to watch your language around the crew, please. Allan has a reputation to protect!"

Everyone settled down and there was still a lot of hushed discussion going on in the room. Casey came over to me and put her arms around me then sat on my lap just like she used to do. She hadn't done that in years and it just felt so good to have her snuggle with me. I was a little surprised with what came out of her mouth next. "Dad, I think I want to go to the farm.

I really want to help and I think I'd be good at it. At least the part about the animals. Please." She looked at me with her big brown eyes and I couldn't help myself.

"Sure, Pookie. I think that's great. The animals would love you and I think you would be great for the farm job!" I said as I hugged her. She held me tight and I loved that moment. It didn't happen that often and I learned long ago to enjoy it when it came. World on the brink be damned, my daughter needed a hug.

Just then Paul Stanford and Candace Carlson came over and sat down next to me. "Oh, that's a great daddy hug, Casey. You need to dish out more of those!" Candace said as she rubbed her back. She was Emily's mom and spent a lot of time with Casey. She knew Casey wasn't always quick with a hug or kiss and recognized what she saw. She didn't waste too much time before she announced "Paul and I are ready to get our farm on! We want to do it."

I looked up from my hug and was happy that Casey still hadn't let go. "That's great guys you'll both be perfect. Remember it doesn't mean you're locked in to doing all the farming. It'll still be a group effort but it's a critical part of our master plan. It's vital we have motivated people involved there early on." I responded as Casey was finally releasing her hold on me. "Casey really wants to be part of the farm experience too. Is it okay if she is part of the excursion with you guys?'

"That works out great! We need a third, Casey. I think you'll be a natural. I hear they have ducks and chickens!" Candace said as she gave Casey a nice hug.

"We'll be a great team." Paul boomed getting in on that group hug. "I had a little farm in my backyard back in Mattapoisett. I remember how great it was pulling a carrot out of the ground and serving in for dinner. I hope we never need to rely too much on farming but if we need it to survive then I want to be part of that. Candace, Casey and I will be ready for action right?" He fist bumped Casey and it was another good moment. The Stanfords and our family had been close for years and spent a lot of winter weekends skiing together. Paul was always watching out for Casey because she was usually surrounded by older boys and sometimes needed a little protection. As she got older she usually stood her ground pretty well and the boys didn't want to mess with her too much, at least in that way. I looked at her and how beautiful she was and how much she had grown.

"Okay, folks." I spoke up and everyone quickly quieted down. "We have our fishermen and our farmers!" There were some 'cheers' and 'hurray's and I could tell there was a general consensus that people were satisfied with things so far. "Dave and Colby are going out to sea tomorrow and Paul, Candace and Casey are headed to farm school! I think they all deserve a round of applause."

Everyone clapped and seemed genuinely happy with the volunteers. I made sure to add once the applause lightened, "This doesn't mean the rest of us are off the hook. There's a good chance we will all need to be engaged in these jobs in the future. We'll have to share the work. I know these volunteers are going to really help us as we start learning the business of providing for ourselves tomorrow. Thanks again, everyone. Here's to *surf and turf!*" I added as I held up my glass of orange juice. That last bit was met with a few snickers and chuckles. I thought it was clever.

Kristin let me know it wasn't that really that funny. "Too much, Honey. We got it. Now that we have that settled can we go shoot some shit?" she asked with a smile. She had let me know on multiple occasions she wasn't crazy with the idea of kids at a gun range but she seemed to be coming around.

I smiled and tried to give her my most appreciative look

as I raised my voice and asked loudly "Hey people. My wife's getting restless to shoot some things, what do you all say about that?"

There was some applause and some whistles as we all got up and started to move towards the range that was right next door.

Chapter 11

SHOOTING RANGE

WE ALL GRADUALLY made our way across the hall to the range. There were a bunch of seats set up and multiple stations that had clearly been prepared for us. The range was pretty old but had been updated recently. Each of the eight stations had a camera on the target that could be used to display real-time images at each station's high-definition monitor. Also set up at each station were a selection of guns and several different boxes of ammunition. As the families filtered in they all were looking at the guns and bullets laid out in front of them. While a few of the dads and boys were experienced for everyone else it was their first time seeing a gun up close. They were anxious but also excited to be in a 'shooting range.'

I saw Terry Roberts getting ready to give the "Intro to Shooting" class which he typically does every weekend. He and I knew each other really well. I actually helped get him his current job and he's been Mr. Stanton's right-hand man ever since he was hired. Terry is a patient of mine and is a veteran. He's a young black man and came back from the War in Iraq with nothing. He never finished college and couldn't afford to go back to get his degree. He was surviving on part time work and truly was a victim of the times. He had followed up every lead he had but was coming up empty for a job. I had gotten to know Terry fairly well and I knew he was a smart, experienced veteran who was in need of a break. I also liked him a lot. I knew Mr. Stanton needed a reliable assistant so I decided to bring Terry to the range as a guest one morning. We spent some time shooting and when Mr. Stanton came through I introduced Terry as a friend. Terry and I were going shot for shot not missing a target. He was clearly a confident but modest fellow. Clever and talented. We were hamming it up with Mr. Stanton but at ten o'clock a class was starting and he had to excuse himself.

"You're still teaching that class? How do you manage the phones? And what about all that paperwork you keep complaining about. When do you have time for that?" I asked knowing all the answers.

"I can't seem to hire anybody with a brain or any talent. High school kids are too young and I can't afford to offer benefits. I'll be doing paperwork and returning phone calls until late tonight but right now I have to teach a class!" he exclaimed emphatically. He stood up and was getting ready to leave when I put my hand on his shoulder.

"Jim, you need help and your business is suffering because you're trying to do too much yourself. What if there was a young, charismatic, responsible veteran who had the skills and devotion to help you out around here for a decent wage?" I asked.

"I'd say they're either an ex-con or an addict. I've been burned before." he returned with some ire in his voice. He again tried to maneuver past me but I held him in my grasp.

"I know you have had a lot of bad luck with your employees but I also know you need a break. You can't do this forever. What are you 70?" I asked (knowing full well he was 75.)

"75" he answered, slowing down a little and not resisting my hold. "Hey Doc, if you want the job it's yours. The class is waiting."

"Jim, let Terry teach the class. He's done it hundreds of times and he's good at it. You can watch him and if he blows it I'll pay for everyone's class. If he does a good job just tell me you'll consider him for the assistant position." I put it out there, knowing I was being a little pushy.

I would never say that Jim Stanton was racially biased but I hadn't seen anyone of color in his range or in his employment ever. He never said anything suggestive of any bias but I hate to say it, he was an old white guy with southern roots. Maybe it was me with the bias but I didn't care. I had known Terry long enough that I knew he was an honest, trustworthy guy. Black or white it didn't matter. He had charisma, knowledge and talent. He deserved a chance.

"I don't have time to prep him and I don't know where the lecture notes are. Sorry." He responded.

Terry stood up and looked Jim Stanton right in the eyes and said "Sir, I have taught classes in gun safety, tactical ballistics and advanced gun warfare. I'm licensed and registered and have a clean record. I don't do drugs and never have. I don't drink and don't want to. Let me teach the next class and if you're not impressed Dr. Braden will comp you for the class. However, if you think I did a good job just know I am willing to take on any role."

What could Mr. Stanton say? He nodded and shrugged his shoulders. He stepped aside and Terry walked right past and into the function room where they held most of the classes. We followed him into the room and found a seat. The room was full of all types of characters. Quite a few men and several women. A number of teens seemed to be mostly looking at their phones. I thought it could be a tough crowd for Terry.

He didn't seem to mind at all. He sauntered to the front of the classroom and seemed to just demand attention as he addressed the class. He had a strong, deep voice with a friendly tone which made you think he should either be on stage or on the radio. Instead he was immediately engaging with the class and making relatively boring material seem downright captivating.

Mr. Stanton and I sat through the class and I could tell from the start that Terry had the knack for this. There was no doubt he knew the material and seemed passionate about gun safety. He answered questions easily and engaged the audience from the start. He got a few laughs and seemed to connect easily with the entire class young and old. By the end of the morning every student in the class had signed up for a year long membership and many left after making a purchase or two. Terry had clearly proved that he could be a vital addition to the range and would be a smart hire. He was still assisting on the range as I made my way to the exit. Mr. Stanton waved me over from his office. I sat down and he smiled at me.

"I'll hand it to you, that Terry is great. He clearly knows his stuff and is a natural in the range. He generated more sales today than I've seen the past month. He's great!" Terry was hired that day and has been there ever since.

*   *   *

It was comforting to see him today and I was glad he was giving the presentation. After a hearty breakfast everyone seemed to be ready for whatever was next. I had already prepared Terry for what to expect with our group. He needed to get some moms and kids ready for real action in a short amount of time. Plenty of hands-on training and top flight instruction. Terry was the best. Even stodgy old Mr. Stanton would say that. Terry gave my kids high five's as they walked past. They had spent some time at the range and loved getting lessons from him. Everyone found a seat and got comfortable as Terry strode out in front of the group. There was a big screen behind him that everyone could see clearly.

Terry didn't need a microphone. His deep voice was easy to hear and he spoke clearly. "I know some of you already are comfortable with guns but this morning my job is to get everyone here feeling that they are able to hold, load, and fire a gun safely. Maybe you'll have some fun along the way. After all, that's the reason a lot of people come to places like this."

On the screen behind him were short segments of video footage revealing all types of people shooting guns at an indoor range, in a field, shooting skeet, and competing in the Olympics.

"Before we handle these guns I need to make sure you folks have a basic understanding of gun mechanics and the appropriate terminology we use when we talk about guns. Believe me, if you understand how a gun works and know what all the words mean when you hear or see them, it will all seem more enjoyable and less intimidating. Let's do this." He smiled and comfortably walked around in front of us all. He had everyone's attention, not a single phone was out.

"No matter how comfortable you are around guns everyone needs to remember these rules. Number one, always treat a gun as if it's loaded. Number two, only point a gun if you're willing to kill or destroy what you're pointing it at. Number three, only put your finger on the trigger when you're ready to fire. And number four, always keep the gun unloaded and securely locked in a safe when not in use."

"Okay, we're going to use a few different guns today and you'll all see how different they are when you fire them in a few minutes. There are three main types of guns: handguns, rifles and shotguns but they all work in a similar fashion and have different applications as you probably know." The screen lit up behind him revealing a man walking through the forest and a giant bear suddenly charged at him. "What are you going to use in this situation? My pistol may not have enough stopping power while a rifle may be too cumbersome to load and aim in time. Most folks would want a shotgun when you need to inflict enough damage to save your life but may not have enough time to take dead aim."

The screen then showed a gun range with a target 100 yards away. "If you add distance and have time a rifle is the best bet. I don't care how good a shot you are with a revolver or shotgun it's not gonna hit that target but a rifle, or long gun, can." The screen showed in slow motion a bullet striking the bullseye.

"As far as rifles go there are numerous styles and shapes ranging from a sniper rifle to machine guns. There are many differences to all of these including length of barrel, diameter of barrel, type of firing action, capacity of magazine and on and on."

"To understand better what I'm talking about and to help you be more comfortable let's discuss some of the standard vocabulary. Let's start with the ammunition." On the screen behind him appeared a cartoon depicting the different components and terms that were displayed exactly as he said the words. When we load a "bullet" into a gun we're really loading a round of ammunition. The round contains several parts including the casing which can be made of various materials but most commonly brass. The casing holds everything together. In the back of the round there is the primer which acts as the spark plug or igniter. This primer typically sits right next to the propellant which is usually a form of gunpowder. In the front of the round there is the bullet which is the projectile that is actually fired. A big difference you likely know already is a shotgun shell which fires multiple pellets in a wider range of distribution."

"There are many sizes and shapes of guns and ammunition. You should only fire a gun if you know that it has the correct size and shape round for that weapon." The display showed numerous bullets and shotgun shells which emphasized exactly what he was saying quite well. "This is critical folks. People can die if they don't know these things. Most guns and ammunition are well-labeled with this information and you will understand it more and more as we go, I promise."

"Let's talk about the gun itself." Again the screen behind him revealed a gun with various parts clearly labeled. "Some of these are common terms but let's review it anyways. You hold a pistol by it's grip and you hold a rifle by placing the stock against the shoulder and holding the forestock with the other hand. The barrel is the long tube the bullet flies down as it's projected. When a round enters the barrel and is ready to be fired it is considered to be in the chamber. Everyone knows what the trigger does. Remember, don't touch it until you're ready to fire. The safety is a mechanical lever that blocks the gun from firing. The magazine is the detachable container that holds the ammunition. The number of rounds held can vary widely and has increased over the years. In the pistols you folks are going to be firing in a few minutes the magazines hold sixteen rounds." As he was talking there were different guns being shown on the screen including images of some very sheik 9mm pistols with very well-recognized designer labels on the grip and holster very similar to the guns Jason had ordered. (We had Terry add those new pictures just this morning!) The wives all seemed to notice those images.

I heard Jaymi Stanford whispering to her husband, "I never knew they had those brands of guns, Paul!"

Terry began again just as an animated video of a car engine appeared behind him "Let's talk about how the gun fires. The purpose of firing any gun is to accelerate an object to a high speed with accuracy. How that is done is similar to another machine you use everyday. Your car engines work using the same principle and rules of physics. Within the engine there is the introduction of gasoline into a small space. A spark causes a controlled explosion and gas expands in one direction forcing a piston to move. This force ultimately turns the wheels propelling the car forwards."

Now a video showing the inner-workings of a gun were displayed on the screen. "Similarly, when you pull the trigger of a gun a spring loaded pin strikes the back of the round at the primer. The ensuing spark within the casing results in an explosion of the propellant. The expanding gas is directed in only one direction and the bullet is propelled forwards as it separates from the casing. Specially designed spirals within the barrel allow rotation of the bullet increasing accuracy significantly."

"It's pretty amazing how quickly all of that happens with a squeeze of a trigger. In fact many guns use the energy generated in the explosive process to fire the bullet, unload the spent casing, and to load the next round. That whole process is called a "cycle" or an "action." Single action guns are no longer very common. Semi-automatic weapons are the most common. That means you pull the trigger and the gun fires and cycles itself ready to fire the next time you pull the trigger. In a few minutes you will all be firing semi-automatic weapons. With some practice you can fire 50 rounds per minute. With training that maxes out at about 100 rounds per minute."

The screen started showing video of a massive gun on the deck of a battleship firing at a blistering speed. Terry continued, "Fully automatic weapons are largely illegal to purchase. With one pull of the trigger the gun keeps firing until you depress the trigger or run out of ammo. These guns can easily achieve 300 to 900 rounds fired per minute and some military grade weapons fire 4000 rounds per minute. We won't be using those today unless Dr. Izzo has any surprises for us."

"Folks thanks for listening to me and now let's get shooting. Today we're going to have one trainer for each station. That means each family has full access to an experienced trainer to help them which is uncommon but I think the best way to learn how to become a safe, confident and quality marksman. Good luck!"

The whole group clapped and whisted excitedly at the conclusion of the presentation. Through the back door entered the rest of the teaching staff and the fun was about to begin.

Terry was working with my family and I watched for a few minutes. He had Kristin and Casey holding and loading the 9mm pistol comfortably within several minutes. "I know Jackson can do this blindfolded. You don't need to be able to do that but with these finely crafted machines you will soon recognize the sound and feel of each round sliding into place in the magazine. You'll be relying on your senses to load the gun but even more to shoot the gun. You should practice lining up the sights on the gun to hit the target. Over time you may not even need to sight or aim every shot. Who's ready to give it a go? Let's do it Jax"

Everyone put on their safety glasses and ear protection. Jackson loaded the magazine expertly. He slid the magazine into the grip and felt it insert properly. He aimed down the range and unloaded on the target missing just once. He was aiming and the torso or heart of a human silhouette. We all clapped but no one louder that Casey. He put the gun down and removed the magazine. Jackson motioned for Casey to come up next. "Come on Casey. Your turn to do some damage!"

Terry chimed in with a big smile, "It's time for trouble. Jackson why don't you take her through it." He winked at Casey but hovered behind her watching closely. She had done this before but it had been a while. She was motivated now for a few reasons. She knew her life may depend on her shooting someone (or something) in the near future. Mostly she wanted to show Jackson that she was good at it. She really was pretty impressive. She loaded the gun with very little help and took aim. She took a little longer but she hit the same target only missing 5 out of 17 rounds. Pretty good.

Kristin was next and she struggled a little to load the rounds and her posture was off. Terry shifted her feet and moved her center of gravity then gave her the green light. She fired several rounds and didn't hit the target but I could see a big smile on her face. "Oh, Terry that felt good! I don't think I've felt as balanced before. That didn't sting at all! I almost hit the target!"

"Do it again Mom!" yelled both Jackson and Casey. She did and they applauded each shot as she actually did pretty well!

I walked around and each station seemed to be doing about the same. I was pretty amazed that everyone was engaged in what they were doing and committed to this. While I was hoping we wouldn't need to shoot anyone I knew that the greater likelihood was that there would be a lot of shooting. I didn't want anyone to get hurt because they weren't ready or prepared to save their life. Or someone else's.

Next came the rifles. An AR-15 was placed at each station with plenty of ammo and magazines. Everyone had to load a magazine, insert it correctly, turn off the safety and fire the weapon. While initially tentative after a few minutes everyone was loving it. In fact, after a few minutes the wives all congregated in one lane watching each other and whooping it up. I overheard Jaymi Stanford shout out as she emptied a magazine, "We should do girl's night here next!" The other wives smiled and nodded knowing that the next girls night wasn't happening for a long time.

The boys also seemed to be having fun with the AR-15.

Everyone had plenty of time and ammo to really get comfortable holding, loading and firing. The sight of the day had to be Casey helping Emily line up her shot with the 9mm equipped with a laser scope. She had Emily sight the scope right on the nose of the target and unload the whole clip. Emily completely destroyed that target hitting it square in the face every time. We all applauded but her father Peter cheered louder than any of us and even louder that he had at any of her swim meets. This was a success.

Everyone had a chance to use a shotgun and a long-range hunting rifle as well. Being comfortable with all of the weapons would surely come in handy if my prediction was accurate.

There were a few more demonstrations and Terry helped everyone understand how to use a taser. I was glad we added it as a feature. While we hoped we didn't need to shoot anyone it certainly would be important to have non-lethal options. Having the whole crew get some first hand practice tasing some dummies was practical as well as challenging. Now I've shot just about every gun there is but never a taser. Terry chose me to do a demonstration for the group. It was difficult and my kids loved seeing me miss the target a few times. Terry just couldn't resist hamming it up for them. He stood right behind me and fixed my posture like it was my first time ever shooting. Everyone was laughing and I heard a few pictures being taken. A good moment for sure. Everyone took a few turns and we all seemed comfortable with all these weapons. It had been quite a morning for us all and it was time to end the session. I couldn't have planned a better training session and everyone seemed to really be motivated and united. It was a good feeling.

Chapter 12

WHAT'S NEXT

I LED EVERYONE BACK to the banquet facility. I had arranged
for the buffet to be cleared and for there to be some cold
drinks and light food ready for anyone who needed it. There
seemed to be good spirits all around. I made sure everyone had
a snack then decided it was time to have a brief meeting. "Hey
everyone, I can't believe what I just saw in the next room. You
guys did great in there. Is someone keeping an eye on Emily?
She seems dangerous. Peter and Candace please watch her
closely!" I joked and everyone laughed, especially Emily and
Casey. They loved the shooting, almost as much as they loved
the breakfast.

Everyone was listening so I kept going. "Okay folks, we need
to talk about a few things. First off, in about ten minutes Dr.
Ashworth is going to call me and I plan on making it a facetime
call on the big screen here just so we'll all be up to date with
what's going on out there. I know there's been stuff on the
news. Jesse and Jamie saw some of the updates and we'll try
to find out what's really going on. In the meantime Scott and I
have been working on a few side projects. He's been working
the phone all morning. Let's try to get through things fast here.
We now are down to two days to be prepared for what's coming

next. If things start to happen how we anticipate we will be glad we took all the steps we did to be ready for . . . whatever is to come. Right now I made arrangements with a local moving company and they have dropped off a rental truck for each of our families right out here in the parking lot. They loaded each truck with extra blankets and six tanks of propane. Being loaded into each truck for everyone here right now is a personal 9mm pistol with two magazines and an AR15 assault rifle just like what you trained with today." I heard some whispering and definity saw a few fistbumps between the boys and yes, Emily was fistbumping Colby and Lucas and Jackson. "Each truck will also be loaded with all the 9mm rounds and AR-15 rounds that we could get from Mr. Stanton and several local shops. We're gonna have a lot of ammunition for sure. Everyone is going to have a state of the art taser. We also have a dozen shot guns and plenty of shells. We'll have a dozen hunting rifles with several crates of ammo. As far as being stocked up with weapons and ammo I'm not sure there's more we can do. What do you think Jason?"

He was standing right next to me and everyone shifted their attention to him. "Well, first of all I wanted to say thanks to Paul, that was one hell of a breakfast. You did not disappoint!" We all laughed and there was a lot of applause and jeers but at least I made sure nobody went hungry. "Terry was amazing and I think the training went well but there was something missing. When I brought Kim, Jayci and Santino here the last time I could tell the girls were unimpressed with the available guns. They weren't quite as upscale as some other things they enjoy and that really got me thinking." Right on time the door opened and Terry entered pushing a cart loaded with big boxes followed by Mr. Stanton with a similar cart.

Jason continued, "I had previously arranged for Kim to have a very special 9mm designed to match her handbag. They even created a matching custom shoulder holster. I thought she would enjoy it and a lot of the other guys agreed that the wives may actually like shooting more with high-end guns and holsters."

Mr. Stanton was never shy to interrupt "That's why Dr. Izzo designed and paid for all of these specially crafted deluxe 9mm setups with two guns, shoulder harnesses and designer magazines for all the wives and young adults! Come on up and get it!"

It looked like Christmas except with deadly weapons. Everyone received a beautifully appointed case containing the two pistols and matching magazines with a beautiful adjustable shoulder holster. All the wives and kids were smiling ear to ear. Casey and Emily had matching gear and Jackson picked out a special edition designed by a rapper I hadn't heard of. Kim and Kristin put on the shoulder holsters and looked great modeling the new weapon couture.

A few minutes later Dave's wife Lori walked over to me, looking very Lara Croft with her twin 9mm guns holstered. I put my hands up and stepped back a little "Hey, I don't want any trouble lady."

She smiled, "I could get used to carrying these around pretty easily." She seemed happy but I could tell something was bothering her.

"What's up?" I asked.

"Some of the wives were talking, we all have a lot of questions about what to bring and what to expect at this fort. We've never been there."

I paused and realized it had been a long time since we'd been there too. It seemed like there was a simple solution. "Well, how about a quick tour this afternoon? They have guided or self-guided tours available all day."

She smiled and exhaled a little bit. It looked like she was

hoping I was going to say that. "That's great. One more semi-normal thing until things go south. Speaking of going south, I just saw some news reports about what's going on in these research institutes and hospitals all over the world. Most cities are describing unusual patterns of violence as well. It's getting bad but still no talk of a viral outbreak!"

I nodded and gave her my best empathetic look straight out of medical school training and said "I know it's hard right now Lori, and we are going to have more information soon. In a few minutes we're going to hear from Dr. Ashworth and I'm hoping he'll give us a better idea of the timeline." I looked at my watch just as Scott was using a remote control to lower a screen in the banquet room. I gathered everyone around and waited for his call.

Two minutes later I did receive a call from Tom. I greeted him then switched it over to a facetime call broadcast to the big screen. Tom was on the screen and everyone could hear him. I thought the whole group deserved to know what was going on and Tom was okay with this too. I knew he really wanted us all to be ready and to hear what was happening. While I know he felt guilty about what was about to happen in the world he never tried to sugar-coat the details or make any excuses. He really cared about me and my family and knew just about everyone in our group personally.

I held the phone so that he could see my face. "Hi Tom, this is Paul and everyone in the group can see you on the big screen. We appreciate you calling and giving us some updates with what's going on. Most of us have seen what's been on the news."

His face looked somewhat rugged. Maybe he hadn't shaved or even slept. It looked like he was in a tent. "Hi folks. I know there's a lot of confusion and uncertainty. Hopefully I can give you some information and answer your questions. I promise to give you the most accurate details we have but you have to remember most of this is still unfolding and it's not easy to predict this timeline. First of all, the news stations are being fed some misleading information purposely. They know something's going on but we can't afford widespread panic yet. This virus and its impact on the public is spreading really fast and the pattern is staying true to the model. By tonight many of the larger cities are going to be experiencing increasing disturbances and there will be reports of violent mob behavior. We won't be able to cover things up much longer. We were hoping our efforts to develop a reversal agent or enough immunoglobulin would succeed but we've used or distributed everything we have and there's just no time for any other hail mary's here. At some point we're just going to have to go into watch and wait mode."

He took a deep breath and continued, "Most of the world leaders and governments are following the same approach. Instituting martial law or quarantining is unlikely to make any difference at this point. I anticipate by Saturday the shit's really going to get serious everywhere and I would recommend being somewhere real safe come Friday night. I will make sure you are all updated sometime Friday evening when we have more data. After I hang up Mr. Stanton will enter your banquet hall and distribute a supply of state of the art satellite phones that will allow you to stay in touch with each other and with me after this weekend. The phone lines, energy grids and cable systems won't stay up long. Folks, I really wish we didn't need to do any of this but I've accepted that things are rapidly deteriorating and we all have to work together to survive. There is no stopping this virus. This is going to be far worse than anything you are thinking."

Scott was standing next to me and gestured that he had a question, I handed him my phone. "Tom this is Scott. Do you feel the vaccines and immunoglobulin are effective from what you know? How safe should we feel around people who receive them?"

"The sooner people can receive the shots the better but as long as they receive it before they enter the transformation there is good data. It works but we just have so little of it." He gave a subtle nod as he looked at the camera and those of us who knew Tom well could tell he was saying 'don't worry Scott, Tracy and the girls will be protected.'

"Tom, do your models tell us how *long* we need to be prepared to shelter . . . when will these things stop or die?" I asked hopefully.

"That's a real tough one because so far these creatures are proving to be vicious, powerful, fearless and really, really hard to kill. They don't sleep but they seem to have periods of dormancy when they're easier to kill. We have some that we have had locked up under surveillance for twelve days but they don't seem to weaken or stop for anything. They do not tire. They attack and destroy with a ferociousness I just can't explain. These things seem to have good vision and hearing. The targeted genetic alteration must have enhanced some other parts of the midbrain and cerebellum. These beasts are in attack mode and don't have off switches. I'll send you some videos of a horde of these mutants and an up close inspection of one. It's not pretty. I can't tell you how long you need to be prepared for but I would say be ready for a long struggle and don't expect much help from the police or local government. Most of them are still in the dark and we didn't have enough vaccine to provide it to them. You will be all alone for many weeks if not months. When and if we can we will reach out to help you." He suddenly looked a little startled as if he heard something. He looked straight in the camera "I've got to go. I will make sure you receive an update tomorrow night. Best of luck. Remember, things are gonna get real bad Friday night into Saturday. Be somewhere safe Friday night. Good luck." And he was out.

There was silence for a few moments then a lot of anxious whispering in the group. That call from Tom answered some questions but probably created more anxiety. These creatures seemed worse than before. I wasn't looking forward to seeing those videos but we needed to know our enemy. I cleared my throat and got everyone's attention.

"Lori has a great idea everyone. What do you say we all take our cars and moving trucks home then meet up for a tour at the fort at 2 pm. I know Kristin wants to get home to get some packages off our front porch and to make room for more. We better tip the delivery drivers well, they're putting in a lot of effort in our neighborhood today and tomorrow for sure." I said with a smile trying to keep it light. I know everyone was up late last night ordering just about everything they could think of and in mass quantities. It's so hard to predict what we'll need but if Tom's right, and he usually is, in two days there will be no more internet shopping or delivered parcels. Everyone might as well order whatever they think they might need while they can.

Everyone seemed to agree on the idea of checking out the fort. I was getting ready to leave when Allan came up to where Scott, Kristin and I were standing. He had a good question "If Tom's right how are we going to get into that fort Friday night? We could sneak in or force our way in. I think we'd all like to be tucked in at the fort tomorrow night rather than taking any chances."

I remembered where Scott and I left off out in the parking lot. I looked over at him and so did Allan. Everyone seemed to stop and we all listened to what Scott was going to say.

"Well, there's still some details I have to work out but I've spent much of the morning working on that very issue. There's good news. I think we can all look forward to attending a gala at the fort on Friday night followed by a group sleepover!" He boomed with some cheers and applause coming from the crowd. "Evidently one of my clients has deep pockets and an even deeper love of Fort Adams. I had to pony up quite a check to the preservation society but they were quite appreciative of the mystery benefactor's philanthropy and his penchant for spontaneity. They are already getting ready for a very special few days at the fort unlike anything they've seen before. There's also a disappointed cub scout den that won't be staying at the fort tomorrow night."

That last comment was met by some sad "Aww's" especially from Jaymi Stanford. "Maybe they can have their sleepover next weekend." she reasoned to herself aloud.

"Jaymi!" Paul said loudly but not in a mean way. She stared for a moment then seemed to get it. She let out another quieter "Aww." as she realized ours would be the *last* sleepover at the fort.

Chapter 13

SCHOOLS OUT?

"CASEY COME RIDE with me. Mom and Dad are going to bring the truck home right behind us." I said to Casey who was still hanging on to Emily. Everyone had already removed their guns and holsters reluctantly but the girls were obviously still excited about the morning they just had.

"Jackson be honest. Who was really killing it back in there at the range, Me or Emily?" Casey called out. They were both in good moods and that was nice to see. If things were different that would have been one of the best mornings ever. When Dad usually drags me to the range it was serious business. No fun and games. Certainly no grand buffet. I think even Dad was having a good time or at least he was trying to seem happy for our sake.

"You both rocked it." I responded knowing that taking sides was just not worth it. "Emily you can come with us too. Just let your mom know."

We all got in the car and pulled out of the parking lot. We would be passing by the high school where we all went and the car got kind of quiet as we approached it. I felt a little choked up with some emotions I didn't expect. "It's so strange. I feel like I want to be in school right now. Even for a few hours just to feel kind of normal."

"Yeah, I know. Me too." Casey responded in a sadder tone than before. "Why don't we just go? I don't need to see that stupid fort. We're gonna be stuck there soon enough! What do you think, Em?"

"School sounds kind of nice." Emily responded, sounding a little more upbeat than the two of us. "I'll call my Mom. She'll be floored but I think happy."

I thought about it a little more. I really hadn't studied and I didn't have my backpack with all my stuff but I didn't care. "Yeah, let's just go for the last three hours of the day. I'll let Mom and Dad know. But remember. No one can know anything about this. This *apocalypse.*"

"Yeah, yeah, yeah." Casey spouted. "Dad said something like when the time is right he will make sure everyone has a warning or gets some type of message from him. If he does it too soon it's just gonna make it harder for us to do stuff and get stuff."

"He will let everyone in on it but the truth is it really won't matter. There's nothing anyone can do by this point. That mutated virus is already widespread and the clock is ticking. We can only save a few people with the shots so why get everyone else in a panic." I was mostly just thinking out loud but the girls seemed to appreciate hearing things as simple as I laid out.

After a little moment of being quiet Emily responded "Going to school might be fun when you think about it. No tests to worry about or projects to get stressed out about. I might even want to listen to some history and science stuff. School would be so much better without all the stress they add to the learning. My 79 in math really shouldn't bother me that much."

Emily got us all in a better mood as I parked and we all went into the school. We entered through a side door right as a bell rang. Everyone was getting out of class and it just seemed so surreal that things were still . . . the same as ever. Emily was so right. None of the kids really were able to appreciate what they had. They couldn't really embrace how lucky they were being in this school. I soaked up everything I could that day and didn't even think about grades or due dates. I learned more in those three hours of school than I ever did prior to this new *reality*. Everything seemed different. Even me.

I even talked to a few girls I never would have talked to before. I didn't have the old excuse of 'next week' or 'maybe tomorrow.' I seemed to have way more confidence as I walked the halls. Perhaps it was the 300 rounds of ammo I just fired with an AR-15 but I felt great. Between classes I walked right up to a girl who used to intimidate me and I looked at her square in the eyes and started talking to her. Just like that. After a slight hesitation she smiled and looked right back at me and we had a real conversation. I even made her laugh. The bell rang and I walked away feeling like I just discovered something amazing. Pure confidence.

I had a few encounters that afternoon with teachers, classmates, and few other girls. I felt so different and was really happy we came into school. I ran into Colby Zanelo in the hall. "This is pretty messed up isn't it?" He said but then adding "But pretty cool at the same time in a weird sort of way. Is it strange that we're going to miss all this?"

"You're right, it's all different now. And I was just starting to figure some things out. I have this new outlook on life and I wish all of this wasn't going away." I responded.

"Yeah, I noticed you chatting up Stephanie! She looked pretty stunned at first but she's been smiling since. I heard her telling some of her friends about it a little later too. All good." He said as we high-fived and went in other directions.

"Have fun on *The Flying Serpent* tomorrow" I said in a quiet voice.

"Aye-Aye" I heard as he turned the corner. I laughed and went into my last class ready to soak up whatever they were dishing out.

Chapter 14

FIELD TRIP

K RISTIN AND I dropped off the moving truck at home. It took some time to clear the boxes off the front porch. I had never seen so many packages, and they were all pretty big! I was teasing her about all the deliveries but in her defense they weren't all hers. The kids and I definitely contributed to some pretty heavy shopping since yesterday! We wouldn't have time to open most of these boxes, we'll probably just load them into the moving truck later on.

We jumped in my car and headed to Newport. We made our way over to Fort Adams through the back roads. It seemed to be a parents-only field trip today as most of the kids chose to attend school after we left the range. We were all baffled at first but I felt it was a great decision for them to enjoy the last bits and pieces of the current reality. They didn't need to come down to the fort but we did. Some of the other parents had never been to Fort Adams. Our family loved coming down to this area but today's trip seemed to have a different vibe. It wasn't too crowded in Newport these days. We weren't in "the season" when all the tourists descend on the *City by the Sea* in the summer.

I had been worried we wouldn't get a spot in a tour because

of the sometimes heavy crowds in the Newport area. I had called ahead to schedule a private tour of the fort after Lori and I spoke. When I gave my name the young man on the other end quickly spit out a very friendly "please hold" and I was listening to very calming music. After about 10 seconds a very animated voice with a strong Irish accent came on the phone.

"Good afternoon, Dr. Braden! This is Lieutenant Gerard of the Fort Adams Preservation Society. We're so happy you called! Mr. Lang has informed me of your intent to tour our wonderful fort this afternoon and I'll be here to meet all of your group's needs." He couldn't have been nicer and told us we basically could have the run of the place. He was largely in charge of the fort and seemed to be the perfect person to be helping us out. He assured us they were rolling out the red carpet and I felt satisfied as I hung up the phone. As we carved our way through the smaller roads of Newport I had some eerie feelings about what these streets were going to look like in a couple days.

"Honey, are we going to have to go in those deep tunnels under the fort?" Kristin asked in a tone that basically was saying 'I'm not going in the tunnels.' We'd been married long enough for me to interpret her question.

"I do want to check out the tunnels, to make sure they don't pose any risk. We need to secure as much of the fort as possible. Scott basically paid Mr. Gerard—forgive me *Lieutenant Gerard* half his annual salary to be a very doting guide to all of us today and an appreciative host at tomorrow night's gala. We need to really take advantage of this access."

Kristin rolled her eyes when I mentioned "gala." She had been to her share of these fancy white-glove affairs and wasn't sure she was in the mood to put up with another one tomorrow night. "Why does there have to be a big party? I still don't know why we have to get dressed up." She moaned a little with a hint of sarcasm. She still seemed to be irritated when we showed up at the fort entrance. We hadn't been here for years but even she was impressed and awed by the mammoth size of the walls as we drove up.

We were starting to park when suddenly a flagman jumped in front of us and beckoned us forwards. "Please proceed to the main gate." he said as he flagged our group of cars forward. We proceeded through the main gate which I thought was somewhat unusual. A host of volunteers lined up and were applauding our six vehicles as we passed through the main gates and onto the expansive parade field. They were certainly happy to see us! We were part of the "rejuvenation" that they needed to get this fort, well . . . rejuvenated. Scott had made sure these people knew that all their hard work was going to be rewarded. Tomorrow night was the big gala but we could feel the energy and enthusiasm in the volunteers as they moved around trying to make everything perfect for us. Everyone on the sprawling parade field that made up the inside of the fort seemed to be in overdrive as they were setting up for a big weekend.

"Good afternoon, everyone!" we could hear a booming voice with a strong Irish accent as we got out of our cars. "I am Lieutenant Gerard and I welcome you all to a very special tour of Fort Adams!" He was clearly excited as he walked by each car and snapped at trailing volunteers to bring us all sparkling flutes of the finest champagne. "Enjoy what is the very first part of our very amazing weekend here at the fort. When you are ready to see this very special place we can give you the most amazing views of the most historically important fort on the east coast!"

We all got out of the cars and made our way over to the lieutenant. He seemed more than enthusiastic about our presence here today. He made sure to let us know that he was the officer in charge and we had the run of the roost. "Good to see you all today, folks! While you are here you will be seeing a lot of trucks entering and exiting the parade fields. Do know that we are setting up for not one but two nights of revelry and celebration within the walls of this great fort. Due to the great generosity of the mystery donor we have pulled out all the stops to make sure this weekend will be the most memorable of any celebration you've seen in these parts in quite some time!"

"Two nights, is that right Lieutenant?" Lori asked as she sipped some champagne.

"Oh, yes madam, this weekend will be a celebration of celebrations for us and hopefully for you." responded the lieutenant. By now we had all circled around him with champagne flutes in our hands. "Tomorrow night will be a smaller 'ceremony of thanks' as we receive you all as our guests. You will enjoy the finest cuisine available and enjoy some local entertainment on these expansive parade grounds. Thanks to some amazing work going on right now by a host of local contractors as well as some of the most philanthropic donations from local companies you will all be sleeping in style tomorrow night. While perhaps not what the soldiers were used to 200 years ago you folks will enjoy some modern indulgences and creature comforts that you all deserve. Ten, yes ten of the previously unrefurbished officers quarters are in the process of being fully restored as completely functional living quarters featuring all the modern wants and needs that will make your stay most comfortable. There will still remain the bunk rooms and the classic, unrestored quarters that are part of the tour. The work you hear going on in the background is most exciting to us all, indeed! Mark my words by tomorrow night those residences will rival the best hotel experiences in the land. The army of contractors and artisans working on this project are the most skilled in New England their work so far is quite impressive to behold."

My curiosity was piqued, "I wasn't aware that such renovations were part of the preservation society's plan?" I asked.

"No Doctor, it wasn't until Mr. Lang called on the board this morning to consider the options available. Full restoration of the fort to its former glory is just not feasible it seems. However, with a mighty inflow of capital there is hope for this fort afterall. The newly restored suites you folks will christen tomorrow night will immediately generate income as we enter the boutique hotel business. We also anticipate opening up a high-end restaurant on the western casement overlooking the channel and nearby Jamestown. The water views alone will make it a top-rated choice for dining. Our once meager kitchen is in the process of being upgraded and doubled in size to accommodate the new hotelery concept. Expansion of our underground cold storage is also going to amaze you if you choose to explore that. What amazes me most is that all of these projects can be kept largely off the grid in regards to cooling and heating. I don't understand most of it but evidently the geothermal heat that uses the earth's natural energy to heat the fort can also cool the freezer. Amazing!" The lieutenant was definitely excited about this new direction the fort was taking.

"Ooh I can't wait to go to the restaurant!" Jaymi Stanford seemed gleeful, "I hope we can all be here for the grand opening whenever it is!"

I immediately glanced at Paul who was keeping it cool. Not knowing what to say we all nodded in agreement and even Paul seemed to just go along with it.

"We'll be there, Honey. And we'll stay in one of the suites that night!" He responded for us all to hear.

Jaymi seemed happy but no happier than Lieutenant Gerard "Aye, I can smell it in the air. This place is going to be very busy and you can sense the excitement around us! Just take it all in!"

He wasn't wrong. We could see contractors putting up drywall, furniture being unloaded, caterers bringing huge amounts of food into cold storage. There was a huge crane on the north end of the fort but I couldn't see what it was doing. "What's going on there Lieutenant?" as I pointed to the crane.

"Just another upgrade courtesy of your benevolence. It seems our propane tanks weren't up to Mr. Lang's standard and he arranged for a ten thousand gallon tank to be installed and that's what you're seeing at present. All of the utilities that aren't powered by the geothermal sources will be propane dependent. So much going on here and so much to see. Let's start with a review of the fort's history."

We definitely didn't have time for a history lesson. Unlike the kids we all wanted to forego the lecture and scope out the fort. Emily's dad Peter was the first to interrupt the lieutenant, "That will be great to hear but first we'd all really like to see some things up close." As he said this everyone breathed a little sigh of relief and I was glad it didn't have to be me interrupting the lieutenant.

Peter kept going "We seemed to drive right into this fort without any difficulty or lowering of a drawbridge. Do the original gates still work? Can this fort be sealed up?"

I have to admit this was probably the most important thing for us to know. If the fort was unable to seal the entrances it was just another building. We all turned our attention back to the lieutenant as he seemed a little surprised at the question but still all smiles. I wonder if he ever got that question before.

"Folks let's start walking because even if I tell you about this gate you would never be able to appreciate the sheer girth and expanse of this piece of art. It took fifty artisans six months to fabricate this mammoth wrought iron structure. It weighs over ten tons but smoothly glides on a rail like a screen door. When locked the gate is essentially impenetrable. We seldom close the fort but I assure you it is still quite functional."

We turned the corner and entered a side door near the fort entrance. Immediately before us was one of the most impressive displays of iron I had ever seen. The lieutenant summoned two officers and they quickly hit a few buttons on the wall and the iron fence began rolling on a rail we hadn't noticed before. It took less than one minute but when the entryway (about thirty feet across) was sealed it certainly looked like a vault being closed. Quite impressive. Nobody was getting through that gate.

We had him show us again exactly how the gate was opened and closed. It was actually pretty simple and he even showed how this massive gate could be closed if the power was out. We all seemed to be happy with the main gate but there was still the next question to ask, "How many entrances are there?" Jesse was the first to ask.

"Only two sir." Responded the Lieutenant "This magnificent structure and what is now the tour entrance just across the way. I assure you it's not very interesting and holds very little historic value."

"Is there a gate there?" asked Jesse.

"Actually there is a fence there that we close at the end of the day but it is not the original gate that formerly existed at that site. The original gate is over there and in some disrepair." He pointed to a large structure under a large tarp. "Right now some chain link fencing serves as the gate."

"Could the original gate be installed at that tour entrance in its current condition?" I asked with some true concern.

"Well, I think . . . that is I believe that . . . well yes. Yes it could." but he didn't seem sure.

I thought quickly, "Lieutenant this issue may seem unimportant but believe me when that gala starts tomorrow night if this fort doesn't have true defensive gates installed and fully functional the donor is going to be pissed. He is a purist and won't settle for a chain link fence."

The lieutenant seemed a little confused but by now he was just going with the flow of our bizarre questions and demands. He reached for his walkie-talkie, "Johnson! McDonald! Get the bobcat and the welding torches. Bring the side entrance gait into position and install it immediately. Work all night if you need to. Make sure the locking mechanism is functional and conforms to the current standards. Top priority!" The Lieutenant looked at me and winked. "She'll be sealed up by nightfall, Dr. Braden. Mark my words. Now about the history of the fort."

Kim was next to redirect the poor lieutenant "I'd love to see the kitchen, freezers and food storage areas. Can we take a look at that part of the fort?" She and Lori were definitely thinking about what supplies we needed to bring and what is already here.

Poor Lieutenant Gerard was caught off guard again and was thinking of his response when Jason asked "How about the well? Is it fully operational to provide water for both the kitchen and the new suites? Is the water drinkable?"

Paul Stanford joined in next, "Is the generator able to provide adequate wattage for the entire fort. What other renewable energy is available?"

All eyes were on the lieutenant as he realized this would be a different tour altogether. He seemed to take it all in stride and took us through parts of the fort few people had seen. By the end of the tour we had seen the kitchen, the cold and dry storage, and had a good idea of what was still lacking. We were all impressed with the water supply. A combination of well water, rain catchment and water purifiers all seemed to be operational. The geothermal heat and cooling systems were impressive and required virtually no energy. We were convinced that the 30 foot walls and massive gates were ready for whatever comes our way.

The hotel suites were most impressive and we couldn't believe how fast the teams were resurrecting old dark quarters into fancy new suites. There were dozens of carpenters, plumbers, electricians, HVAC teams, and other contractors all going in and out of the suites and kitchens. It was quite amazing. The army of contractors were scheduled to work through the night and were on schedule to finish before the gala starts. Trucks of brand new furniture, appliances, artwork and just about everything you can think of were rolling in bringing more and more beds, chairs, sofas, lamps, tables, ovens, refrigerators, TVs and everything you would find in a nicer hotel. Even Scott would be quite impressed.

Chapter 15

TWO IF BY SEA

A T THE END of the tour we thanked the lieutenant and departed the fort. It was almost 5 o'clock. Scott was on his way down and he wanted to have a quick meeting at the far side of the parking lot near the seawall. An odd location but we did need to decide a few more things before night set in. When you exit the fort into the large parking lot you are immediately surrounded by panoramic views of Newport harbor and thousands of boats. There was one giant yacht that was docked just across the lot that wasn't there when we arrived earlier. It was more of a ship really, the kind you would expect to be owned by a sheik. We were standing on the sea wall marveling at this massive yacht when a small door opened halfway up the side of the boat and a pretty-faced young woman suddenly appeared. "How was the tour folks? I bet you're all tired of walking around that fort. Why don't you come aboard and have some delicious food we just prepared."

We were all caught off guard a little but something really smelled good and she seemed so nice. She sounded Australian and appeared to be in a steward's uniform.

"Are you talking to us?" Kristin asked, wondering if

this woman was confused, "And what is that aroma? Is that hibiscus?"

"Yes, it's the chef's favorite secret ingredient in tonight's special but don't let him know I told you. And yes I'm talking to you, Mrs. Braden. Mr. Lang has briefed me regarding your party's arrival and he is en route. He should be here in five minutes. That should give us enough time to get you all on board the *Resilience* with a drink in your hand and a comfortable place to sit."

This was a mammoth vessel! It was at least 250 feet long and rose 50 feet out of the water. We were all excited about boarding this beautiful yacht but we couldn't see *how* to board. It was about twenty feet away from the seawall and not tied to any dock or pier. Just then a panel opened up below the stewards door and what appeared to be a gangway emerged silently and kept extending until it was just in front of us. It then lowered to the ground. A moment later from each side of this gangway rose a series of posts with a velvet rope leading from shore to the ship. It was beautiful to watch. If the gangway was that impressive we couldn't wait to see what else was on board. Kristin led the way and we all boarded the ship and were handed a beautiful cocktail as we stepped onto a sprawling deck. This was no regular boat deck. There was plenty of room to walk around and beautiful chairs and couches and tables set up unlike any boat design I had ever seen. Everything was perfect if not over the top. It felt good to sit down for a moment and take in the scene.

Just then we heard the distant sound of a helicopter as the steward checked her watch. "Right on time. Mr. Lang is arriving now." she said into what appeared to be a microphone on her wrist. We could see several other stewards immediately appear from a door at the front end of the boat and help the helicopter land. Very quickly the copter landed and the rotors started to slow down. We could all see Scott unload and he was led towards us. He looked right at home surrounded by all of this opulence and grandeur. He approached the group and was handed a cocktail by the steward.

"Thank you, Abby. Hey team, can anyone guess what I bought today?" He asked the group. At any other time we would all be blown away but today it just seemed like an accessory. He probably had a good reason to be spending his time and energy with this venture but we weren't going to question anything he's done so far.

I was laughing as I responded, "Between the hotel you spawned across the road, the helicopter you flew in on and this enormous cruiseship what haven't you bought?" and everyone joined me teasing him a little.

He smiled and as the steward disappeared down a stairwell he explained how he came to be a yacht owner. "I had no idea I was going to buy such a vessel. My intention was to purchase a small boat that could sleep five comfortably so the girls and Tracy had a safe place to quarantine. While I was in the process of buying a much smaller boat the trader mentioned that he had a major headache. It seems this boat and this crew just returned from a two month cruise out at sea. There was a small collision with an oil rig and after an inspection this boat was deemed inoperational for cruising. It may remain at anchor and can travel no more than 5 miles from shore due to the structural damage. I basically stole this thing for pennies. The real attraction is a crew that should be contagion-free by my calculations. They haven't left this boat in one hundred days. I paid the two of the crew to stay on board for the next three days too. It was not cheap to get them to stay on board but I just couldn't risk them getting exposed to the virus. The other three crew members I plan to send away. I'll send them to Boston for an all-expenses paid week at the Ritz.

We all agreed that for now it would be smart to have a back-up plan if things went south at the fort. It would be tight but if needed we could all cram aboard *The Resilience* at least for a short span of time. It's main purpose was just temporary. Tracy and the girls would enjoy being on this beautiful yacht more than an old, decrepit prison cell across the street. When they were confirmed immune there would be a beautifully appointed suite at the fort for them to move into.

"It seems I'm not the only one spending some money." Scott continued, " I did receive several calls from high-end auto dealerships today to confirm what some would call 'previously unheard of credit limits many of you seem to be enjoying. I can't wait to see what you all are driving tomorrow night at the gala."

"Hey, we all can't just walk to the gala from our yacht!" Jesse replied good-naturedly.

I'm pretty sure Jesse bought a Bentley.

We needed to talk about tomorrow. We finalized some details regarding the fishing and farming excursions. Everyone was still ready and willing to put themselves out there for our team. The gala started at 7 pm promptly and we needed to have as much as we could inside the walls of the fort by then. Big John would have his RV convoy delivered here by 5 pm. We would deliver our loaded moving trucks into the fort whenever we chose (Lieutenant Gerard resisted at first but ultimately guaranteed we could bring all of the vehicles into the fort and onto the parade field for our big sleepover.) Everyone would be in gala attire including any family and friends we immunized. We would then have one final meeting on the *Resilience* at 6:30pm. Finally we would each drive our car through the gate and into the fort by 7 pm. We would try our best to enjoy the night before the party ended at 10 pm. Any remaining gala attendees would vacate the gala and once we were satisfied the fort was cleared the gates would be sealed tightly.

As we were finalizing the plan the steward showed up and looked a little concerned. Scott spoke with her briefly and she used a remote control to lower a video screen near where we were all sitting. We turned on the news station and watched closely.

"This is Dan North reporting from Providence where there have been multiple bizarre and horrific attacks occurring with a seemingly random pattern today. Similar outbreaks of violent attacks have been reported worldwide and the police have yet to comment on the nature of these events. Theories of gangland violence, drugs laced with PCP, and even human rabies outbreaks have riddled the internet. Governments have been tight-lipped thus far but as smaller cities begin to be affected there may be no safe haven from these attacks. We are going to show footage from a camera at the Providence Mall but we warn viewers that the footage is quite disturbing."

We then saw what looked like several people running towards innocent bystanders and attacking them. Biting, clawing, ripping and eating flesh. Other people would try to help but only meet the same fate. Some of these *creatures* jumped through panes of glass suffering major lacerations but it didn't even slow them down. A security officer shot one of these wild attackers point blank in the shoulder and chest and it didn't flinch as it jumped on the officer and mauled him savagely. Only when about 6 police emptied their guns into one of these monsters did it stop. All of these images were just like what Dr. Ashworth showed us. It was all too real. It was scary and it was happening everywhere now.

We turned off the TV and agreed to stick to the plan.

It was getting dark and we all just wanted to get home.

Everyone had a lot to do but I took a moment to discuss a

few other things while we were all together. There were still a few things I felt we had to accomplish before everything around us came to a screeching halt. I went through some of the items that we still needed to get done and availed on some of the group to handle some of these big jobs.

Casey, Candace and Paul Stanford would be on the farm working their tails off.

Dave and Colby Zanelo were boarding *The Flying Serpent* and Lucas would be needed to help Lori.

Scott was getting Tracy and the girls from the airport and was working closely with the fort rejuvenation details and making sure everything went smoothly and remained on schedule. Huge sums of money had a way of doing just that.

Jesse was the guy who had the most technical abilities and I wanted him to get some necessary hands on experience just in case it was needed. He was going to spend the day with an electrical engineer I knew. The engineer was semi-retired and was teaching at the local technical school. I needed Jesse to be able to wire anything we needed and fix any glitches we might encounter. He needed to be comfortable with generators and using the power of a generator to get anything up and running. A store, a gas station, a house, anything. How can we power up something we need electrified. We needed Jesse to be completely comfortable with electric panels and circuits. I felt he was pretty capable already. He would also be outfitted with all the tools and equipment we may need. He was also permitted access to bring the electrician into the fort so they could inspect closely the circuitry of the fort and it's massive generator. He would also inspect the new propane tank and familiarize himself with it's operation and maintenance.

I decided my brother Mark would be my point person for renewable energy. He had just installed solar panels on his roof and was always reminding me that he got paid for his extra energy while we were dependent on the grid. The panels he owned turned sunlight into solar energy. The energy went to a distributor box and some of it was used by the house and some of it was routed back to the grid. He had an electric car that he could charge directly from his distributor box too. It was pretty amazing and he was really into it. He was a chiropractor and had already canceled all his patients for the rest of the week after he got his shots this morning. On my urging he had contacted his solar panel company and paid a hefty sum of money to get the behind the scenes tour. This would allow him to see the inside of their shop and learn everything he could in one day. They mostly installed solar panels but also dealt with wind, geothermal and hydroelectric sources. They were stocked with all the necessary gear and equipment that we could be interested in. Mark's job was to make sure if he had to he could acquire, install, and maintain these systems if we ever felt we needed them. He was already pretty savvy with his own system. Mark also had access from the lieutenant to bring a technician to inspect the fort's geothermal design in case it needed any maintenance.

Mark and Jesse were more than motivated to take on their roles. We were going to need them to be capable and ready but it was still too difficult to know what challenges we were going to face.

Jason was going to get his hands on more technical equipment we may need including some additional weapons. We thought it might be good to have some more powerful long range guns with bigger ammo. We didn't know what else could stop these things. He would get plenty of explosives, equipment for an electric fence, different types of mace. He had an empty van and planned to fill it with whatever he could as he combed southern New England legit businesses and some less reputable sources. We didn't want to be underprepared. I also charged him with trying to get some type of communication equipment that would work even if phone lines and wifi went down.

Allan was planning on "borrowing" some fire station equipment. He and Kenny (another neighbor I vaccinated this morning) would work together to orchestrate this under the radar. Allan rattled off a list of things that I never thought of but seemed worth the effort. There were trucks loaded with potable water, refueling trucks, an ambulance stocked with everything we could need for a medical emergency, and a boat with a water cannon rounded out the list. We were protecting a fort surrounded on three sides by water so *why not* have a water cannon?

Amy's job was to pull every string she could and secure as much equipment and medications she could liberate from the hospital where she worked. I gave her a list of medications we could use, mostly antibiotics, epi-pens, suture kits, bandaging, some IV lines and saline. I already had a bunch of stuff from my office but the hospital had big storage areas that were likely going to be ransacked real soon. She needed to get there first.

Everyone had their jobs not to mention packing up their moving trucks with everything they needed. The clock was ticking. The gala started at 7 pm tomorrow. We had less than 24 hours to prepare. Would that be enough time?

Chapter 16

THE FISHING TRIP

IT WAS PRE-DAWN Friday morning and all the lights were on at the Zanelo's house. Colby and Dave were getting ready to spend the day on the high seas aboard *The Flying Serpent* and they were trying to get in the right mood. At any other time it would be an amazing experience for someone who loves fishing to spend a day seeing how the professionals do it. With so much going on in the world and at home Dave found it hard to leave for the day and Colby admitted he'd rather go to school. Lori wasn't too happy about it either but she believed in the plan and knew how vital this day at sea could be for the group. She knew that the food they were bringing would run out and the farm just may not be accessible in a world filled with those flesh-eating monsters. She tried not to think about it as she made their lunches. When she was worried she would gravitate to the kitchen. When some families go through a crisis neighbors often bring over a casserole or a meal. Not in Lori's house. When she was feeling stressed she would start baking and cooking. We all knew she would be up early cooking and no one was surprised when Colby or Lucas showed up at their front door with a pie or a lasagna fresh out of her oven. No wonder she really wanted to check out the kitchen at the fort. That may be where she finds some solace in this fast-approaching nightmare. For now she was making her boys sandwiches and some treats for their long day.

"Ok Lori, after this you got to shut down the kitchen and keep loading the truck. Lucas will be here to help you with packing and loading and you know Paul's two doors down if you need anything." Dave said as he tried not to sound nervous or anxious. He was worried and hated to leave home with so much happening. "You gotta stop cooking. Just start packing up whatever you think you may need."

"I know, but I'm just glad we got a chance to look in all the cupboards and drawers at the fort's kitchen. I was mentally preparing to pack my whole kitchen but they had just about everything I think we'll need. We may need some essentials for our own suite's kitchen. I wish I could have checked that out!" She put her arm around Lucas and Colby who were eating breakfast as she continued, "I think I know what we need. Lucas and I have plenty to keep us busy today and keep our minds off . . . everything else."

"Mom, Dad and I'll be okay. It's just one day and we're not really going out that far." Colby tried to reassure her, "I hope they let us reel in a Tuna!"

"You know they're probably gonna have us pull in nets, bait some traps and mostly just learn all the technical stuff we can out there Colby. It may not be as fun as you think." cautioned Dave.

They each brought their lunch and a bag of essentials with them. They wouldn't be coming back to the house. After their sea voyage they'd be changing on the *Resilience* and going directly to the gala. They loaded up Dave's old car with their gear and got ready to go.

"Dad, why can't we take the new truck? You said it was your dream to have one of those!" Colby asked.

Dave looked over at the sparkling new pick-up truck with all the bells and whistles. It had top of the line everything with a safari package, bullet-proof windows and tires, heated and air-conditioned seats with massage in the front and back row. He decided to take his older car down to the docks this morning. Lucas would drive the new truck to the fort later. It had tons of room in the bed plus they had the moving truck to fill. It was still dark as Dave and Colby left home for the last time and drove to the dock to meet up with the crew. They both had a pit in their stomachs as they exited the neighborhood not knowing if or when they'd see it again.

They tried to get excited about the day ahead of them and they knew a lot was in the balance. Fueling the boat. Starting the engine. Checking the oil. Getting bait. Setting traps and lines. Storing all the fish. Learning all of this in one day was going to be a challenge.

They arrived at C dock just at 4:45 am as Allan recommended. They were right near Fort Adams and when they returned it would just be a quick walk to the *Resilience*. It was still dark but many of the boats were lit up and there was plenty of activity. They grabbed their backpacks and walked towards the very end of the dock and there she was *The Flying Serpent* herself. Not quite as impressive as the last boat Dave was on but it appeared seaworthy.

"David and Colby I wager!" came a booming voice from behind them. "Didn't think you'd make it but I'm glad you're here. Two of the three crewmen are AWOL this morning so we're all going to be working hard today! Hopefully you city boys can keep up! I'm Joe, Captain Joe." he said as he reached out to shake hands with his new crew.

Dave was surprised at the welcoming tone from the captain but it did make some sense. He was just handed a boatload of money to do what he was going to do anyway just with more help. There would be some added requirements that were understood. The captain agreed to give the visitors full access to everything they needed to know. Everything was included including how to operate the boat, the best fishing locations, where he could guarantee the best results, legal or not.

"Morning Captain, I'm Dave. That's Colby. Hopefully we won't slow you down too much." They all finished shaking hands and boarded the ship. "Any idea where the missing crew might be?"

The captain shook his head, "No. It's really not like them either. They're usually here by four in the morning. I just hope they're not in jail. Or caught up in this violence we see on the TV. Either way it's time to go with or without them. I just hope you're both still upright by the time we reach the lines. You may not need those packed lunches if the seas are high. Shouldn't be too bad." Captain Joe said as opened the door to the crew's break room.

They were given a quick tour of the ship from the crew's quarters and locker room to the engine room. They mostly followed the captain around as he conducted his usual morning preparations. He performed all types of tests and calibrations and Dave did his best to make mental notes of everything. He added some lubricant and checked a bunch of levels in the engine room. He was naming a bunch of machinery and turning some valves as he spoke pretty fast. Fortunately, Colby was filming things with his phone and getting it all documented. Finally they went up to the controls and the captain identified the most important knobs and gauges. He grabbed a key out of a coffee can and placed it in the ignition. He pressed another button as he turned the key and we could hear the engine below roar to life and the whole panel lit up brightly. He then turned the engine off and turned to Colby and said "put that machine down for a minute and have a try!"

Colby tried a few times and finally got the sequence right and the engines came alive again. "That was pretty cool, Captain!"

He led them through a series of tasks and seemed to be quite happy to tell them about running this boat. "If you boy's have a good time tell Mr. Lang we're willing to take out cash paying customers whenever he wants!" It was pretty clear he wanted to make us happy. "Let's hope we have a good haul today.!"

The other crewman, a short stocky boy about Colby's age named Gil was already on board. It was decided Colby would work with Gil and Dave would shadow the Captain. Colby and Gil set out to start preparing some traps and loading up ice in the storage areas.

Dave watched closely the captain threw off the lines and maneuvered out of his slip deftly. He looked over at Dave and winked, "You'll get your hands on the controls a little later. It's a little easier to drive in the middle of the ocean." He let out a good natured laugh. He drove a few hundred feet to a fuel-dock. "Come with me, we'll top'er off. Not sure why this is all so interesting to you folks. Kind of like filling up your car, but with 400 gallons."

Dave witnessed the entire process and just had a few questions about the fueling process, "How is that pump powered and what happens if the power's out?" He looked at the fuel attendant who shrugged his shoulders. He was just a summer kid.

"Aye they've' got a generator over in that shed. Down here we still work when the power doesn't" Captain Joe was pointing over to what looked like an old cabin.

"Where does the gasoline come from? Is there a tank over there too?" Dave asked.

Captain Joe looked at the boy who again just shook his head as if to say 'dude it's way too early for this.'

"Oh yeah, there's a tank under that same shed just like at yer mobil station where you fuel yer Mercedes, Mr. Zanelo." Just then the fuel gauge clicked, the tank was full and it was off to Block Island sound for the day's journey. Within an hour they arrived at the first bouy. Pulling up full lobster traps, unloading lobsters then resetting them with bait was hard work but pretty cool at the same time. Hauling in nets with hundreds of fish was thrilling although it seemed to lack some of the elements Colby enjoyed with shoreline fishing. Pulling in lines hoping for a tuna or a swordfish was the highlight of the day. It was actually quite thrilling for these first-timers. 'Long-lining' is a commonly used mode for bringing in bigger fish. The main line can run a huge length with shorter lines or 'snoods' with baited hooks dangling at various intervals. Every 200 yards or so the crew could tell if there was a fish on right away. Sometimes it was just a bass but every fifth or sixth line brought an exciting challenge. It was amazing to see an enormous tuna pulled onto the deck but somewhat sad to see it beaten and gaffed until it was lifeless and put on ice. Dave and Colby were amazed at the enormous fish being caught so close to land. Swordfish, tuna, some sharks. Not all were keepers and the crew tried to humanely unhook most of the throwbacks. After thirty or fourty of these even the Zanelos were ready to move on.

It was hard work and even Captain Joe gave the Zanelos credit. At the end of the day another boat came by and they transferred all their bounty for cash. Lobsters, various fish types and sizes all on ice were bought and sold out here in the middle of Block Island Sound. The fish was sometimes even processed and packed out on the water on these huge processing boats before being shipped elsewhere. They emptied all the product, cleaned up and Dave and Colby each took some turns driving the boat and playing with the controls and sonar. Nothing too complicated out here but it got a little more difficult the closer you get to inland waters.

"Colby you can work on my boat anytime. Got plans for next summer?" The captain asked which really was a compliment considering his initial low expectations.

"I think I'll be available, Captain." Colby said as he took off his gear at the end of a long day. He, Dave and Gil the other crew member were in the locker room changing after a physically demanding day's work. They were really beat but Dave and Colby had held their own and even Gil was complimentary of their willingness to get their hands dirty. Most importantly they learned a tremendous amount and felt pretty good about their mission—being able to do this for real if and when they needed to. Colby was ready to be heading back and he was starting to worry about what was happening in the real world. "How long of a trip until we're back on land?" he asked the Captain.

"We're actually pretty close to port. Twenty minutes." the captain responded "We kept it close to shore as part of the agreement. To get to the outer banks is a two day trip but it sure is worth it. At least it used to be. Don't worry, I'll get us back quick while you fellas change and relax. I'm ready to get back myself, I feel like crap. I think I'm coming down with something." He left and was off to the pilot's cabin and the "crew" kicked back and relaxed.

Chapter 17

FARM CAMP

EVERYONE WAS UP early in our house. Candace was going to pick Casey up at 5 am sharp so we were all getting ready for what would be a big day. Casey was trying on different jeans and boots to get the right look down. We wanted to ensure she was pulling her weight so we reminded her that this was not a game. She actually did have some farming experience. Every spring we would go up to Maine where Kristin's cousins have a farm. They worked hard from sunup to sundown and had taught Casey and Jackson the meaning of a 'full days work.' Cousins Johnnie and Jeremy didn't take many days off but they were certainly willing to have some fun nights. We would crack open some beers at the firepit while the kids would beg to go to bed early. We called them the *Mainiacs* and they always lived up to that moniker. Small doses of farm life seemed really attractive during those trips north but neither Kristin or I had that kind of work ethic. Casey never seemed happier than her time on the farm so we weren't surprised when she volunteered to be part of the farm squad.

"Mom, can I wear my new boots? I know they're brand new but I was just thinking . . ." she asked trailing off a little. "I already packed all my other gear and clothes for the fort.

I wonder if there's going to be any birthing today. That would be so great! Maybe I could help like when Aunt Cassie let me get my hands right up in there with the lamb deliveries." Seeing first hand the amazing miracle of birth was eye-opening for Casey as she saw multiple baby lambs join the fold. She stayed up all night with Cassie not wanting to miss any of the action. Those were great times. We would have to call the Maniacs and let them know the need to isolate and protect the farm over the next few days and weeks. They were pretty good at that. Maybe they would be ok. Maybe they hadn't been exposed. We would have to let them know what the new reality is but that would be another tough call.

"I hope I can birth a cow today! Jackson can I borrow your waterproof ski gloves?" she giggled as she asked.

"Come on Casey, I'm eating! That's not cool!" Jackson yelled from the kitchen but we could tell he was having some fun with her too.

Kristin and I made sure Casey was going to take things seriously. She had already worked pretty hard packing all her gear and was ready to leave her bedroom perhaps for the last time. She was going to bring all her favorite items with her to the fort which was okay with us but she begged us to let her bring her sidearm to the farm. We promised we would bring it to the fort and it would be waiting for her there.

"Don't worry. Mr. Stanford and Mrs. Carlson will be ready for anything. You'll be safe at the farm. Remember it's only a short walk from the farm to the fort." Kristin reminded her. "We'll meet up on the yacht! You won't believe this boat Casey! Scott said they have a diving platform that's thirty feet up and you can jump right off it into the harbor."

"Yeah, you probably *should* jump in the harbor after being on that farm all day. Man that's gonna stink!" Jackson just said what we were all thinking.

"I'll do the thirty foot jump if we all do it together!" she responded to his taunt.

"Deal!" I said before Kristin could protest "It will be a family jump!"

Just then Candace opened the kitchen door and didn't say much as she walked right over and poured herself a coffee. This was a pretty typical occurrence in our kitchen. We were morning people but Candace definitely wasn't. The girls carpooled to school together most of the time and we sometimes had to *remind* Candace it was her turn to drive. After a few sips she perked up a little. "Casey are we ready to show these farm-people how to do it?"

"You know it Mrs. C!" Casey sang, "We're gonna be seeding and feeding!"

We gave Casey big hugs even though it was only one day on the farm. She hugged back which felt great and then she was off. They were going to meet Paul Stanford at the farm at 5:20 and I was really hoping that this effort was going to pay off. Allan seemed confident that the farm owner and his daughter were truly willing to share the important aspects of running their farm and teach them as much as possible in just one day.

Paul was waiting for Candace and Casey at the farm. Once they were all there they went around the house and into the barn. They introduced themselves to the crew and spent a few minutes with small talk but then it was time to get to work.

The owner of the farm, Mr. Carpenter, welcomed the new members and made sure they were prepared for a long hard day. He admitted he didn't know why they were there but he had accepted money to try to make three farmers and he wasn't going to let anyone off easy! He split up the group and sent Paul into the fields to work on harvesting and planting. Casey was tasked with animal management including milking, egg harvesting and feeding/grooming the many animals. Candace was going to learn all about farm management including lessons on seed and feed, storage basics, farmhouse maintenance, vehicle maintenance and about thirty other categories that proved to be quite overwhelming. Fortunately much of the details were written down in a journal. Allan had thrown in some extra money to secure a written summary of all the things that seemed vital to run this place.

During the morning's lesson Mr. Carpenter was being quite emphatic at the cost of running this small farm and the skyrocketing cost of materials and overhead. From grains to fertilizer, from fuel to bales of hay, it was a hardship for them to afford to run the farm. They were forced to cut corners elsewhere which was another part of the lesson. Candace took an opportunity to get something big done quickly in the very spirit of Scott Lang. "Mr. Carpenter. I really appreciate what you're doing for us and I do intend to learn everything I can. We appreciate you agreeing to do this so we're adding another incentive. Allan wanted me to offer you folks one additional challenge today. We are offering to purchase all the goods this farm needs to operate for the next twelve months as long as you can get it delivered here by 8 pm tonight."

He raised his eyebrows but she definitely had his attention. "Twelve months? That's a lot of money and a lot of bulk items to procure and store. Gas, propane, fertilizer, seed, grain. That's at least a thirty thousand dollar check that I'm not sure you're ready to write.

"Do you think you can do it and get it all here by 8 tonight?" she pressed.

"Oh, I think I can get what we need ma'am." She gave him an envelope with cash and he didn't even count it. He shook his head but did allow himself a little smile. He took out his phone and started making calls. After about 20 minutes it was back to the lesson.

At noon a bell rang from the house and everyone finished what they were doing and gravitated to the main house for lunch. Candace looked like she was emerging from a deep study session with all her folders and documents. Casey had a chicken tucked in her arms and a few pigs following her as she walked through the field. She shooed the animals away as she entered the back door of the house with a big smile.

One of the crew came in with her and really seemed impressed with Casey. "This girl is a natural. She already knew just about all the things pertaining to the chickens, pigs, lambs, goats and horses. She said something about 'learning it all from *Mainiacs* and she wasn't kidding. We spent most of the time with cows. Feeding, milking, processing the milk and cleaning the barn. It was a banner day for cow poop."

"Holy shit that stunk!" Casey exclaimed and even Mr. Carpenter laughed out loud.

"You can get used to that real quick. I don't even smell it anymore, young lady." he said with a fatherly tone. He looked around through the window, " I wonder where Mr. Stanford is. I didn't hear any sirens. I don't see an ambulance. Turning over a field is back breaking work. He probably went home."

A few minutes later Paul did enter the house panting and drenched with sweat. He was working with Sandy, a younger member of the team who happened to be Mr. Carpenter's daughter. She was about 25 and definitely knew what she was doing.

"Ah, Mr. Stanford. You look like you could use some lemonade . . . and perhaps a shower." Mr. Carpenter jabbed as he handed him a tall glass of cold lemonade. "Unfortunately for you, it's back out to the pasture for more harvesting and reseeding after lunch."

"What? There's another pasture?" Paul raised his voice a little and looked dejectedly at the Sandy

"Actually, no Paul there isn't. Dad the thing is . . . we're finished with that." Sandy blurted out reassuringly. "We started out at a good pace and this guy didn't slow down in fact he sped up. He wouldn't take breaks and to tell you the truth he was really good out there. He drove all the machines, even the combine. We're done. But you're right about one thing Dad. He does need a shower!" and everyone had a good laugh, especially Paul.

The rest of the day Paul was able to float around learning about different machines, harvesting techniques, and a host of things he may not have seen had he still been out in the pastures. He had plenty of extra time and absorbed a lot of potentially critical lessons the rest of the day. Mr. Carpenter asked him a few times if he wanted to make a career change. There was also perhaps overuse of the word 'son' and everyone smiled at that. It bothered Sandy a little at first but she saw how happy her father was and she just left it alone. Besides, she was actually quite impressed with big city Mr. Stanford who just had a certain way on the farm. She knew she didn't have to protect her father either. Mr. Carpenter was as tough as they come. He probably just saw some of himself in this hard-working and humble newcomer.

Casey and Candace also made fast friends on the farm. Everyone working with them expressed the initial apprehension about letting in some outsiders. By the afternoon they weren't outsiders, they were family. The various farm hands took turns with all three of the new 'students' to show them something different or teach them something that wasn't on the agenda. More than a few of them mentioned to Mr. Stanford about the outdoor shower. Paul finally relented and took a nice shower with animals all around him in the middle of nature. He even put on a pair of Mr. Carpenter's old overalls. Everyone had a good time poking fun at the city slicker and marvelled at the change they saw in both Paul and Mr. Carpenter. More than a few pictures were taken of those two together in matching outfits!

It was a full afternoon but by the end of the day Candace, Paul and Casey bid everyone farewell and left for the yacht. Casey said it was the best day she ever had and they made her promise to come back to visit the animals. She was over the moon. She knew she was going to miss the farm so much she decided to take a little 'reminder' of her time at the farm. She just couldn't help but stuff one of the little baby chick into one of her pockets with a handful of seeds. As they drove off property and towards Fort Adams they all seemed to know it was time to get back to reality. The problem was that reality was changing day to day. There was still a gala and some role-playing to get through tonight. Then the waiting game. Waiting for God knows what.

They drove up to the parking lot next to the yacht. Abby operated the gangway and they all boarded, even the chick.

Chapter 18

THE WAR ROOM

A FTER CASEY LEFT in the morning I urged Jackson to go to school. He did go but planned on coming home after lunch. We heard how different he felt yesterday at school when he wasn't worried at all about grades, exams and projects. His face lit up when he described his heightened confidence in himself and his ability to 'take in the moment' without getting so caught up in unnecessary worry. He loved his new attitude and confidence when he found himself around girls, teachers, and people who represented authority or danger. He felt renewed. This was great but I also knew it was eating him up that so many things in his world were going to go away. He seemed okay with it and promised to enjoy the day as best he could. He was already packed for the trip to the fort. We all were for the most part.

After he left I set up our dining room as a command center. I had a TV in the corner showing the news station. There were more and more stories on the nationwide spread of violent outbreaks, bloody attacks, murders, shootings and increasing police presence especially in big cities. Many states had activated the national guard. Still nothing about a viral epidemic or any connection with the REMfab trial. I suspected the government was working hard to put a lid on that chatter. I had drawn a timeline on the wall with the day's events and the critical aspects of the next 24 hours. It felt strange using a sharpie on a newly painted wall but stuff like that just didn't matter anymore. I still had to make a bunch of calls and take care of all kinds of loose ends. Meanwhile every 5 minutes the doorbell rang and another delivery was arriving at the door. Kristin was taking care of most of these interruptions. She was used to that unfortunately and knew most of the delivery men by first name (a lot of jokes about that have been told around the household and neighborhood.) The phone was also ringing non-stop but mostly quick things. One call caught me off guard.

"Hey Dad, good morning!" I said as I picked up the phone. "How's it going?"

"Just fine, Buddy. We're good. We're at the cabin." my father said.

"What? Why? I thought you were coming to the fort with us later on. The dinner's only a few hours away then we're going to seal things up." I was a little frazzled with this twist.

He sighed a little and I could hear the emotion in his voice. "We came up here to get some supplies and we just have so much stuff that's here and so many memories. Part of us wants to be with you but we have decided that we can ride things out here and when the dust settles we'll meet up with you folks. You know this place is safe and we have enough supplies for however long this takes."

It was true. Dad had been preparing for this since I could remember and long before. He was as tough as they come and was a survivor. He had prepared himself just like he had prepared me over the years. And talk about fully-stocked. The cabin was unassuming at first but it was built as sturdy as they come. It was built to be completely off the grid. It was fireproof and unbreachable. It contained an underground bunker that

was fortified to withstand a nuclear attack and had enough
supplies for a family of four to last two months at least.

"We'll be okay and I have the satellite phone you gave us.
We've got a generator and plenty of fuel. There's a whole bunch
of old home movies we plan on watching." he spoke sincerely
and I could tell he was torn on this decision. "We're only an
hour away but we both feel this is right. The news, Paul, it looks
pretty bad. Nobody seems to know what you know and it's
getting worse quickly. I hope you all get that fort squared away
fast. If you get in any trouble you just call me and I'll be there."

He was speaking the truth. He was always there for me
and for the family. He would do anything for my family and
my brother Mark's family without hesitation. He loved the
grandkids to death and it was going to be tough for him to go
without seeing them regularly.

"I know Dad. Ok. I wish you were going to be with us and
we could sure use your experience here but I understand. I get
what you're saying and I won't pressure you. You've got about
eight hours to change your minds. I'll call you later and we'll set
up some tentative plans to reconnect."

"Son, be careful. I love you. We love you and we *will* see you
soon. Goodbye"

I hung up and had to wipe a few tears from my eyes. I sat
down and allowed myself to have a minute. I did tend to keep
things in too much and sometimes a few tears served as a well-
needed release. After a few minutes I was startled as the doorbell
rang for the tenth time. Kristin must have been upstairs so I
went to see what the next delivery was. I found four giant crates
on the front porch and the delivery guy was coming with more.
He seemed a little perturbed but his attitude changed when I
tipped him with a one hundred dollar bill.

He was smiling as he turned away and headed to the truck,
"Have a great weekend, sir! I sure will!"

I waved and kept my mouth shut. Unfortunately nobody was going to have a great weekend. London had basically been shut down. More concerning was New York City and LA. It really looked scary in the big cities. Tracy and the girls would be landing at 4pm. Cutting it close I thought. The highways could be a problem by then. People were starting to panic a little even around here in Rhode Island.

I pulled the crates into the house and opened them. I wasn't sure what to say. Enormous amounts of lipstick, mascara, eye-liner, blush, foundation, make-up brushes and mirrors. I initially was going to see why Kristin needed all these things when I noticed the invoice. Casey had ordered all of this. I just had to smile and let out a laugh. Whatever will make her happy. I could just picture her right now milking a cow or cleaning up after a pig while wearing eye-liner and lip gloss. She was a riot. I kept smiling as I loaded everything into the moving truck.

I did receive a call from Lieutenant Gerard. "Good Morning, Doctor. I am checking in with you folks about tonight. You've seen the news and I do have some concerns about the gala. While I'm confident we can make this all happen safely I do want to make sure you folks are still planning on keeping to the schedule."

"Yes, Lieutenant. We all plan on keeping to the schedule. We can't let these news reports get us too alarmed." I said. If only he knew.

"Very good, sir!" he responded cheerfully. "There's a lot of activity here. Hundreds of workers spent the night working on the residences and kitchen. They are almost done! They are spectacular. The catering trucks are here bringing all the supplies for tonight and tomorrow night. Thank goodness we have tripled the storage here. There is a lot of food and goods they are delivering in anticipation of this weekend's events. The caterer informs me that it was Mr. Lang's recommendation to bring it all ahead of time which is perfectly fine with us. Hopefully, the news will change and the ghastly violence in the big cities will stop."

"I agree and do know that we will all be there by 7 pm. We should make it clear that everyone who is not staying should clear out by 10 pm. They can leave anything they want behind. That means caterers, service, contractors, engineers. Let's clear the fort by 10 pm sharp." I wanted to be sure it was understood ahead of time.

"I think that's a great idea, sir. I'll actually feel good closing up the gates tonight. I do admit I enjoy the security of living in a fortress." he admitted to me.

I was a little shocked and confused. How could I have missed that key element. He ran the fort and controlled the fort, that much I knew. The lieutenant lived in the fort? My mind was racing a little as I made a quick decision.

"Lieutenant where are you now? There's a couple of things we need to discuss, in person." I asked hoping he was available.

"I'm at the fort of course, sir. Just let me know when you'd like to meet." he answered with some surprise in his voice.

"I'll be there in twenty minutes."

I told Kristin what my plan was and she agreed. We needed to bring the lieutenant in. I was about to leave when I caught some news footage that was disturbing and I stopped. Things were getting worse. I opened up my safe and grabbed my 9mm and shoulder holster. I put a jacket on and sped to the fort. I was going to have to admit to the lieutenant that we had been using him and lying to him all along. He'd have to believe that we were in the midst of a historic pandemic that was unfolding before us in the cities and on the news. I'd also have to convince him to receive an injection that may or may not work. Ultimately, he'd have to be quarantined like the rest and I was hoping he would do this all voluntarily.

I called Scott on the way down to Newport. He was pretty busy working the phones but at this time there weren't too many things left to do. We were almost out of time. He had sent most of the *Resilience* crew away for the weekend except for the captain and the head steward whom we had all met. They were father and daughter and had no local ties, they really had no place to go. They were both Australian without any real family except each other. Steve was essentially the captain, the helicopter pilot, the chef, head of security and a very caring father. Abby was the head steward, the assistant-chef, the housekeeping and a very good soul. I could sense he was building towards something and wasn't sure exactly how to ask. I took that moment to tell him about the lieutenant and why I was heading down there. I felt we could really benefit from his services and he seemed like a valuable addition to our team. I added that I had several extra vaccines in my pocket. He agreed with everything I was saying.

I also mentioned, "It sounds like Steve and Abby could be good candidates for the group as well. What do you think?"

Scott seemed relieved to hear what I just said and I could sense he was right there with me in terms of these last minute curveballs. "Perhaps you could invite the lieutenant over to the boat. I'll get the media room set up for a presentation that will be convincing as well as exceedingly comfortable with custom build hand-sewn leather recliners."

"See you in twenty minutes." I said with a smile.

"Ok, thanks Doc." he responded. He was relieved after this change in plan but I knew he wouldn't be able to breath easy until Tracy and the girls were safely on the yacht.

I met the lieutenant in the parking lot outside the fort and I thought I should ask him some important questions before we brought him in. "Lieutenant, we're going to be discussing a few things that are really important and somewhat frightening.

You're going to be absorbing a lot of information that relatively few people in the world know. Before we start I need to ask you a few personal questions."

He seemed quite focused on what I was saying and quickly blurted out "Yes, yes of course, Doctor. I'll tell you anything you want to know. I just want to know what's happening."

"You live at the fort? Alone?" I asked directly.

"Indeed. For ten years now. I have a little apartment, it's really not much but it's good enough for me. I don't pay rent. It was the only way I could afford to get paid next to nothing."

"Do you have family?" I asked, feeling guilty that I hoped he was a loner.

"I'm long divorced and my two sons were both casualties of war. Afghanistan and Iraq. Tragic. They were American soldiers please know, and proud of it." he answered. "Don't really talk to my brothers. It's just me."

I had heard enough. Perhaps it wasn't his answers that I needed to hear. I really didn't know what else I needed to ask this man. It was mostly instinct that he was a good person that I could trust and rely on. Bringing him in would also help us transition into the fort with greater ease and he would likely be able to help us out in numerous ways.

"Okay. I understand. Let's go on board. I want you to meet some people." I said as I led him up the ramp.

We boarded the *Resilience* and met up with Abby and Scott who led us to the media room. It looked like it belonged in a mansion on Bellevue Avenue a few miles away. This well-appointed room had beautiful leather wallpaper and acoustic ceiling tiles. A massive video screen had been lowered on one end of the room. Scott wasn't wrong about the recliners either. Steve met up with us and everyone took a seat. I gave them the full story sparing no details. They saw all the video footage and it didn't take much to convince them to join our team and receive the shots. We discussed some quarantine protocols. We couldn't guarantee the injections would work but it may be their only chance. We could test them regularly for seroconversion with our test kits.

Steve and Abby were thankful to be invited into our group and I made it clear that they were no longer employees but members and part of our family. They provided some more detail regarding their life stories and I could see why Scott saw so much value in these two amazing people. It was clear that they would enhance our group with their personalities and skill sets.

The lieutenant was also appreciative. "I'll be honest Dr. Braden, I'm relieved. The group tour we provided you folks yesterday was the most bizarre thing I'd ever been part of. Now all the unusual requests coming from you and Mr. Lang are all suddenly starting to make sense. I knew something was off!"

"Okay then." I addressed the new team members, "The gala is at 7 pm across the way. Newport gala attire. You'll all meet the rest of the group but there will be many others who are not clued in to what's going on so tight lips. Lieutenant, remember we've got several hours to get everything we can use inside the walls. We need all the food, fuel, water, and anything else you can get with your authority. Most importantly we've got to get all the non-essential workers out of there by 7 pm. Tell the contractors to get everything done that they can and the caterers should be leaving all the food and supplies possible before we seal that gate."

Scott and I made sure that the lieutenant, Steve and Abby knew that they had a few hours to take care of any last minute needs. The window for getting any supplies or necessities would soon be closed. They seemed to appreciate the gravity of the situation. Scott assured them that there should be no financial restriction in any effort they made to purchase and secure anything they needed. Items such as food, water, personal items like medications, ammunition, fuel for the helicopter or boats. They understood the challenge they were up against and seemed confident that they could handle all of these new obstacles. I also gave them each a packet which contained pictures and brief bios of each member of our group. I thought it would be useful especially for the lieutenant. He will be meeting some of these people for the first time tonight.

We ended the meeting and everyone went in their separate directions. I stopped at the farm to check on Casey and the farm crew. I drove around the back of the farmhouse and couldn't believe what I saw. Paul Stanford in a pair of overalls walking around the pasture with Mr. Carpenter. They were both smiling and laughing. Casey was in an enclosure surrounded by chickens and pigs looking like she was in her happy place. One of the farmhands came over to me and I introduced myself.

"Casey's just a natural with the animals and we didn't need to teach her much at all. We'll be sad to see her go. That Mr. Stanford is something else too but I'm sure I don't have to tell you that. We expected him to be dying to get out of here after a little hard work but he put on an impressive show for us all. He completed two days of work by lunchtime. He worked his ass off just so we could go over more and more of what it takes to truly run a farm. It's no wonder Mr. Carpenter took a shine to him." she said.

I couldn't wait to hear that story. 'Classic Stanford' I thought to myself.

I decided everything was fine on the farm and headed back to the house. There was still a lot to do. It was already 3 pm and time was starting to go by real fast. While driving I was thinking about a mass text I would send out later this evening. I wanted to let everyone we knew and cared about to have a little extra time to prepare for the inevitable. I couldn't save them all but could I help some of them survive? I didn't want to incite panic and I didn't want to have people showing up at the fort. All the advanced data suggested they were all infected and it was only a matter of hours now until the virus transformed them all to killers. We couldn't afford that to happen within our walls. But . . . what if . . . there were some immune out there. Perhaps there would be some survivors. I had to let them know where they could find refuge. I figured I had to send the text by 6 pm and make sure people got somewhere safe tonight. A few hours can give them time to get provisions, medications, and a safe place to hide out for a few days. If they can survive for a day or two we could test them for antibodies and possibly give them safe harbor.

I arrived home not surprised to find another UPS delivery truck. A young lady was just coming down my steps and was smiling ear to ear. "Good morning sir! You sure are getting a lot of deliveries today." I smiled back and suspected the word was out on our address. I didn't hesitate and handed her a crisp hundred which made her day.

I brought the boxes in and Kristin was opening up more boxes upstairs. I went up there and filled her in with what was going on. She was so glad Casey was having a good day on the farm. Candace had sent her some pictures and was keeping her in the loop too. She also showed me a picture Candace sent of Paul Stanford in overalls and nothing else standing arm in arm with Mr. Carpenter and we both couldn't stop laughing for a minute.

She held up a package and I smiled when I saw it. I had managed to order about 5 years worth of contact lenses and I was relieved they had arrived. It was almost too late to get something if you need it online now. Anything we ordered now had to be delivered to the fort. The delivery trucks sure were busy. Our neighborhood was crowded with them. Our whole gang hit the internet hard Wednesday night so we weren't the only ones receiving deliveries today. I wonder if they were tipping as well as I was? The stores were still open but a lot of the essentials like bread, water and coffee were flying off the shelves. New Englanders were known to stock up on these items with even a hint of bad weather on the horizon. The news channels definitely were getting people nervous and many stores were having a tough time keeping the shelves stocked. Plus, anywhere there were a lot of people there was an increased chance of being attacked. We didn't want anyone from our group to be around stores or malls after what we were seeing on the news.

I turned on the TV and got caught up with the afternoon developments. Many downtown businesses were shutting their doors tonight and the hospital emergency departments had lines out the doors. Things were getting a little hairy.

The lieutenant called me with some updates as well. The caterers and the Preservation society called on him regarding the gala. He assured him that the event was on and there was no reason to deviate from the agenda. He again pushed for the caterer to bring anything and everything they could by 6 pm. He even had them agree to store the rest of their dry goods, beer, wine and liquor on the fort premises. He wouldn't even charge them. The decision to bring in the lieutenant was looking better and better.

He gave me some additional updates, "Your brother-in-law has been bringing in all kinds of equipment to this fort. It looks like a legitimate fire department within this fort. Plus I'm glad you tipped me off to Big John. That man is quite something. He delivered ten beautiful RVs each packed with goods and drove in his own mammoth mansion on wheels. He parked it right in the middle of the fort's parade lawn and kept asking for someone called "Langaroo." I suspect he meant Mr. Lang and I told him I would be sure to pass the keys on. He kept telling me about these RVs and how spectacular they are."

"Yeah Big John is a salesman through and through. How'd you finally get rid of him?" I asked honestly wanting to know.

"I bought an RV." he said with a laugh.

I joined him in a good chuckle. He has a wad of cash in his pocket from Scott, he has lived in a one room apartment for ten years and he just learned the modern world is at the brink. Why not buy an RV?

"Great job. See you in a few hours." and I hung up.

By then Jackson was back from school. I knocked on his door and walked in. He was packing up his gear and seemed to be in a good mood. "Hey Jax. How was your day? Did you have another day like yesterday?" He had told us about his revelations about life, authority, stress, girls and how he seemed to 'figure out a few things.'

"Yeah, dad. I don't know what gets into our heads and makes us shy and nervous. I mean, I know things are different now but I really just feel . . . comfortable with myself and with the people around me. Teachers, girls, other boys whatever. Why be shy or nervous? I'm so done with that!"

"It is hard for a lot of people to realize some of these things. You're figuring out some things at seventeen that others don't realize until seventy! Some people never truly live their life due to unnecessary fears and uncontrollable anxiety. Even people who seem confident are often scared on the inside." I replied but I did want him to keep talking. This was great stuff for a Dad to hear.

"I know. And I know what that's like and how frustrating that can be. Confidence is great, and it multiplies too. I spoke to a few girls yesterday and actually had real conversations. I listened. They seemed to listen. Other people notice stuff like that too. Some people *I never* talk to came up to me just to talk like I was a safe person to talk to. No attitude or judginess. I like that so much more than worrying about such unimportant stuff. Crappy time to figure all of that out but I also realized . . . can't do anything about it. Embrace it."

"Embrace it." I echoed. I wasn't sure what else to do but *embrace him.* We had a good hug and it just felt so great to have him around and part of our team. He was turning into a man before my eyes. "You're right. There isn't much we can do about it other than try our best to survive and we will."

"Yeah, I get that now. Hey Dad, I think you're doing a great job leading our group. I'm proud of you." he said with that very confidence not too many young men possess. I let him go but he left his arm around my shoulders. "Putting yourself out there, trying to get everybody to go along with all of this . . . craziness. It must be so hard but I really think you're doing great. I think everyone appreciates what you're doing for all of us. I know we do."

"I'm proud of you too." I responded "I don't know if I can do any of this without you. Let's stick together. Always."

"Deal. I still wish Papa was going to be there. And Baba." They called me earlier and explained that they were going to lie low and meet up with us in a few weeks. Do you think they will?"

"Sure. You know Papa. I pity any of these infecteds that goes after him." I said with complete honesty. He was a great father and doting grandfather but he was probably the last person you wanted to tangle with in close combat and if he has weapons, forget it.

"No doubt. They'll be sorry." he walked over to the closet. "Do I have to wear a suit tonight?"

"How about just a golf shirt and that blue jacket we got you for the Fourth of July."

"Oh, yeah. I looked buff in that. Too bad Stephanie won't be there." He said but it didn't seem to bring him down too much. I didn't tell him who *would* be there. He'd find out soon enough. If I was right about my son, in a few hours he wouldn't be thinking too much about Stephanie. I kept that little tid-bit a secret.

"Okay, we'll leave here at 5:45 sharp. I'll drive the moving truck with Mom. You can take your car." I said as I walked out of the room.

"Wait. What? What car? What do you mean?" as he sprang out of his room.

I reached into my pocket and threw him a keyless fob. "Oh, didn't I tell you? Mom and I had a lot of deliveries today but one of them was dropped off especially for you. It's out at the curb."

Kristin poked her head out of the bedroom with a huge smile, "I hope you like it! Something tells me you will! You only told me it was your dream car like a thousand times."

"NO WAY!" he ran over to the window. "NO WAY! That's the Lamborghini SUV. Midnight blue. High profile wheels and rims. Sport package. Sun-roof."

"V8 twin turbo." I added. "Bullet-proof windows, run flat tires,"

"You guys rock!" he yelled as he ran down the stairs.

I yelled before the door closed. "One lap around the block then come shower."

He jumped in the car and took off.

I jumped in the shower. I was really proud of the things he said. Why worry too much about things you just can't control. I wished it was that easy. I was going to try like hell to control what happens to my family over the next few days. Some things I couldn't control and some things were going to go to hell. As for right now I was only thinking about my wife and kids and despite what was happening in the world things were pretty good. Strange thing to think but it was true. I knew things were going to get real bad, real quick but as for right now, I had a seersucker suit to put on and a gala to attend.

Chapter 19

PREGAME

WE ALL HAD a busy Friday and as it got later in the day the minute hand just seemed to go faster and faster. I had finished my shower and was almost dressed when Jackson knocked on the door.

"Dad, you *have* to drive that car! It's intense! I can't believe you bought it!" he said with a huge smile on his face.

"I'm glad you like it and I hope you have plenty of fun with it in the future. But to be honest, I leased it." I said with a wink and a smile. He and I both knew we were all just buying a little happiness before everything crashed. We were going to be stuck in a fort and he may never get to go out with a bunch of friends or on a real date. He deserved a little fun in a cool car. Now he has that. It seemed important to him and we didn't want to take anything else away from him.

"I'm going to finish packing all my gear and then I'll finish loading up the moving truck." Jackson reported. "We have just about everything in there. Hey can I bring my dirt bike? That would be good to have, right?"

"Yeah, that's a great idea. Bring the extra oil and spark plugs." I said. "Throw everything you want in the truck. I'm not sure what's going to be here if we come back for anything."

We had packed all the sentimental items already. Pictures, albums, books, some furnishings. Anything we thought we might want or need. The kids had most of their favorite things packed and most of their clothes. Both of them had ordered lots of new clothes for the next year or two just to have stuff to look forward to wearing. What a strange time. They kind of liked ordering all of these things but they also knew the underlying cause was so awful. The two of them seemed to get that it was *okay* to be sad and upset while a little excited and happy at the same time. We all felt that way.

It was a strange time and even I had a little bit of a challenge knowing what emotions to feel. 'Just go with it!' we kept saying. We would get through this together.

I couldn't believe that 48 hours ago everything was normal. We were all experiencing a whirlwind of emotions and it was amazing how well everyone was keeping things together. At about 5:30 pm we were all ready to go. We were getting ready to walk out of our house perhaps for the last time ever. Kristin looked great and so did Jackson with his dinner jacket on. I was proud of him but on this night there was something missing and it truly was a sign of the times. I said to him, "You look great but you forgot just one thing."

He looked down at his outfit. He did his usual run through of everything he was wearing. Phone, wallet, watch, deodorant. He looked at me unsure of what was missing.

I opened up my jacket and he saw my shoulder holster and my gun. Immediately he lost his smile and he became very serious. He realized things were different and he had to be prepared.

"Gotcha, Dad." He grabbed his backpack and quickly put on his shoulder holster and loaded 9mm pistol. "Ready to roll." He looked at me and I definitely saw a man who I respected, trusted and admired. He was as ready for this as anyone could be.

It was time to go but Jackson did have a good question. "Isn't there gonna be security at the gala? Are they gonna pat us down?"

"I would worry about that. We have an inside man running security." I told him with confidence.

Jackson really wanted Kristin to go with him in his new car and she wasn't too upset to be missing a ride in the moving truck. They both got into his beautiful new ride and I got into my 'gentle ride' truck which was packed to the brim with propane, guns, ammunition, furniture, clothes, food, bikes, and every random thing we could stuff into it. Plenty of make-up that's for sure. We had everything we thought we could possibly need and were ready for whatever was going to happen next.

Just then Peter Carlson came by in his moving truck with Samantha and Emily just behind him in a brand new Range Rover. He rolled down his window, "Which way to Fort Adams?" he hollered and had a big smile.

I couldn't help but grin. It seems Peter was trying to get in the mood as well.

"Just follow us!" Kristin yelled to him as Jackson eased out of the driveway with me on his tail. And just like that we were off.

I listened to the news on the way down to Newport. Some sports and weather but a lot of attention was on the strange happenings that were now occurring in most cities and towns. More and more bizarre stories coming out describing vicious attacks, violent atrocities and increasing police presence everywhere. It wasn't just in the bigger cities. It was happening in small towns and rural settings. I was starting to look around more intently at people walking on the sidewalks or crossing the roads. Fewer people were out and about. I still hadn't seen one of these maniacal creatures. How long until they were all around us? I knew it was a matter of hours. We would be hearing from Dr. Ashworth later in the evening and I wasn't looking forward to his update.

We arrived at the parking lot outside the fort just after 6 o'clock. We got out of the trucks and cars and were making our way over to the *Resilience* when we heard a familiar voice call out "Mom, Dad, Jackson . . . check this out!"

Casey was aboard the *Resilience* and was about 20 feet above us on a platform wearing a bathing suit. The boat was about twenty feet away from the seawall. She waved to us all and jumped off the platform and we couldn't believe it as she plunged into the water below. She came to the surface and waved to us as she swam back to the boat. The rest of the farm team had followed Casey to the platform. Paul and Candace didn't look as excited as Casey but they grabbed each other's hands and jumped overboard together. We laughed and applauded as they climbed aboard at the waterline. We came aboard via the gangway and it was good to see some of our team members already there. I made sure everyone knew that Abby and her father Steve were now part of the team and aware of what was happening. Abby had set out a little spread for the group and we had a few minutes to relax. I was glad to see that they were both planning to join us at the gala.

Abby approached me to give me an update. "My father and Mr. Lang are en route with guests." She smiled and then added, "I just wanted to say thank you again but my Dad and I both had a hell of an afternoon. Flu-like symptoms and sweats for several hours after the shot but we feel better now. Should we be worried?"

"No, Abby. That's a good sign. A very good sign." I told her with some confidence. She had an armful of warm towels and she sped off to Casey, Paul and Candace to help them find their quarters. The Izzos were also downstairs in one of the suites changing for the gala. There were plenty of rooms and suites that were stocked and ready for whoever needed a place to sleep or simply change outfits before the gala. It was an amazing ship! At about that time we all heard a familiar sound. It was distant at first but we all turned to see a helicopter quickly approaching. It was the same beautiful black helicopter we saw just yesterday and it quickly approached and landed towards the bow of the ship. We all watched as Steve lowered the steps and Scott exited the copter. After him came Tracy and the three girls. They all ducked a little as they followed Scott towards the back of the boat. As they made their way towards us Jackson grabbed my arm and casually asked, "Dad, is that who I think it is?" His grip was getting tighter

"Yeah, Jax. That's Scott." I deadpanned. After a moment I added, "Oh, and Cameron is there I think. Yes and Peyton, Sawyer, and Tracy."

"Why didn't you tell me she was coming? Why wouldn't that be something I knew?" He asked in a half-whisper.

"Well, to be honest I really didn't think any of the Lang girls would be here but I'm awfully glad they are all here and safe. Believe me when I tell you a lot of effort went into getting them here. LA is really a disaster right now. Let's be glad they're safe. And *alive*." I said to try to give him a little perspective.

He nodded and seemed to get it. He was right. I should have let him know that Cameron would likely show up today. They hadn't seen each other in a few years but when they were together in the past they were inseparable. On a few vacations and during some summer breaks they had spent a lot of time together but a lot of time had passed since then. They were kids back then but we did joke about the two of them and 'what if . . . ' None of those 'what ifs' ever dealt with world-ending pandemics and being sole survivors yet here we were. A lot of things had changed since those days.

Scott led the girls into the large deck area where we were congregating and made a general introduction of Tracy and the girls to the group. Many of our close neighbors knew the girls already as Scott had brought them out to Rhode Island several times.

Jackson seemed slightly nervous and unsure of what to do. Just this morning at school he felt like a new person brimming with confidence and without any hesitancy or anxiety. Why did he feel so nervous about talking to Cameron? He realized he shouldn't be nervous and he summoned up the courage to approach her. He first went to grab her a lemonade from the bar and when he turned around she was right there in front of him smiling right at him. She looked so different but still had the same beautiful face and eyes and he immediately felt any anxiety or fear melt away.

"Hi Cameron, I was just going to bring you a drink. Good to see you!" he said.

She smiled and came right in for a hug. He hugged her back and looked up to see just about everyone's eyes on them. He didn't care. He realized how much he missed her and how they were so compatible. She was a little older than he was but he was tall and well-made so they actually looked great together. Both had grown quite a bit since they last saw each other on the slopes of Deer Valley.

Kristin was catching up with Tracy and Abby was with them. I walked over to Scott and Steve and was about to make some wisecrack remark when my phone rang. It was Dave so I took it right away .

"Hey, Dave. How are you *seamen* doing?" I asked not really trying to be funny.

"Paul we've got a big problem! Shit."

I summoned Scott and Steve into the next room and put the phone on speaker.

"Dave tell us what's going on." I said.

"It's the captain." Dave was out of breath and clearly there was trouble. It sounded like screeching and banging in the background "We were in the crew locker room. He barged in and looked deranged and out of it. Before I knew it he attacked Gil the crewmember. He looked just like what we saw in the videos. He was attacking and going berserk and all we could do was to get out of there. I'm trying to hold the door closed but he's trying to get at us!"

"Are you and Colby okay?" I asked.

"We're okay but we don't have any weapons and I don't know how long this door is going to hold up. This thing is relentless and powerful! Colby's steering the ship!"

Steve asked calmly "Dave, can you see land? Can you tell us where you are?"

"Colby says we're coming up to Castle hill on the right. We don't have much time!" Dave responded with some panic.

I really wasn't sure what to say. This was not a contingency I had anticipated.

Steve began to slowly and calmly give directions for which I was thankful. "Dave tell Colby to turn around and slowly head out to sea. Try to barricade the door and we'll be there in 5 minutes. Take off any boots or heavy gear you are wearing and put on a life jacket. Keep us on this line."

"Got it." Dave said breathlessly.

We looked at Steve who seemed to be the most cool-headed. "I need two men to come with me. Preferably good with guns." He reached into his vest pocket and grabbed a device and pressed several buttons. We could see the helicopter lights turn on and the engines came alive. The rotors started to turn. He grabbed Abby and spoke to her briefly. She immediately disappeared down a flight of stairs as he turned back to Scott and I and said cooly, "Let's go get Dave and Colby."

Steve, Scott and I ran to the bow of the ship and climbed into the helicopter. Before we had even buckled in or put on our headsets we were in the air. Steve quickly accelerated and we flew directly over the fort. I could hear him giving directions to Abby from his headset. We were quickly over water and searching for the *Flying Serpent*. It took Steve no time at all to locate the boat and he instructed Colby to put the boat in neutral. In what seemed like two minutes we were hovering over the fishing boat and getting ready for whatever came next. Steve pressed a button and the right door opened smoothly and a rope ladder was being lowered down to the deck of the boat.

"Guns out, gentlemen. I'll bring Colby out first. Once he's on board with us then Dave's going in the water. We're taking no chances with that thing." Scott and I did what he said and did not question the plan.

Steve again pressed a button on his headset and was speaking to Dave and we could hear everything over our headsets. "Dave, we are here at the fishing boat and ready for Colby. Can you keep the door closed another minute?

"Oh, thank God! Yes. I think I can. This thing is crazy strong!" Dave exclaimed breathlessly.

Steve calmly responded. "Good, Dave. Send Colby out to climb up the ladder. Stay on the line."

"Okay! Colby go climb the ladder! Here he comes!" Dave sounded exhausted. "This thing is inhuman. It won't stop!"

Steve cautioned us, "Colby's coming out first guys. Scott you help him up the ladder and Doctor keep your gun sighted on the deck of the boat."

Colby came onto the deck and right over to the rope ladder. He came up quickly and Scott pulled him into the safety of the helicopter. Next Steve backed the helicopter away slightly from the boat. Then returned to the headset.

"Dave, we have Colby. He is safe. Do you think the door will hold him?" Steve asked.

"No. As soon as I let go this door's coming down. This thing is powerful and I'm gassed." I could tell he was on empty.

"Do you think you can run as fast as you can and jump overboard on the port side of the ship? There's a boat waiting for you and we have three guns trained on whatever is on your tail." Steve said calmly.

I looked down and was amazed that Abby was just off the port of the ship on what looked like a jet boat. She also had a semi-automatic rifle trained on the boat railing.

Dave paused a little then answered, "As long as Colby's safe then I can be in that water so fast you won't believe it."

Steve was back on with a calm voice. I was glad he was in command. He acted like he had done this hundreds of times. "Okay everyone. Colby is safe and Dave is going to come out next on my go. We have to light up whatever is on his tail! Ready team. Dave is coming out hot and going over the rail in 3..2..1.. *GO* Dave!"

Scott and I were ready as Dave ran out of the cabin and onto the deck. We could see behind him the door fly open in tatters and a blood-covered creature crash out of the doorway. It was immediately barreling towards Dave. Dave climbed over the railing as quickly as he could but not fast enough. We really didn't have a clean shot at this monster as it gained on Dave. I feared it could reach him before he was able to jump overboards. Just then what used to be Captain Joe got blown off its feet and we could see it sustaining multiple torso shots and it went down. We looked over and saw Abby still with her rifle aimed above her at the ship but she couldn't see the downed captain now. Dave was finally able to jump in the water but we were amazed to see the bloody beast was back on its feet and headed right where Dave had been. Scott and I had a clean shot now but Abby was still too low. We aimed for headshots but this thing was moving quickly. It's head and face were already covered in blood from smashing the door non-stop. Scott and I unloaded our guns and I know I hit it multiple times including the head and chest but it kept moving. Abby took dead aim at it's head with her larger caliber weapon and this thing finally went down for good after what seemed like four of five direct headshots. Unbelievable. Dave was floating in the water safely but clearly exhausted.

Steve's relaxed voice came over the headset again, "Okay, people. Target is down. Everyone appears to be okay. Except for the captain. Dave is swimming over to the jetboat. He looks pretty spent. I'll take him, Colby and Scott back to the *Resilience*. Paul you bring the jetboat back while Abby will bring home *The Flying Serpent.*"

We were all somewhat in shock but these two professionals were as calm as ever.

"Then it's time to party!" came Abby's voice over the headset. "I haven't worn my Lilly Pulitzer dress in years."

I helped Dave up the ladder and onto the chopper then climbed down to the deck of the *Serpent*. The Chopper flew off as Abby tied up and came aboard the bigger boat effortlessly.

"Abby. You guys were amazing. You have to tell me. Before you worked on the *Resilience* what did you really do?" I asked her suspecting that she hadn't told me everything.

"Australian SAS. Special Air Service. Much like your special forces. Dad was top level and I was an instructor." We decided we liked being on boats and flying helicopters more than killing people." She handed me some gloves and a hose. "You put Captain Joe on ice and I'll take care of the crewmember. We have 5 minutes to clean this up then we'll motor back to port." And like that she was gone and I did exactly what she ordered.

She returned a moment later. "The deckhand is still alive but barely. If you get bitten by one of these do you turn into one?" she asked.

Honestly, I didn't know. "I'm not sure Abby. I don't think so. But let's not take any chances." We both went into the locker room Gil was in really rough shape and was hemorrhaging from a deep neck wound. I knew he would not survive this.

"Gil has no chance of recovery, he could be infected." I cautioned her.

She didn't pause as she raised her handgun and put a bullet in his brain. She immediately started to pull his body towards the door and I returned to the deck.

Within a few minutes they were both in plastic bags and under a foot of ice. I hosed off the deck and then jumped into the jet boat.

"Are you comfortable at the wheel of one of those, Doctor?" She asked.

"Never drove one of these but I have a Whaler." I responded

Then you better put your harness on. Keep your helmet on too. Bring it to the stern of the ship. Help will be there. See you back at *Resilience*." she said with a devilish smile.

I followed her instructions and put on the safety harness. Smart move. I put the throttle down and this thing surged faster than any boat I'd ever been on. This acceleration was even more powerful than my Porsche. It was a great effort to even hold onto the steering wheel but within 60 seconds this thing was already almost back at the slip. Steve was already down at water level and helped guide me onto a ramp under the stern of the boat. The boat was quickly lifted into the belly of the boat. We were surrounded by other toys: Jet skis, kayaks, mopeds and everything you need on land or sea.

"Good job, Doctor." he said as we shook hands "That was something else. Pretty scary."

"Scary? You seemed like you were almost bored. Thank God you and Abby are on our team. And please, it's Paul." I said

"Well then good job, Paul. But it's still you I want to thank. Without your trust we would be turning into one of those things pretty soon. I prefer things this way. Let's go get changed and get ready to party."

"Yes, sir." and we went up the elevator and everyone was there getting ready to go.

Dave came up to us immediately and offered a hug to me and a bigger hug to Steve. "I thought for sure we were both goners out there. I don't know what kind of training you guys do on this boat but it was awesome to see in action. Thank you!"

"We're all glad you're okay, David. I love fresh tuna and I hear you're the man." Steve responded dryly as we all laughed a little. "That thing was vicious but it was just one. I'm more worried about big groups of those things."

Abby appeared on deck a few minutes later after bringing into port the *Flying Serpent* and I could see Lori giving her a big hug. I'm sure Dave told Lori most of the story. He may have left out how close he and Colby were to getting killed but Lori certainly seemed appreciative of Abby's help. Kristin joined them in a hug and they clearly looked like they would all be fast friends.

I saw that Kristin's parents had arrived on the deck and sauntered over to them. "Quite a vessel, eh? Not bad for a *motor boat*. What do you think Pa?" I asked. He was a sailboat enthusiast and typically didn't care for motorboats, large or small.

"I tell ya. I kind of like this." he responded as he took it all in. "If we don't like our accommodations at the fort can we come here?"

"What?" I asked incredulously, "I have a beautiful RV picked out just for you!" knowing the RVs definitely ranked far below motor boats on his list of things to sleep in. "But I know the owner and if you guys want a suite in here it's not a problem. In fact Scott already penciled you in as a squatter here. He still talks about sailing on your old sailboat and how you convinced him *not* to buy a boat."

"Looks like he forgot about that lesson. I'm glad for our sake." he responded, gesturing at all the opulence and grandeur around us.

At that time I took a head count and everyone was here. I stood up on a stool and put my hands up, "Okay, it's 6:30 and we'll be heading to the gala shortly. I think this is a good time to have a few introductions and go over a few important things. First of all, I want to introduce to some of you two of the newest initiated, or shall I say inoculated, Steve and Abby Kensington. Most of you know they were captain and crew of the *Resilience* up until now but they are so much more and take my word for it people, we are lucky to have them."

"Cheers!" came from Dave who was raising a glass to his two heroes.

"Why not?" I agreed. "Cheers to our new team members." We all toasted them and I went on. "Not present but well-known to most of you is Lieutenant Gerard. He was the tour leader from yesterday afternoon. He is currently our inside man across the street and has been quite helpful at making sure our objectives are being met. Secure the fort and maximize the resources available. He's trustworthy and capable and lives at the fort. I just couldn't evict the fellow from his own apartment. He's military and a good man."

"Many of you have met the rest of Scott's family in the past but who are these young women?" I paused, gesturing towards them. "Tracy, Cameron, Peyton, Sawyer we're so glad you're here and safe. I know you'll all have many new friends soon. Welcome to all of you."

I continued to introduce the various families so that everyone could match a name to a face. "My wife Kristin deserves a medal for what she's been putting up with over the past few days."

"You mean years!" she interrupted with maybe more laughs than I expected.

"But good years, really good years." I agreed. "And Casey put in a full day on the farm and I'm really proud of all the hard work she, Paul Stanford and Candace Carlson put in today. We really thank you all." I paused for some applause. "Jackson is here and he has really made us so proud and I know he's ready for whatever happens next. He actually went to school yesterday and today. I couldn't believe it. I don't think I'll ever understand teenagers."

"Next to them is Dave and Lori Zanelo and their boys Lucas and Colby. As many of you know we had our first skirmish with one of these beasts aboard the fishing boat that I asked Dave and Colby to board. I didn't anticipate what happened and for that I'm sorry. I also didn't anticipate seeing what we can do if we work together as a team when someone is in trouble. Dave and Colby were heroic while Steve and Abby were nothing less than spectacular. Everyone's safe and that's what matters." (a few more whistles and applause from the gallery.)

"Jason and Kim Izzo are next to them. Santino and Jayci were impressive on the range. Jason I think there's still quite a bit of buzz around those designer 9mm pistol sets with matching Hermes shoulder holsters you had shipped. You think there's a few more for the Lang girls?"

"Definitely! Abby and I already made sure there's a full set for each of them in their suite. I hope you girls like them. Welcome!" Jason said to the girls warmly. The Lang girls seemed elated that there was some type of fashionable gun waiting for them in their rooms. Scott had prepared them well.

"Jesse, Jamie, Logan and Ethan are next to the Izzo's. They're all critical members of the team and Jesse proved it by spending all day today at New England Tech learning valuable skills I thought we might really need. Thanks Jess for becoming our well-needed electrical engineer."

"The Stanfords are here. Paul spent all day on the farm and I heard he has found a new calling. I will admit I was surprised when Paul volunteered for the farm experience. He doesn't strike me as farm-material but I guess I was wrong. I heard from the farm hands directly that he really was a natural. I never would have guessed he had that in him. Did you Jaymi?"

"I don't know what he has *in him* but I do know what he had *on him* after being on that farm, my Lord that smelled bad!" she answered with quite a bit of applause and some laughter from the group.

"Colin and Tyler Stanford also had to endure that I'm sure, welcome boys. I mean men!" I said warmly.

"The Carlsons most people know. Candace put in a full day on the farm and we really appreciate her hard work. Samantha and Emily both put in impressive performances at the range and Peter crushed it at the buffet." Which was met with some laughter and some applause, meant mostly for the buffet I think.

"You didn't disappoint with that buffet, Paul" Peter responded to even more laughs.

"Next is Amy Grey, Kristin's sister and a talented nurse. She's married to Allan who we all should thank for the great leadership he has shown. We started without much of a plan two days ago and look where we are now largely with his help and guidance. Evan and Miles are their boys and they did a great job shooting guns for the first time."

"Rick and Judy Browne are my in-laws. Judy will be a great contributor wherever she goes while I'm sure Rick is just hoping to finally get a round in at Newport Country Club." He laughed and nodded in agreement.

"My brother Mark and his wife Megan are next to them. My nieces Madigan and Ellery just love this boat. The good news is their whole family tested positive for antibodies and they're moving into the fort. The bad news is they won't be on this boat tonight. Madigan, did you know there is a pool and a waterslide on this boat?" I asked.

"No way!" she snapped but she seemed intrigued. "Is that true Ms. Abby?"

"Yes, dear. The waterslide's my favorite. There's a lot of fun toys on this boat that you'll be able to enjoy in the very near future. There's a movie theater, a karaoke machine, a bowling alley and for you Mr. Browne a top notch driving range on the top deck. I made sure we had a massive supply of eco-friendly golf balls." She responded with that great Australian accent that makes just about everything sound just perfect. "We also have skeet shoot for when the Lang girls are ready for some lessons."

"Kenny, Holly, Gian, and Sienna are newer additions and they may spend some time onboard the *Resilience* here until they test immune. Kenny, I think the Lang girls may be able to babysit for you folks while you're aboard the ship. Just be forewarned, they are used to working in Bel-Air. They net fifty bucks an hour for babysitting and they don't even change diapers." A few laughs but people were getting ready to go to the gala by now so I needed to get to some more business.

"Okay team, next we need to get into the fort. Lieutenant Gerard will be manning the front gate and he will make sure to direct us exactly where he needs us. Let's not leave anything outside the walls. If anyone has vehicles outside the fort let's get them all inside the walls now. Cars, trucks, vans everything. The lieutenant will greet us all at the gate and get everyone inside quickly. He knows who everyone is. He will direct everyone where to go. Don't worry about that. Remember, tonight is just dinner and a band will be playing. Perhaps a few words of appreciation from the Commodore. He's the lieutenant's boss and head of the fundraising committee. He can't pass up a chance to address an audience full of potential donors. At 10 pm the gala will end and I want the gate closed and sealed tight right away. Once it's sealed it's sealed. We'll be in and that's really all that matters. The bigger event and check presentation is tomorrow night. Unfortunately, all the reports we have suggest that event is just not going to happen. From what I've seen on the local news things are getting bad everywhere, not just big cities. It's only a matter of time until the truth is out and then there will be widespread panic. It's going to be too late for a lot of people. We will get an update tonight from Dr. Ashworth. There also is an announcement scheduled from the Governor this evening. Things are happening fast. I am prepared to send out a group text tonight to family, friends and neighbors that we couldn't bring here explaining what is going on. Perhaps we can give them a few hours head start just like Dr. Ashworth did for us. Feel free to forward it to anyone. Remember, we can't bring people here or inside the walls of the fort. I'm not releasing our location at this time. It kills me to not extend a helping hand or invite others. It's too risky. Just ask Dave. Even one infected within the walls is not worth the risk."

I paused for a minute and looked around the room. "I know you've all seen the news and are aware of what's going on around Rhode Island and around the country. Scott, what is the latest update?" I asked him knowing that he had just seen the latest news feed.

Scott didn't hesitate to address everyone. "Things are getting bad and no state or city is being spared. Most of the airports are being closed. There are more and more reports just like we've been seeing and the details are pretty horrific. It's like the videos we've seen but even more intense. There's been reports suggesting some type of government coverup and a possible viral pathogen outbreak being reported but nothing firm. It looks like just a matter of time, perhaps hours, until things really go south. I'm predicting sometime tonight we go into lockdown and people are told to shelter-in-place." He put his arms around Peyton and Skylar and they both held him tight. I kept going as long as people were paying attention. "It's here. This is it. But we're ready and we are not going to be surprised by anything now. We have just a few hours until the gate closes and we can't risk anything happening that could jeopardize this plan. We need everyone with guns loaded and eyes open. Dave already told us that it was just a matter of minutes. Captain Joe said he didn't feel good then ten minutes later he was attacking them. We can't afford to be caught off guard." I took a few breaths and decided that was enough reality for the moment. These people have done so much over the past two days but it was going to be a really long night. I knew they were as ready as possible.

I continued, "Okay, enough business. For a few hours lets enjoy some good food, some good company and a feeling of accomplishment. Lieutenant Gerard has made it his mission that we have the most fantastic experience tonight and he really wants to embrace us all with an over the top dinner and top-notch entertainment. I for one am looking forward to a little fun. Let's go party." I stepped down from my stool and joined my family. Most people were starting to leave the *Resilience* and head down to the parking lot where the vehicles were. It was time to go to the fort.

Chapter 20

JUST LIKE OLD TIMES

"**H**EY DAD, NICE speech. Did you really just come up with all of that on the fly? You had some good ones!" I said as he stepped off the stool and came over to us. It was true. He was trying to keep everyone upbeat during a really dark time. Everyone knew he was totally committed and devoted to the group's survival. That was the end-game. Survival.

"Thanks Jax. I didn't want to go on and on but I thought a brief introduction of everyone was in order. I didn't want to miss anybody, we'll all get to know each other better real soon. You guys ready to go?" He asked, not aware that he still had some questionable splatter on his suit (he hadn't had time to change after Dave's distress call came in earlier. Cleaning up two mutilated bodies without getting a blood stain was a tall task in a seersucker suit.)

"Oh, honey! Is that blood all over your sleeve and pant leg. If we were at home I could get this out but you're going to have to change that jacket for sure." Mom chimed in "There's another one in the cab of the truck. Go ahead. We'll meet you out there."

"Okay." Dad said as he looked at his suit and seemed a

little bummed. "I'll see you guys out in the parking lot in a few minutes."

He went along with some of the others leaving the *Resilience*. "He really wanted to wear that suit." Mom shook her head a little then turned her attention to me. She was looking at me with that look like she was trying to read my mind. "So, how's it going? Everything okay so far?" she asked with a not-so-subtle smile.

"Mom, really! Don't you think . . ." but then I stopped. Cameron had walked over to us and quickly was right between us. "Hey Cameron, sorry my dad kept talking and talking. He's been doing that a lot lately."

"No, it was really nice. He made us really feel welcome and I think I understand things a little bit more now. I'm actually glad we're here." She said with a bright smile. "I wanted to ask you a few things, Mrs. Braden."

"Sure, honey. Fire away." Mom responded in an all-too-motherly tone.

"So this is a gala? Is that fancy or is it more laid-back? Me and the girls need to know how to dress."

My mom seemed more than happy to talk a little fashion with Cameron. "Oh, you'll see tuxedos and you'll see some casual dress from the men. Many of the ladies will have gowns but any dress is fine. Some color is preferred. My advice is to wear flats not heels. It's mostly grass on the parade field."

Cameron nodded and moved on to the next question. "Is there dancing at a gala? It sounds like there should be dancing."

I was starting to feel a little uncomfortable with this line of questioning but I just couldn't walk away.

"Oh, yes dear! There's music and dancing. All kinds of celebrating. We will likely have to put up with a few speeches but nothing too formal. Your dad's going to say a few words I think but it's really all about having some fun."

"Gotcha. So do people bring dates to a gala? Is that part of the fun?" Cameron asked and glanced a couple of times my way.

Mom didn't hesitate to respond, "Now you make sure your sisters know that dates are not required or necessary but, between you and me, it sure can make it more fun! At these types of events men somehow naturally become more gentlemanly and gallant. The spirit of the gala can even get these guys on the dance floor if you can believe it"

Just then Tracy came over to us and seemed to be all smiles, "Hi everyone! I'm going to go get ready. Kristin, do you think you can help me pick out some outfits for the girls. We've never been to a gala at an old fort before."

They disappeared down a stairwell leaving me and Cameron alone. My first instinct was to escape and evade but I didn't let that urge overtake me. I thought about how great I felt at school earlier this morning and once again allowed myself to feel confident and cool under pressure.

"I guess I'll go get dressed too." Cameron said and started to turn

"Before you go, Cam . . ." and I reached out and put my hand on her elbow, "I think my mom's onto something. This gala could be a lot more fun if we went together. I know we haven't seen each other in a long time but I really like being with you. I'd love to go together if you don't already have a date." I smiled at her and it was a real genuine smile too.

She blushed a little and smiled right back at me, "Yeah, moms are sometimes smart when it comes to these things. I like that you're being honest, direct and kinda ballsy. I'd love to go with you, Jax." She had that look in her eye that made me feel like everything else just didn't matter. "I know you have to go and I have to go pick out a dress. I'll see you inside the fort?"

And then she did it. She grabbed my hand, pulled me closer and kissed me right on the cheek. Then she was off.

I stood there for a minute just thinking about what happened and wasn't really sure what to do.

"Cameron seemed happy about something." Scott said as he suddenly appeared next to me. "You have any idea what she's smiling about. I haven't seen her like that in a few years." He looked casually at me but had a smile on his face. I knew that he knew what just happened so I didn't even try to deny it.

"I didn't even know she was gonna be here til you guys got off the helicopter. I wish I had known." I confided in him feeling a little confused. Scott was like an uncle and I knew he could keep things we talked about confidential. "I guess I was just caught off guard."

"It sounds like you were pretty smooth asking her to the gala, right?"

"Yeah"

"You're excited that she's here and part of this, right?"

"Of course."

"In the past 48 hours you figured out a few really solid life lessons. You're a vital member of our team, maybe the most important. And now you have a date to a gala with a girl who really likes you. As shitty as some things are in this world, it seems like you're having a pretty good couple of days." He winked at me, smiled and was off.

It was all true. What a confusing time. I sat there for a minute just trying to take it all in.

A few minutes later Mom came up the stairs and seemed happy. "Everyone's getting ready. Let's go get moved in across the street."

"Thanks Mom. You were pretty cool you know. I'm gonna give you an assist on this whole thing." and I meant it. "Let's go help Dad. Where's Casey?

Mom walked over to Abby to see if she knew where Casey went.

"Oh, I think I know!" she responded with a smile "Casey, Skyler and Peyton asked me if there were any seeds in the kitchen. I found them a bag of seeds and they were still down in the dining lounge when I left. They were acting a little cheeky."

"Casey has a way of getting into trouble or making a mess. We call it a lot of different things but *cheeky* makes it seem so innocent." Mom responded as we all took the grand stairwell down to the kitchen and lounge area. Tracy joined us too. She was looking for her youngest girls.

The lower level was just so beautiful and the kitchen was bigger and nicer than what you would find in most larger homes. Of course there was a much larger kitchen in the lower level for the chef and staff who do the real cooking Abby informed us. This is more of an 'entertaining kitchen' adjoined to a large dining and lounging area. We saw the girls sitting on the floor laughing and giggling. As we got closer we could see the cutest little baby chick in the middle of their circle.

"Casey, did you take that chick from the farm? I asked but it did seem like a stupid question.

"Uh, he just kinda followed me and by the time we got to the car we had really bonded." she said with a huge smile.

"I think it's great!!" Mom said and I really couldn't believe my ears. "You girls don't make a mess and make sure you keep him safe.

Tracy was smiling too. She said softly to Kristin, "My girls are a little shy and a little freaked out by all of this. A little baby chick seems to be the perfect way to let these girls reconnect and have a little *girl time*.

After a few minutes we convinced Casey to come with us

and the girls made sure they could all sit together with the chick at the gala. Everyone was reassured and the three of us finally left the yacht and joined up with Dad and the other families out in the parking lot.

Chapter 21

MOVING IN

I NEVER REALIZED I had this much blood on my suit as I disrobed in the back of the moving van. I had a few flashbacks of how gruesome Captain Joe looked. Abby basically unloaded a whole clip into his chest while Scott and I went for headshots. That vicious animal just kept coming and coming. We put two bodies on ice and Abby docked the boat. How long until he or Gil is listed as missing? Will the cops or coast guard try to call Dave or Allan. That was our first real foray into the blurry legal territory we all would be realizing soon. It didn't matter. I didn't have time to worry about that. There were too many other moving parts right now and the clock was ticking. We were always getting closer to the ultimate chaos. When exactly would it all happen? Hopefully, Tom would have some news for us later on tonight. Good news or bad we just needed some kind of guidance from whoever was overseeing all of this. Was there still any real leadership out there? Was Tom truly connected with whoever was running the show? We needed to know more but for now everyone seemed to be on the same page around here. Secure the fort.

The time for obtaining goods of any type was over. Food, guns, ammunition, fuel, clothing, and knowledge. We tried to get our hands on what we could and I actually think we did a pretty good job. The full moving truck was a testament to that. I was so proud how everyone stepped up to do whatever they could for the cause.

It was kind of nice having that minute in the moving van surrounded by my family's stuff. I took off the blood-stained jacket and pants but wasn't quite sure what to do with them. I had waited so long to wear that outrageous suit and now I was considering throwing it out. "I just can't do it." I muttered to myself as I stuffed the suit into a clothes hamper I discovered. I was glad Kristin had a back-up summer jacket and khakis ready for me. She was good. I put on the new outfit and a little extra deodorant. It was going to be a long night. A minute later I stepped down onto the pavement and could hear Lieutenant Gerard in the distance giving directions. I could see some of our neighbors driving their cars in through the main entrance. The massive gates were open and the Lieutenant was right there at the entrance. I could see him shaking hands with Jesse and Jamie and their boys. I could sense from 300 feet away a pretty amazing moment. I saw Jamie get out of the car and give the Lieutenant a hug. Not just a hug but a hug that said 'you are one of us. I am with you!' It was comforting to see that and even more surprising when Jesse got out and gave him a bro-hug. There was good chemistry happening and we were generating one of the most necessary elements we needed for success, trust. Many of us knew each other well and already had that confidence in each other. We had grown even closer than ever over the past 48 hours. Now we had new members to the team that I already had great faith in. Soon they would be like family too. So far, the extra members we absorbed seemed like pretty good choices. While some of it was by choice I couldn't help think that there was a lot of fate involved. Regardless, I was content with the group we had.

There was a line of cars and moving vans moving into the fort. There were also cars, vans and people moving out of the fort. Just then I saw Kristin, Jackson and Casey walking towards me. I just stood there and looked at them. They were smiling and laughing. They were dressed up and looked great. What was going on? I knew by now to just take the good times when they come. They looked happy so I put on my best smile and approached them and we had a good ol'fashioned family hug right there in the parking lot.

"Dad, don't squeeze too tight. Be careful about Greg!" Casey said in a friendly tone. She was guarding her left jacket pocket.

"Uh. Who's Greg?" I asked, honestly not knowing what she was talking about.

She reached into the pocket and pulled out this little chick. I looked at it and at everyone else. At the same time we all started laughing and everyone came in for another big squeeze. I had already accepted that these moments were not to be overlooked or taken for granted. It was nice while it lasted but Jackson was the first to break it up.

"I can't wait to drive my car again." he said with excitement. "Casey, come with me. You will love it. Dad, can we drive up to the entrance and back?"

"Sure, just don't waste too much time. And don't get in any trouble." I warned.

The kids were all smiles as they jumped into the *lambo* and drove off. He had really gotten the hang of the manual transmission and we loved it that he wanted her to go with him for a drive.

Kristin and I got into the moving van and I started it up. "Honey." she started "I don't know how to say this and I feel like a terrible person but. . . ."

"What? The kids? Let them have fun." I said.

"No, it's something else. The kids. Us. Everything. It's just kind of . . . exciting and different. I know it's awful to even say it but things just seem to be so . . . *good*! What's wrong with me?" she sounded as conflicted as I'd ever heard her.

"Nothing. Nothing is wrong with your feelings. I have them too. I know we should be feeling dread and fear but there is just that strange sense of excitement." I confided in her, "I felt it too. Until I saw one. When I saw that creature withstand a barrage of bullets and just keep coming I realized what we were truly up against. We are going to quickly learn what the new world is like but how about this." I paused as I put my arms around her. "As far as tonight" another pause as I kissed her gently, "we just let ourselves have a good time?"

"Deal." she responded with a longer kiss and she seemed to be more at ease with her state of mind. I carefully pulled out of our parking spot and started towards the fort entrance. I noticed that the previously used smaller entrance had been sealed with a reinforced iron gate. Careful attention had been made to ensure all the access points were closed up tight except for the main entrance. The massive iron gates were open and inviting but I knew that at a moment's notice they could be closed by pressing and holding a button or manually by turning a giant wheel. By bringing in the lieutenant I was able to trust that no shortcuts had been taken. He knew what was at stake.

We were almost to the gate when Jackson and Casey returned from their spin and pulled in front of us. They stopped when they got to the lieutenant. We could hear him and his excitement as he introduced himself. I had sent him an information packet on the entire group including pictures of everyone. I know he studied all the details and knew exactly who he was aligning himself with. There was going to be a lot going on in the coming days and we were all going to have to trust each other from the start. I let him feel that he was in charge of fort security and he really appreciated that responsibility. He was decked out in his military formal suit complete with white gloves. I noticed the sidearm he had on his belt which looked like part of his normal uniform. I knew it wasn't his normal attire for such an event but it was a smart way to dress up and give everyone a sense of security. The guests were sure to be rattled by what they've seen on the news. Most of the evening's crowd weren't going to be wearing loaded weapons. Our group was not your typical group. We were all armed and we were all ready for anything. We had to be.

"Good evening, Jackson and Casey! I'm Lieutenant Gerard and I'm so proud to meet you both and look forward to working with you. Are you ready for a good night?" He asked with clear unbridled enthusiasm.

They both seemed to be happy to be greeted with such excitement. "I think you both will find the accommodations to your liking. I've designated the Captain's suite for your family. It was the original home to the Captain of the fort and his family. There's a lot of interesting history to soak up and I'm sure you'll find it captivating. We've spared no expense to maintain some of the historic charm of the officer's quarters while creating a luxurious 5 star hotel suite experience. There's lots to explore and quite a few surprises you both will like."

"Thanks Lieutenant. Can't wait to check it out." Jackson responded with a smile. "How much time do we have until the gala starts?"

"Fifteen minutes, sir" he responded "Just enough time to unpack a few essentials and spruce up a bit."

"Lieutenant?" Casey leaned over to ask.

"Yes young lady?"

"Are baby chicks allowed in the fort?" she asked as she showed him her new pet.

"Of course they are, my dear!" He nodded immediately. Evidently Abby had tipped him off earlier about this. "You'll find a small enclosure outside your accommodations for such a pet. I hope you like it."

"Thank you! See you later!" she called out. He waved them on and Jackson pulled through the gate.

We pulled up to the Lieutenant and he seemed to be glad to see us.

"Good evening Doctor and Mrs. Braden. You are right on time. You look particularly stunning tonight, Madam."

"Thanks, Lieutenant. I like your dress uniform. It seems like the perfect choice for tonight!" she responded honestly. "And I like how you accessorize too!" glancing at his sidearm.

"Indeed." He responded as he placed his hand on the holstered weapon, "I don't wear this to many fundraising events but something tells me I won't be the only one packing tonight. Am I right, sir?"

"I think just about everyone in our group will be armed." It was true although some of the ladies may not be able to wear their holster while decked out in their dresses. Some would be sure to have their trendy evening clutch designed to inconspicuously hold a 6mm pocket pistol. "I've already emptied a clip from a helicopter this afternoon. Not the Friday I imagined three days ago for sure. I'm hoping to leave my gun holstered the rest of the day."

We were all hoping for a quiet night.

"Let's hope tonight's event is, well, *uneventful*." He said with a wink. "I'll just be glad when everyone is within these walls." He stepped back and waved us through.

As we drove through the gates I couldn't help but feel the weight of the moment. For the past 48 hours we had been preparing and planning. Allan had given us the idea of coming to Fort Adams and everything else was based on updating, fortifying, supplying, occupying and protecting this home base. This new *home*. We were ready. The time for preparing was over and we had confidence that we had done enough and made the right decisions along the way. Our lives depended on it.

I drove the truck towards our quarters. I had already been briefed earlier on where our family would be located. I did protest to the lieutenant as I didn't want to have the nicest living space at the fort. The lieutenant had essentially ignored my pleas.

"Doctor, please. Someone has to be in that suite and it should be you. No one will question that, believe me. We all know that if it wasn't for you none of this would be happening and we'd all be helpless victims. You have given us all a chance to survive and everyone appreciates what you have done." He responded with more emotion than usual. "But I'm not sure about it being the *nicest* living space. That title just may belong to a rather surprising residence, an RV no less. Have you seen Big John's RV? It's nothing less than magnificent!"

I smiled knowingly and could just picture the moment Big John dropped off his monster RV and made sure everyone knew who he was and how much he wanted to see his 'little buddy Langaroo.'

I parked in front of the 'Captains Quarters' and couldn't believe my eyes. I know there had been a lot of construction going on but I didn't anticipate such a complete transformation!

"This is gorgeous!" Kristin exclaimed with a little bit of a dropped jaw. "It looks like the Ritz! Do we have a few minutes to look inside? I'd love to freshen up."

Jackson and Casey got out of his car and ran over to us with big smiles. "Can we check it out? The lieutenant said we have time!"

"Sure." I said as I hopped down from the truck. I had a key to the door and gave it to Jackson. "Let's do it."

The kids ran to the grand looking door and it felt just like when we were checking into a hotel and they couldn't wait to see the room. They opened the door and ran in as we followed. The place was amazing and we all stood together and said in perfect unison "Oh . . . my . . . God."

It didn't even look like the same room we saw on the tour. While it had a few accent pieces that appeared to be antiques and some historical photographs on the wall it looked like what you would find in a modern hotel magazine spread. There was an entryway that led into a large living area with a fireplace, large sectional sofa, huge TV and an enormous window looking out onto Brenton Cover and Newport beyond. To the right there was a small lavette and a sizable kitchen all on the main floor. We were about twenty feet above ground so we were safe from anything gaining access from outside. It was all quite breathtaking! There was a beautiful wooden stairwell and on the second floor was a hallway with some bookcases and a sitting area. Off the hallway were several rooms. First we checked out the large laundry room which Kristin just loved. On the right was a large, beautifully appointed master bedroom. The master bathroom complete with a large walk-in shower was straight out of architectural digest. Kristin teared up a little. I could tell she had been picturing us unpacking in the less-than-attractive apartment we viewed on the tour. This was a pretty nice surprise.

"I call this room!" we heard Casey call out.

"I want this room." Jackson rang out from the other bedroom with youthful exuberance. The kids rooms had beautiful hand-carved beds and had been decorated for a teenage girl and teenage boy with pretty cool furniture and wall art. *Nice job* Lieutenant, I thought. Their jack-and-jill bathroom was not a disappointment either. The stairwell also led up to the roof. We checked it out and there was a beautiful rooftop terrace. A sitting area with some gorgeous views and a firepit! This could be a cool little escape when the fort didn't seem big enough.

All in all we were glad we checked things out and we were all in a little better mood.

"Okay, everyone grab a bag or two of essentials from the truck. Take five minutes then we'll head over to the gala." I said and we all went back downstairs. I took a look in the high-end refrigerator only to find it stocked with water, fruit, eggs, general essentials and a couple bottles of our favorite wines. *He's really good*, I thought once again appreciating what the lieutenant had done for us.

We all freshened up and I put the news on real quick before we left. The only story these days was of the mystery plague of violence and people turning into monsters. Was it drugs, terrorism, gang warfare, infection? Whatever it was, it seemed to be worse than ever.

It was Dan North again reporting and I turned up the volume.

"So far hundreds of people around the state have been victims of this senseless, ruthless and seemingly arbitrary violence. Adults, children, elderly, hispanic, white, urban, rural it just doesn't matter. The reports are rolling in every minute. People are being attacked and killed as more and more people are arming themselves on the streets. Stores are now being looted and other crimes are being reported as the police just don't have the manpower to respond to all of the 911 calls. Let's go now to Patrick Littleton at the state house. Patrick, what's happening there and are you safe?"

"Good evening Dan and I do have a security guard with me. Am I safe? Based on what we have seen and what we are reporting, no. None of us is safe. There is a higher level of fear than I have ever seen and it seems to be justified. The video you are about to see was shot by the cameraman in front of me just thirty minutes ago at the downtown train station."

A video started playing of people running around in the

Providence Amtrak station. You could see what appeared to be three of the infecteds racing around attacking people and tearing flesh from bone. Someone would try to rescue a victim only to get attacked themselves. A few braver men tried to wrestle an infected but they didn't stand a chance with these berserk creatures biting and gnawing at any flesh they could reach. It was a bloodbath. A policeman fired at the infected and the bullets did not slow them down. They quickly descended on the cop and he was quickly mauled himself.

"We barely escaped the station ourselves and scenes like that are playing out all over Rhode Island and the world. It's scary and it's still not clear what's behind all of this. Dan"

Dan North was listening to his earpiece. "I'm now being told the Governor is going to be making a public address at 9 pm tonight regarding the escalating violence and at this time the Providence Police Chief is being interviewed at headquarters. Let's go to a live shot now."

There was a camera on the police chief as he stood at a podium. He looked like he hadn't slept in two days as he addressed the roomful of reporters. "Good evening. As you know there have been innumerable assaults, gruesome attacks and seemingly random murders over the past twenty four hours on the streets of Providence and throughout Rhode Island. Detectives are working around the clock examining the evidence and interviewing the victims. There's no lack of video as no doubt you all have seen. Security footage, webcams, personal phone videos . . . there's massive amounts of footage of this senseless carnage. And so far that's the conclusion. The assaults are seemingly random, these do not appear to be planned. There is no attempt to hide these awful attacks and the most troubling aspect is that the perpetrators are all . . . impaired."

A slew of reporters barraged him immediately with the same

questions. "What do you mean by 'impaired' and "do they have some disease" or "have you ruled out rabies?"

"Folks, I've been doing this for 34 years and I have never seen crimes like this and in the numbers we're seeing." He responded, not answering any of the questions. "It's getting worse. There are no good answers yet. More people are dying as we speak. Shortly I'll be meeting with the governor. We anticipate input from the FBI and CIA who are involved at present. You will be getting an update tonight at 9 pm tonight. That's all I have." He walked away from the podium.

I realized Jackson was standing behind me watching with me. "Hey Dad. This is messed up. It's worse than I thought it would be don't you think?"

"It's happening fast. Maybe faster than we thought." I said, agreeing with him. "I wonder if they know the truth yet. I'm pretty sure the government does but they also know that there's not much they can do."

"At 9 o'clock maybe they will announce that it's the virus. What will happen then? Do you think we're safe?" Jackson asked.

He was being brave but I could tell he was scared. The truth was we were all scared and there was a lot that we just didn't know. "I know we're safer here than anywhere else. I know we did everything we could to prepare ourselves and this fort for whatever is to come. Everyone has done a great job and I couldn't have asked for more. In a couple hours I think there's going to be an announcement and everyone will be told to shelter-in-place. This is the best place to shelter if you ask me."

"Honestly, I wasn't expecting all this." He gestured to the beautiful living room we were standing in. "Mom seems especially relieved with this. Kinda makes it confusing. Some things going on in the world are so awful and scary but the past few days . . . there have been some really good moments and I can't help feeling this sense of change and almost . . . anticipation and excitement." He looked away from me as if I might be ashamed of him for feeling that way.

"It's okay, Bud." I put my arm around his shoulders and squeezed. "I feel that same sense of . . . conflict. Just remember we didn't choose any of this to happen. It's happening out in the world and there's nothing we can do to help any people out there. Nothing. All we can do is try to survive. We are doing such a good job surrounding ourselves with comfort and protection and some indulgences it's only natural that there's a sense of . . . thrill. It's okay to feel that way. But always remember, it's about this group surviving. That's what we're doing here but we can't do it without working together and teaming up. I like our team so far. What do you think?"

"Yeah. I'm good with the team. And our clubhouse." he said with renewed certainty.

"That reminds me. I have a text I'm sending out to a bunch of family and friends. I'll send it now and at least they will know it's time to get shelter and food and to hide out as long as possible. There may be some people out there who are immune or who don't get this terrible . . . infestation. Hopefully there will be some survivors out there."

I sent the text just as Kristin and Casey came down the stairs looking beautiful. Everyone was looking good and we had enough time to take a quick family selfie. Something to look back on from the gala when things hadn't all gone down the tubes. Just then some music started playing out on the stage and it seemed the party was starting. We left our new place for the first time and while it felt so strange to be going to a party we all seemed to be in the right mood for this evening. Conflicted but together. Scared but confident.

Chapter 22

THE GALA

WE EXITED OUR new home away from home and we were all suddenly taken in by all the activity surrounding us. Jackson and Casey quickly ditched us to go hang with some of the younger crowd. Kristin and I started walking but after a moment we stopped and just looked all around us. It was an amazing site to take in and we were feeling such opposing emotions. We saw a grand stage with a band all decked out in uniforms, the musicians just playing their instruments and following the conductor. It was entertainment, it was whimsical, it was fun and we just let it keep on going. We felt a little guilty that all these people were here for us. While I felt somewhat sad for them I would be watching them all closely. If any of them started to look a little too sweaty or pale or whatever I was ready to pull out my 9mm. It was great that the caterers all showed up but if one of them started to look like they were infected they would be spotted and handled. We were all going to be ready. I had grabbed my taser and put it in my pocket just in case.

Kristin and I slowly walked over to the grandstand and listened to a little music. After a couple minutes just being together we sauntered over to where others were gathering on the other side of the lawn. Many of the team were starting to congregate. Dave and Lori were dressed up nice and looking great. I was happy to see them ready for the evening. Dave and Colby had been through quite a bit just two hours ago but they both bounced back pretty well. What choice did they have?

"How is the new place?" I asked hoping the other suites were as nice as ours. "Better than you thought?"

Dave responded honestly "We were expecting a shit-hole! All I can say is Damn! This place is 100 times nicer than we thought it would be. Totally nicer than when we checked it out on the tour. How the hell did they do this?"

Lori added "The place is great, Paul. Having a country-style kitchen in our new home is so nice. I know the fort has a brand new massive kitchen and we'll be using that mostly but. . . . It's just really nice that our place has what I really need to feel at home. I think we'll have to thank the lieutenant for sure."

The Stanfords, Brownes, Carlsons, and the rest gradually emerged. Each family that came out of their new home shared the same opinion. They were stunned and happily surprised that such an effort had been made for their happiness. We weren't sure how the contractor's had done all that work so quickly but they had done an amazing job.

We joined up with the Izzo's and then my brother's family. Kenny and Holly and the kids were talking to Kristin's parents. Amy had texted with really good news. After the meeting on the *Resilience* she had tested Kenny and Holly and that they were immune. So were Kristin's parents and my brother Mark's whole family. The shots worked! It was amazing and I was glad they would all be able to join us in the fort immediately. There may be some regretting that they wouldn't be on the Resilience but there would be plenty of time to be on the boat in the future.

Steve and Abby were just arriving. No site of the Lang's yet. Everyone here seemed to be in a good mood. I felt I had to just make sure everyone was in the right mindset before we all sat down.

"It's going to be an exciting night one way or another!" I called out as everyone quickly stopped and listened as I made an impromptu address on the fly. "I'm not sure how many of you caught any news updates. It's bad out there and it's getting worse. By the hour. At 9 pm the governor's giving an address and I expect she's going to order everyone to shelter-in-place. It's not safe anywhere. We need to be watching everyone for any strange behavior or signs of illness and we need to be ready. I know you're all prepared for anything and I am too. Let's have some fun but be careful and let's watch out for each other." I paused for a moment then caught a waft of something being prepared in the kitchen.

Kristin smelled it too. "Oh, that aroma is amazing. I just realized how hungry I am. I hear the catering company is fantastic!" she said with a big smile.

"I can't wait to enjoy a nice steak with all the fixins'." I said as we all started to walk towards where all the tables were set up under strings of lights. It was beautiful. We found our assigned tables and everything looked perfect. The band was playing and many other guests had arrived or were just entering the grounds.

I could see the lieutenant working hard at the gate. He was an ambassador and really the face of Fort Adams. He knew most of the guests on the invitation list and was greeting them all personally. He was watching closely for anyone who didn't look healthy or seemed out of sorts. He was periodically reporting updates on arrivals or cancellations. He wasn't updating other staff or security. He was updating several of us who had special transmitters in our ears. Thanks to Dr. Izzo and some nefarious business partners he sought out earlier in the day we had a brand new state of the art bluetooth communications system that we were just trying out. This communication system, or 'com' for short, was supposedly superior to anything used by the government or police. The lieutenant was keeping us informed of what was going on at the gate and on his scanner. Scott, Steve, Allan, Jason, Jackson and I all were wearing the same earpieces and were all being kept in the loop. We could all speak on the channel and hear each other quite clearly. It was really impressive technology especially since it required no phone or wi-fi signal. It was free-standing and we would be able to use it when the grid fell. So far most of the invitees were showing up which surprised us. These people didn't want to miss a society function for anything! It was surprising just how normal this all felt. There were many catering staff passing around hot appetizers and glasses of champagne. Everything was perfect.

We had all found our seats and we were sitting at a table with the Zanelos and the Stanfords. Kristin decided that some dancing was in order before anything else. She grabbed me and signaled all the wives to grab the husbands. We all had a dance and it felt good to have at least a couple of minutes to relax. We danced. We laughed. We had some fun. We did not lose our site of the big picture. We were watching everyone.

A few minutes later a report came in from Lieutenant Gerard. He sounded a little exasperated. "I'm trying to check in guests, watch for signs of infection, direct the staff but I'm spending most of my time receiving shipments from Amazon and UPS! Many of these delivery drivers are asking to deliver *personally* to Dr. Braden. Is there something I should know?"

I let out a little laugh as I realized what was going on. "Sorry, Lieutenant. I had our deliveries forwarded from our house to here. I guess I got a little carried away tipping the drivers earlier. I was giving them 100 dollars for the deliveries but they really deserved it. Kristin has had them working their tails off and I guess it's not over."

"Well I've got six separate drivers each waiting for their tip out here. Should I send them on their way?" He asked, sounding frustrated.

Just then Scott chimed in on the com, "The Lang family is just arriving at the gate now gentlemen. I'll see to these delivery driver's so they can be on their way."

I kept dancing, "Thanks Scott. Let me know what I owe you later." I laughed a little and Kristin asked what that was about. "Oh nothing. Just some more deliveries."

Her eyes lit up. "Ooh, I'm so happy! I hope those are the new shoes I ordered! Can we go get them before dinner starts?"

I smiled as the song finished. I liked to dance but didn't mind a reason to *stop dancing*. "Sure honey, but something tells me there are plenty more deliveries coming. Probably even more shoes."

She and I headed to the gate and continued to enjoy the music, the hanging lanterns, the fancy outfits everyone was wearing and the delicious aroma in the air. If things were different it would have been an incredibly wonderful evening. I wasn't sure how it was going to end but whatever happens tonight, it certainly is going to be memorable.

Chapter 23

THE DANCE

"THIS IS PRETTY cool Casey." I said as we were checking our new rooms. "We'll have plenty of time to move our stuff in tomorrow. I was expecting a run-down crappy room or motorhome. This is sweet!"

"Jackson look at this!" Casey pulled me over to look out her window. "You can see the Newport Bridge, all of Newport, Brenton cove. Look at all the boats! There's Scott's boat. It's huge!"

"That's a great view. Hey what's this?" I saw what looked like a door but it had a keypad and it was locked. "I don't think I have one of those in my room."

She didn't know what it was either. As we looked around there seemed to be a few different knobs and buttons we couldn't figure out. There would be time to investigate it later. Casey seemed happy and that helped me relax a little. I put on a little cologne before going downstairs. Casey decided to change her dress. I went down to find Mom and Dad.

Dad was watching the news on a huge TV screen. It was bigger than ours and clearly brand new. I stood next to him and saw some footage of people getting attacked somewhere. It looked like a train station. It was horrifying and looked unreal. But it *was* real and it was a reminder that terrible things were happening out there and we'd be seeing it for ourselves really soon. Just two hours ago one of the infecteds attacked Colby and Mr. Z.

It all just seemed so strange still. "Hey Dad. This is messed up. It's worse than I thought it would be don't you think?" I said trying not to sound like a scared little boy.

"It's happening fast. Maybe faster than we thought." He responded, "I wonder if they know the truth yet. I'm pretty sure the government does but they know that there's not much they can do."

At 9 pm there was going to be some type of announcement. Maybe for a couple hours we could have some fun. Mom and Casey came down a few minutes later and they were all dressed up. They both looked great and seemed happy. After some quality family moments including a photo-op we left for the gala.

Casey noticed I was wearing cologne. She didn't want to admit that it smelled good, "You know a little goes a long way, Jackson."

I knew she was just teasing but she was right. I was glad we would be outside so it wouldn't be overpowering.

"Hey Casey, there's the pen the lieutenant made!" I point out a little circle of chicken wire outside the front door. There was a little dish of water and some seeds on a little plate.

"Oh that's so cute!" she screamed out. I'll leave Greg here for a little while but I'll come visit later.

I could hear the band playing and I wasn't sure if I should go pick up Cameron or meet her in here. I was going to ask Mom but she and Dad were headed to the gala so I decided it was okay to text Cameron. We used to text all the time but haven't for so long. I really didn't know why.

Hey Cameron. Do you still have my number? JK. I thought your family would like some alone time but I can come pick you up if you'd like.

She responded almost right away.

We're leaving now. I hear music. Let's meet on the dance floor!!

Sounds great.

I was starting to get a little nervous and again had to remind myself of my new inner confidence. It was just so strange. Whatever it was about Cameron when I thought about her I just felt a little nervous, but a good nervous. I know Dad would say she made me 'weak in the knees' or something cringy like that but it really was spot-on. I took a few breaths. I reached in my pocket and grabbed my key fob and locked my new car. The lights on the Lamborghini flickered and the coolest sound signaled the alarm was on.

"Holy shit! Is that your new car?" Tyler Stanford yelled out as he was walking past it towards me. "That is so cool! You gotta let me drive it some day!"

"Sure. Why not?" I responded. "I heard you got a new toy too."

"Oh, yeah! Collin and I both got new dirt bikes. My dad bought an awesome jet ski too! I'm just not sure *when* we'll be able to use some of these new things, you know."

I looked around the fort. "This place is pretty big. We can do some riding in the parade field! We can build a jump!"

"Yeah! Collin can film us jumping with his new drone!"

Just then most of the other kids were emerging and meeting up near the parents but not too near. It was pretty cool that everyone got along for the most part. I made sure everyone met my cousins from Barrington. Madigan and Ellery were the same age as me and Casey. They were going to get along great with Cameron and the other Lang girls I thought. And there it was again, that feeling. *Calm down Jackson*, I said to myself.

Everyone was looking good in jackets and ties. It was a little warm for jackets but we all had them on anyway. We had all talked about this before with some of the dads including mine. I knew most of the guys had their guns loaded and ready under those jackets.

I decided this was a good time to make sure a few things were clear with everyone. Dad had actually asked me to have some kind of meeting with the younger group. He wanted everyone to know that they were key contributors no matter their age. Everyone had to be committed.

"Hey guys and girls. Let's talk for a minute." I said in a voice loud enough for everyone to hear. Everyone gathered around and seemed to be listening to me.

"Okay, in a minute we'll head over to the gala and have some fun." I took a deep breath but didn't feel nervous, it felt good to be confident and calm. "You all look good. The music's playing. The food smells great. There's a lot going on." Everyone was nodding and smiling as they listened. "It's okay to have a little fun but we can't get too distracted. Who's wearing a gun?" Most of the guy's raised their hands. The girls didn't but dresses just didn't make it easy. "Okay, good. They should be loaded. Safeties on. Go ahead and check. Fingers off the trigger. No mistakes." A few of them clearly had their safeties off. "Okay, jackets stay on and guns remain holstered from here on out. Most of the people you don't know are clueless about what's happening. There's going to be some major announcement at 9 pm and whatever is announced we are all staying here. No one leaves the fort no matter what anyone tells you. You leave here and you may not get back in." Everyone was listening and paying attention.

I continued, "Everyone should have their phone on. If anything goes wrong or if there is any change of plan the group text line will update everyone. Check it regularly." The next point was important to stress. "My dad sent out a text to alot of our friends and neighbors about what's going down out there. We can't let them in here. It's too dangerous. If anyone tries to find out where we are you cannot tell them! Let my dad know or Mr. Lang. Anyone we know could be infected and just one getting in here is way too risky. Right Colby?"

He didn't hesitate to answer "Those things are for real. My dad and I couldn't handle one of them. This thing just kept coming and coming. It was bloodthirsty and it took three mags to put it down. It would have killed all of us. These things are scary and worse than in the movies." He was shaking a little and Lucas put his arm around him. Lucas was the oldest of us and was the biggest.

Lucas said to me and to the group "Our dad told us the same thing. Don't worry, Jax. Let's all work together and help watch for trouble. We can't leave the fort for any reason." Everyone seemed to nod in agreement.

Colby spoke out again "Remember. The captain said he didn't feel well just a few minutes before he turned. It can happen fast so we gotta watch for any signs. If any of the guests looks questionable go check it out."

I agreed "That's a great idea, Colby. And don't do it alone. Let's stick together. If there's anything that catches your eye grab a buddy and go check it out. We have to keep an eye on each other."

"So Jackson, who's your *buddy* going to be tonight?" Santino Izzo teased me a little in front of the group. They all knew about Cameron but there was a sense of mystery about her. She was one of these girls who got whisked in on a helicopter and there was some buzz that she and I were a couple already. But everyone had met her and the other Lang girls earlier and it was really not a big deal. Cameron was part of the team and part of our family. Santino just wanted to poke a little fun and it didn't bother me at all.

"Hey come on!" I laughed a little and returned a few fist bumps. "I will be watching everyone closely, just from the dance floor. Speaking of which. I'm late for a date. Let's roll. Safeties on!"

"Safeties on." Everyone responded softly in unison as if they had practiced it. We all started walking towards the gala. When I look back at that moment I realize it was a really important impromptu meeting. My history teacher would have called it a 'galvanizing moment' and we all would roll our eyes a little. I wasn't the oldest and I wasn't the biggest but I had a voice that these guys listened to. They knew they could trust me and that I was invested in the survival of the whole group, young and old. I wasn't trying to be a leader but we needed someone to be making sure everyone else remained focused on the right things and ready for whatever happened. I didn't know what was going to happen tomorrow but I knew what we needed to do now. That was enough, we were a strong group and for now we all had a clear goal. Survive tonight. Tomorrow is tomorrow.

We started towards the party and we could see our parents sitting at some tables or on the dance floor. My parents were dancing. They looked happy. Casey, Madigan and Ellery were next to me. They looked happy. For now things were okay.

We found our seats and there were several 'kids tables' which was fine with us. As much as I wanted to be 'grown up' I didn't mind that we could all be kids at the same time. So far things were going well within the 'kids' circle. We all got along real well and there wasn't any fighting or power struggles yet. There would be some tough times to come but not tonight. We shouldn't feel guilty about having some fun if it came our way. My dad made sure I understood that earlier. I found a table and decided it would be good to have the Lang girls and the Braden girls all together. Casey and I agreed it would be the easiest. Just then I received a text.

Just entered fort for 1st time. Wow. Place is beautiful. ICU.

I looked over at the entrance and saw the Lang family talking to Lieutenant Gerard and then there was Cameron looking over at me. We were 200 feet apart but it was like there was no one else here. I could see her eyes and everything else was just in slow motion. She started walking towards me with her family and she looked great. I started to walk slowly to the dance floor. 'What was I doing?' I thought to myself. I wasn't really sure but I was just trying to do what felt right. I saw my parents and the Zanelos and Stanfords all dancing. Everyone was smiling and allowing themselves to have some fun. I found a little area near the middle of the dance floor and was trying to feel the beat of the music. I wasn't sure what song it was but suspected it was Frank Sinatra based on how into it Dr. Izzo was. I was admiring the band and they were all decked out in white tuxedos. Someone tapped on my shoulder and I turned around. Cameron was right there and she looked amazing. She was smiling and looked so happy. It just felt like we were never apart. I reached out my hands and we started dancing. It seemed so easy with a big band sound and everyone else around us dancing too. It was pretty loud so I didn't even try to talk. We had a great time dancing for two songs then decided to take a break. She turned to walk off the dance floor but didn't let go of my hand. We held hands all the way to the table and it felt . . . normal.

I kept my eye on every person we passed and was still watching for anything that didn't look right. I was having a great time but I was still looking at people's eyes and making sure I didn't get *too* caught up in the moment. I felt like I could do both. I saw several of the guys walking around and patrolling the dance floor and tables. Some of them were over at the fancy high end porta-johns keeping an eye on the guests. I met eyes with some of the guys and there was a subtle type of recognition we gave each other. It was almost imperceptible but to me it was a simple nod of the head that said 'I got you' or 'I'm on top of things' and I didn't detect anything negative about me dancing with Cameron. I felt great and really had no feeling of insecurity or anxiety. I was feeling even more comfortable when I was around her. It felt natural.

We were about to sit down when I felt a hand on my shoulder. I looked at Cam and based on her expression I knew who it was. I turned towards Scott and he was smiling. He looked happy. I glanced at Cameron who was smiling too and I only had good vibes.

"Would you mind if I had the next dance, Jackson?" he asked without any hint of sarcasm or attitude.

"No sir." I responded and they strode off as another old song started playing.

I watched them dance as I sat down and got sucked into a conversation with the Lang girls and Braden girls regarding chickens. It appeared that they were planning a 'chicken heist.' Yes they were plotting to sneak out of the fort and steal more baby chicks under the cover of darkness. I was pretty sure they weren't serious so I helped them figure out some of the logistics. How many baby chicks would fit into a backpack? We were laughing and having a good time. Just then the song ended and someone in a very formal outfit appeared up on the stage with a microphone.

"Good evening ladies and gentlemen. I'm Commodore Hamilton. I have the privilege of being the president of the Fort Adams Foundation and it is especially rewarding to me to be here on a night like this. As everyone here knows there is a very generous donor who has pledged ten million dollars to the foundation and we couldn't be happier. You can already see the massive changes here at the fort and the energy that this funding brings is palpable. Tonight has been designated a night for celebration whereas tomorrow evening the mystery donor will make the presentation here on stage." He paused for some applause and whistles.

During this whole speech I continued to watch for any strange behavior within the walls. People were walking all around and there were several areas with some activity. The ultra high class porta johns were popular tonight, a few people waiting in line looking somewhat uncomfortable but not sickly. There was an open bar so people were definitely mingling around there but no one who looked suspicious. So far no problems.

"On a sadder note," the uniformed man on stage continued, "you all are aware of the tragic state of things outside these walls and the violent outbreaks that are occurring. We will be broadcasting the governor's announcements at 9 pm. Until then everyone please find your seats. Dinner is served!"

There were more applause as he left the stage. So far there were no major problems. It was so strange that I wanted to get this party over with just so that we could get to the end of the world. Why wouldn't we want to enjoy these last few hours of fun and music. I decided that I would try to have some fun, at least until 9 pm.

Cameron came back to the table and sat down. She seemed to be all smiles and I was too. She told me I danced better than her dad but I didn't really believe her. I told her how the girls were going to rescue some chicks and she found it hysterical. I had the whole table laughing and we were all having a good time. I found that I could laugh and enjoy myself but still scan the whole crowd for anything wrong. That's when I saw him. Heading towards the bathroom. He was about 50 and a little overweight. He seemed to be coughing or gagging a little but I really couldn't tell. I excused myself and casually strode towards the luxury porta johns. I walked by a table of guys. Three of them had their eyes trained on this guy. I walked by and I held out 1 finger and Collin Stanford stood up. I kept walking and Collin trailed me by ten feet. We went over to the porta johns and I stood in line behind this guy. There was no one else here right now. Collin was waiting next to me. This guy was coughing and sweating and looked like he was a little out of breath. The door swung open and someone exited the john and this guy rushed in. We heard some continued coughing and hacking and I was really starting to get nervous. My mind was racing and I really didn't want to unholster my gun but I thought I should. Just then I heard a very calming voice right behind me.

"Hey guys you enjoying the gala so far?" Dad asked in a smooth relaxed tone.

I looked at him and he looked at me and without saying any words I could sense he was right on the same page as us. While looking at the porta john he continued "Seems like we got lucky with the weather, what do you think Collin?"

There was more coughing and some wretching in the bathroom and I could tell that he very subtly reached and turned off his safety. I did the same.

He said under his breath to me and Collin "Taser first. I have mine ready, stand down but be ready, okay? Jackson? Collin?"

We both nodded and about ten seconds later we heard this

guy just start throwing up. We could tell he was heaving again and again. He just kept going until he finally stopped. My heart was beating fast but I definitely felt a certain calmness about me. It felt like things were moving very slow and my reaction time was very fast. I felt like I would be able to read the situation and make split decisions without any hesitation. We waited. We heard him wash his hands and gargle a little then stumble out the door. He seemed a little off balance but he did not look infected. We all were calm as he walked right past us looking a little better than before.

"False alarm, gents." Dad said to us, "But good eyes and good team work. That guy looked pretty bad. A few too many Dark and Stormies. Let's get back to the party."

We started walking back all a little more casually. Dad spoke again "Collin, can't wait to see the new dirt bikes. Jackson brought his too. Should be a fun diversion."

"Yeah, do you think we can ride them tomorrow?" Collin asked?

"Sure. It'll be a blast." Dad said calmly, "Let's go finish dinner. Those steaks looked good."

Collin and I walked back to our tables. I said quietly 'safeties on' and we both reached casually under our jackets. A fist bump and then we separated. While we were away dinner had been served. I joined the girls who were clearly enjoying a little red meat, all except for Madigan, our family's vegan. She had a salad of some type and she seemed happy with it. I took my seat between Cameron and Ellery and checked out the damage.

"Oh my God this is so good!" Cameron exclaimed as she went to town on the sizzling steak in front of her. In LA she mostly had sushi and salads. A thick dry-aged porterhouse isn't the typical go-to entree in her circle. I loved that she wasn't afraid to really take down a good piece of meat. Just like mom. She didn't grow up in New England and she had never had a stuffie before. She just couldn't stop herself from finishing one. I am a stuffie-snob but even I admitted they were really good. Not as good as Grandma's but really good. Throw in some calamari and we were both full. Neither of us had eaten that much before but it was just so much fun to eat with another foodie! We all had such a great meal, even Madigan. A song we recognized started to play and Cameron and I danced some more. Madigan danced with Tyler Stanford and Casey pulled the Lang girls and Ellery out on the floor. What a good time! Everyone was getting their groove on. Cameron and I were both so full and admitted we overdid it a little. After one more dance we both had to sit down again. I couldn't believe she went for dessert too!

Chapter 24

THE ANNOUNCEMENT

THE BAND WAS playing, the stars were out, we were all having a good time. The dance floor was full, even most of the kids were dancing. I was keeping an eye on Jackson and Cameron. Not because I was worried about them. I actually really loved seeing them both happy in that moment. They deserved to have just a little bit of fun before things changed. Scott was enjoying the moment too. He came over to me as we watched them.

"Hey, if they get married do you think this place will be available for the reception?" he asked, smiling.

"I heard it's booked for the next year or two. And there may be some unruly squatter's you have to deal with too." I answered.

He was smiling and seemed at ease. The girls were safe and seemed happy. Tracy was being more than civil, even nice. Things were good but we all knew it was just a matter of time. We saw the lieutenant wheeling out a big screen and he had someone with him holding some type of projector. They were going to make sure everyone saw the announcement. We had agreed it seemed like a good idea for everyone to know what Governor Raymond had to say.

The band finished the song and the commodore came back on stage. He approached the microphone. "Okay folks, it's almost 9 pm and the governor is going to make her announcements. We wanted to make sure you could all see it. Lieutenant, go ahead."

Lieutenant Gerard turned on the projector and we could see the empty podium on the screen. He came over and stood next to Scott and I as we waited for Governor Raymond to give us the update. I was curious if she was going to reveal the truth or just spin more conjecture. Regardless, we were expecting her to send everyone home and enforce some type of shelter-in-place ruling.

While we waited the lieutenant gave us some updates. "Sounds pretty bad in Providence and not much better in Newport. The infecteds are increasing in number and are starting to accumulate. They are running around the streets and attacking people and besieging homes filled with innocent people. It sounds awful."

It did sound awful and I continued to watch over the crowd. I could see Jackson and the boys all standing up and paying attention to the screen but also scanning the crowd and watching for anything that looked suspicious. I spoke over the com, "Let's watch this newsfeed but everyone keep their head on a swivel. Things are heating up out there and we can't be caught off guard in here. Remember, no one leaves the fort."

Finally, Governor Raymond came to the podium and adjusted the microphone. She wasn't smiling and didn't look happy at all. "Good evening people of Rhode Island. I am making this public address tonight because the safety of the state's citizens is paramount during these troubled times. We are in the midst of an epidemic. An epidemic of violence and atrocities against innocent people that we have never seen before. I have spoken with the state police and with the

National Guard and after several meetings held earlier today I am prepared to make several announcements. It is with regret and with sadness that I announce . . . we are losing this battle. As fast as we can respond to one attack two more are occurring. The assailants in these attacks are requiring two, three, sometimes four policemen to take them down and sometimes more. Good citizens are dying and so are good policemen and guardsmen. After my brief presentation we will all be seeing a direct feed from the headquarters of the US response task force in Washington. It has been promised that we will learn more about the nature of the attacks and the violence at that time. Our office has still not been informed of this information despite our pleas. Regardless, I am bound to govern this state with the main goal of keeping people safe. With that in mind I am enforcing a shelter-in-place order as of this moment. All citizens are to return to their homes immediately and will stay there until this order has been lifted. This order will be enforced by the police and the National Guard. Violators will not be tolerated and will be arrested and placed in jail without a court hearing or judicial process. Stay home. Don't leave home. Lock your doors and if you have a safe place to be without windows or easy access from the outside stay there. Please do your best to protect yourselves and your families. There will be briefings on all networks, on line, and on the radio at 12 noon and 6 pm daily. I will be praying for all of us." She paused for a moment and seemed to be listening in to her earpiece.

We all looked at each other during this brief pause. While none of this came as a huge surprise it was a surreal moment to see it all unfold. We were trying to remain calm. There were a lot of guests getting their coats on and starting to head to the exit.

The governor again made an announcement. "I have just been informed that we will be hearing from a medical consultant for the government in several moments. While most unusual to hear from a non-government source it seems that in this case they have elected to have a lead scientist make several announcements regarding the current worldwide crisis."

A different podium appeared on the screen with the White House logo. There was no sound for a moment and we all watched anxiously. Someone was approaching the podium. I could not believe my eyes. It was unmistakable. Dr. Ashworth was at the podium and preparing to address the network, and likely the world, regarding the recent violence. We all looked at each other in complete shock and amazement. This was very real.

"Good evening. My name is Dr. Tom Ashworth. I am a liaison to the CIA and CDC and I am addressing you tonight as I have the most in-depth knowledge and awareness of the current global crisis and viral pandemic. I represent a company that developed a revolutionary treatment for insomnia. A novel treatment was created using a modified virus carrying genetic material designed as a trojan horse. The target of the virus was the sleep center of the brain with the goal of improved REM sleep. An unintended consequence was an up-regulation of the sympathetic nerve connections and complete destruction of frontal lobe neurons. The frontal lobe dysfunction removes all reason, judgment, and executive function in the brain while the activated sympathetic system creates an aggressive, primitive and unfortunately violent host victim. Secondary effects appear to be loss of any sense of pain and seemingly unlimited energy due to the genetic mutation. As you have seen in the videos these things are hard to kill. They do not have an off switch. We have some of these..things . . . in holding cells that are still as violent as they were over two weeks ago when we first realized we had a major problem."

Tom stopped for a moment and caught his breath while we all caught ours. The world was hearing this all for the first time and it had to be creating quite a bit of anxiety, along with some hostility regarding this vaccine therapy. All of this was caused by a pharmaceutical company trying to make money! I could already hear people getting angry and upset behind me. Sadly, it was just too late for anyone to do anything but try to survive.

"These infected beings are not human. Their brains are damaged beyond repair. They are not people. Do not try to save them, they cannot be salvaged." He took his time and took a few deep breaths. "We made every effort we could to reverse this viral infection but we could not do it. The vaccine was created using an altered, inactivated virus combined with fragments of human DNA material. The inactive virus regained it's replicative properties and became virulent. It spread quickly and it spread everywhere. What you are seeing is the effects of this virus on the population. It will continue. It will get worse. Most people will succumb to this. There is no available antidote. We had a small amount of immunoglobulin and vaccine that was targeted for high value subjects and it has been exhausted. We delayed this announcement while we searched for any cure. We have none. There may be a small percentage of survivors with natural immunity and some people may have a delayed infection. Please heed all warnings of the government and seek shelter and remain hidden. If you are on the street or outside of your house you are at risk of being attacked by an infected or being eliminated by the military response. Wait for messages from us. If it is safe to come out we will inform you. Until then, God save us." He walked away from the podium and off the stage. The screen went dark for a moment.

The news channel came back on and it was clear that the news anchors really didn't know what to say. They were in shock and not sure how to handle the enormity of what we all just learned. Finally, the camera closed in on Dan North. He was listening to his earpiece as he started talking again.

"Quite a lot to take in. Dr. Tom Ashworth giving us the long-awaited explanation for the attacks. A pharmaceutical research project designed to help people with insomnia now the cause of a world-wide pandemic of epic, no *biblical* proportions. We are going to have commentary from the National Guard and from the state police. Right now. . . ." He paused

He started again, "And now we are joined by. . . ." He paused again.

"No. No. I'm not doing this. Everyone listen to what that guy said. Go home and guard your families. Protect your kids. Hope for a miracle. I'm leaving here now. Good night." He stood up and walked away. The co-host looked just as rattled and after a few awkward moments followed Dan off the set. The camera stayed right where it was and there just remained an image of the abandoned news desk. The cameraman and crew likely were already in their cars and it was kind of an eerie site on the screen.

Lieutenant Gerard turned off the TV. This was it. Right on time.

We all just sat there taking it all in. Even though we were some of the only people in the world who knew all of this ahead of time it still seemed so shocking. None of this was easy to digest. Being mentally prepared for this was almost as important as being physically ready. We were going to find out soon how well we did. Did we do everything we could do? Now that everyone else knew what we did how would things change?

It still seemed scary and the kids were definitely a little freaked out. They were all coming over to our tables and seeking out a little comfort with their families. We all just huddled there as all the other guests were making it towards the exits quickly. Just then Commodore Hamilton came over to our table. He clearly looked upset and I couldn't blame him at all. The very weekend that the Fort Adams Trust was receiving it's huge windfall and all this had to happen! Little did he know that it was all part of our master plan. This was all just a ruse and he was an unwitting player. We were granted nearly unlimited access and provided anything we asked for. All the people working so hard to transform this old fort into our impenetrable castle had been serving just one purpose, helping us survive this massive surge of relentless, primordial violence. It had all come together well but as he approached us I wondered what he might have to say.

"Well, folks this certainly wasn't how I imagined this night would end. I'm not sure what's going to happen next but we have to get out of here now." He said with some urgency. He seemed slightly perplexed that we were all just sitting around and not panicking.

"I'm sure you all are interested in getting home and back to your families. You saw the news!" He seemed even more animated. A few other members of the Trust came over to his side.

"Our families are right here." I answered him calmly. "I believe Dr. Ashworth said to seek shelter." I held my arms up gesturing at the giant walls around us. "We're going to stay right here."

He was clearly upset and perhaps not used to anyone defying him. "No, no that's not what's happening. We're closing up the fort. The governor said go home. We can't have anyone working here or staying here. Everyone must go. Clear the fort. Now!"

He was getting angry and this was not entirely unexpected. He just didn't know how little power he had. "I'm calling the lieutenant."

"Why don't you just go home? Go somewhere safe." Allan said to him. I was interested in hearing just how much he was going to press us. He probably wanted to get home just like everyone else headed for the gate. "Send all the staff home. Most of them are gone anyway. We are here and we are not leaving. None of us."

The commodore screamed into his phone "Lieutenant, we have a problem here! You need to clear this group and close the fort. Get security down here if you need to! Everything shuts down. Now!"

We could hear the lieutenant on our earpieces. "I will take care of everything, sir. The fort will be secured. You should go home. Mr. Jacobson doesn't look well. He's here near the exit gate. He may need *attention*."

Some of us immediately stood up. That was our code word for if one of the guests was acting peculiar or suspicious tonight.

"Let's get to the gate." Steve spoke calmly. Scott, Dave, Allan, Jason and I all started toward the exit.

The commodore seemed somewhat pleased at the turn of events. These stubborn people were finally listening to him. He turned and followed us. Jackson and a few other boys also came with us. I didn't mind. They needed to feel a certain level of responsibility. If there is a threat it must be dealt with. Quickly. Having numbers was critical. Especially with these things. One-on-one was an unfair fight, even with a gun.

The rest of our group stayed put and watched the throngs of petrified guests head to the gates. So far nothing suspicious. Some of the kids (and moms) were checking their phones. I knew the internet must be lighting up. This was not just another Friday night.

We quickly reached the gate and met with the lieutenant. He looked relieved to see a support team show up. He pointed towards a man sitting on a bench just inside the walls of the fort. "He's been sitting there for a few minutes. He's sweaty and looks terrible. I called out to him a few times but he didn't answer."

"Oh good, Lieutenant Gerard. Glad you're still here." exclaimed the commodore as he caught up to us. "This group seems reluctant to vacate the fort. Please help me convince them the gala and their night at the fort is over."

"Aye, sir. Will do. Right now Mr. Jacobson is looking a little distraught. I'm a little worried. He's acting very peculiar."

"Barney? Yes, that does look like Barney. No, he doesn't look good. Here comes his wife in their car. She'll get him home." The commodore sounded confident as he shouted at his friend. "Barney! Linda's here! Go get in the car! It's not safe!" He started walking towards him.

Linda got out of the car and started towards the entrance. She looked a little worried too as she approached the gate. Barney seemed to startle a little as the commodore approached. He lifted his head up and seemed to look around at his surroundings. We could all tell at once he looked infected. We had seen enough film.

The commodore continued to walk forward but the lieutenant grabbed his arm.

"What are you doing? Let me go help him!" called out the commodore, clearly irritated.

"Linda, please stop there!" I called out as she was approaching her husband.

I called out a little louder, "Commodore don't get any closer. He is infected. This is very dangerous. We can't let him attack her, you or us. Gentlemen, let's flank him. Guns on target. Jackson, boys, flashlights on Mr. Jacobson please." Night had fallen quickly and this was a dark corner of the fort. We were lucky the lieutenant spotted Mr. Jacobson. This could have been a disaster although it wasn't over.

We all took out our guns and turned the safeties off. We were locked and loaded. The five men moved into position each about twenty feet from the subject, guns drawn. The boys each took position behind us. Each had a bright flashlight helping us see him clearly. It looked like we had trained for this a hundred times.

The commodore was dumbstruck and clearly frightened at what was happening.

We surrounded Mr. Jacobson who was looking more and more infected each minute.

"Mr. Jacobson!" Allan called out "We don't want to hurt you. Please get up and go home. Your wife is here. Get up now!"

He didn't move. The instinct was to approach him but that was exceedingly dangerous.

I didn't want to wait for him to fully transform. "Steve, taser and zip tie handcuffs?"

"Agreed." Steve responded. "Best not to wait. Allan and Dave taser on the count of three. Once he's down Paul and I will approach. We both have cuffs. Support right behind us. Keep those lights on him boys."

Mr. Jacobson stood up slowly and looked really scary. He was snarling and looking at all of us it looked like he was getting ready to move.

Allan and Dave approached to about ten feet away. Armed support just behind them. They had tasers drawn and aimed on target. Steve began in a calm but confident tone "One. Two. Three."

Dave and Allan fired at the infected. They both shot once with both direct hits. Mr. Jacobson flailed his arms and turned around. He didn't fall. They immediately reloaded and shot again. He finally went down and we were quickly on top of him. We turned him on his stomach and both sat on him. Steve used a zip-tie handcuff on his wrists and I got his ankles. This all happened in about fifteen seconds. The commodore seemed completely overwhelmed with what was happening. We turned Mr. Jacobson over carefully avoiding his head and mouth. He started to bite and gnash. He was writhing around and his body was shaking. I was concerned he would break out of the cuffs. We carried Mr. Jacobson away from the fort and placed him on the ground next to his car.

He continued to writhe around and snarl and hiss. His wife was in shock and was only now figuring out that he was infected. He was gone. The commodore was looking at him on the ground and then at us. "Well now, what are you going to do?" he asked us.

"That's up to you, Commodore. We're going back in." I said to him as the nine of us stood there holding our 9mm guns and not showing a hint of fear.

Steve added, "If I were you I'd get in my car, drive home, lock the doors and hide in the basement with as much food and water as you can store. But get this straight," he brought his gun up and directed it at the commodore, "We are staying here and there's not one thing you can do about it. Get going." He lowered his gun and we all watched to see what would happen next.

Linda tried to lift her husband into the car while he just tried to bite her. We just weren't sure what to do so we helped her put him in the backseat. I put an extra set of plastic zip-ties on his wrists and ankles before she drove off. Could we have done more? Not sure. She might make it home. She would likely start to change soon too.

We turned to go back into the fort. We all walked straight past the commodore who seemed stunned by all of this and not sure what to do. We entered the gate. The commodore turned back and clearly was angry.

"I'll come back here with the police if I have to. You will all be cleared from these premises. Mark my words! Lieutenant you are relieved!" The commodore yelled but his animation was met with very little response. This seemed to aggravate him even more but he did finally leave.

We left two men at the gate with AR-15s. There were still some people and staff exiting so we couldn't close the gate yet. Right now that still remained our main priority. Seal the fort. We split up in teams and the lieutenant directed each team to clear an area. We had to be certain every nook and cranny and porta john was clear. We could not afford any infecteds hiding out all quiet and low-key like Mr. Jacobson.

We systematically cleared the parade field and all areas guests and staff had access to. We made sure the fort had been adequately checked and rechecked then the lieutenant gave the official order "Close the gate!" He pushed a button and the gate slowly moved and when it finally closed it was with a heavy thud. A thud that felt very comforting. The fort was secure.

Chapter 25

AFTERPARTY

Wᴇ ᴀʟʟ ʜᴇᴀᴅᴇᴅ back towards the rest of the group. We paused for a moment as I ducked behind one of the abandoned bars. I grabbed a couple of bottles of champagne. We made it back to the table to a few cheers. We relived for our group some of the details and I thought it would be a good opportunity to have another impromptu meeting. It was as good a time as any to clear the air and bring everybody up to speed.

Jaymi Stanford was the first to weigh in on things. "Not for nothing but our apartment is completely amazing. We have a beautiful master bed and bath, the kids have their own rooms and the kitchenette is probably nicer than our house's. What's happening?"

I had to agree with her and I'm glad she helped us start to talk on a lighter note. "Jaymi we're just as blown away as you are. This transformation is amazing and there are two people to thank for a lot of hard work and effort. While no one will be surprised that Mr. Scott Lang orchestrated much of this I want everyone to know that he busted his ass making sure that this fort was transformed into what it is today." There was loud applause and Scott's girls who sat on or next to him all hugged and kissed their dad the hero. Kristin poured champagne into a bunch of glasses and handed them out.

I continued "There's another unsung hero who deserves attention tonight. Lieutenant Gerard. We decided that trusting you was a good idea. We decided that bringing you into our group was the right decision. We agreed that you were someone who would make our group even stronger. And we were right every step of the way. You have proven yourself to be invaluable as a member of our group. Welcome and thank you. A toast to the lieutenant and to Scott for their hard work which allowed us to establish our group within this magnificently redesigned fort!"

'Salud!' 'Cheers!' 'Here, Here!' and everything else you'd expect to hear with that toast. Everyone enjoyed some champagne and it felt nice to relax a little. What I didn't expect was for the lieutenant to jump on a table.

"You people have been nothing but fantastic! Dr. Braden came to me with such a cockamamie story I thought about calling the police but I didn't. His story was so crazy it just had to be true. And sadly it was. I immediately understood my role in helping to transform and redesign this fort. With Mr. Lang's help I think we did an amazing job. Mrs. Stanford I'm so glad you enjoy your new home away from home. You folks all deserve to be happy during your time here. I will be. I already feel blessed to be part of this group. In fact I would like for you to all think of me as one of you and to call me Sam. It would be my honor."

We all clapped and cheered and both Sam and Scott received plenty of love. There were hugs and high fives and everyone seemed to be happy we could take this break and breathe easy with the fort finally secured. No one was happier than Sam. He already had our trust but it was a good moment that brought us all closer together.

We just hung out there at the tables for a little while and everyone seemed like they had plenty of energy. I stood up and got everyone's attention. "What a night. What a good night we had. It had some surprises. Seeing Dr. Ashworth woke us all up and affirmed what fears we already had. The unfortunate transformation of Mr. Jacobson was sad and unsettling. It did serve its purpose. We saw what we saw and we handled it. We can handle this. We are ready. Right now I think things are relatively calm out there in our immediate vicinity around the fort. It's going to get crazy at some point but for now I think we can just plan on getting things settled down here. Kristin, how should we tackle this tonight?"

She stood up and looked around at everyone "First of all, I want Sam to know we are so happy to have him as part of our family and I agree with Jaymi's shout out! Great job Sam and Scott!" Again everyone applauded and I could see a lot of the boys exchanging high-fives and fist bumping. It was not lost on them that their new rooms and living conditions were not a downgrade.

Kristin continued, "Lori, Kim and I discussed earlier and agreed that if we had a few hours tonight there could be several valuable things to accomplish. First of all, we have ten RV's with a huge amount of food and non-perishable items within them. We don't know what's in there but whatever is there it's worth saving. The RVs should be emptied and the food should be brought into storage. Next, we have the catering trucks that are sitting within the fort that should be emptied into our storage. The bar areas should also be emptied and all the bottles stored below in the kitchen. There is plenty of room. Also, I know many of us ordered tons of food and don't have room for it all. Whatever you can't fit can be brought into storage if you'd like. Lastly, I want to make sure that our good neighbors on the *Resilience* are feeling welcomed here. There are suites ready and waiting for the Lang family and Steve and Abby. Everyone's welcome here once we know you are immune, we can test you every day. I know the *Resilience* may be hard to leave but we look forward to everyone being within these walls eventually. You are all family and we welcome you all to this fort. Hopefully, you can accept this place as your home away from home away from home. We're all family now!"

Abby stood up and ran over to Kristin for a hug. Lori, Jamie, Kim, Candace and basically all the mom's joined them in a girl hug. Abby seemed to be overwhelmed but happy to be aligned with such strong women. She had only just met them yesterday but already she had seen so much. She had witnessed what these women could do to save their families and these were the type of people you could quickly trust and believe in. There was a true sense of family that was palpable. While she had spent years in the military and was a strong woman herself (she had already shot 14 rounds into an infected with an AR-15 today) she was really happy to be accepted into this group of women. She had never really had this sense of unity and she truly felt grateful.

I stood up and applauded the women hugging. It was a feel-good moment when we needed it. The greatest thing was that it was organic. Kristin had a great feeling about Abby before she even really knew who she was. Abby risked her life for some people she had just met. It's just not everyday people like this come together.

"We are all really lucky. In this world. In these times." I was reflecting a little. "It's okay to enjoy a little bit of human kindness when it happens. To be honest, I've been seeing it everywhere and in everybody. I see it in the parents. I loved it when Jamie Browne got out of her car to hug it out with Sam. Those are good hugs, I know. The younger ones are amazing too. I see it when the Lang sisters immediately helped my daughter feel like she's got new best friends and sisters she never had. I've seen the boys behave like a well-oiled marine unit and still want to protect their moms. I've seen everyone here respond to hardship the best way possible. With teamwork and by doing it the right way. When you do things the right way it usually gives you the best outcome. So let's continue what we're here to do. Survive and thrive."

"Here, here!" along with a few more clanging glasses.

"Sam, Steve, as far as tonight what do you think we should do for security here at the fort?" I asked. I had already discussed this with both of them but wanted everyone to be privy to the discussion.

Steve responded first. "While we were all saddened by Mr. Jacobson's plight let's not forget we are in a tactical advantage out here on the peninsula. I don't see many infected making a beeline for the fort. Allan's idea to make this fort the home of the group is just as advantageous now as it was 200 years ago. It's a great location. If any infecteds make it up here it will be in small numbers and much less than other sites you may have considered. It was a great choice Allan. As far as tonight, I think we are in good shape. We should have one lookout between the fort and the *Resilience*. Up on top of this east wall. Four hour rotations I think are appropriate. Sam?"

Sam stood up and echoed much of what Steve said. "I'm not too worried about tonight. We're far enough removed from Newport that we won't see the volume of infecteds. We must still understand that all it takes is just one. I agree with Steve, one lookout along the top of the east wall I think is sufficient." We all had been familiarized with the east wall. The main gate sat within the east wall and the scout positions designed atop the gate gave the lookout great views of the parking lot, the *Resilience* and beyond. "If the gate is opened we need to have a team approach no matter how small the task. A simple walk across the parking lot is not worth taking any chances. We can have a vehicle ready to bring the Langs and Steve and Abby in no time. We'll have to be methodical whenever we open the gate or leave the fort. We can't let our guard down."

It was just 10 pm and we had decent energy. We decided to take advantage of things and get the food all stored away. We were all so stuffed it made it easier to put all the delicious prepared foods into cold storage. There was a huge amount of leftover steak, ribs, salmon, potatoes, calamari, etc. A fair number of guests did not show up, not a big surprise. Sam had been explicit with the catering company that they bring and store everything today in anticipation of a full turnout tonight and tomorrow night. It was a massive amount of food that we would not waste. Each family had also managed to purchase cratefuls of food that were being brought over to the storage area. I thought Kristin had gone a little overboard when all the huge boxes of snacks and chips and cookies started arriving but now it made more sense. Any sense of "normalcy" would help with this transition. I couldn't believe how much food we had stockpiled but I also knew it wouldn't last forever. Everyone helped out with this important task of getting things stored away. Lori and Kim directed this part of the operation. They were getting the kitchen prepped and making sure everything that we could store was well-labeled and cataloged. They kept it quite organized and we nearly filled the storage area. Once everything was accounted for they planned what we would have tomorrow (mostly leftovers of course.) It had taken just two hours but everyone had pitched in. Steve and Abby were used to working as chefs and running a kitchen but they were more than happy to be assistants and consultants when it came to this job. They knew first hand it was tough work.

The boys enjoyed emptying the RVs not only to discover what food was there but also to check out what each RV was like. These RVs were really amazing. Each one was like a self-contained home with all the amenities. They had full kitchens and bathrooms nicer than most homes. Widescreen TVs, satellite dishes, generators, heating/air-conditioning and expanding rooms that basically doubled the size of the living area. Master bedrooms with attached bathrooms and walk-in closets. One had stairs that went up to the roof where there was a sitting area, a fire-pit and space for a grill. Amazing. The boy's decided that they were going to pick out one of these RVs and turn it into a cool place for just younger folks to hang. It would be kind of nice to have a place away from parents but still be in the safety of the fort.

It was almost one in the morning and we decided to get Steve, Abby and the Langs back to the *Resilience*. They could easily walk the 300 feet but it just seemed a little too soon to take any risks. It would be good to practice some of these mini-excursions too. Steve and Abby could take care of themselves but the Langs weren't trained soldiers. The girls were a little nervous as they made their way over to the exit. Casey was hanging with the girls and was pleading to go have a sleepover on the boat but we said no. They were still under a makeshift quarantine. During the day they could leave the *Resilience* but needed to be with someone at all times. All of the recently immunized would be tested for antibodies daily. For now the Lang family would be fairly comfortable aboard the yacht which had all the creature comforts of any multi-million dollar mansion. Once they tested positive they would have an amazing new suite similar to ours within the fort. Water views, four bedrooms, beautiful bathrooms and a well-appointed kitchen. Their new accommodations would have all the bells and whistles although perhaps not quite as many as the *Resilience*. Scott helped design all the suites so he was pretty sure the girls were going to love it. Right now they were happy with their cabins on the yacht plus they were ready for bed.

Casey was eager to get to bed too. I sent her back to our new home and reminded her she had a brand new queen size bed waiting for her. She didn't argue much. We would see the girls tomorrow and there would be so much to do. Madigan and Ellery walked her back to our place and made sure she got home safely.

Now it was time to focus. Such a short trip should be easy but we needed to be careful and take no chances. First we needed the right transportation. We had so many new cars and trucks to choose from. We had a bullet-proof Lamborghini, an armored Humvee, an armored limousine SUV, several vans, firetrucks and the most powerful tricked-out Chevy pickup truck ever made. Jesse had the limousine all gassed up and ready but Sam thought the best option for tonight was his duck boat. He had bought it several years ago after he went on a tour in Boston and thought it would be perfect for life at Fort Adams. I had to admit the duck boat was pretty cool. We went on the same tour up in Boston and the kids loved it. So did I. The tour started out on Boylston Street and toured through the Boston Commons and by Quincy Market. The duck boats then drove right into the Charles river and it was really quite thrilling. Sam loved his experience too and it was a thrill he wanted to recreate in Newport. He had fixed up his duck boat and often brought it out into the harbor just to test it's capabilities. It would also be fun for the girls to be on such an unusual vehicle.

Sam drove and Steve rode shotgun. I joined them on the duck boat along with Dave, Abby, Tracy, Scott and the girls. The adults sat on the sides with guns ready and the girls sat in the middle on the benches. They seemed to be enjoying themselves and it did feel just like we were preparing for a tour in Boston. Allan and Jason would provide gun and rifle support driving in a van behind the duck boat. This was mostly a test ride but it was still dangerous and everyone had their head on a swivel. We all were wearing the com device in our ears. They had really worked well tonight during the gala. We all felt that communication over them would be another good thing to practice tonight. It was pretty amazing to be able to talk to each other so easily and clearly without holding a phone or relying on a signal or wi-fi.

We sent two guys up to the east wall and they had a great view of the whole parking lot and the *Resilience*. It was Jesse and Peter who were atop the wall and they were spying over the parking lot. Jesse had a long gun and was prepared for long distance shooting. He also had some night vision goggles that helped him see everything clear as day. They were amazing and seemed pretty useful for an occasion such as this. Peter had an AR-15 and was prepared to provide some support but he was a little far away to help out too much if we had any problems.

Sam asked Jesse if the lot was clear and was given the green light. He gave the order and the gate started to open. The duck boat and the van left the fort and once they were gone the gate immediately closed. The procession slowly crossed the parking lot and approached the *Resilience*. As they approached Steve held up his hand and Sam stopped. Something was wrong. The gangway had been activated and was connecting the boat to the sea wall. There were also some lights on in the lower level where the crew slept. What was going on? As we inched closer we could see there was a body on the gangway It was too far away to tell who it was. Steve immediately informed the team of the situation.

"Gangway's already been deployed, it's unclear who activated it. Someone's on the boat. Could be a deckhand. One down on the gangway. I cannot identify who it is. We need two more on east wall with long guns and visual support."

I requested some immediate support "Paul Stanford and Mark up to east wall with long gun support. Mark bring the nightscope lens. We need info on the *Resilience* and potential unwanted guests."

The parking lot seemed empty. Steve was suspicious that the other crew members had come home early from their all-expenses trip to Boston and at least one of them had turned. He tried to call Pete who was one of the stewards. As we sat there we could hear a phone ringing. It was coming from the gangway. It was obvious that the body on the gangway was one of the crew, probably Pete. Steve hung his head for a moment. A few moments later he called crew number two. No answer.

Next he called crew number three, Mike. The call was quickly answered.

"Steve? Oh thank God it's you! You have to help me! I'm in the engine room and Marty is one of those infected things. He's outside the door and trying to get in. Pete ran to get help. I don't know where he is, he hasn't answered my calls!"

Steve knew where Pete was. Pete was dead. We knew we had to try to get on board and take out Marty quickly, at least we knew where he was. We needed to act quickly but we needed to be exceedingly careful with this.

Steve laid it out over the com, "We've got one down on the gangway and one hiding in the engine room. The third is an infected. He's on board and we need to take him out."

"Why don't we try to lure him out with sound or something?" I asked. "That may work."

Steve looked at me and Sam and nodded. Sam held up a microphone from the duck boat dashboard then handed it to Steve.

"Guns trained on the boat." Abby directed over the com.

"Allan and Jesse watch for unwelcome guests, men on the wall let us know if you see any activity to the north or south."

Steve spoke into the microphone "Marty can you hear me? Marty please come out here. I need to see you Marty. I have something for you Marty."

Nothing. We couldn't hear anything. He tried a couple more times but nothing.

Steve spoke on the phone to Mike. "Stay put. Coming on board now to take out Marty."

The first thing we decided to do was to move Pete off the gangway. Steve had his shotgun loaded and ready with his loaded 9mm holstered as a back-up. He led the way and Dave and I followed to grab the body. It was pretty gruesome. Parts of Pete's face were missing and he had multiple deep bites on his neck, chest and abdomen. There was a lot of blood. We carried him off the gangway to the parking lot and put him down behind a fence. I signalled to Allan who came right over. I suggested he clean up the gangway with the hose once there's an all clear. I didn't want the Lang girls to see that sight on the boat they'd be sleeping on tonight.

Steve waited for us and we joined with guns drawn and ready. Steve knew the ship well and we didn't. He was in charge

"The engine room is two floors down. There's a long hallway with a right turn then a left turn. That's where Marty will be. There are several rooms on the right and left that have locks in case there is trouble. My plan is to sneak right up behind him and take him out with this." He held up what looked like a semi-automatic shotgun but it was much bigger than a typical 12 gauge. It had a magazine on it and it looked bad-ass. "This is a Browning 4 gauge semi-automatic rifle with laser sighting. If this doesn't take Marty out then I think I want no part of this battle we're starting." He looked at us both and just seemed so calm. "Let's do it."

He led us quietly down the stairwell. We could hear Abby's voice on the com, "Dad those rooms may be locked already. Don't assume they'll be available for safe entry."

"Right, Abby. Gents, these stairs are the go-to escape plan for now."

We descended down the second stairwell and we could hear banging and some guttural snarling that made my hairs stand up. It was so unmistakable for an infected. We began down the hallway and Steve tested each door. They were all locked except for one. That could be a safe zone if things got hairy. We took the right and the banging was louder and the hissing and grunting was just awful. I could just picture this nasty thing around the corner just waiting to charge us. Calmly Steve approached the next turn and after a brief pause and cautious glance around the turn he proceeded quickly. He took two deliberate steps towards the infected and took aim. He fired the gun and the sound was much louder than a typical shotgun. I expected more shots but he lowered his gun as we turned the corner. He approached the body. He kicked this thing but there was no mistaking it. This thing was dead.

"Infected down. Checking on Mike. Then we'll sweep the ship." Steve said calmly over the com.

"Roger." came Abby's voice.

Steve knocked on the engine room door and Mike opened it quickly. He smiled and gave Steve a big hug. "Thank God! I thought he was going to break this door down any minute! Is Pete okay?" Mike asked, looking hopeful.

"No, Mike. Marty took out Pete. I took out what was once Marty." Steve said in a softer, comforting tone.

Steve quickly got back to business. "Mike this is Dave and Paul. Dump this body out the starboard hatch. Do a two minute clean then meet me at the gangway. Quickly. Was anyone else with you?" Steve asked. Mike shook his head then Steve was off to check the ship.

"Right. Guys thanks for saving me. This is crazy! I'll open the side hatch." It was only a few feet away. We quickly disposed of Marty right into the cove. We cleaned up the blood the best we could in two minutes and threw all the blood-soaked rags and sponges into a garbage bag. It was a pretty good job. I was getting too good at this. We quickly ascended to the main level and Steve was there. He waved the rest of the waiting team on board while Allan and Jason stood guard.

Abby and the Lang family boarded the yacht over a freshly cleaned gangway. The girls looked like they were half-asleep and hopefully they would go right to bed. Dave and I said good night and left for the waiting duck boat. We had already decided we'd have group breakfast in the fort at 9 am. There would be a lot to talk about. The gangway withdrew into the side of the boat silently and it was sealed shut. That boat was pretty much impenetrable from the outside. They would be safe tonight. We took Mike with us and headed back towards the fort. It was too dangerous to leave him on the boat.

"Looks clear from atop the wall. No activity visible around the parking lot." Peter announced.

As we approached we used a spotlight to check around the fort entrance then we gave the signal and the gate started to open. Both vehicles entered and the gate closed tight behind us. It had been a long day and I was glad it was over. We decided to have just one man on watch atop the east wall tonight. Four hour shifts. It would give everyone some added security knowing that someone was watching over the fort and the *Resilience*. We could switch the earpiece communication to walkie-talkie mode. Everyone headed for their new homes. I showed Mike to an RV and made sure it had everything he needed for the night. The plumbing was working. It had clean drinking water and plenty of food. There was a TV and cable. I gave him a five minute explanation of why he was going to spend the night in a locked RV in the middle of a locked Fort Adams. He seemed to get it and understood that he was going to be in the RV until we knocked on the door and unlocked it from the outside. One last thing to do. I pulled out two syringes from my pocket and he understood why this couldn't wait. I gave him the shots and he didn't complain. He just wanted to go to bed. So did I.

I went over to our new "house" and Kristin and the kids were wide awake which was nice. There was music playing. They had made popcorn and seemed to be having fun unpacking and getting settled. When I entered they all stopped what they were doing and came over to make sure I was okay. I told them about the "mission" and how even a trip across the parking lot could get dangerous. I Informed them of the two casualties and one surviving steward. They wanted to hear all the details so I filled them in. Again, our team worked well together and there was a feeling of trust we were developing with each other. Trust that seemed to multiply when lives are on the line and nobody gets hurt. Despite some surprises and unexpected excitement things worked out and the team was safe. The *Resilience* was sealed up tight. Jackson had already heard some of the details from Cameron. She had texted him from the duck boat and he tried to help her feel calm. He gave Cameron and her sisters a virtual tour of our new house and they loved seeing the inside. They were relieved just like Kristin was that it wasn't decrepit and disgusting. It was 'super nice' and Scott assured the girls their place would be similar in size and style. Scott and Tracy appreciated that Jackson was able to help all the girls feel relaxed during those tense minutes. I'm sure everyone would be talking about our first mission over breakfast.

Jackson wanted to know more about Steve's four gauge shotgun and I promised he could try it out sometime. I wanted to try it too, it was badass. I reminded him that they had a shooting platform with trap shooting on the top deck of the boat. "Thay boat is so awesome. Do you think we could stay on it sometime?" Jackson asked. "And that jetboat Abby drove! That was amazing!" "Sure, we can hang out there and we will. That yacht is pretty amazing." I responded and also shared a little about my afternoon excitement. "I drove the jet boat in from the Block Island sound, after the rescue. Now I've driven some fast cars and have flown in a lot of jets. I love to drive fast but pushing the throttle on that boat was absolutely the most hair-raising and adrenaline-pumping thing I've done in a long time. I can't wait to see what other toys they have!"

Kristin chimed in, "Abby was saying that they're going to host a dinner for everyone on the *Resilience* in a few days. They really do appreciate being welcomed by us. I just love her and her dad. I heard he's a great cook, too."

I agreed. "We got lucky with those two. Steve's the guy you want next to you when there's trouble." I knew that first hand. "Abby's as tough as nails. Sam has been a great addition too. We have a good team."

Kristin came over and hugged me and both kids joined us. "*We* have a good team too. Guess who I want next to me when there's trouble?" She asked as she gave me a kiss.

"Steve?" Casey responded innocently as she enjoyed our group hug.

We all burst out laughing and I think we were all happy to have that needed release. We were all tired and it would feel good to sleep knowing that everything was sealed up and that we had a lookout on the east wall. Peter Carlson was on the wall tonight. I grabbed the walkie and checked in with him. "How's it looking out there Peter? Any activity?"

"The coast is clear but I can hear some activity in the distance. There's been some explosions over in downtown Newport. A few alarms are going off. Not much on the scanner." He responded.

"I'm just not sure any policemen or firemen are even on the job tonight. Allan called a couple guys earlier and everyone seems to be home and sheltering."

"Well, I'm glad we're sheltering *here* where it is safe." He said with a little emotion, "I can't imagine what I'd be doing if we were back at the house learning all of this tonight like everyone else. I didn't have a gun or a saferoom or any real protection. Now I'm guarding a battle-tested fort wearing a holster with two loaded 9mm handguns and have a sniper rifle in my hand and an AR-15 strapped over my shoulder. I think my chances are a little better here. Thanks for saving us, Paul. We all know without you we'd be in big trouble."

"Hey, that's what neighbors do." I responded humbly. Just then a call was coming in from Tom. "I'll see you at breakfast Peter."

I put down the walkie-talkie and grabbed my phone. "Hello Tom."

"I figured you'd be up." he responded dryly, "I hope you're all safe. I imagine you saw the address. How'd I look?"

"You looked like shit, Tom. Where are you?" I wondered.

"I'm at the Pentagon right now. My family is here with me. We have a whole wing set up like a dormitory. Wish we had a nice yard like you guys do." He sounded like he just wanted to talk to someone he trusted.

"Yeah, I'll have to pay Jackson big dollars to mow this lawn."

"By the time he finishes with his push mower it'll be time to start mowing again."

We both laughed a little. I let him get to the business of the call.

"Things are getting hairy. Everywhere. Pretty much what we anticipated. I didn't expect most of the police, firemen, and National Guard to all abandon the job and go home. Other than some key military bases the defense network is pretty dark. How are you guys holding out?" he asked.

"We are safe thanks to you and your help. The fort is secure and we seem to be well-supplied for now. We've had three encounters with infecteds. Those things are hard to kill." I replied.

"No doubt. And they have endurance. We continue to test some of them that have stayed alive for over two weeks now and they haven't weakened or slowed down. I'm not sure how they have so much stamina. They don't sleep and they don't stop ever. This thing could go on for a long time. Months. Hope you got plenty of food and water." He did really care about us.

"I think we'll be okay." I responded. "We have a fishing boat ready for action and a farm that's nearby and operational. If you want to get out of there you and the family can come here. I can offer you a pretty nice RV that has all the upgrades Big John Mills could offer."

I think Tom enjoyed having a little laugh with someone he trusted. "I just may take you up on that one of these days. Sounds like you guys are ready for anything. Speaking of that I anticipate the power grid, gas lines, phone lines and cell towers will fail within the next day or two. Nobody's at the helm. We have military at key facilities but across the board most locations are going to go dark, everywhere. Your satellite phones will work. Let's plan on talking Monday, Wednesday and Fridays at 9 pm. Sound okay?"

"Sounds good. Thanks. Talk to you soon." I answered.

"Stay safe." and he hung up.

It was late, well after two in the morning. I usually didn't feel tired at this time. It had been an especially busy day and I actually felt like I could get some rest. I crawled into bed and hoped that I'd be able to fall asleep. There was no news and no websites to check out. Sleep was really the only option. I closed my eyes and hoped and tried not to think about any of the horrible things I saw today. I couldn't help thinking about all the things we still had to do. The list was pretty long. I'm not sure how far down the list I got but eventually it all faded and for the first time in our new home, we were all safely asleep.

Chapter 26

A NEW DAY

I USUALLY GET UP before five am but this morning I could have slept 'til six. Then I heard the gunshots. One, two, three, four, then a pause . . . then a different gun. Automatic. At least fifteen rounds. I immediately put in my earpiece. "What's going on Paul?" I asked and I already had my shoes on and was walking out the door.

Paul Stanford was on the wall from 4 am to 8 am. He quickly responded but was clearly out of breath, "It was Sandy. From the farm. Mr. Carpenter's daughter. She was running through the parking lot and was being chased by an infected. She kept circling and trying to get away from it. She was getting tired. I had to take it out. She seems uninjured but she looks exhausted. I'm coming down the stairs now."

"Right. Be careful. I'm on my way to the gate." I said as I jumped on my bike and started for the fort entrance.

Sam's voice came over the com next, "I'm at the gate. The infected is down. The girl seems ok, just exhausted. I don't see anyone else."

"Wait there Sam. I'm almost at the gate." I called out as I rode towards the front of the fort. I jumped off the bike and met Paul and Sam at the gate."

"Looks clear. " Paul said as he looked out between the iron bars of the massive gate.

"Okay." I said as I was thinking quickly, "Sam let's open the gate enough for us to slip out."

Sam was right on it and the gate opened two feet then stopped.

Paul and I exited the gate. Guns drawn. I could see Steve walking down his gangway with that 4 gauge. We approached Sandy who was sitting down. She looked exhausted and afraid. She put her hands up as we all had our guns out as we approached her. She suddenly looked at Paul and realized who he was. She had just spent hours with him the day before and couldn't believe he was here this morning in a random parking lot in front of Fort Adams. She stood up and ran to him and hugged him hard. She was crying and looked like she needed a hug. We all sat there a moment. By now Steve had joined us.

"Let's get back inside." I said and we started for the gate. "Morning, Steve."

Sandy was shaking and freaking out a little. Paul kept his arm around her and we all stepped through the gate. The gate shut soundly behind us and we stopped to make sure Sandy was okay. She wasn't wounded but she certainly looked wiped out. She looked like she had run a marathon.

"What happened at the farm?" Paul asked. We tried not to crowd around her.

"Well, we all watched the TV last night and were freaked out a little. We decided we would only do the most critical tasks at the farm this morning. Dad didn't want the animals to suffer too much. None of the farmhands showed up. They're gone. It's me and Dad and the animals. I went out there and after about five minutes I saw some guy running after me. He looked like one of those awful things. He was so fast. I couldn't shake him and I didn't want to bring him inside the house so I just kept running. That's how I made it down here. I was just about ready to jump into the water when I heard shots fired. I didn't know who they were shooting at until that thing went down."

"These things are scary, Sandy. They are fast, strong and just don't stop." Paul responded still with his arm around her comforting her. "I'm glad you didn't give up."

By then some of the wives had come and joined us. Kristin took Sandy by the arm. "Hi Sandy. I'm Casey's mom. I heard so much about you. Why don't you come with me and we'll get you something from the kitchen."

"Mr. Stanford, will you call my dad and let him know I'm okay?" Sandy pleaded.

"Sure. I'll do it now." Paul responded without hesitation.

The girls walked away and we all took a few deep breaths. We had been lucky so far. We had a few run-ins with the infecteds and we knew it would get worse.

Abby's voice came over the com. "There are two more in the parking lot. No wait. Three." There was a pause "Make sure that gate is closed. They're looking around for something. Maybe they heard the shots and were attracted to the noise."

"Thanks, Abby. I'll stay here for now." Steve responded "You stay on the boat and keep an eye on things. We'll keep someone on the wall. Let's hope they just go away. We have a couple hours until breakfast."

"Roger. Will contact you before breakfast to confirm the transportation plan." Abby responded.

Sam's voice came over the com next. "Perhaps the duck boat isn't the best choice for such an . . . active environment."

I answered back. "Agreed, Sam. We'll get the Humvee gassed up and ready. It's got a mounted large caliber machine gun. We're not going to take any more chances."

We headed back towards the kitchen area. Things were just getting going at the fort. The gunfire had woken everyone out of a good sleep. Lori had jumped out of bed and instinctively ran to the kitchen. She had started a pot of coffee when she realized what was happening. She was bringing out a carafe to Kristin and Sandy as we were arriving.

I could tell it was going to be another full day based on the early developments. It was the new normal and everyone would need to adjust. I couldn't believe how well everyone was doing. The guys, the wives, the kids. Everyone was adapting to life in this new world of no rules, no laws, and no promise of an end. I was just glad Jackson and Casey were still at home. Hopefully they were sleeping in.

I heard some pounding coming from one of the RVs. Dave heard it too and we both pulled out our sidearms and approached the RV cautiously.

"Mike is that you?" I yelled. "You got to let me know it's you."

"It's me, Mike. I'm okay! I'm good. Just wanted to get out of here for a minute." he responded.

"Do you feel normal?" Dave asked.

"Yeah. I'm not feeling bad, just a little claustrophobic."

I unlocked the door and Dave and I both stepped back with our handguns ready for any bizarre behavior.

Mike opened the door and stepped down onto the grass field.

Steve was right behind us and added, "Hey guys, I know he looks absolutely hideous and terrifying but holster your weapons. Believe it or not that's what he really looks like in the morning."

We both started laughing and those two enjoyed a good hug. We sat down at one of the tables and relaxed for a minute. Kristin brought us all some coffee. We needed it. Steve and Mike told us a few stories of life on the high seas and some of their more harrowing experiences on the *Resilience*. While not quite pandemic level they had been through some pretty stressful situations and Mike confirmed what we already knew. If things were getting gnarly there was no one you'd rather have on your side than Steve.

Paul came over to the table and motioned that he wanted to speak to me privately. I got up and we walked a few feet away from the others, "What's up, Stanford?"

"It's about the farmer, Mr. Carpenter. I was talking to him on the phone and everything was okay at first. He seemed just fine but he said he had to put the phone down for a minute. I waited for a minute then I heard some strange sounds like some slamming and some heavy breathing. After another minute I could hear some of the snarling and grunting sounds those things make. He never picked up the phone. He's definitely infected. What should I do? Should I tell Sandy?" He asked. He seemed a little shaken by this. After hearing the stories from the farm it was no secret Paul had quickly developed a strong attachment to Mr. Carpenter. It was a punch in the gut for Paul but he probably was the right person to tell Sandy.

"Yeah. Let her know Paul. Take her over to a more private area. She'll appreciate that." I said and he agreed.

He approached Sandy and they went over to a different table. It wasn't going to be easy but he had to tell her the bad news. I ducked into the kitchen. There was all kinds of activity going on. I could only compare it to a busy restaurant kitchen on a Saturday night. Four different chefs working at four stations with some smoke, some sizzling and all kinds of great smells. They clearly didn't need me in there so I snuck out and sat down with Steve and Mike and listened to some more entertaining tales. I was hoping that the excitement of the day was over. Sadly, I knew it was wishful thinking. This day had all kinds of problems in it's potential.

Chapter 27

CONFLICTS OF INTEREST

'WHAT A GREAT night's sleep' I thought to myself as I curled up in my new bed. I usually don't sleep this well, a family curse. I'm not as bad as Dad but it's totally frustrating. I feel pretty refreshed this morning. Who'd have thought it. New house. New bed. New everything. What a cool night! The gala. The dancing. The late night texts with Cameron. I was slowly waking up and strangely felt really good about facing the new day. Then I woke up for real to the sounds of shooting in the distance. The east wall.

One, two, three, four, then a pause. Then a different sounding gun. An AR-15. At least fourteen rounds. I heard Dad talking in the next room. His door opened and he flew down the stairs and out the door. I turned on my walkie-talkie and listened to everything as it unfolded. An infected in the parking lot chasing someone. It sounded like Mr. Stanford took it out. He couldn't get it with his rifle so he grabbed the AR-15 and smoked it. I wanted to go check things out but I knew we had enough numbers based on what I heard. Besides, it was a late night of texting back and forth with Cam. She had a pretty scary evening after leaving the fort and I tried to help her feel less freaked-out as she and her family sat out in the parking lot. I didn't know what else to do so I gave her a virtual tour of our new home and she and her sisters loved it. She was so cool. She seemed cheery most of the time but I knew it wasn't easy for her to be here. I really felt great about how things were going and it just felt so strange that it was like the end of the world. It just didn't seem to make sense. What else is new?

I did finally get out of bed and went downstairs. The first thing I noticed is 'wow, what a beautiful view' as I looked out onto the harbor and Newport. I could see the *Resilience* and knew that Cameron was over there and probably sleeping. There were lots of boats but no activity. Normally there would be boats heading out for a sail or to work at this hour. It was a pretty amazing location we had and the new living room and kitchen helped me feel that this transition wasn't going to be as hard as I thought it would be. I grabbed a bagel and some juice and turned on the TV. There was no network news or anything but reruns. I did find a cable news show so I left it on in the background. The cable still worked but I knew it wasn't going to work for long. That was the deal and we all knew it. I was surprised that a reporter was still working. I suspect most of them just quit and went home like we saw them do last night. Freaky. Same with police, firemen, storeowners, just about everybody. This guy on TV seemed to be watching a video of infecteds running around in a mall or something. It looked like it was somewhere down south.

I turned on my walkie-talkie to check out the activity. The person from the farm was named Sandy and they brought her into the fort. Interesting. The farm was virtually next door to the fort and Mr. Stanford knew her from yesterday. Casey had spent most of yesterday there too and loved it. We all might be taking turns working on the farm once we were sure it was safe. It didn't seem too safe yet.

That's when I got my first text from Cameron.

I heard that gunfire. Are you ok? It seems so close!

I'm ok. My dad went to check on it. An infected just got taken out.

I hate all this. But I did have a good time last night. Did you?

I had a great time. Seems so weird to be so happy and so freaked out.

So right on. Can't wait for some breakfast with you. Bye.

Mom came downstairs and seemed to be in a rush. She gave me a quick kiss then was gone. She didn't seem to know anything I didn't. I was pretty sure Dad was going to be okay. I knew he'd be careful.

I felt good about how things were with Cameron, too. We had a fun night talking and I was hoping we could just hang out today without any major stresses. I told her she could drive my Lamborghini. She was a little older and lived in LA but I was pretty sure she never drove a Lambo. Hopefully we'd be able to take it out onto the road and really go fast. There wouldn't be any cops. No laws to break. No speed limit. So cool but also kind of sad. Would there ever be laws and police and real order again? Pretty heavy thoughts for so early. I tried to not think about those things too much.

I felt a lot of different emotions and I think a lot of people were going through that too. Over the past three days so many amazing and so many awful things have happened to us all. I was trying to focus on the good things cause I can't control the bad things. Gun training with the whole neighborhood was so cool. Getting my new car, a lamborghini no less, how sweet was that? My last two days of school and feeling like I had it all figured out. So many great things and then to see Cameron get off the helicopter. For a minute or two I worried she wouldn't have any interest in me but things couldn't have worked out any better. Can't wait to spend time with her. I was going to try to just focus on the positive and good things. I was going to help Casey and Mom and everyone else feel better about things especially if I sense they're struggling. That was going to be another focus of mine. If Casey and I can try to be happy then Mom and Dad won't be as stressed out.

I heard Abby's voice over the walkie-talkie, "There are two more in the parking lot. No wait. Three." There was a pause "Make sure that gate is closed. They're looking around for something. Maybe they heard the shots and were attracted to the noise."

I walked over to the window and could see a couple 'people' out there but it wasn't a good angle. The *Resilience* looked like a sleek modern castle. I picked out an outfit that I would look good in but didn't want to look like I was trying too hard. I put on my holster and my 9mm was loaded. No jacket. No need for hiding anything anymore. I kept a taser on my belt too. I put my com in my ear so I could hear all the updates. I looked like I was ready for anything. I stepped outside and realized I didn't have my phone. I had to laugh. All these weapons and ammo and attention to safety but I forgot my phone. New priorities.

I grabbed the phone then left again. Casey was probably gonna sleep for another couple hours. I pulled my mountain bike out of the truck. Didn't need a lock. I pedaled over to the gate and Sam was there too. He was looking at the infecteds, studying them. He saw me and waved me over then gestured for me to be quiet. I joined him and watched for a minute. There were three of them walking around looking in every different direction. It looked like they didn't really see us, maybe they could smell us.

Sam whispered to me as we watched. "I don't know what they're doing. I wish they'd just go somewhere else. So ugly."

"How long have they been here?" I asked quietly.

"About fifteen minutes. One of them chased a local farmer here. Mr. Stanford shot that one and saved her life." he answered. "Perhaps they heard the gunshots. I don't know."

"Do you think we'll need to shoot them? I don't think we can open the gate with them around."

Sam nodded. "I agree. If they stick around we'll have to take them out."

They were gradually walking towards the far north end of the parking lot. We could not really hear them but we could see them still. They were probably 400 feet away. That's when two cars came into the parking lot and stopped near the gate. I couldn't believe my eyes that people were out driving around. Sam couldn't either. He had his communication piece in his ear and spoke for everyone on com to hear. "It looks like the commodore has returned. He brought some backup too. Four men just got out of their cars in the parking lot. Are they *mad*?"

I recognized this guy from last night. He gave a speech and I think he was in charge of the fundraising for the fort. He also tried to get us all kicked out at the end of the night but we didn't even budge. That's when one of the guests turned. It was pretty gnarly to see that happen. It was so quick. We were lucky Sam noticed him. They tased this thing before it became fully infected and loaded it back into his wife's car. They used zip ties but who knows how long they held. Must have been a tough ride home for his wife!

I heard Dad on my com, "Don't open the gate. Try to get them to stay in the cars. We're coming."

"Lieutenant! Open this gate immediately. I don't want to be out here. Those things are around!" the commodore belted out.

"Sorry, sir. The fort is closed and the gate is locked up tight. I might recommend you get back in your cars before the infecteds see you. There's three just over there!" and Sam pointed to the end of the lot but we could barely see them.

"I said open the gate! You'll do it now if you know what's good for you!" the commodore yelled angrily.

I instinctively put my hand down and just rested it next to my gun. I didn't even mean to do it but these guys quickly became aware that I was armed. The commodore looked at me and recognized me from last night.

"What are you doing with a gun? In the fort?" he asked with a crazy look.

I just had to smile a little at what he said. It seemed like a fort was one of the only places where people *would* carry a gun. "A better question is what are you doing without a gun? In that parking lot teeming with blood-thirsty infecteds?" I asked.

I heard footsteps just behind me. I looked at Dad who obviously heard what I said. He gave me a subtle wink and a nod of approval.

Steve was right next to him, "I was just thinking the same thing. You men need to look at your surroundings. The infected are wandering around out there and you're on the wrong side of a ten ton gate."

"If I were you I'd get back in my car and go somewhere safe. Go home." Dad added

One of the bigger guys next to the commodore pointed threateningly at Dad and Steve and said "Enough talking. Open this gate or there's going to be trouble. We're going to kick all your asses then get the police to haul you to jail for trespassing." We all laughed a little. By now there were eight of us and these guys were just blowing smoke.

Steve responded "The only fighting that's going to happen in the parking lot is you guys getting your faces chewed off by those three monsters just around the corner. Did you know they were attracted to noise?" And he took his enormous, scary looking four gauge semi-automatic shotgun and slid it between two of the iron bars of the gate and aimed it right at the commodore. It was about two feet from his head and the poor old guy looked like he was pissing his pants. "Get in your car now or I'll invite them over myself." He cocked the gun and this thing just looked and sounded like the scariest thing I'd seen in a long time. Dad had told me about it last night after the events on the *Resilience* and I definitely would not want that thing pointing at me.

These guys quickly smartened up and all turned and walked quickly to their cars. It was pretty good timing because we could see three infecteds running over straight at the two cars. They started up the cars and the commodore rolled down his window. "We'll be back with more men!" and he pointed at us menacingly.

We could hear the other guy screaming, "Roll up the window! Quick! Let's go!"

These infecteds were so fast. It was now four of them that we could see and they were running right at the cars. An infected was sprinting right at the first car when it left its feet and dove right at the passenger window. The window shattered and so did part of the infecteds head. It didn't stop. It was going right back at the passenger when it's head seemed to explode. We heard a shot fired probably from the east wall just above us. Mr. Carlson was up there and he definitely saved this dude's life for now. Another infected dove at the front windshield of the other car and it cracked. A second one dove at the same spot and part of the windshield collapsed. Another two rifle shots but these things kept coming! Dad had his 9mm out and stepped up to the gate. Three of us with guns did the same. We lit up the three infecteds while Mr. Carlson kept firing as well. One of the infecteds came running towards us and Steve fired his shotgun and he completely blew this thing's head and shoulder clean off. The sound was deafening.

The two cars finally peeled out and got out of Dodge as fast as they could.

Meanwhile the two remaining infecteds were staggering towards us.

Dad held his arms up for everyone to stop. "Jackson take the one on the right. Head shot."

Santino Izzo had shown up too and was standing next to me. Dad said calmly but with authority, "Santino, you take out the one on the left. Headshots men. Don't hesitate. Aim and take them out when they are at twenty feet."

We both stepped forwards, held up our guns and unloaded our clips as these things approached us fast. I knew I was hitting this thing right on the bullseye and couldn't believe it didn't stop. One, two, three, four, and finally after five rounds it collapsed about 5 feet from the gate. Santino put his down too. We holstered our weapons and then there were a lot of fist bumps and high fives. It was a tense standoff and then a shoot-out that nobody really anticipated so early in the morning. I was shaking for a minute but quickly regained my cool. I was glad I had a chance to get that first kill out of my system.

Dad put his arms on both of our shoulders, "Nice shooting guys. Great job Jackson, Santino. You did well." He then changed his tune a little and called out, "I don't know Steve. I'm pretty sure you missed with your shot. Maybe the boys could help you out with your accuracy!" Again we all had a good laugh and started back towards the rest of the group. Steve was smiling and walking next to me. He could tell that I was staring at his shotgun. He removed the shell from the chamber and handed the massive gun to me "Check this out, Jackson. This is a custom built Browning 4 gauge semi-automatic rifle with laser sighting. This thing can shoot through an engine block and stop an elephant. It can hold 12 shells and fire them all in under ten seconds. You don't want to be on the wrong side of that gunfight."

"This is the heaviest gun I've ever held!" I marveled, "It must weigh twenty pounds!"

"Twenty-four loaded. These shells are not for duck hunting." He responded and held up a shell the size of a can of soda. "When we have some down time you boys can give it a try. It's a lot of fun!"

"That ammo must not be easy to find, or cheap." I thought out loud.

"No, it isn't. When your Dad allowed Abby and I to join your team he gave me enough advance time to get all the supplies I thought I might need. Mr. Lang made sure there were no financial restrictions so I made sure I had everything I needed to help our team. I have plenty of boat and helicopter fuel in storage. I have an entire cabin on the yacht filled with ammunition. I've got all the shells I need. You guys can shoot all day long. The boat is stocked. We have tons of food and necessities on the *Resilience*.

"That's such a great boat. I'm glad you guys are with us. My Dad's really happy too. He said it was the luckiest thing that happened to us yet." I told him honestly.

"I appreciate that. *We* appreciate that, Jackson." he replied.

"In a few nights we'll have a party aboard the ship and I'll show you all kinds of things that will knock your socks off! Did you see the Jet Boat?"

"Oh, yeah! That was amazing! Can we wakeboard off of that? That would be fun." I had thought about that and how great it would be. Steve was easy to talk to. Maybe it was his cool Australian accent. He seemed so calm and confident. I was starting to know what that's like and maybe that's why I really enjoyed talking to him.

"Absolutely! Abby loves wakeboarding." Steve told me and I couldn't believe it. "There will be a time for fun and games but something tells me we're going to have our hands full with these infecteds for quite some time."

We reached the rest of the group and Dad and Steve told the whole story. It sounded like they had to be embellishing or making some stuff up but everything they said was totally true. It wasn't even 8 am and it felt like so much had happened already!

I heard over the com Scott's voice sounding snooty, "Excuse me, neighbors. Would you mind keeping it down? We really would like some peace and quiet here on the *Resilience*."

We all laughed and I had kind of forgotten they were just a couple hundred feet away from all the action. The discussion turned towards logistics. We had to figure out all the details of how the Langs and Abby would be picked up and transferred over here to the fort. They had all tested negative for immunity so they'd have to stay on the boat at least one more night and everyone had to be chaperoned by someone else at all times, especially when they were over here. I received my fair share of ribbing about that last detail. The guys teased me but I didn't care. We all sat around a table and had some coffee while we waited for breakfast. Santino and I told our versions of the shooting. I mostly remembered how hard to kill these things were. Multiple head shots and these things just kept coming. Santino remembered the sounds the infecteds made when they were so close. Awful, terrible sounds. I agreed it was creepy and we all knew we'd be hearing a lot of it in the coming weeks.

Chapter 28

BREAKFAST PARTY

WE WERE FINISHING off the plans for our next objective. It should be fairly simple to just pick up a family across the parking lot and bring them inside the fort but there were a lot of details that we needed to go over. We had decided that we would pick them up at 9 am sharp. We would use the Humvee with the mounted heavy machine gun for muscle and the stretch limo with armored windows for style. We would have four long guns on the east wall and four shotguns arming the gate in case there were any uninvited guests. That's when Peter came over the com.

"We have six infecteds entering the parking lot. It looks like they heard some noise and they all look very angry that they weren't invited to the party."

"Thanks Peter, and again good job this morning. I'm sure the Commodore appreciated you saving his life." I said sincerely. "But I don't think he'll be back to thank you.

I ducked into the kitchen to see how things were going. Lori and Kim were doing great. They had Colby helping out with the pancakes and Jayci tending to some corned beef hash.

Colby saw me walk in and put me on notice. "Hey, Dr. Braden, that breakfast at the range was great but the spread we're putting out this morning's gonna blow you away!"

"I bet it will Colby. It smells great! How's this kitchen ladies? Is it at least operational?" I asked.

Kim answered first. "Dr. B it's better than that and I love cooking with Lori. We're so similar and neither of us needs to be in charge. I've learned so much from her already! She's my sister from another mister!" They both seemed just happy to be distracted in a busy kitchen.

Lori just laughed. "I love this too! This is my escape. If I wasn't working for the department of health I think I would have opened a restaurant. This is pretty close to that! And Kim is so fun to work with. So easygoing. Hopefully, our spread won't let people down after that breakfast at the gun range. That was so good but we're up for this challenge right, Kim?"

"Oh, that bacon was good! And Santino loved the eggs benedict. But *hell yeah* we're gonna put that buffet to shame." Kim shouted out.

I laughed as I replied "As far as I'm concerned if people show up it's a success. Remember, I didn't do any of the cooking either. I'm sure your food's gonna surpass that spread. There is literally a team of people delivering a family through a sea of zombies just to get to this breakfast. I think that's pretty high praise." I turned to leave but added as I was walking towards the door, "Remember, you guys shouldn't feel that you need to spend any more time in this kitchen than anyone else." It was true and they knew it. Right now I think they both appreciated having an escape from some of the awful things going on in the world, that's how they described it to me.

"Santino was great this morning, Kim. He's a man." I said as I was exiting, "And I don't need to say anything about Colby.

I'm glad he's on our side." I gave him a thumbs up and came back out onto the field.

I announced to the crowd, "It smells good in there! There's a lot of work happening in that kitchen."

I joined a table where they seemed to be finishing up the plan. It was Steve, Sam, Dave, Paul and Mark. "Everything good gentlemen? Got it all worked out?"

Sam answered first, "Shouldn't be a problem. As long as more infecteds don't show up we'll be okay. We're just debating how to take them out. Shoot 'em or run them over."

"What do you think, Sam?" I asked. "We have had success with shooting them so far."

"I'm worried shooting them just draws more of them towards us but there is more risk in sending people out there to run 'em down."

"Maybe a stupid question but is there a silencer for a long gun?" I asked.

"Yes, a suppressor is a silencer for a rifle and it can reduce the sound and percussion of the blast." Steve answered. "I have one on the boat. It does work well on a sniper gun but not for my 4 gauge. That thing's just going to be loud no matter what."

We looked at Sam but he shrugged and said "No, not something I've used before or have access to, sorry."

I was pretty confident we had the guns to take these things out without them jumping on (or in) our cars. "I say we take them out with guns. I don't want to take any chances. We can draw them to the gate and take them out with small arms. Once they're down the gate will open and we'll get the Lang's and Abby. If we see any infected we can stop the process and take them out. We get our people in and we're done."

Sam took it from there. "I like it, Doctor. I will drive the limo out first and Jesse will be with me armed with his AR-15. Mark will drive the Humvee out next and Steve will man the mounted gun turret. Meanwhile we'll have four men on the wall, Peter, Dave, Santino and Jason. At the gate we'll have Dr. Braden, Paul Stanford, Colin, Colby and Jackson all on shotgun. We've got it covered. If anything goes wrong we bring it all back."

I responded "I think it's a good plan, Sam. Good job. Steve?"

"Agreed. As much as I admire Sam's duck boat I think it's a little vulnerable. Perhaps in a few weeks we can all take a ride into the harbor but not today." Steve replied honestly and I agreed.

I spoke up so everyone could hear. "Okay, guys we're going to go pick up the Langs and Abby at 9 am. Sam has a good plan. First we're going to draw the infecteds over to the gate and take them out with headshots. We'll clear the lot. Then it's going to be Sam driving the limo with Jesse riding shotgun. Scratch that. Jesse riding AR-15. Behind them it is Mark driving the Humvee with Steve manning the turret. We'll have four men on long guns on the east wall. Peter, Dave, Santino and Jason. At the gate will be me, Paul, Colin, Colby and Jackson all armed and ready. Kenny will have the gate. We will all be on com so put it in now or have your walkie-talkies on. Grab what you need and be loaded and ready for action. Ten minutes until departure. Get your minds right. Everyone ready?"

There was a collective "Oh, yeah!" from the team and we all stood up.

Abby came over the com next. "We are ready and watching. I like the plan. Great job guys. We will be ready for pick up. Be careful."

Peter came over the com two minutes later. "Update from the wall. Now there's eight bogies in the parking lot. They're wandering around looking for a breakfast place."

"Okay then. Seems like everyone's just about ready." Steve's voice could be heard over the com. "Let's get everyone at the gate first to take out the infecteds. We may have to move some bodies. Anyone have a brand new pickup truck ready to transport fourteen of these ugly bastards?"

"Oh, come on guys I just got it!" Dave lamented. He had a beautiful new truck with barely twenty miles driven.

Everyone was laughing but Dave took it in stride. "Okay, I'll go get my truck but I'm gonna wash it right after breakfast!"

The rest of us lined up and pulled out either our 9mm or shotguns.

"Everyone ready?" I asked. After everyone cocked their guns or chambered their round they all seemed ready. "Ok, Tyler Stanford. Call 'em over!"

Tyler stepped up to the gate and yelled out, "Breakfast time you ugly bastards. Come and get it!"

We all chuckled then got ready for the action. Almost immediately all eight infecteds started running towards the gate.

"Wait til they're twenty feet!" Steve called out. "Pick a target . . . Aim . . . Fire!"

Several infecteds dropped right away. Some seemed to drop on the second or third shot. Two of them made it just about to the gate when they dropped.

"Ok." Sam yelled out. "Four rifles to the top of the wall. Watch for approaching bogies. Everyone listening. Kenny ready at the gate. Let's get out there and clear a path for Dave's shiny truck. Jason and Jesse on shotgun duty."

Once everyone was in position Sam yelled "Open the gate!"

It looked like a thing of beauty. Jason and Jesse led and watched for trouble with their guns raised. About eight of us followed them outside the gate and quickly picked up the infecteds and moved them out of the way. Dave drove through the gate and we lowered his tail gate. We quickly tossed the bodies into the bed of the truck. I jumped in the truck with

Dave and rode shotgun. True shotgun. Jackson and Colby jumped in the backseat of the cab. We sped over to the sea wall and Dave backed up into position.

Dave exclaimed over the com, "This back-up camera really works great when you got a lot of bodies to dispose of. This truck is awesome!"

We threw the bodies into the water quickly.

"No bogies around gentlemen. Good work!" Peter announced over the com.

We emptied the truck and high-tailed it back to the fort. Dave parked and we jumped out. Everyone quickly got into position for the next part of the plan. When everyone was ready and we got the 'all clear' the gate reopened. The limo and humvee exited the gate cautiously.

"Everything looks clear from up here." Peter announced from atop the wall.

The limo drove quickly over to the far edge of the lot in front of the boat and the gangway had been deployed. Jesse jumped out of the car and opened the limo doors. Abby came over the gangway first with her M16 rifle. She and Jesse scanned for infecteds as the Langs crossed the gangway and loaded into the limo.

At that time we all heard Peter call out "Infecteds coming in hot. Looks like six. Five hundred feet up the road and closing fast. Let's go guys!"

The Langs and Abby loaded up efficiently and the doors were closed quickly. Sam peeled out and steered towards the gate. These things were moving so fast it was going to be close with the two vehicles. I started to panic that we wouldn't have enough time to get everyone inside and shut the gate. What if one or two of these things gets in here? Oh shit!

Steve came over the com next. "Sam, get the limo inside the fort as fast as possible. Kenny get ready to close the gate once the limo's safely in. Mark and I are going to take out this squad of bogies."

He just sounded so cool and didn't waiver at all. The limo sped through the gate and the gate shut with a thud 5 seconds later. We all looked out to see what happened next in the parking lot. "Okay, Mark turn the humvee to the right and start driving north towards the bridge at running speed. Go now!"

Mark accelerated quickly, turning the humvee and swinging it around in front of us driving towards our left. The infecteds all trailed the massive truck by about thirty feet. Steve aimed the heavy machine gun and systematically aimed at and completely obliterated each target. It was quite magnificent to watch especially after seeing how resilient these things were to small arms fire. They were all down within about fifteen seconds. Amazing! The humvee slowed down and slowly turned around and headed back towards the fort.

Steve came over the com before they got to the gate. "Hey Mark, let's take a drive up the road a bit. Gentlemen, keep watch. We'll be back in a minute. Just going to see what's over the hill."

I responded, "Roger. Don't take too long. You don't want to miss this breakfast I've been told."

Mark drove the humvee slowly up the road until they could see an expansive area of grass and another large parking lot. Two soccer fields sat side by side in this area of the park.

"Let's stop here, Mark. Do you see this?" Steve asked.

"I see it but I don't believe it. There's hundreds of infecteds!" Mark spoke quietly.

"Thousands." Steve countered, "Just milling around waiting for something to attack. Let's just quietly back down the hill. We don't need any more company.

Mark stopped and just put the huge truck in neutral and let it quietly coast down the sloping hill towards the fort. Luckily they went unnoticed by the huge herd of infecteds. They turned around and drove back in through the gate which shut snuggly behind them. Mission complete.

Everyone headed back towards the tables. Lori, Kim, Jamie and Kristin were putting out all kinds of food buffet style. Everything looked and smelled great. We were all milling around talking and laughing a little. It almost seemed like we were resuming where we left off at the gala last night when things got interrupted. Casey was just emerging from the house. It was pretty clear she just woke up. She grabbed her chick and she was happy to see Emily, Jayci and the Lang girls all at a table together. She joined them and they all seemed to be in good moods.

Lori and Kim stepped up on a table and rang a cowbell. Lori started out with a greeting, "Welcome everyone to our first breakfast at the fort! (some applause and cheers) We're so happy everyone's here. We all had a cozy night in this new home and we're glad Steve, Abby and the Langs made it here safely. I heard the Commodore decided not to attend this event, what a shame! (laughter and some applause)

Kim was next, "We had so much fun hanging out cooking in this beautiful Kitchen! Kudos to Scott and Sam for providing such a great set up here. You guys did a great job, we love it! Let's all enjoy a relaxed breakfast and the company of friends and family. How about that table of teen girls come up to the buffet first. I know they're hungry!"

We all enjoyed a beautiful breakfast under the blue sky and everyone was talking about the events from the night before and from this morning. I sat with Kristin and we enjoyed talking to Abby and Steve along with Dave and Lori. I watched Jackson sitting next to Cameron. It looked like he was telling a story and the whole table was listening closely. I'm sure it was about the morning's events. He looked happy and very at ease. Casey was at the next table. A baby chick was walking around the table and visiting everyone's plate and nibbling a little. All the girls seemed so happy to be together and to enjoy such a neat breakfast. I was so proud of all these kids.

Next to the girls was a table with Paul and Jaymi, Peter and Candace, and Sandy. Sandy knew Paul and Candace from the farm and I was glad she seemed to be smiling and having a good time with people she felt comfortable with. It had only been about an hour since Paul told her about her father and the phone call. She cried but seemed to take it in stride. I was glad she was able to be with people who cared about her.

A few minutes later I noticed Sandy stroll over to the girls table to visit Casey and saw the chick. I could tell Casey was a little nervous at first but Sandy went over to her and gave her the biggest, tightest hug and Casey was just beaming. She wasn't mad at all that Casey had taken the chick. She was happy the chick had a happy home. Sandy took a strawberry from a plate and cut it in half. She put it in front of the chick and all the girls couldn't believe how fast that baby chick started devouring it! They all clapped and cheered. They all seemed happy and so did Sandy. It made me think about what we should do about the farm. We'd have to have a discussion about when we needed to go over there. From what Steve said it wouldn't be such an easy trip. Infecteds were everywhere and any trip outside the fort was risky.

Everyone was finishing up breakfast and the kids were starting to get restless. I thought it would be a good time to have a brief meeting and decided to get it started. I discussed a couple of things with Steve, Scott and Sam before I jumped up on a bench and held up my hands.

"Was that a great way to start the day or what?" I asked. "Some applause for Kim and Lori! And for that pork belly!" (loud applause and the ladies stood and waved.) "I think you set the bar pretty high ladies. I love that you both enjoyed this morning in the kitchen but I'll just say it again that cooking and working in the kitchen is a job we *all* need to share. We're lucky to have people like Lori, Kim, Abby, and Steve to assist us but everyone needs to help out. It's hard work. For the first few days Lori and Kim have agreed to be in charge of food and meals but they'll need help. So far they haven't needed to ask. That's the overriding feeling I get when I see us all working together today, last night and the past few days. Everyone helping each other and no selfishness. No arguing. It's been nice. In case you haven't seen things out in the real world it's not so nice. Everything has pretty much come to a grinding halt. For now there is electricity, phone service, wifi, and cable. It's going to end. Soon. I spoke to Tom late last night and he looked like shit. He's at the pentagon and believe me we have it better here. The government is manning some critical infrastructure for electric, gas, and oil but eventually the bulk of the country is going to go dark. Probably today or tomorrow. The advance warning Tom gave us was on the money and without that head start we'd be in big trouble. Right now we're here. We're as well-prepared as we could possibly be and we have each other."

There was some applause and some whistles. I took a few breaths. "We have two new people here. Mike is a deckhand from the *Resilience* and I've gotten to know him a little this morning. He's a good guy and Steve feels he'll be a helpful addition to our team. He'll be staying on the boat with everyone else until he is immune. Sandy is well known to some of you and came here this morning after being chased away from her farm by an infected. Paul Stanford saved her and he wanted to make sure Sandy knew she was welcome to stay here if she wanted. Sandy we have an RV with your name on it once you are immune. (more applause and Casey ran over and gave her a hug.) We'll meet a little later about sending a scout party over to the farm to check things out. For those of you who don't know, the infecteds are completely covering the soccer fields next to us and we will have to be very careful about leaving this place. Don't worry Sandy, we'll get there. Finally, I want to make sure we are careful about family and friends. I know we're all getting texts, calls and messages. For now we have to be quiet about where we are and what we have here. It's just not safe to bring people here. Not yet. Ok, let's all help clean up. Remember we are going to be really strict with garbage. Essentially there is no garbage. Any food scraps go into the well-marked barrel. The napkins and paper towels are all biodegradable and go into the green barrels. Try to clean your plates and silverware the best you can. When you're on dishwashing you'll appreciate it. Ok, I'm done. Have a good morning!"

I stepped down and sat at my table. For a few minutes we just talked and enjoyed a second cup of coffee. It didn't seem like anyone wanted to do anything else and we were okay with relaxing for a little while. For the past few days it had been constant work and watching the clock tick faster and faster. Today it just felt different. It felt good to just sit for a while. Right then I felt a hand on my shoulder and it was Allan.

"The deckhand doesn't look so good. I think he needs *attention*." Allan said quietly. He used our code word from last night and it made my pulse quicken immediately. Allan continued, "He was acting different and he had a real strange look to him. I saw him stagger across the field and he's sitting over on that bench."

I could see him sitting on a bench with his head between his knees. We had to act. I tapped my com device and immediately everyone listening could hear me.

"Allan has spotted a problem. Mike the deckhand isn't looking good. Steve if you can go across the field to the bench and attend to him. Sam and Dave grab that wheelchair from the gate area. Jesse, Peter and Paul each have a taser and zip ties at the bench location please. We have some time, keep guns holstered. If he's turning he needs to be removed from the fort."

Almost immediately I saw everyone stand and go into action. The right people were going to the right places and it felt satisfying. I could see Mike still sitting still and Steve was already there talking to him. The right people were approaching the bench quickly.

Steve came over the com next, "He doesn't look good at all. We need to get him out of here. Ok, the guys are here. Zip-ties to the wrists and ankles. Here comes the wheelchair."

Suddenly, over the com Mark's voice brings more bad news. "Hey guys, just an FYI there are more infecteds in the parking lot now. They just started marching down about three minutes ago. We got about ten of them milling around. A few more coming this way."

This complicated things a little but it was important to know. "Okay, we heard you. Thanks Mark. Keep us posted." I responded. "Let's still get Mike into the wheelchair and up near the gate."

Just then Sam and Dave arrived with a wheelchair likely used for tourists who had a few too many cocktails before their tour.

Steve and Dave lifted Mike onto the wheelchair. There was a little resistance from Mike. He was starting to growl and snarl. It was happening so fast. Once he was in the chair Steve pushed him towards the exit. We all had a heightened level of urgency knowing that Mike was quickly turning and the parking lot was full of infecteds. We only wanted to open the gate if we were confident the area was contained.

We arrived at the gate and Kenny got ready to open the gate if I gave him the signal. We could see all the infecteds milling around just yards away from us. Mike was writhing around and was looking scary. He was still in the chair but looked like he was trying to get up. His ankles and wrists were bound but this was not a good situation! He was a big guy and might be able to break free and attack. He was arching his back and trying to lung at Steve. He was biting and hissing and it was clear he was gone.

"Should we open the gate and toss him out quick?" Dave asked.

"Too risky." Steve said. "Those things will be sprinting over here as soon as they hear the gate open."

"He's going to break those zip ties any second!" I yelled.

Steve was behind Mike and I could see him now holding a pistol. He looked at me and Scott and we both knew what he was planning to do. We both gave a nod of approval and Steve held his 9mm up to Mike's temple and fired twice. Mike's body slouched and we were pretty sure he was dead. I breathed a sigh of relief but this wasn't over. Not unexpectedly the gunfire drew the other infecteds over towards the gate.

Some of the guys drew their sidearms and I noticed Sam holding his hand up and running to a nearby storage area. "Hold off on firing your weapons." Sam implored

I wasn't sure what he was doing but I felt it was okay to delay capping these infecteds. Now that Mike wasn't a risk to us the gate would stay closed.

Sam returned holding a long box. Jackson helped him open the box and inside were four ancient-looking weapons. They looked like bayonets!

"We were going to display these artifacts in one of the museum sections of the new fort. I don't mind putting them to use. These would be used to protect these walls from a breach so we are only doing what we're supposed to do, I guess" Sam declared, sounding a little unsure. "I'm not sure how sharp they are."

By now the infecteds had reached the gate and were reaching in and the sound they made was awful.

Sam handed a bayonet to Dave, Allan, Jason and took one himself. The four men approached the gate slowly and first Sam plunged his blade into one of the infected's heads. The hideous, snarling beast quickly dropped to the ground and lay still. They brought down each infected and we were glad that we didn't have to fire a bunch of rounds. Those old bayonetts worked pretty well, assuming there's a giant ten ton gate between you and the intended victim.

Steve was kneeling next to Mike's limp body. Abby had told me how much Steve liked having Mike on the ship and how happy he was that he had been welcomed into our group. It looked like Steve was just taking a moment to either say a prayer or have one last moment with Mike.

I approached Steve and quietly spoke, "We could bury Mike or have some kind of ceremony. Whatever you want us to do."

He looked at me and shook his head. "This isn't Mike. It's some beast. I just want to get rid of this sight. He'd want to be in the water anyway. But thanks." He took out his knife and cut the zip-ties. Mike's body flopped out of the wheelchair and Sam wheeled the chair away.

"Okay guys, I know we did this about an hour ago but let's do it again. Now that Dave's truck is broken in it won't be so hard for him." I called out. "Let's get three other guys up with Mark on the wall with long guns. Four in the lot with shotguns. The rest of us will load all the bodies into the truck. Jackson,

Colby and I will go with Dave for the dropoff. The same drill we just went through."

"All clear out there, Mark?" I asked over the com. Mark was up on the wall and we would need about five minutes to dispose of these corpses.

"All clear for now. I'll let you know if there's any action." he replied from up above us.

Dave pulled the truck up to the gate. I nodded to Kenny who opened the gate. Everyone was serious and we loaded up the bodies efficiently and within two minutes we were throwing them into the water. Deja-vu all over again.

"All clear out there. You guys are getting really good at this!" Mark said over the com.

We finished up and we all piled into the cab. Even the boys didn't want to travel in the bed of that truck. It was nasty with various body parts and gallons of infected blood coating every surface. Dave started towards the gate quickly but we didn't see any infecteds. I was tempted to take a little ride to see the upper fields or even the farm but it just wasn't safe. Especially with the boys. We were back in the fort and the gate shut with a thud behind us.

"Four and a half minutes. A new fort record!" came Allan's voice over the com. "Dave, do me a favor. Take a right and drive towards the northwest corner of the field.

We were all a little puzzled but Dave took a right turn and we saw Allan standing there next to the fire engine with a hose in his hands. He even had his fireman's hat on for the occasion. We all laughed a good laugh. We parked over some gravel around a drainage grate and all got out. We watched as Allan sprayed the truck down and cleaned out the bed. He made sure all the blood was gone from the brand new liner. Hauling almost thirty bodies full of bullet holes can really make a mess. Most fire trucks have tanks that hold water when there isn't access to a plug. This one had five hundred gallons and I think Allan used most of it. The brand new pick-up truck looked shiny and new again. Dave was happy and Allan had come through again!

We returned to the rest of the group. I was interested in getting back to check on Sandy. She looked just fine and seemed to be enjoying talking to the other women. After what happened with Mike there was a heightened level of anxiety about immunity and this virus. Steve and Abby may not have been exposed and they both received their vaccine/ immunoglobulin shot as soon as possible. Sam received the same injection and he was doing well so far. They would all be tested daily to check for seroconversion. Mike didn't do so well. Sandy was certainly exposed if we are to assume her father has already succumbed to the virus. I didn't have any more vaccine. I had only some immunoglobulin to offer her but it could be too late.

I needed to ask her if she would accept the treatment soon. I sat down at the table she was sitting at. They were discussing the fort and some of the beautiful views we were all enjoying. It really was true. It was a great location. I decided to interrupt and ask Sandy some specific questions and I didn't want to wait much longer.

"Sandy, I'm not sure if you know much about what we're all doing here at the fort and what's going on out there in the world. Has anyone filled you in?" I asked her.

"No, not really. I just thought you folks were really enjoying a sleepover or something. Maybe too afraid to go home after that news show last night." she responded honestly.

"Okay, good. You saw that update. Yeah, everything you saw is real and it's happening everywhere. There are a few pockets out there of people who were identified early as being candidates to receive an immunization or who were already immune. We here represent a group that is immune to the virus. This is a secure location with contacts at the pentagon including Dr. Ashworth who addressed the nation last night. Most of us are immune. Some people here received a vaccine and immunotherapy to protect them. I have a shot I can give you that *could* protect you from turning." I paused letting her think a little.

"So . . . I could turn into one of those things and you suspect my dad already did, right?" she seemed to grasp it all, "Is there any way to predict when or if I'll turn?"

I shook my head. "I don't think so." Which was completely honest. I didn't.

I continued "But I do have an immunoglobulin shot that has antibodies in it that can provide you rapid protection with the hope and expectation that your body starts making its own antibodies."

"Kinda like when I had to get those rabies shots after my cousin's pet raccoon bit me?" she asked.

I was a little surprised at how very similar the two scenarios truly were and couldn't help but smile widely. "Actually it's exactly the same. Very good." I responded. I felt the same way as when I'm quizzing medical students rotating through my office and they actually know an answer.

I guess Kristin noticed my tone as well. "Oh Lord, Paul you sound just like when you're teaching one of your students. And you have that same look on your face!"

"Do you think that shot could protect me?" Sandy asked

"I think it's the only chance you have. If you're willing we shouldn't delay this." I said with some gentle urgency.

Sandy consented and I asked Amy to give her one of the remaining immunoglobulin injections. Before she left with

Amy she looked at me and at Paul and asked very pointedly. "So yesterday at the farm. Paul, Candace, and Casey . . . let me guess. You were using us to learn how to take over the farm when we turned into those monsters?"

"Yeah, Sandy. We wanted to be able to have some resources like a functioning farm and a functioning fishing boat to help us survive." I conceded.

"And all those supplies you paid for and all the stuff you had my dad procure was really for you and your group?" She was really asking good questions

"Yeah. Guilty" I responded.

She nodded "Okay, okay. I get all that. What I don't get is how Mr. Stanford was able to single-handedly turn over three fields and do three days of work in one morning?"

I scratched my head, "Yeah, Sandy, that wasn't part of the plan at all. That was Paul just doing what he thought was best. I guess. Paul. Any explanation?"

Paul shrugged his shoulders "Just kind of seemed like the thing to do."

Sandy answered quickly "Well by turning over those fields there's a chance that in 6 weeks we are going to have a bountiful harvest and enough food to provide for this group many times over. So . . . it seemed like a really great thing to do!" She smiled at Paul and her eyes were full of tears. "And my father had the best day he'd had in years thanks to you." Paul had to wipe his eyes too. We all did.

She left with Amy to go get her shot. I also reminded everyone that although the shot would provide her with immediate protection we needed to be very careful with Sandy. She should be chaperoned at all times. I also know she wanted to check on the farm and the animals. She had told us that without being watered the fields were at risk and the animals needed to be fed. I wanted to check on a few things outside these walls too. It was risky to drive so I decided it was time to use a little technology.

I walked over to the table with Jackson and some of the other boys. I knew Jackson could help me but it could even work better if it were a group effort. "Ok guys, I'm going to need some help. Who has a drone here at the fort?"

Chapter 29

OFF TO A QUICK START

I WAS A LITTLE nervous when the group took off to pick up Cameron and the rest of her group. I was really looking forward to seeing her and was hoping they'd all be safe. I wasn't too nervous about being with her but I still felt that *wave* come over me whenever I saw her. That didn't really bother me. There were too many other things to worry about. My calmness and confidence seemed to be even stronger after this morning's developments. Seeing, confronting, and shooting an infected allowed me to get over some type of fear that was lingering there. I had been wondering what that first kill would feel like. Would I be afraid? Would I wimp out? Would I feel remorse?

No.

It was good to be a little nervous sometimes. I actually liked that feeling of adrenaline just like before a big game. A little goes a long way. Too much and it can be counterproductive. I liked being in that sweet spot. I liked feeling the confidence that comes from being well-prepared mentally and physically for whatever challenge arose. That surge of energy was something I appreciated, kind of like being able to go into a higher gear that isn't usually there. I was hoping that this wasn't going to go away.

The limo returned and the gate shut behind them. I was listening to the com and Steve and Uncle Mark were going for a little recon. I wanted to go see Cam but I wanted to be ready to help at moment's notice. I ran up to the top of the wall and tried to watch the humvee but it disappeared up the road to the South. There was a wing of the fort that might offer a better view but I didn't have time to get there. I would talk to Dad later about maybe getting that lookout area prepared for use.

One minute later the Humvee came back and reentered the fort. With the fort sealed up my attention turned to the limo. I wanted to give her plenty of space. I let the family get out of the limo and proceed towards the tables that had been set up closer to the kitchen. I watched Cameron walking with her two sisters. They adored her and since the divorce Cameron had to assume some motherly roles especially when they were visiting Scott. I liked seeing her walk across the field and I noticed she was looking at all the tables and looking around for something. I like to think she was looking for me. I hoped she was. I wanted her to know that if I wasn't there it was only because I was working hard to make sure she was safe and that her family was safe. She was with her father and ordinarily that would be a major obstacle for a teenager. While this whole situation sucked and I would love for the planet not to be threatened at least I knew some things were working out in my favor. Scott knew me as well as just about anyone. He knew I was a good guy and respected all the things he and my dad always talked about. He knew I cared about my family and friends. He knew I was honest and reliable. Scott and my Dad often used a term I didn't really understand. They would refer to themselves as 'old school' all the time and I never really felt it made sense. Now I kind of knew what that meant. To them it's how people who really love each other treat each other just like they did in the old days. It meant that if a family member or friend was in need or in danger everything else kind of went away. It meant you don't let little things get in the way of friendship and family. As long as you are true to your word and you protect your family and friends the rest of the stuff didn't matter. I get it now. I am 'old school.'

I jumped on my bike and reached the tables at about the same time everyone else was starting to sit down. Cameron ran over to me and gave me a hug. She looked and smelled great and I could tell that any worrying I was doing was unnecessary. She was honest and open with me and didn't really concern herself with what other people might say. She was 'old school' too.

We sat at a table with some guys and some girls. My cousin Madigan had met Cam in the past and then they got to spend some time together last night too. Cameron having some friends here did make things easier. Plus most of the guys at the table were pretty cool with her and they all thought her dad was awesome. The whole breakfast was nice until my walkie-talkie started to chirp. I quickly put in my earbud and listened to what was happening. Cameron knew what I was doing and gave me some space. She talked to Madigan as I slowly stood up. I scanned the field and located Mike and the bench he was sitting at. I knew Cameron wouldn't be upset or annoyed that I wasn't focused just on her. As long as someone is doing something that is for the greater good it shouldn't be held against them. What's more important than the safety of this fort right now? That had to be our first priority and I was sure she knew that.

I left the table and allowed myself to go into "battle mode." I liked to be able to detach from my emotions and feelings and enter a mode that was all business and very serious. Mike the deckhand was infected. Uncle Allan spotted him first and alerted the team. We were lucky, again. As I approached the bench where Mike was I saw that there were already five guys in support. Steve was sitting next to him. They had a plan to get him over to the gate and away from everyone else. I would hang around in case they needed help or if any other problems arose. One minute later we were made aware of more infecteds in the parking lot. This was a problem. We can't open the gate if they're out there and we can't risk Mike turning inside the gates. Some of the other boys my age were with me in support as we all proceeded to the gate. It was always good to have numbers. So far there hasn't been much of a power struggle. I was impressed with how well the dads, Sam, and Steve all worked together to handle any type of problem that developed. It was happening all too often and we haven't even been here for twenty four hours! Rescuing Dave and Colby off the fishing boat, the infected at the end of the gala last night, rescuing Mike from the *Resilience*, saving Sandy from the infected, the face-off with the Commodore this morning. Each time the team pulled together and handled things smoothly. Whether it was my dad, Steve, or someone else making the decisions they didn't let anything get in the way of the ultimate goal. The safety of this group.

All of these experiences were also bringing us all closer together. Relying on each other with our lives really helped seal bonds of friendship and trust. I wondered if Cameron and I were also getting closer because of the dangers we were facing. If it was just another family trip would we have gotten so close so fast? I wasn't sure and I wasn't sure it mattered. We both seemed to be happy and if we could find any kind of happiness in this strange bizarre world it was worth holding on to.

After we eliminated some more infecteds I realized what a long morning it had been. I made my way back over to Cameron and the rest of the table. They wanted to know all about the infecteds and what they were like. I gave them a run down of what happened but I spared some of the nastier details. It wasn't like a movie or TV show when you're looking at something that wants to kill you and eat you. It was awful and there was nothing entertaining or good about it. I hated that part of it all. They didn't need to know about that. At least not yet.

I looked at Casey and some of the younger girls playing with the chick and laughing and I was glad that they were spared the experiences I had already seen and been part of. Protecting the family. Protecting the group.

Casey showed all the girls the new pen for the chick that Sam had made. Cameron and I went over to them and everyone smiled as the chick seemed to be exploring it's pen and really seemed to be happy in the grass.

Scott and Tracy came over and watched too. After a minute Scott asked "That chick seems to love it's new home. Hey girls want to check out our new home?"

Peyton looked confused. "I thought we were staying on the boat?"

"For a few days we need to stay on the boat but very soon we'll be staying right here." Scott gestured over at their new condo just next to ours. "It's totally rebuilt and restored and I think you're gonna like it!"

"Are you sure we have our own rooms?" Cameron asked.

"Yep." he answered

"Are you two both living there? Together?" Peyton asked.

"Well, we have separate rooms. But we'll all be together. Want to go see it?" he asked. "Let's go check it out! Come on Jackson and Casey, join us!"

Cameron smiled widely and grabbed my hand, "Let's go check it out!"

We all let out some 'oohs' and 'wows' and some 'cools' while we explored their new home. It was similar to ours but with different decorations and a slightly different layout. Great water views and a cool open kitchen with a huge island. The rooms upstairs were also impressive. Cameron had her own room and bathroom. The other girls had their own rooms and shared a bathroom.

Cameron looked so relieved, "I'm just so glad this place is nice. I thought it would be old and nasty. I really like it. And I really like the boy next door!" she said so that only I could hear.

Casey noticed that in Sawyer's room was the same door that had no knob or way to open it.

"Hey Dad, what's this door all about? Casey's got one too!" Sawyer asked.

"I know what that is. Stay here, I'll open the door." He left the room and within a few seconds the door clicked and swung open.

We walked in and saw all kinds of computer screens, telephone equipment, food, water and some weapons. There was another door on the other side of the room.

"That must be my room!" Casey said. "That's so cool!"

"This is a panic room or safe room." Scott informed us. "This is a place you can go and be safe if there's trouble. All the units have them. We'll talk about how to use them and be safe at a later meeting. I wanted to be sure we had these installed. These are impenetrable."

"Dad, I like this even better than the boat!" Peyton said, "It's so great! Thanks for letting us see it. I thought it was going to be a cave or something!"

Tracy let out a laugh, "Yeah, me too. This could work. Girls you should see my shower it's the nicest one I've ever seen!"

Scott nodded and was smiling "I'm glad you're all happy. I'm happy too. After this morning's events and seeing all those infecteds we may decide just to stay here and not go back to the boat. Is that okay with you guys?"

They were all okay with it but Peyton wanted to be sure they still could go back to the boat if they wanted.

Scott nodded, "Oh yeah, I think Abby really liked having you girls stay there and you're welcome to keep your room on the boat as long as you want. After all, it is our boat. I bought it two days ago!

I was glad they were all happy and so was I. Casey and I left them to have a little family time and I went back out to join the guys. I had just sat down to catch up with everyone when my dad came over.

"Ok guys, I'm going to need some help. Who has a drone here at the fort?" he asked. "That was not what I expected him to say.

Four hands went up. "Great. Do you think you can go get them and meet me back here in ten minutes?"

All of us with drones agreed and I went back to get mine. I wasn't sure what he was going to do but at least it wouldn't put anyone in harm's way. Besides, I was kind of curious what was going on outside these walls.

Chapter 30

DRONE SUPPORT

I've flown a plane and have some experience with model airplanes but flying a drone is a whole different thing. Fortunately, Jackson was really good at it and operating the onboard camera system. I brought out a few TV screens and a long extension cord. I set up a little outdoor viewing area as the boys prepared their drones for flight. The drones each had cameras that could transmit video to a phone. That video could be displayed on a bigger screen for us all to see.

I wasn't sure Sandy would want to see what's going on at the farm but she really wanted to know all the facts. She was aware that her dad was probably infected but that didn't change her mind at all.

"I just need to see it. If he's one of those . . . *things* then he's gone and I won't have to worry that he needs me or needs help."

I understood what she said about her dad and what Steve said about Mike. Once a family member turns into a bloodthirsty stone-cold killer it's much easier to distance yourself from them. Trying to have a funeral or burial for one of these beasts just doesn't seem right.

She hung back with some of the moms. They were talking about starting a garden inside the fort. Seemed like a great idea to pass some of the time. It probably wasn't good to get too bored during what could be some long days ahead. Sandy would be an ideal resource for a project like that and chances are she had access to the equipment they would need. At some point we would need to go back to the farm but at least for the first few days or week they could come up with some plans and design something to do within these walls.

Now it was time to take a look *outside* these walls. By the time the drones were going to be taking off we had quite an audience watching the TV screens. Jackson and the other boys went up to the top of the south wall to make it easier to navigate the drone flight. From the top of the wall you could barely see the farm in the distance.

The four drones sat in the grass just a few yards away from us. Over the com I said to the boys "We've got a full house here ready for the show. Whenever you're ready."

Jackson quickly responded, "Ok, ready for liftoff. Stand back."

The drones all came to life and one after another they shot straight up in the air at least one hundred feet and gradually started towards the south wall. It was quite impressive to see and to hear them fly. We could see them all gracefully depart over the south wall and then our attention shifted to the TV screens. Two of the cameras were directed towards the ground at about a 75 degree angle. The other two were directed straight ahead to help with navigation once they were at the farm.

The drones were over the wall and heading towards the upper fields. We were all looking intently at the screens and all of a sudden we could see thousands of figures milling around on the soccer fields. Huge amounts of infecteds out there not far from us. It was pretty chilling. Jackson had the drones drop in altitude to about twenty feet just to see what would happen. As the drones got closer to the ground we could see the hideous creatures in greater detail. We saw them look at the drones but they just basically remained where they were and did not give chase. That reassured me. I didn't want to lead a full herd of infecteds to the farm. That wouldn't be helpful for us. The drones covered ground quickly. Within three minutes they were at the farm. Amazing. The drones circled the farm once just to check things out. We could see a lot of animals all around the farm. Sandy kept pointing out all the pigs, goats and chickens on the screen. They seemed healthy enough. Slowly the drones lowered and began to approach the main farmhouse. They slowly navigated to the back windows and we were actually looking inside the farmhouse.

I spoke over the com, "That's great guys. Let's just keep in that same position for a minute. Let's see what's inside."

We were looking inside the kitchen and everything looked totally normal. We couldn't see any irregularities within the kitchen. The boys had come back down to the video area so they could see all the images on the big screens while they were directing the drones.

After about one minute Jackson gave the next instruction "Let's move to the north. We're moving left fifteen feet to the next window."

Sandy spoke up. "That's his bedroom. He could be in there. I don't know if those things can open a door."

The drones sat there looking and just when Jackson was going to give the next order we saw a figure. A hideous figure suddenly came to the window and seemed to be shrieking and growling. It was beastly and clearly infected.

I felt a pang of sorrow and I couldn't imagine the sadness that Sandy must be feeling now. Paul put his arm around her to comfort her.

"That's not Dad!" Sandy shouted out as she stood up quickly.

"That's not him! I'm sure of it. That's his friend Jack Williams from next door. They were hanging out earlier. That's not my Dad!"

"Roger that, let's go to the next window. Fifteen feet to the north." Jackson gave the order.

The drones moved and we watched intently on the screen. One of the drones came very close to the window. We could see a figure approaching the window. We couldn't tell what it was but as it came closer to the window it's features became clearer. It pulled some curtains to the side and it looked like an old man. He didn't look like he was infected. We all looked at Sandy.

Sandy gasped "It's Dad! It's him! He's not infected!"

She gave Paul Stanford a big hug, they were both excited to see him in his own flesh.

"He looks okay. He's not infected." Paul agreed

"He's in his study. There's no way out except for the bedroom and that's where Mr. Williams is. He's trapped but he's okay!" Sandy exclaimed.

On the video we could see Mr. Carpenter rush to the door and try to brace himself against it. Then we saw him push a dresser against the door. The infected must have been trying to get in.

Jackson called out again "Back to the bedroom. Fifteen feet to the south."

The drones slowly moved and within a few seconds we could soon see the ghastly image of an infected slamming itself against a door. This beast looked like it was in some type of rage as it slammed against the door head first again and again."

"Dad built that door real thick." Sandy burst out, "He wanted it private and quiet and made the door with his own hands. He'll be ok! He probably doesn't have his phone. He's trapped but he's safe."

She hugged Paul Stanford again and he gave me a look as if to ask 'What do we do?'

Jackson gave the next order, he really was good at leading without being pushy or bossy. "Let's inspect the farm again real quick then check on the marina."

The boys navigated the drones around the farm and we could see the animals seemed to be relatively unfazed by all of this. There were several infecteds near the barn and some in the fields just wandering. The drones left the farm and headed back towards the fields and then over Brenton Cove where all the boats were. Jackson did a flyby of the Flying Serpent and everything looked fine. We couldn't see anyone on any boat. Next they flew over the *Resilience* which looked like a fortress. They circled it and it looked clear which was reassuring. They checked out the parking lot which was clear as well. Lastly they flew around the fort and checked out the entire perimeter. Other than a few infecteds everything was largely quiet. They brought the drones back to the fort interior and back to their launch pad.

"Great job men, great job!" I said and I meant it. I couldn't believe how well they did and it was completely safe without risk. It was impressive.

Sandy ran up to me and gave me a hug. "He's okay. You saw it right? He's okay!"

"Yeah, I saw him. He looked good for sure, Sandy." I returned but I wasn't sure what we were ready to offer. I gave her a hug and as I did that I met the eyes of Steve. I looked around at Allan, Jason, Dave and Mark. They all seemed to be waiting for me to give my response. I looked at Kristin who was holding onto Abby and Lori. They were looking at me.

"Sandy, my Dad's out there too." I said honestly, "If he needed my help I'd go get him. Your dad needs our help. You're one of us and we're going to get him."

Allan agreed which was a relief, "We've got to go get him. We can do it."

Dave was on board too. "We'll get him, we have to."

Steve finally chimed in, "He still may be infected. He could turn any minute but we can take care of that if it happens. I agree with Allan and Dave. Let's get him."

Sandy went over to Steve and Dave who were standing together and hugged them both. "God bless you both, my dad's worth saving. You'll see."

Chapter 31

RESCUE MISSION

I KNEW WE HAD to come up with a plan. That door was secure for now but for how long could it withstand the constant pounding from an infected. Two hours? Three hours? Eventually it would collapse. We had to get there and save him before that happened. We couldn't call him or warn him we were coming.

Paul Stanford was the first to approach me. "I'm coming on this one. I want to be there for him. Please let me get in on this." He looked at me like someone who was desperate but also like someone who really cared about what was happening here. Saving a man's life and saving a daughter's father.

"Okay, Paul. I think that's great. In fact you know that farm and that house better than any of us. I was going to ask for your help anyway. If you want to come you're in." I told him and I meant it. He could be useful and we had room on the rescue team.

"Great. Thanks. I think I'm ready for anything. If you need me to kill one of those things I won't let you down." Paul said with certainty.

"Alright, let's sit down at the table and come up with a plan."

I led him to a big table and we sat down. Steve, Allan, Dave, Jesse, Abby and Mark all sat down with us.

I took out a Newport map and set it down on the table. We looked at the proximity of the farm to the fort and it seemed like we should have no problem but we all knew the real obstacles that lie ahead.

"Those things are going to follow us to the farm and affect our rescue and then they'll follow us to the fort and impact our return." I said stating the obvious.

"We could drive right through them at a high speed and rescue the farmer before they get there." Dave said first. It was true it could be a quick rescue.

I wasn't so sure it would be that easy. "Dave, there are thousands of infecteds between us and that farm. There's also several infected on the property and one in the house. That all poses just too big a challenge don't you think? We can't have multiple people stranded in that farmhouse with a horde of these things surrounding the house and our vehicle. Speeding in and hoping for a clean getaway seems too risky." I replied honestly. "Do you agree, Steve?"

"With these things and their tenacity it would be a risk just trying to plow through them and hoping for the best." Steve answered. "We have to come up with some other plan."

I countered, "We don't have to drive right to the farm. We could drive in a circle and outrun them. We could approach the farm from a different direction and not worry as much about that horde."

Steve nodded and added "We could also use a diversion. Something to take the bulk of these things away from our main objective."

"The drones didn't seem to really captivate these things." Dave added, "What other diversion do we have?"

"I have a helicopter. It's a little louder but maybe something in the sky doesn't draw their attention. They didn't follow the drones so why would they follow a helicopter. We don't know." Steve responded.

"Maybe we just need to keep it simple." Allan said, "Three guys in the Humvee go full throttle and head to the farm. Crash and grab. If the horde doesn't follow you then save the farmer. If they start following we can have some kind of decoy car to divert their attention somehow. If it doesn't work out you can turn around and come back."

"That is so simple it just might work Allan, I like it." Steve said. "Those things aren't going to be jumping through the window of the humvee.

"Okay, so it sounds like we have a plan." I said with some relief. "Steve should be our back up with the helicopter so he's out. I think Mark should drive the humvee. Paul Stanford is going and I'll go. We'll keep it simple."

Steve added matter-of-factly, "You guys should bring Abby. She's battle-tested and can operate that heavy machine gun on the Humvee. She's got war-time experience and more balls than any of you guys."

I had no problem following a war-trained soldier into the battle but I wanted to make sure she was on board with the plan. "Abby, I think you would be a huge addition to this rescue mission and I absolutely would appreciate it if you'd join us. The lead is yours if you're willing to take it."

Abby was right next to me and had her arm around Sandy. She responded confidently, "I'm ready to join you guys on this mission to save Sandy's dad. I know that if my dad was trapped like this I would not stop for anything to rescue him. We have to do this and we will deliver. Trust us." She said as she looked into Sandy's eyes and it really hit home to me. Trust was such a huge commodity and it was something that we had right now. It was palpable as several other men volunteered.

Jackson had been sitting with us the whole time. I was hoping he wasn't planning on joining us. I didn't want him to be taking so many risks here on day one. Unfortunately, it seemed like he was eager to be involved.

Jackson stood up and cleared his throat. "Abby, I really think I'm ready to be part of this mission. I'm confident I would be a useful team member and I want to contribute. Even if it's in the decoy car I want to help. I'm ready."

She was smiling and she gave a subtle look to me. Part of me wanted him to stay within the safety of the fort but the other part knew he was just as ready as any of us to be on this mission. I gave a subtle nod and that was all Abby needed to see.

"Great, Jackson. I think we could use your skills and thanks for volunteering."

"I agree. He's a stud. Ok, let's come up with our final plan." Steve suggested and pointed at the map "Sandy, tell us exactly where we need to be."

Sandy gave precise information on where the rescue team needed to be. She gave info on the local roads, the house layout and the best way to enter the house. She was very helpful and informed us that they never locked the front door or back door until yesterday. That was the first time her father ever locked the doors. That information was useful and so was her house key which she handed over to Abby.

Abby asked about deadbolts, alarms, bulletproof windows that couldn't be smashed. It was a simple farmhouse and it seemed like getting inside was something that should be manageable. Taking out the infected was another story.

After discussing things for a few minutes it seemed that we had a plan.

We had a Humvee that would serve as the main rescue vehicle and would be driven by Mark. Abby would be the leader of the party and she would man the heavy machine gun.

Allan, Dave, Paul Stanford and myself would be in the humvee party and hoping for a very boring trip. We knew that there was always the chance of unforeseen horde activity but it seemed like we had a pretty good plan.

We had another vehicle that was going to serve as the diversion. Jesse had driven to Boston to purchase a stretch Navigator with armor-plated siding, bullet-proof windows, and run-flat tires. It seemed like the safest vehicle to use as a vehicle diversion and it also had a twin turbo V-8 400 horsepower engine. This thing was badass. Jesse himself volunteered to drive on this mission and Jackson and Peter Carlson were going with him. They would hopefully lead the herd of infecteds away from the fort and away from the farm. Everyone heard the details of this mission and was given a chance to back out or to ask questions. We were all silent.

The two teams walked towards the vehicles. Everyone had their earpieces for the com. We had a chase car ready if we needed it and a helicopter that could be in the air in three minutes. We would have an eye in the sky to help us with navigation in the form of a drone. The rescue mission was as prepared as it could be with so little time. Everyone was confident and optimistic as we loaded up the vehicles and got ready to deploy. First was the Humvee with Mark at the wheel, Abby at the turret, and Dave, Paul, Allan and I as crew. This vehicle was an amazing machine and we all felt safe inside it's armored walls. With the heavy machine gun up top and plenty of weaponry inside we felt ready for anything. The Navigator with Jesse, Jackson and Peter followed the Humvee. Peter and Jackson each had two shotguns ready for action and they both had AR-15s loaded and at arm's reach. They were ready for just about anything.

We sat there for less than a minute until Abby got on the com, "I'm not sure what we're waiting around for gentlemen.

I've got a nail appointment and a bikini wax I don't want to be late for. Is there any reason I'm not on my way?"

Sam replied uncomfortably, "No sir..I mean ma'am . . . no reason at all."

Abby definitely asserted herself as a fearless soldier during the rescue mission at sea yesterday. We knew she was experienced and no one questioned her abilities. We felt confident she would be as cool under pressure as her father. She had that vibe that she was ready for anything that happened.

"Open the gate." Sam ordered and it was Kenny opening the gate.

Abby was on the com. "Alright team, we're exiting the fort and entering the real world. Time to have your head on a swivel and your finger on a trigger. I'm in the turret and have full vision. Let's move out."

"Roger, that." came Jesse over the com. "*Love you long time.*" He let out which was a fairly common Jesse-ism and it made us feel good about the moment.

"I'm feeling a lot of good energy, boys." Abby returned. "Let's get out there and spread the word. We are large and in charge."

Steve came over the com, "Why don't you save some of this bravado for when you actually save the farmer, commander."

"Yes, sir. Let's save the farmer, gentlemen." Abby responded without any tone or hint of resentment.

Colby came over the com. He had his drone in the air observing everything. "You still have the main herd at the soccer fields. It has grown. The road still looks fine."

The two trucks moved out of the fort. The gates closed quickly after the exit. They took a right turn and headed up the hill towards the fields. Our group in the Humvee was first then Jesse in his Navigator behind us. We were off and heading up the hill. The hope was that we could plow through the crowd of infecteds and just maintain our speed to the main road. We knew these things were tough and fast but there was a sense of optimism that we could get to the farm safely with our plan. At the top of the hill we started to see the infecteds. There were more now than when Mark was here earlier. We were going slow but we didn't slow down. We were hoping to slip past them but it was pretty clear they noticed us. They were all looking straight at us and they started running directly for us.

Abby came over the com, "Okay, gentlemen it's time to get going. Too many of these things to use weapons. Let's just plow through them and remember that these aren't people. These are monsters."

Mark was driving the lead vehicle and was ready for that order. "You got it boss. Pedal down."

He sped up and it was quite unnerving to see the bodies jumping at and on the cars. As we accelerated the infecteds just seemed to bounce off or go right under the wheels. It was awful but these vehicles were so heavy and well-armored we felt pretty good about things so far. We were traveling with good speed trying to put some distance from us and the main pack. It took about one minute of this until we reached the park entrance and by then we were about three hundred feet from the main horde. The farm was to the right and the Humvee turned and headed that way quickly and at speed. The Navigator had trailed the Humvee and waited for the infecteds to catch up. Jesse honked his horn and tried his best to attract attention. He did a good job attracting most of the herd and then he gunned it and took a left going the opposite way.

As predicted the infecteds followed the Navigator the easterly direction and away from the farm. They kept heading away from the fort and farm at a moderate speed that would hopefully keep the infecteds running after them.

The Humvee drove around a smaller road in a circular

fashion and seemed to be in the clear with no infecteds in sight. The plan was to get us to the farm without an army of infecteds and we had succeeded so far. We proceeded down the lane where the farm was located. This was a fairly rural area and we didn't see many people or infecteds. We turned a corner and there was the farmhouse ahead of us. We approached slowly and watched for any activity. There were no infecteds on the road but as we turned into the driveway we saw at least three walking through the fields and one in the middle of the driveway. The Humvee slowly approached the house and we became aware of how close these things were to us and we knew how fast they could move in on us.

"Okay, boys we've got at least three in the fields and one ugly son of a bitch right in front of us." Abby's voice came over the com. "I don't want to shoot any of them, it'll just attract more."

Mark responded, "I could just run this guy over and then position us closer to the house. Maybe it won't make a lot of noise."

It seemed like it could work. The other infecteds were far enough away they might not hear us as long as we don't shoot our guns.

"Ok, Mark. Give it a try. Try to go right over it with the wheels." Abby gave the order.

"I'm gonna line it up just like at the carwash. It's like I've been training for this all these years." Mark had a smile on his face and as he was talking he hit the gas and hit the infected square directly in front of the right front tire. The impact caused its body to fall directly back and down on the ground. Mark kept going and we could feel the right tires run right over the infected. It seemed to get dragged under the Humvee for about twenty feet at which point we were right at the back door of the house. The truck stopped and Mark kept the engine running.

At first I didn't know what the sound was but we could all detect something under the Humvee. It sounded like a scratching or a clawing directly under the right rear axle. There was the faint but unmistakable snarling and hissing of the infected still trying to attack from under the right rear wheel. It felt like it was reaching towards the body of the truck and towards us. These things had no off-switch as it kept trying to kill whatever it could get its claws on.

"Ok, boys. We know where the farmer is and we think there is one infected inside there." Abby reviewed our earlier discussion. "Mark will stay at the wheel and I'll keep the gun trained on any bad guys that approach. Dave, Allan, Paul and Dr. B will enter the back door with shotguns ready for close encounters. Once we start firing I anticipate we'll have company. We don't have a lot of time for this rescue. Seconds count once the first shot is fired. I'll be on the com with any updates. If it's getting busy out here I will call you back to the Humvee. Everyone ready?"

"Check." I responded as she handed me the house key Sandy had provided.

"Ready." Allan came over the com.

"Now or never." Paul seemed ready.

"Let's roll." Dave said as he opened up the door.

We all got out of the Humvee and immediately were met with two distinct and disturbing sensations. We could hear the awful sounds of the infected as he groaned and shrieked from under the truck. The second thing we noticed was the smell of fuel and an expanding puddle of gasoline under the Humvee.

"This could be a problem. Fuel leak." Allan was first on the com.

We looked where the noise was coming from and this infected had rolled up into the body of the humvee and it was reaching up with it's arms into the inner workings of the rear chassis of the truck. It was trapped but wasn't dead. We couldn't shoot it either with all the gas.

"That thing must have reached up and grabbed the fuel line." Mark said, "The level's dropping. Down to a half a tank already. Shit."

"Let's get the farmer. Focus on the task." Abby said firmly and confidently.

"Right. Let's get him and get out of here." I answered as we turned to approach the back door. "Okay guys, we may encounter the hostile immediately. Be ready to fire. Let's be careful." We all made sure our shotguns were loaded and ready for immediate firing.

I reached the door and unlocked it with the key and quietly opened it. Things were quiet at first as we all slipped into the kitchen. We then heard a loud crashing sound coming from the next room.

"I know what that sound is." Dave said as we approached the door to the next room. We peeked around the door frame and could all see an infected with a bloody head and face that looked like it had probably been crashing head-first against the next door for hours. Dave experienced that non-stop pounding yesterday while on the fishing boat. He could understand how afraid the farmer likely was. It was amazing the door was still upright. We could see some broken pieces of wood within the door and two of the hinges looked broken.

I held up my hand as we all waited for him to hit the door and then we all entered the room and spread out. When this thing sensed we were in the room it didn't hesitate at all to attack. It lunged right at Allan and we all shot at this thing simultaneously. We definitely hit this thing multiple times as parts of it's head and chest exploded and it collapsed in a pile of bloody flesh.

"Infected down." I said over the com, "Dave and Allan watch our six. Paul and I will get the farmer."

"Ok. Good job." came Abby "Let's hurry, we're down to a quarter tank and it's dropping fast. Here come more of these infecteds drawn in by the noise. I'm going to have to fire. Be prepared for more company!"

"Got it!" I said and we knocked on the door.

Paul called out "Mr. Carpenter. It's me Paul. You're ok. We killed it. Open up, please."

We could hear some furniture being moved on the other side of the door and then the door opened. He looked somewhat dazed and confused but realized that we were there to help him. He looked down at the infected that terrorized him for a few hours and then back at us.

"How did you know ... ? Where did you ... ?" he didn't know what to ask.

I walked into the room and looked him over for injuries. He looked okay. "Mr. Carpenter we're friends with Sandy. She's okay. She's at our secure location and we are going to bring you there now. Please come with us."

"Mr. Carpenter. It's me, Paul Stanford." Paul reached out to him.

At first Mr. Carpenter didn't seem to recognize who this person was with a gun and with all the commotion. After a moment he looked a little closer and realized just who this man was. The biggest smile came over his face and the two men hugged. It was really quite moving and if we weren't being overrun by infecteds I would have let them have their moment. We had to get out of here now.

"Let's move, guys." I called out to them.

I led the way and Mr. Carpenter followed. He seemed to understand we were in a hurry and didn't hesitate. He followed us outside and that's when we heard some loud gunfire. We could see Abby up in the turret and she was aiming at several approaching infecteds running at high speed. She was shooting in bursts of two or three rounds trying not to make too much noise. It didn't matter. That gun was loud! She didn't waste any rounds. She blew those things away with an efficiency that seemed to run in the family.

"Time to go, guys. Get in, we're on fumes!" Mark was getting anxious.

There was still a snarling infected under the truck and the overpowering smell of gas. Poor Mr. Carpenter seemed shell-shocked. We piled in the Humvee and closed the door. Immediately Mark took off and Abby finished firing. The Humvee was laboring and sputtering but it was running. The gas line was leaking but perhaps not totally severed.

"We can fill up with gas. I have plenty." Mr. Carpenter answered. "We just received one thousand gallons."

Just then Jesse came over the com. "I've circled a couple of times and can't escape the horde. They're coming from everywhere. It's getting worse each minute. The roads are filling up. We've got to get back!"

"Sorry. No time to fuel up." Abby answered Mr. Carpenter. "Let's get back to the fort."

Colby was on the com again, "I'm on top of you guys with the drone and you got infecteds headed your way. They're on the roads and in the fields. They're everywhere. Get out of there now! Get back to the fort!"

"I'm not sure we can make it!" Mark answered, sounding frantic. "We're on empty and this thing feels like it's ready to stall on us. We can't afford to get stuck out on the roads with the hordes out there. We'll be stranded. I'll see how far we can get."

We pulled out of the driveway and turned onto the main road but the Humvee was sputtering and laboring.

"We'll be out of gas any minute. Dead in the water." Mark called out.

"Did you try the reserve tank!" Abby called out.

"I already did. They're both empty." Mark responded frantically. It was clear the Humvee was just not going to make it.

We were starting to encounter more and more infecteds and just driving right through them. It was getting more dense as we drove and it would be another 300 feet until we turned left towards the fort. We were coming to a cross road and I was just thinking that this was a particularly bad place to be stranded. It was going to be difficult to meet up with Jesse on these roads and get into his Navigator with all these beasts swarming around. That's when I saw a sign and immediately did some calculations in my head. I called out with authority "Mark, take the next right!"

I looked at Abby who was leading this mission, "Abby, we just can't get into Jesse's rig out here in the open. It's too dangerous."

Mark had already turned down the side road as I directed.

"What's your plan, doctor?" she asked without any anger or wounded pride.

"Jesse can you meet us at Newport Country Club?" I asked over the com.

"Uh . . . there's no time for golf right now but sure, I'm just around the corner." He responded, "I can get there in about thirty seconds."

Mark steered the truck up the small road and we were suddenly out in the open surrounded by fairways and greens. We could see the majestic clubhouse perched on a hill. It looked just like it was any other day with no hint of bloodthirsty killing machines.

Colby came over the com again. "I don't see any infecteds

around the clubhouse but in just about every direction the roads are swarmed. No path open to the fort."

We headed up the hill towards the clubhouse and were about fifty yards away from the clubhouse when the Humvee stalled and finally came to a stop. It was completely empty and we all knew it.

Abby was first to give the order "Grab all the gear you can and let's move towards the clubhouse. Let's go!"

We opened the doors and grabbed everything we could. We each had a shotgun, our 9mm handguns and a backpack with shells and rounds.

We started running to the club and Jesse came over the com. "We're turning the corner now. Plenty of bogeys on our tail. Will get to you guys as fast as we can but it's gonna be tight!"

"They're coming at us from both directions. Jess there's just so many of them!" I said on the com. *This is not good* I said to myself as I ran at top speed.

We finally made it to the clubhouse. It was locked but Allan immediately broke a small window and reached to open the deadbolt. I entered the clubhouse first and was prepared for any squatters. It seemed quiet and peaceful. I briefly recalled my last visit here to play in a member-guest tournament. This majestic clubhouse was the centerpiece for the very prestigious Newport upper class. White glove service, string quartet, the smell of old money . . . . not today. What was happening here today and the approaching horde was such a stark contrast to that beautiful memory. I couldn't let myself get caught in the moment.

"It's clear!" I called out and everyone entered behind me. We took up defensive positions and watched for Jesse. Down the road but within view was an approaching mob of infecteds. They were all headed this way and closing in fast. Ten seconds later Jesse was speeding up the road and just plowing through the masses. By the time he got to where we were there were two infecteds on his hood and one on the roof.

Abby gave the next order "Jesse stay inside until we clear your vehicle. Dr. B, Allan and Dave shotguns out. Dr. B and Dave take out the infecteds on the hood Allan the one on the roof. Let's go!"

The three of us exited with shotguns loaded and ready. The navigator came to a screeching halt. One infected rolled off the roof and Dave immediately approached it and took dead am right at its head. He didn't hesitate to blow it clean off. One down.

The other one on the hood was snarling as it had its head pressed against the windshield. I knew it was bulletproof glass but I couldn't risk hurting my team. I knew Jackson was in this car. I approached from the side and as the infected was arching up preparing to slam its head against the windshield I pointed the barrel right at the base of it's skull. I pulled the trigger and it was a direct strike removing most of the skull and brain. At the same time Allan fired at the third infected and knocked it off the hood of the tall SUV. It wasn't dead but Dave immediately approached it and blew it's head off. The whole sequence lasted no longer than ten seconds. We were ready for this. After what we all saw and experienced earlier today we knew we couldn't hesitate to take these things out.

With what looked to be thousands of infecteds closing in on us there seemed to be no chance that the limo could escape through that mob. It would be too risky to strand ourselves in a vehicle out in the open. We'd have to take our chances here at the clubhouse.

"All clear!" Abby called out. "Unload quickly and let's get inside."

Jesse, Peter and Jackson exited the vehicle with their gear in tow.

We took just a moment to scan the horizon. In every direction we could see fast approaching infecteds. They were now running at full speed towards us. Attracted by the gunfire no-doubt. There were tens of thousands and the sound from the huge mass was an eerie haunted sound that made all of our hairs stand on end. This was a terrifying scene and there was no way out. Even if the Humvee had a full tank it would have struggled to make it far through that swarm of infecteds. It looked like the odds were against us making it back to the fort.

That's when a different voice came over the com, "I'm three minutes away from your position. I can load the whole group. Just get up to a rooftop location. Quickly people." Steve's voice was as calm as ever. Just another weekend. It was great to hear his voice and he gave us all renewed hope that there was a chance of escape. We didn't hesitate to all jump to action.

We ran into the clubhouse and locked the doors behind us. There were also a few windows next to the doors. We threw some sofa's up against the doors but quickly realized that was useless. This was an old stout mansion with thick doors and sturdy glass but tens of thousands of those rabid monsters that didn't feel pain or ever slow down would find their way in. How quickly we didn't know but we couldn't afford to sit around to find out.

Abby whistled from down the hallway. "Let's go team. Up to the roof. Who knows the layout?"

I knew that the only way to get to the offices upstairs was to head to the left and up an old stairway.

"Follow me!" I called out and we all ran through the grand foyer then up a narrow hallway. We opened a door and went up some older stairs. At the top of the stairs we exited into another hallway. Mr. Carpenter was slower than the rest of us.

Allan and Paul were helping him as much as they could. On the second floor was a long hallway with a bunch of doors to what appeared to be standard offices.

I yelled out "Check out the offices. We're looking for one that has a window that will give us easy access to the roof." Everyone looked in a different office. I forced open a door and quickly went to look out a window at the other side of one of the office. No roof access. Just a thirty foot drop into a massive crowd of bloodthirsty monsters.

Abby was on the other side of the hall, "In here!" She called out. "This window will put us right onto the roof."

Allan tried to open it. The window wouldn't budge, it was an old window that looked like it was painted and sealed. Dave raised the barrel of his shotgun but Allan held up his hand.

"Wait, Dave. That will just break the glass and probably slow us down." Allan instructed. "This will just take a second." Allan was a veteran firefighter who had to deal with these types of situations every day. He knew how to get doors and windows open quickly and he's had to do it with lives on the line including his own. He used a blade to cut through some old paint and caulking. In about ten seconds the window was open without a bunch of glass shards and especially without a shotgun blast attracting more infecteds. Once we opened the window we were aware of several different things. The horde of infecteds was immense and we could see and hear the tens of thousands of hissing snarling beasts just below us. It was clear any truck would not have made it through such a thick mass of bodies. No way we would have been able to navigate through that sea of infecteds. We also could hear the helicopter approach somewhere above us. We couldn't see it but I couldn't imagine how Steve could get the copter anywhere near us soon enough to save us from this mob of infecteds right on our tail.

The other scarier noise was coming from downstairs. We could hear sounds of crashing, stomping, running, grunting and pretty much the scariest sounds we could imagine hearing. The floors and walls seemed to be shaking. Was it from the helicopter? No, it was definitely coming from the angry swarm of monsters filling through the downstairs and pouring into the rooms and hallways. The sound was quickly getting louder as the mob was finding the stairs. I knew we had to escape this place quickly. I called out, "Let's go! Out the window and up the roof. Load up into the copter! Fast!"

Allan and Peter pushed together a bookshelf and a desk so that the door wouldn't open. Could that slow them? Mr. Carpenter spun a sofa sideways and wedged it against the wall to create a pretty solid defense. He looked at us and added, "Just one of these things will get through that door eventually. This mob will get through in less than a minute." We needed every second.

Steve came over the com, "I'm just above you folks at the top of the roof. Plenty of room. Abby should come first to man the gun." He was so cool and composed.

One by one we exited the window and climbed up the roof. Abby shot out of the window and quickly disappeared as she ascended upwards. Mr. Carpenter was actually pretty capable and didn't need much help. Paul, Dave and Allan helped him and once he was out they followed. By then there was pounding on the door and the walls all around us.

Once everyone else was out I started to climb through the window and out of the office. I could hear the sound of infecteds crashing against the door but it was holding solid for now. I also heard some nearby office windows shattering open too. I didn't want to wait around any more. I started to climb up the shingled roof. The downwash from the rotor was strong and I had to really concentrate to scale upwards on the roof. Despite the deafening noise from the copter and the powerful wind in my face the sound of the swarming infecteds was still overpowering. I was about halfway up and it looked like everyone else was on the copter. Abby was on the side of the copter and was seated on a mounted large caliber machine gun. She had it directed to my left. I looked back briefly. I could see that the window at the nearby dormer was smashed open and I could see some infecteds start to emerge. Some of them were pushed right over the edge and plummeted to the ground. Others that I could see were already on the roof and starting to run directly towards me. My god they were ferocious and fast! They had no fear and were sprinting towards me with that ghastly undead look in their eyes!

Just then Steve came over the com sounding like he was in a hot tub or just had a massage. "We're all waiting for you Doctor. Jackson's on board safely. This is a full flight. Standing room only unfortunately."

Abby came over the com next, "Keep coming Paul. I'm going to take a couple of these things out. Do not stop!"

I answered quickly "Got it. I'm coming. Shoot!"

The sound from the machine gun was unfamiliar. This was another badass weapon. It was a side-mounted belt-fed six-barrel fifty caliber gun and Abby let loose small bursts seemingly right over my shoulder. It sounded like each two second burst was about twenty rounds. As I reached the copter and put my foot on the skid both Allan and Dave grabbed me and pulled me in.

"We got him!" Dave gave the signal to Steve who immediately lifted the copter directly up. Abby continued to direct bullets at infecteds just feet away from us. They were coming from both sides and once we were about ten feet clear she stopped shooting. By that point there were hundreds of these things on the roof and I couldn't believe how close we were to catastrophe!

"All clear!" She said as she took her hands off the firing mechanism.

We slowly backed away from the clubhouse and could see the horrifying magnitude of these monsters completely enveloping the majestic building. I could see the faces of these awful beasts as they all swarmed onto the roof. Boy were they angry!

I couldn't believe we all made it away from there. That clubhouse was a deathtrap and we all could have been lunchmeat for that giant horde of killing machines.

For a few moments we all sat there just catching our breath.

"Hopefully everyone enjoyed their time at Newport Country Club." Steve deadpanned as we slowly turned away from the clubhouse. We all remained quiet as the chopper gradually flew over the masses. Where did they all come from? The Navigator and Humvee were completely enveloped by infecteds. Some windows had been broken and it was clear we had made the right decision to abandon our original plan. The side trip to the country club was a close call but it had probably saved our lives.

Sam came over the com next "Everything okay guys? Some nervous people here at the fort want to know if everyone's safe."

"The whole team is accounted for and safe." Abby responded. "The farmer has been retrieved. So far the mission is a success. The bad news is that the country club was a let down. The people there were quite rude."

We all smiled at that. I again reflected on my previous trip to the club and the different type of experience we had today.

I added "The club's just not what it used to be. You should have seen the element they let in there today."

"Can we *not* go there again, Dad? That place sucked!" Jackson responded sarcastically.

"I agree Jax." Steve added from the cockpit. "Seems like a nice day up here though. Who wants to take a look around Newport?"

Right about then Mr. Carpenter had caught his breath and realized that we were all safe. He didn't have an earpiece in like we all did so he couldn't hear everything we were saying. He looked at Paul and asked "So, who are all you people and where are we going?"

He didn't seem angry or afraid. Anybody would be a little shell-shocked after what he just went through. Paul was next to him and he gave Mr. Carpenter a headset so he could hear what was going on. "Mr. Carpenter, we are part of a group of survivors. I'll explain everything when we get back. Sandy wanted you to join us at our place where it's a little safer. We're some of the few immune to the virus and we have made Fort Adams our main headquarters. That's where we're going next. But first we're going to take a tour of Newport and check out what's happening."

"As long as my Sandy's okay you can take me anywhere!" Mr. Carpenter responded with a smile and he sat back and closed his eyes. He must have been exhausted.

It was a pretty good idea to do some investigating as long as we were in the helicopter. Why not? We left the golf course and headed towards town. We flew over Brenton Cove and within thirty seconds we were in the heart of Newport. We could see thousands of infecteds milling around Bowen's wharf. From afar it looked like just a normal Saturday afternoon in this tourist destination. Tons of foot-traffic on the wharves and crowds milling around Thames street. We knew it was bad down near the fort but it was even worse over here in town. It was all pretty amazing. A few buildings were on fire. I could see one or two cars that were on the road and moving but they were completely surrounded and engulfed by infecteds. It wasn't going to end well for those people but there was nothing we could do.

Abby came over the com next. "We could probably get a table at the Cooke house today." We all knew the popular Newport restaurant and it's reputation for always being crowded. "Maybe not. It looks pretty crowded."

It was true. We could all see the infecteds roaming around the wharf just outside the popular eatery.

Surprisingly, it was Kristin's voice next on the com. "Oh no, you are *not* going to the Cooke house without me! Get your butts back to this fort now! Besides, we all decided we are going to have that second night of the gala after all. We're going to have music and dancing and maybe a movie under the stars!"

"That sounds pretty good right now, Honey." I answered.

"Roger that." Steve responded. "We'll be landing within the fort in three minutes Sam. Please make sure we have a safe landing zone, thank you . . . *Honey*."

The whole helicopter erupted in laughter none louder than mine. I was ready to go home and so was everyone else. We all survived and except for two vehicles we came out unscathed. We saved the farmer and it was time for another gala!

Chapter 32

HOMECOMING

STEVE STEERED THE helicopter towards the fort and we enjoyed the views of the harbor one more time. As we approached the fort I could count several dozen infecteds in the parking lot outside the gate. We could see the upper fields and there were still hundreds of wandering zombies just waiting for something to stir them into a frenzy. The helicopter was sure to get some attention. We could see many of their heads turn and look our way as we approached.

"Let's see how smart they are." Steve hovered the aircraft at about ten feet over the water and about fifteen feet from the seawall. The infecteds all seemed to be aware we were there but didn't really react beyond that. They resumed the slow roaming they typically exhibited despite our presence.

"I don't think they know what this helicopter is. They probably can't see us in here." Jackson was the first to point out.

"They just see the can." Steve was agreeing, "Shall we show them the sardines?"

Abby was next to the door and she turned a latch so she could manually slide open the cabin door. As she did that the sound of the engine became much louder and it was clear we wouldn't be able to attract them with noise. Still not much action from the herd. Maybe they couldn't see us inside this thing. Maybe they don't like sardines.

Abby attached some type of retracting cable to her harness and stepped out onto the helicopter skid. She started waving her arms and dancing a little to try to get their attention. It definitely worked. The slow-roaming infecteds seemed to immediately identify her as prey. They quickly turned and started running towards the helicopter. As some began to run it caught the attention of others just like animals hunting in nature.

I wasn't sure what to expect. As the infecteds got closer it was clear that they could see us as a meal and not just noise. They kept running and even when they got to the wall they did not stop. They kept going and were running right over the edge of the wall and dropping right into the water. One after another they splashed and landed right on top of one another. They weren't swimming. They were still reaching for Abby. Eventually they were all sinking and disappearing as more landed in the water to join them. They kept coming. It was chilling to see them all careening off the sea wall in 'attack mode' but it was also encouraging that we figured out at least one way to eradicate them with minimal risk.

"Interesting." Steve remarked over the headset, "I'd love to stay all day but I don't want to get Kristin upset. She did tell us to get our *butts* back to the fort."

A few more laughs and smiles, Steve couldn't resist any chance to crack a joke or tease someone gently. Nothing mean and always in good humor.

Abby returned to her seat and closed the cabin door. Steve lifted up and maneuvered the chopper over the walls of the fort and landed gently in a large open area. He immediately flipped a few buttons and the rotors started to slow down.

"Okay, team. Safeties on. Holster your weapons." Abby's

voice came over the com. I hadn't even realized I still had my handgun in my grip and ready for action. I wasn't the only one caught up in all the drama and excitement. We all listened to Abby give instructions as she opened the door and helped us all get out. I could see the whole group watching us from a safe distance. Kristin and Casey were smiling and waving. They were standing next to Sandy who had a huge smile on her face. Paul walked Mr. Carpenter over towards them and Sandy ran forwards and gave her Dad a big hug. After a few seconds they both reached out with an arm to Paul and pulled him in to have a little group hug. They were all smiling. We all witnessed that heart-warming moment and it made our little mission seem like a huge success. It brought a smile to everyone's face. Candace and Casey also joined them for a mini-reunion. Mr. Carpenter gave a big hug to everyone and seemed like he was happy to see faces he recognized.

I watched as Amy approached Mr. Carpenter a few minutes later and I knew what she was doing. I saw her and Allan bring him and Sandy into one of the RVs that they had set up as a little urgent care center. Amy was going to give him the last dose of immunoglobulin we had. So far, Sandy seemed to be doing well but we were still watching her closely and not leaving any non-immune people alone for very long. Just in case.

We all enjoyed a little down time. Kristin and I ducked into the kitchen where Lori and Kim were hanging out. We had a little impromptu meeting. We still had tons of food from last night that was still good and there was even more meant for tonight's event. Unfortunately, night two of the gala seemed likely to be cancelled but that didn't mean we couldn't have a smaller celebration. The ladies all thought a little revelry was a good idea.

"I think we could all use a little fun." I agreed with them. "I don't know about you but last night I couldn't really relax.

I kept expecting things to go south and eventually it did. Tonight I think we can finally breath a little easier."

"I think we all need a little break from the tension." Lori seemed to agree. "We weren't on the mission today but all of us were feeling stressed out with every update. I think we can figure out a way to relax a little tonight."

"Just remember, make sure you ladies don't work too hard." I reminded them. "We're a team. I'm happy to help out here. But first I'm gonna grab a twelve pack and bring the rescue team a refreshment." I opened the freezer and grabbed some cold beers.

"We still have power which is great." I said. "I bet it's going to turn off any minute. If it does the generator will kick on and the kitchen is on the circuit. We should be okay."

The ladies were happy to hear that. "The lights flickered a few times but I'm happy we won't be cooking in the dark tonight." Lori responded as she was unpacking what looked like some beautiful calamari. "So how about drinks and appies at six o'clock and dinner at seven?"

Kim nodded, "Yeah, that's what I was thinking. Maybe a family movie at eight o'clock? Jason was going to see if that sounded good with you Dr. B."

"It sounds great. As long as it's not a zombie movie." I chuckled as I turned and left.

I approached the tables where the team was hanging out. Most of the group was sitting around Steve as they relived parts of the mission. He had everyone in stitches with more of his one-liners and good-natured ribbing. I put the twelve pack in the middle of the table and everyone smiled and were happy to grab a cold one. Jackson was hanging with Cameron and some of the younger crowd a couple tables away. I could see that he was happy and I saw Casey nearby with some of the other girls. She was smiling and laughing with her cousins and new friends and that allowed me to relax for a little while.

Abby grabbed a beer and asked curiously, "Dad, when did you attach the machine gun to the helicopter? That's a tough job. One person can't do that alone. You need three people and about four hours to get that done."

All eyes on Steve and I was wondering the same thing. That gun wasn't mounted yesterday. It probably saved my life up there on the roof of the country club.

Steve responded, "Well, I thought it just may be the difference between someone living or dying. So I asked Scott for a hand and we stayed up much of the night working on that. We did need a third person for some critical steps so young Miss Cameron also stayed up with us and probably only got about two hours of sleep."

He paused for a moment and looked at me and gave a subtle smile. Then in as honest and as humble a tone I'd ever heard him speak he said, "They're very special people. I got to know them both well and it made me even more thankful to be here with you all. And that Cameron has sincere affection for Jackson. She talked about him quite a bit. He's very lucky."

I did get a little emotional as he spoke and I appreciated everything he said. "Well, I think *we're* lucky you did what you did and I'm also glad you didn't wait for our distress signal. You were there when we needed you. Without you and Abby we'd be in trouble. We're thankful you're both here with us." I held my beer up and everyone else did too. "To a successful mission, to our great leader Abby, and to a very special team. Cheers."

Everyone enjoyed the toast and the cold beer and we had a good bonding moment. It had been a very eventful day and we were all hoping for a more pleasant evening. Abby told us all a few more stories about Steve and she had us all howling.

She didn't hold back. He didn't mind it at all and was laughing at himself good-naturedly. We sat there for a while and soaked in a little sun. Jackson, Cameron and Colby came over to us and hung out for a little while. We made sure they knew how important they were to the team and to our success.

Steve wanted to make another point. "You know Dave, I was fully prepared to come help you guys but if it weren't for Colby I wouldn't have been there in time. He called me directly when you turned towards the country club. He knew immediately that I should be airborne. I was flying towards you within a minute. Any delay and we would have had a different outcome."

The whole team let Jackson, Cameron and Colby know how much we appreciated them. We were all having a good time reveling in the moment. I slid three remaining beers over towards our junior team members and they each sheepishly grabbed a can and opened it.

Steve held up his beer. "Here's to Jackson, Colby and Cameron. Your bravery, commitment and effort helped get us through this day and we're happy to have you all as members of our team."

"Cheers!" from everybody and we had a few more laughs before everyone went their separate ways. We'd be meeting up at 6 o'clock which was just a couple hours away.

Chapter 33

A LONG DAY

I WAS HAPPY TO be back at the fort and it felt great to just chill and spend some more time with Cameron. It had been quite a first full day here at our new home. It started really early when Dad, Sam, and Steve had the early confrontation with the commodore. I couldn't believe it when Dad had me actually shoot one of the infecteds. It was awful and terrible because I knew that just a few hours ago that thing was probably someone's dad or husband or brother.

I felt awful pulling the trigger but there was also a feeling of exhilaration and relief. I knew I could do it but I wasn't sure how I'd handle that moment. My first kill. Ultimately, I was able to be calm, cool and composed. I was able to pull the trigger and not hesitate.

I was nervous and so was Santino but now I knew that I could do it. I also went on a mission to save a farmer I didn't even know and it was by far the scariest thing I'd ever experienced. Being chased by twenty thousand snarling bloodthirsty monsters and jumping into a helicopter to escape them was as terrifying as it gets. Next time I feel some pressure or stress I'll think about that and I think I'll be able to keep my cool.

The only thing I just couldn't figure out is why I feel nervous and jittery when I see Cameron. It's not fear. It's not anxiety. It's not a *bad* sensation and I actually kind of like it. It's weird and I think it's love but I don't know.

I felt it again after I got off the helicopter. I felt happy to be back and I gave my mom a hug first. Then Cameron came right over and put her arms tight around me and hugged me close. It felt great and I didn't want her to let me go. She did finally loosen her grip and whispered in my ear "I'm glad you're safe. I was worried about you."

"I really felt I needed to go with the group on this mission. But the whole time I just couldn't wait to be back here with you." I whispered back to her. I just said those words and didn't even really need to think about it. The words just came out but they were the complete truth.

She let go of me and grabbed my hand tight as we walked for a little bit. She asked me all about the infecteds and the details of what we did. I described how crazy it was at the country club. She had seen some video from the drone so she knew I was not just making up stories or bullshitting her.

"I thought you guys weren't getting out of there alive." She said again with some tears in her eyes. "I'm not sure what I would have done. Everything in this world is just so awful and terrible. I should be upset and angry and sad but when I remember you're here it's all . . . okay. Without you I'm not sure I could put up with this."

"I know what you mean." I said honestly. "I really like being with you and it seems so wrong to say but . . . you make all of this . . . kinda good."

We sat down at a table with the other girls and Casey was designing a chicken coop. Each girl was going to have a chick and each chick would have it's own little apartment. Sandy had already promised that as soon as it was safe they'd go back to the farm and secure some more chicks. Casey was so excited but she knew they would need to have a better home for the chicks. They needed a new coop. Sam had already told Casey he would build a big chicken 'apartment house' for her. She had thanked him earlier for the pen he made and they talked for a while about chickens and farms. Sam really got a kick out of Casey and her free spirit.

"Hey Jackson, I decided to change the name of the chick. Guess what it's new name is?" Casey asked me as we sat with them.

"Hmm. I bet you named it . . . Chuck." I threw out a name. "Or how about Beli*chick*?"

Cameron joined in too, "No way. Those are lame. I bet you named it . . . Alfonso."

Casey smiled at that, "Well that is pretty good. But we're going with Sam Jr." she smiled clearly happy with the name. "Guess who we're naming him after?"

"Sammy Davis, Jr?" I guessed. It was a pretty good guess I thought.

"Samuel L. Jackson?" Cameron guessed.

Casey just laughed. "No, you guys are way off. I named it after Sam."

We all laughed as little Sam, Jr. walked around the table visiting each person expecting a little treat.

Some of the other boys came over and hung with us. It was a good group and everyone seemed to be getting along just fine. The older boys also got a kick out of the chicken coop. A little innocent fun and a chance to be a bit silly just seemed like a nice diversion during these times. We were all able to be ourselves and be happy for what we had. No tension or bad vibes.

I noticed Colby had pulled his chair right next to my cousin Madigan. She was my age and he was a year older but whatever. They were laughing and he was holding out a strawberry for Sam, Jr.

Even young Evan and Miles joined our group and we all felt better with more people around us. We were a big family. We had to be strong. We were.

Mrs. Izzo came over to us and didn't say anything for a minute. She just seemed happy that everything was good and the younger folks were happy. "I need four volunteers to work dinner tonight. Some cooking. Some serving and some cleaning."

Nearly every hand shot up and her smile got even bigger. "Thank you all so much. Tonight I'm gonna select Jayci, Casey, Lucas and Collin. We'll need you in the kitchen at 4 pm. It's only 2 pm now so you can hang out for a while. See you at 4 pm. Thank you!"

We all hung out and enjoyed the sun and being together. After a while some of the kids asked me about the mission and what I saw. They really wanted to know what it was like out there so I told them.

"For the first twenty minutes I was in the diversion car. It was scary but we just drove around and sometimes drove right over the infecteds. We heard from Uncle Mark that the Humvee was out of gas. They had run over an infected and this thing reached up behind the gas tank and damaged a gas line and the thing just stalled on the road. It might have been a good thing because we probably couldn't have driven through this huge mob of infecteds even in a Humvee. We escaped on foot to this golf course and went into the clubhouse which was a super huge mansion. These infecteds just crashed right into the locked doors and windows and eventually broke through the walls and chased us right to the roof. The helicopter was waiting for us and it was so close to being a disaster. We were lucky to get out of there."

Cameron squeezed my hand tight. It felt good

"Did you cap any of them?" Logan asked.

"Not on this trip." I answered honestly. "But I shot one earlier this morning and it still is kind of hard to think about." "Why? Those things are monsters." He asked. "Yeah. I know. It wasn't that it used to be a person or anything. It's that it was so hard to kill. I shot that thing five times in the head at close range! Five headshots to bring it down. That's what makes it hard to think about. That's what we're facing. Those things are just superhuman. Colby saw it up close yesterday, right?"

"Oh, yeah." Colby answered. "Talk about badass. This thing was like a terminator. My dad was using his full strength for like twenty minutes to keep this thing from coming out of the locker room. When we did get rescued the infected got shot like ten times by Jackson's dad and Mr. Lang. Abby had to shoot it with a whole clip from her AR-15 to put it down. It was scary. I can't imagine twenty thousand of those things trying to kill you."

Madigan grabbed Colby's hand and tried to reassure Colby. "You helped save them with your drone, Colby. You did an awesome job!"

The younger crowd hung out for a while and we all talked about things we were going to miss and things we were kind of looking forward to. It was a chance to hear that other people were having some of the same conflicting thoughts and emotions. It was a safe place to say things and be honest. Pretty heavy stuff. Not quite *Lord of the flies* stuff but some heavy things were going on.

Cameron, Colby and I decided to walk over to the big table where the rescue team was hanging out. They were reminiscing about the day's events and it was extra special when my dad let us grab a beer and join in a toast to the successful mission.

It just felt good to be part of that team.

* * *

A little later I walked Cameron to her new house. The Lang family had decided that until the herd thins a little they would stay in the fort. After our rescue mission left this morning most of the infecteds had cleared out of the area for a little while. The parking lot was basically clear. Sam, Scott and a few others with shotguns had all gone over to the *Resilience* to get some of their luggage and essentials. It would really make the new Lang residence seem like home with all their stuff.

We got to her place and she begged for me to come in so I did. Tracy and Scott were putting things away and they had some cool music playing. They were so happy to have all their luggage at their new place. They knew they could always go back to the *Resilience* if they needed to but this would be the new headquarters for the Lang family.

"Hey, Jackson!" Scott called out when we entered. "Sounds like you guys had a fun time at the country club. How were the greens today?"

"The greens were rough. The conditions weren't great to tell you the truth." I smiled as I thought about the whole experience. "Hey, this place looks great. So different from this morning."

Tracy was hanging a picture on the wall. "Thank you, Jackson. I'm so glad I brought some of these old pictures with us. It's going to make it feel like home for the girls."

"You know there were a lot of cool paintings at the country club." I mentioned. "Something tells me they may be available."

"Hey, why stop there?" Cameron asked. "We could go to the Met and get some Picassos for my bedroom!"

"I want the Mona Lisa." Peyton claimed.

After she said that there was a little moment of quiet. A moment when we all reflected that everything was different now. Everything.

Scott broke the silence. "I haven't been to New York in a long time. Maybe we could take the *Resilience* right up to midtown and go shopping!"

"Yeah!" Cameron shouted out, back in her bubbly mood. "We could take a helicopter tour like when we were there last time as a family. That was great!"

"We are going to have some fun field trips I'm sure, Cam." Scott replied, "But let's wait for a little while. I don't think anyone wants to relive what Jackson and his team experienced a few hours ago. Am I right?"

"No doubt." I said as I looked out their picture window. About a dozen infecteds were wandering around the parking lot. "I don't want to take any chances with those things. Let's just stay here for a little while. This place might be an old run-down fort but it's safe and secure and we have pretty much everything we need."

"So you're glad Newport Country Club wasn't our home base?" Scott asked knowing full-well those infecteds went through its walls like they weren't there.

"I'll take twenty feet of granite for walls any day." I said with full honesty. "I really can't think of any place as safe as this. I also really appreciate the recent upgrades. This is all pretty fantastic!" as I gestured to the beautiful high-end hotel suite we were standing in.

"This wasn't easy to pull off. None of it was. But so far it's working out." Scott replied with his typical modesty.

Cameron chimed in "Yeah, I was dreading the whole living in a fort thing but I'm kinda liking things so far. You know, except for the giant, bloodthirsty horde of killer, bionic zombies surrounding us." She couldn't help but break into a smile.

We all smiled.

"Yeah. Except for that." I echoed her.

A few minutes later I excused myself. It was time to get

ready for another gala. We all agreed this time it would be very casual. We were hoping for no excitement whatsoever. Food, family, friends and a movie under the stars. Sounded good to me.

Chapter 34

END TO A LONG DAY

AT ABOUT SIX o'clock our family headed over to the main gathering area. We were all very casually dressed. The kids were still getting along together well and Kristin and I appreciated that so much. They seemed to be figuring out that fighting each other and arguing just weren't worth it. There was too much badness going on all around us. We all needed to try to be supportive and understanding of one another. They were doing great. I couldn't be more proud of Jackson. He had shown himself to be brave and calm under pressure. He had emerged quickly as a leader amongst the younger crowd. He had plenty of respect from the older crowd too. It was great to see that the budding romance he had with Cameron was going so well. Maybe they both realized that it was better to seize happiness when it's there for the taking. They both seemed happy.

We were some of the last to arrive at the 'gala.' There were all types of heavy appetizers being served by two of our own. Jayci and Collin had found some aprons and name tags from the catering service and were playing-up that role nicely. There were plenty of soft drinks and beers set up at a bar and Dave decided he would be the bartender for tonight. There was an air of relaxation and relief that felt well-earned. We still had a watch stationed on the wall. Sam was guard tonight and on the com. We had agreed that every twenty minutes or so he'd give us an update. A handful of us had the earpieces in but most of the group was not wired for sound.

I told Kristin I would make a couple of announcements. She said okay but to keep the mood light and airy. "No doom and gloom!" she said just before I jumped on a chair.

I looked at her and winked. "Light and airy." I whispered just to her.

"Hey, everybody. Can I just say a few words?" I started with my hands up calling for some quiet.

There was a collective moan as everyone seemed to mutter 'oh no not him again!' but in a fun teasing way.

"I know. I know. Enough business. I get it but everyone is here and I just want a minute. I even convinced Lori and Kim to come join us but they made me promise to keep it brief." That was met by some applause clearly meant for the ladies responsible for the great spread *and* for making me be brief up here. I stepped up onto a table and everyone quieted down.

"So it was just a little over 24 hours ago when we met across the parking lot on the *Resilience* and had a little meeting just like this. I just want to point out a few of the things that we accomplished in that time. We responded to a distress call from the *Flying Serpent* and first witnessed the awful reality that we were facing as we took out the infected captain. We enjoyed a nice gala and even some dancing. We heard from Dr. Ashworth that this fast-moving plague was coming to a head across the world just as he had warned us. We witnessed the first ghastly transformation within these walls at the end of the gala which was certainly eye-opening. We then discovered the *Resilience* had been breached. We handled that with no harm coming to our team. We brought Mike into the fort and learned how potentially tragic that could have turned out. Mike was a casualty of this virus but we handled his hideous transition as a team. We took in Sandy after she was being attacked outside our gate. We immunized her quickly. She looks healthy so far. We repelled the commodore and a team of henchmen although I won't be surprised if he tries to crash this party tonight. That man really loves this fort and a good gala. We went to rescue Mr. Carpenter and that turned into the scariest trip I've ever been on. Steve rescued us in the nick of time but we completed our mission. We did all of these things as a team. Everyone here is a vital part of the team. We're prepared. We're ready. We're together. So let's have a good night and enjoy being together. We deserve to have a peaceful evening. Thanks."

I climbed down off the table and there was more applause than I was ready for. Everyone was standing and applauding me. Even my family. Even Casey was smiling at me and clapping. I looked around and people seemed genuinely happy and were holding each other. These were proud people and I was proud to be one of them. While I'm sure we were going to have a good night together I knew there were tough times ahead.

But we were ready.

Everyone had some good food and some good fun. We dined. We danced. We watched a movie on a screen someone had made out of sheets.

During the evening the power went out and our lookouts told us immediately that the power went out everywhere. It had happened. It wasn't a surprise at all. No one was at the helm at the local electric company. They were either at home or more likely a bloodthirsty infected. All of Newport went dark, except for the fires that dotted the harbor. The power grid was down. Our generator kicked in and everything lit up again at the fort. Our families kept enjoying the night and the younger folks loved watching a movie under the unusually bright stars.

We said goodnight to all the other families after an evening we all deserved. We had some fun and didn't feel guilty for a second allowing ourselves to be happy in that moment. I wasn't sure what tomorrow would bring but I made sure I was going to enjoy the present. We went into our home and got ready for bed. The kids were tired and happy to retire to their rooms. Kristin and I crawled into bed and for the first time since I could remember I fell asleep first.

INFECTEDS

BOOK TWO:
SURVIVING THE SURGE

I HAD PROBABLY BEEN sleeping about ten minutes when my phone rang. I was in a deep stage of sleep but after twenty five years of being on call I roused quickly. I recognized the name and number. It was Jay Wagner. I got out of bed and made my way downstairs as I answered the call.

"Hello, Jay. How are you?" I asked but knew this call could only spell trouble.

"Hey Doc, things really aren't good. I'm kind of wishing I hadn't ignored your earlier text about the violent bloodthirsty hordes and all! We are currently getting crushed here in the neighborhood. Pretty terrifying place to be with hundreds of these awful things running around all over the place. It's really bad."

I could hear some yelling and screaming in the background. There was gunfire. Jay sounded serious and desperate. I hadn't heard this tone from him before, he was usually the jovial, fun-loving guy who was always cracking a joke.

"Where are you, Jay?" I asked "Who's with you?"

"Three families. Mine, Joe's and Ira's. We got fifteen people. That includes Terry." He responded.

"Terry? From the range? And you're all healthy?" I was somewhat surprised.

"Yeah, we're all okay but we're surrounded by these things. The whole neighborhood is out in the street attacking anybody in sight. I've seen these things rip people apart. We're hiding out in my attic. We've got food and some guns but nowhere to go."

"Can you get out of the house?" I asked.

"We tried to make a run for it but some of these things jumped right through the windows and they're still downstairs. Thank God Terry was here. He took out five or six of them but we had to barricade ourselves up here in my attic."

"Do you think you can make it through the night? Do you have enough ammo?" I asked.

"Yeah, I think so." he responded but he didn't seem too positive. "We went to the gun range yesterday evening to get whatever weapons we could get our hands on. That's where we met up with Terry. He was stranded there and couldn't get home. We grabbed all the guns and ammo we could and brought him to my place."

"Ok, good. I'm glad he's there to help you all." I thought for a minute but I just couldn't ignore that our friend's were in trouble. These were good friends and their kids. We knew them all well and hung out all the time. I had introduced Jay, Joe and Ira to Terry last time we all went to shoot together. "Jay the power went down and I expect the phones to go down soon. Be ready at ten in the morning. We'll come get you."

"Ten am." he repeated. "Got it. I think we can hold them off but I don't think any of us could make it to our cars. I tried and I saw one of these things put its head right through a window.

Didn't even phase it. These things are god-awful and vicious. Be careful!"

"Stay safe." I said as I hung up.

I sat there in bed for a couple of minutes just thinking about the logistics. It was frightening to consider leaving this fort again after what happened earlier in the day. I didn't want to put anyone at risk but I just couldn't strand our good friends in a deathtrap. Our happy little neighborhood was now overrun with bloodthirsty infecteds and three good families were surrounded. Terry was there so they had a better chance of surviving the night but I just didn't think they would make it very far even if they could get out of the attic. I had a flashback to our extraction from Newport Country Club. We barely made it out and we had all kinds of gear and weapons at our disposal.

I decided to text our group to let them know the situation. I wanted to call for an early meeting to discuss this. I needed to be careful. We had a good group and have been lucky so far that no one had died or been injured. If I ask too much or extend us too far on this rescue mission I knew there could be dissent. I needed to make sure the group agreed that the means were justified and that the risk was acceptable.

I started typing on my phone. I was pretty slow at this and I chuckled to myself a little. If Casey were here she would roll her eyes and take my phone. She would type for me just so she wouldn't have to endure watching me "slow-text."

After about a minute I decided to use voice recognition instead.

"Apologies to all for the late text. I know we all could use some sleep. I received an urgent call from Jay Wagner. He's with Joe and Ira and their families and they are all stranded in Jay's attic. They are surrounded by infecteds. If you don't know them they are good friends of ours and their kids are great just like our kids. They have guns, ammo and have teamed up with Terry who is military. They are desperate. I would like to meet at 6:30am in the dining hall (next to where the camps have the sleepovers.) We can discuss this more then. Goodnight."

I checked for any auto-correct errors before sending but it looked good.

I received a few confirmation texts. Couldn't tell the tone but nothing hostile.

If they make it through the night I will be relieved. Amazed but relieved. I don't know how many survivors are out there. I went through different rescue scenarios in my head but they all seemed like there was too much risk. What were the chances we could get a rescue unit to our old neighborhood, remove fifteen people from an attic, and get them all back here without a casualty?

What we learned so far is that no plan is guaranteed no matter how well prepared you are. In this new world the legions of infecteds were an overpowering force. Like a hurricane or a flood there was really no way to escape or defeat the hordes. We would have to be smart. We needed a good plan. We needed to come together as a group just like we have already.

Luck favors the prepared.

I don't think Louis Pasteur was thinking about our current situation when he first stated that phrase but it fit pretty well. We would be prepared.